# Readers love
# MARGUERITE LABBE

## *Other Side of the Line*

"This story is so well written. It is captivating and riveting. The author drew me in and wouldn't let go. I couldn't put this book down, and in the end, I wasn't ready for it to be over."

—*Divine Magazine*

"…I'm left with a feeling of awe from having just read a book that will live in my memory for a long time to come."

—Scattered Thoughts and Rogue Words

"…this book was beautiful, heartbreaking at points and painful but also so very sweet!"

—Inked Rainbow Reads

## *Ghosts in the Wind*

"All I can say is read this one with plenty of lights on and a box of tissues by the bedside—but don't miss it, it is worth every moment!"

—Gay Book Reviews

By Marguerite Labbe

All Bets Are Off
Ghosts in the Wind
Make Me Whole
Other Side of the Line
Playing Ball (Multiple Author Anthology)

GEEK LIFE
A Little Side of Geek

TRIQUETRA TRILOGY
My Heart is Within You
Haunted by Your Soul
Our Sacred Balance

Published by Dreamspinner Press
www.dreamspinnerpress.com

MARGUERITE LABBE

# A LITTLE SIDE GEEK

DREAMSPINNER PRESS

Published by

DREAMSPINNER PRESS

5032 Capital Circle SW, Suite 2, PMB# 279, Tallahassee, FL 32305-7886 USA
www.dreamspinnerpress.com

A Little Side of Geek
© 2018 Marguerite Labbe.

Cover Art
© 2018 Kanaxa.
Cover content is for illustrative purposes only and any person depicted on the cover is a model.

Trade Paperback ISBN: 978-1-64080-475-3
Digital ISBN: 978-1-64080-474-6
Library of Congress Control Number: 2018930568
Trade Paperback published May 2018
v. 1.0

Printed in the United States of America
∞
This paper meets the requirements of
ANSI/NISO Z39.48-1992 (Permanence of Paper).

This is for all the wonderful people in the comic book convention circuit for changing the lives of my entire family. You are some of the most creative, openhearted, generous people I have ever met. My son has grown up from a rug rat playing behind a table to volunteering at shows. My husband has found his calling and is living a life he's always dreamed of, and I've met friends that I will have for life. So to all the vendors, artists, writers, cosplayers, podcasters, and producers, these books are for you.

With a special shout-out to my favorite comic book artist, my husband Keir, and my favorite chef, my brother Adam. I love you both.

This book is dedicated to the memory of Mansa Herndon. I am at a loss for words. Your smile, your laugh will be missed. There is going to be a hole at our gaming table and among the con family. Bless you, my brother, and thank you for the memories.

# Chapter One

"DON'T GIVE me that big-eyed bullshit." Morris Proctor leveled an accusing finger at Cassie, perched on her cat tree as she stared him down. She turned her attention to the neatly piled supplies, her silver-tufted ears flattening as he tied back his dreadlocks before kneeling next to the suitcase. "I am *not* abandoning you. It's only for one day."

Cassie shot him a flat green-eyed look that struck straight at his sense of mounting guilt. She was a cat. How could she get to him like this? "Look, I'm with you all day, every day while other pets are left to their own devices. Don't you want some time to yourself?" Morris argued as he flipped open his suitcase and loaded it with extra art supplies.

Cassie sniffed and narrowed her eyes as she wound her tail primly around her paws. Her expression said plainly what she thought of that tactic. "Look, when I want to spend time with you and cuddle, you don't want me to touch you." Morris held out his hand to show her his still-healing scratch. "Sometimes my job does take me out of the house. I'm not your food bitch. Catering to your needs is not the sum of my life."

Cassie jumped to the floor and stalked down the hallway, the tip of her black tail twitching in annoyance. Morris winced. He'd better make damn sure to close all the closet doors before he left. He did not want to come back to find she'd hacked a hairball in his boots or left a dead cricket on his pillow.

Morris sat back on his heels, taking a mental inventory of what remained in his apartment and what he'd already packed in the trunk of his car. He didn't think he was forgetting anything, but a persistent voice nagged at him. He checked the time and dismissed the unhelpful mental prod. No point in having breakfast now, not if he wanted to set up in time. He grabbed his business cards, shoved them in the suitcase, and zipped it up.

As he stood his phone rang. Morris glanced at the name on the screen and considered ignoring it before common sense returned. One of the lessons he'd learned in life was he could not ignore his sisters, especially his twin, and expect to get away with it.

"Hey, Makayla, can't talk." Morris tucked the phone between his shoulder and his ear. With one hand, he grabbed his suitcase and with the other, the luggage handcart piled high with lashed-down crates and boxes. "Have a show today, got to hustle."

"So you're not joining us for dinner?" Makayla replied in a voice thick with exasperation. "You've been dodging us for weeks."

The nagging voice smacked him in the back of the head. He'd meant to return his family's calls. It must've slipped his mind among getting pages finalized before sending them to the printer. "I had a deadline." Morris shouldered open the door and Cassie streaked outside between his legs. "Fuck," Morris cursed under his breath as the black-and-silver shadow darted under his car. "Then I had to get ready for this show."

"What time does the show end?" Makayla demanded. "Where is it? Maybe you could still meet us."

The cool spell of the last week had ended, and hot, sultry air swirled around Morris. It was going to be miserably humid later on. "Not happening today, sis, sorry. Show is in Southern Maryland. It doesn't get out until after five, and I still have to break everything down." Morris abandoned his baggage and crouched to look for Cassie, but she had disappeared. "By the time I get to you, it'll be too late for dinner."

And he'd be starving. He'd already skipped breakfast, and he knew himself well enough not to have any illusions he would pick up lunch at the show. By the time he'd be ready to roll out of there, he wouldn't want a ninety-minute drive, even for his mother's cooking.

"Can't you sneak out of there an hour early?" Makayla wheedled.

Morris grabbed a hold of his patience. One of these days, his family would understand he had a real job. "No more than you can sneak out of an event at work. What would happen if you did that?"

"Chaos and mayhem."

Well, Morris couldn't say the same unless the promoter took offense, but it could equal lost revenue. He had a reputation to maintain.

He might get to a show a bit late, but he never left early. "I swear I'll come up soon. I'll spend the whole weekend."

"Next weekend is Memorial Day." Makayla's voice brightened. "It would be the perfect time." Morris hesitated, mentally running through his calendar, and she jumped all over the hesitation. "Laila misses you."

Oh, that was a low blow. Morris adored his niece, and she reciprocated wholeheartedly. He usually made a point to spend a day with her every few weeks, and they talked on the phone often. He realized with a pang of regret he'd been neglectful lately. "Tell Laila not only will I be there, but I'll pick her up early on Saturday so we can be the first people to celebrate the pool opening."

"She's going to be so excited. We can make a weekend out of it, have a cookout on Monday. I'll pull together a menu with Sierra, Monica, and Mom." Morris half listened to her rambling plans as he scanned his yard, looking for his wayward cat. If he was late because he had to chase her, they were going to have some words. Not that she'd listen, but they would have them.

"Do you want me to bring anything?" Ah, there she was, sitting behind the little statue of a dragon he'd put in the mulched bed. Cassie stared at him from under a half-raised wing. Morris crouched down and made the little clicking sound that sometimes drew her to him.

"Grab some tortilla chips and beer. I think it'll be enough."

A curtain twitched in the upstairs apartment over the garage. Morris had the impression of a figure in the window, and then it was gone. His neighbors were home. Ever since they'd moved into the top of the split-level home they shared, Morris had never seen them. They'd arrived one day while he was at a show, but they were gone before he woke up in the morning, and he often heard them arrive late while he was up trying to get the last of his work for the day done. He supposed he ought to be neighborly and go introduce himself, but the alarm on his phone reminded him he was running late.

"Look, I've got to go. I'll call Laila later and let her know when I'm picking her up." Morris grabbed his burdens again and popped the trunk open. Well, if calling the silly cat wouldn't work, maybe ignoring her would. "Love you, bye." He hung up without giving her a chance to respond. If he let her, Makayla would keep him talking for an hour no matter how many times he tried to let her go.

"Girlfriend?" a smooth male voice called from the walkway.

Morris glanced over and straightened in interest. Hello, ridiculously adorable. The guy probably hated being told that, but it was true. Morris bet he had girls all over him all the time, such a shame. He had a baby-faced boyishness about him that made him look as if he'd just graduated high school. But Morris knew their landlord. He wouldn't rent to tenants until they were well out of college and financially stable, so he must be older. His tumbled shock of sun-streaked brown hair and heavy brows framed friendly clear gray eyes.

"Sorry?" Morris felt his cheeks heat, suddenly awkward, and grateful his complexion hid the reaction as the other man smiled easily. His new neighbor was shorter than Morris, but at well over six feet, Morris was taller than most. The bare hint of stubble shadowed pale peachy-pink skin that added to his boyishness. Yeah, definitely adorable, heaven help him.

"Nothing to be sorry about," the other man said, coming toward him. "I shouldn't have jumped in on the end of your conversation. It was your tone of voice as you hung up. Made me think you were either talking to family or a girl." His seeming youthfulness faded as he carried himself with an innate confidence and authority that Morris envied. He had a determined jaw and a long nose that would've been straight if not for a kink from a past break.

"Both, actually. My sister." Morris slipped his phone into one of the many pockets of his khaki utility kilt with a shake of his head. "Giving me grief about not coming to dinner tonight."

"Ooohh sister guilt," the other man said with a grimace of commiseration. "I have a couple of them myself. I feel ya."

"I have three, all older, including my twin by ten minutes." And Makayla never let him forget that. "They think it gives them free rein to boss me around."

"Age has nothing to do with it, trust me. I'm the oldest, and they still try that number on me." The man stepped forward and hefted Morris's suitcase. "Let me help you."

"Thanks, man." Between the two of them, they managed to store the rest of Morris's gear to his satisfaction. The back seat of his too small car was filled. It was getting trickier to put it all together. He needed to scale back on his product or buy a bigger vehicle. Morris thrust his hand out to his new neighbor. "Pleasure to meet you. I'm Morris Proctor."

"Theo Boarman." He had a nice handshake, firm but without the macho testing bullshit some men tried to pull. Theo jerked his thumb toward the house. "My brother's Lincoln, but he's not likely to be up for another hour."

"Hell, if I didn't have work, I wouldn't be either." Morris inched toward the car as his alarm rang again. "Sorry, hate to rush, but I'm already late." Wait, the damn cat. He couldn't leave until he'd gotten Cassie back inside.

"No, I understand. I work most Saturdays too." Theo stepped back from the car, and as if she heard Morris's thoughts, Cassie appeared and wound herself around Theo's ankles. She was such a sucker for meeting new people. "Hey there," Theo said in a soft voice as he crouched down to scratch her ears. "Aren't you a gorgeous big girl?"

Cassie shot Morris a look as if judging his level of jealousy and Morris froze. He knew the game. If he made one move toward her, Cassie would streak away. "In the interest of neighborly relations, would you mind grabbing the minx who's trying to charm her evil way into your heart?" he said in a conversational tone, in case Cassie read his voice and decided to bolt.

Theo didn't hesitate, bless him, and caught Cassie by the scruff of her neck. "What kind of a cat is she? I've never seen one this size."

"Maine coon and half that bulk is fur." Morris scooped Cassie up as her tail lashed and she let out a squawk of protest. "Every damn time I bring out the suitcase, she pulls an escape artist act. Thank you, again," Morris said as he turned away.

"You are a troublemaker." He kissed the top of her head and carried her back inside as she vociferously announced her disapproval.

Brendan would have kittens if Morris didn't make it to the con in time to get his stuff set up before the front doors opened. Delays set the fussy, anal promoter into a tailspin, though he ought to be used to it by now. Despite his tendency to be a little too controlled, Morris liked him. He was a methodical soul who truly desired to run a good show and to make sure everyone profited. Unlike some others who were only in it for themselves.

When he came out again, Theo was standing on the front steps to the upper apartment, his thumbs hooked through the belt loops of his cargo shorts. Morris cast one last regretful look at him before he got in his car and backed up. He wasn't sure if that was interest in the man's gaze or if it was wishful thinking on Morris' part, but he was looking forward to another conversation.

At least having a hot neighbor would make things interesting— when the man was at home, which seemed to be never. But a little eye candy was better than no eye candy at all.

# Chapter Two

"DON'T SAY I never do anything for you," Theo told his youngest brother Lincoln as he parked outside the comic con. The last thing he planned to do on a rare Saturday he wasn't scheduled to work a double shift was spend it among a group of geeks, whom Theo suspected didn't understand where the line between reality and fiction blurred. That included his brother.

Lincoln bounced out of the car dressed in a full Knights of Ren getup. His eager fidgeting ruined the ominous effect of the dark costume, but Theo let him have his fun. This was the last weekend before the craziness of summer hit, and he'd been busting his ass alongside Theo. He was due a little fun. "Thank you!" Lincoln said fervently from behind his mask. "You are the best brother ever."

Theo shook his head, taking a mental bet on how long Lincoln would last swathed in all black when the Southern Maryland humidity ramped up. He had to be seriously mental. Theo got out of his car and eyed the fire station dubiously. "Seems a little small for a con," he said as Lincoln retrieved his lightsaber and hooked it to his belt. "Not like the cons I see on the news."

"Those are megacons," Lincoln said, in the superior tone only a fifteen-year-old could adopt, as if Theo should know the difference. "Those focus more on pop culture than comic books. I want to go through some long boxes and pick up a few new titles."

"Maybe you should've dressed up as a comic book character," Theo retorted.

"Can't," Lincoln said with smug regret. "I grew out of my Deadpool costume."

Lincoln had put on one hell of a growth spurt last year and at only fifteen, he topped Theo by a good inch. He was doomed to spend the rest of his life staring up at his baby brother because Lincoln ate as if he wasn't stopping his upward momentum anytime soon. "Then stop mutating," Theo said with a good-natured push toward the firehouse. "You're absorbing too much radioactivity from your comics."

Lincoln ignored that as he practically bounced on his toes on the way to the door. He hiked up his costume, digging for his wallet, and Theo stopped him with a hand on his arm. "I've got it." He didn't get many days out with his brother. Two of their siblings were in college, and Theo realized Lincoln would be following them in a few short years. The little pang of weakness was why he'd agreed to this outing in the first place. He'd pay anything to know Lincoln was smiling for a day and not worrying over issues he shouldn't have to worry about at his age.

"Sweet." Lincoln was not one to argue over a free ticket.

Theo paid for their passes, amazed at the number of people who were already there. Despite the crowded parking lot, he'd expected a small, sleepy con. After all, it was at a fire station on the edge of a small, sleepy town surrounded by miles of former tobacco farms interspersed with shopping centers. Those fields now held neat rows of corn and barley. Not much happened around here aside from local fairs and church functions. When Theo wanted excitement, he headed up to DC, but those days were long gone.

The booths laid out in neat rows gave plenty of room for people to walk by or shop without crowding anyone. The firehouse's high ceiling, wood beams, and the wide windows dominating one entire side gave the area an open, friendly look. Colorful banners rose above the booths, announcing this vendor or that artist.

"Do you have your cell phone on you?" Theo asked as he stepped to the side of the entrance to let other attendees get by.

"Yes," Lincoln said with a long-suffering sigh and, leaving Theo behind, made a beeline toward one of the stalls.

Theo looked around, trying to get a feel for Lincoln's world. His brother attended every show he could get to with his friends and came home animated and loaded down with purchases. Lincoln hadn't been to one in ages, so when he diffidently suggested it as if Theo's answer didn't matter, it would've taken a harder heart than his to deny him.

There were tables full of collectibles and a looming wall of T-shirts to his left. On the right, large areas full of long comic boxes enticed people to browse, and booths of toys and games lay straight ahead. Theo walked along the outer row, watching all the activity with interest. It wouldn't hurt to keep an eye on what Lincoln looked at either. He could pick up his Christmas present early and call the day a win.

Theo shoved his hands in his pockets as he wandered up and down. Mixed in with all the vendors were artists, writers, and all kinds of crafty people. He did have an admiration for creativity. Theo couldn't draw a stick, and those who could always fascinated him. He didn't understand how someone could take a vision from their mind and translate it onto paper and canvas, but he supposed it wasn't any different from taking a bunch of ingredients and creating a new dish that pleased both stomach and heart. He might not be able to draw, but he was an artist in the kitchen.

He found his attention drawn again to the artists. Some stood, conversing with people at their tables; others were hard at work with their heads bent over a pad. He even saw one messing around with a tablet as the image he drew appeared on the screen at his table. Theo inched closer to those working, not wanting to disturb them but captivated by the way their hands flew over a page and how lines came together and images emerged. A sign advertising commissions piqued his interest. A one-of-a-kind drawing for his bedroom or the living room might be nice. Neither he nor Lincoln had done much to make their new place seem like a home.

He made another circuit around the floor, this time poking through the sketchbooks set out for people to peruse, searching for a style that grabbed him. His family's restaurant displayed local art with Chesapeake Bay themes. He wanted something a little different for their home. Not that he saw his home much these days. He was going through prints of various characters he'd heard his brother mention when Lincoln appeared again.

"What are you doing?" Lincoln asked and pointed to the wall of prints behind the artist. "Cool Green Lantern. I thought I'd find you playing games on your phone."

"I thought I might commission something. Get a picture for our living room." Theo shut the book with a sigh as nothing caught his eye. "What damage have you done to your wallet so far?"

"Not too bad." Lincoln held up a bag. "I bought some new sleeves for my card decks, some new dice because you can't ever have enough of them."

"So says the man who has never stepped on them in the dark."
They hurt like a motherfucker.

"Seriously, are you having fun?" Lincoln asked as he shoved
his mask on top of his head and searched Theo's face. He looked like
Theo with his sandy brown hair and baby-faced features, but there the
similarities ended. Lincoln's heavy brows and quiet hazel eyes gave him
a studious look that Theo lacked. "We can leave if you're not."

"It's okay, bro," Theo assured him with a smile. "There's more to
see here than I thought. I'm good."

Lincoln relaxed a little, though the line that had permanently etched
its way along his brow in the last year remained. "Okay…. I'm going
to the panel on tabletop games. Trask Briscoe, the guy who owns Old
Dominion Magick Den, is running it."

"He's here?" When Theo had first walked into the man's shop last
December, he'd been skeptical about his prospects. It looked like a dump,
part new age store, part comics, and part games of all kinds. But the
silvering, tattooed hipster who ran it saved his sanity by suggesting the
perfect game for a gift. Theo didn't know where to begin to find something
Lincoln didn't already have, and he'd wanted the first Christmas without
their parents to be memorable for reasons other than their loss. Material
gifts wouldn't make up for it in any way, but the smile he'd gotten had
made the day for him, and they'd had fun breaking out the game after
dinner. It was a new tradition he wanted to continue this year, hopefully
this time with all his siblings.

"Yeah, he's often at cons, trying to drum up new business or stock
up on toys." Lincoln turned and pointed to the back corner of the fire
hall. "His tables are over there."

"I'll have to stop by and say hey." Theo gave Lincoln a light shove.
"Go, have fun, be geeky. I'm going to keep looking around."

Theo watched Lincoln walk away, wondering if he should join him
at the panel. Lincoln was mercurial. One moment he'd cling close, and
another moment he'd accuse Theo of not giving him any breathing room.
Some days it felt like every step Theo made was the wrong one. But
Lincoln didn't look back, and Theo decided he wanted the space.

He turned down the final row where booths backed up against
the massive windows. There was a station set up on the end with kids
doodling and coloring at tables covered with scraps. As Theo scanned

the row, a newly familiar face caught his attention. Morris Proctor sat behind a table, his long body hunched over a board.

Theo watched him work, attraction striking him again as it had when he'd first caught a glimpse of Morris from his window. If Lincoln had realized he'd been ogling their new neighbor, he would've been mortified. The table covered the long, muscular bare calves Theo had admired earlier. Theo had never appreciated the idea of a man in a skirt outside of Scotland until he'd met his neighbor. Now he hoped it would be a common sight.

Morris tilted his head, his broad brow drawn in concentration as his hand moved rapidly over the board propped against the table. His chin tapered from prominent cheeks and ended with a sexy little cleft. Thick, dark lashes framed heavy-lidded eyes, and their sensuousness echoed in his full lips. The dreads he had pulled back earlier now spilled around his broad shoulders in thin richly brown twists.

He wore his emotions in every flicker that crossed his face. Theo found it as fascinating now as he had that morning when Morris had tramped across their driveway, his mouth hard with aggravation and impatience.

A meshed frame arced over his booth loaded with poster-like pictures of all sizes, some with characters Theo knew from Lincoln, but most he didn't. Beside the booth rose a banner emblazoned with the title *Beneath the Surface* by Morris Proctor, and a picture of a young black girl in a wheelchair with a glint of steely determination on her thin face. At her side sat a gray-and-black cat that looked suspiciously like the one who gave Morris such a hard time earlier.

His hot neighbor was an artist and a writer. That explained why he was always at home. Theo was beginning to think he was a hermit. Theo moved toward the booth with quick steps, eager to revisit their earlier interrupted conversation.

When he paused in front of Morris's booth, the man kept drawing, his long fingers gripping the pencil lightly. Curiosity outweighed manners, and Theo went up on his toes to get a better look. The girl in the banner sat amongst a cloud of butterflies with an expression of delight on her face as she leaned forward in her wheelchair, fingers stretching to touch them. It was only a rough sketch, but it was alive with movement and emotion. Theo could imagine it finished, colors blazing.

He wanted it.

"How much for the picture when it's done?" Theo gestured toward the board.

Morris's head jerked up, his eyes wide with surprise, and then his gaze warmed when he saw Theo. "Hey." He glanced back down at the half-drawn sketch. "I'd actually planned this for a new promo banner. I've had that one up for over a year now."

"For your comic?" Theo picked up one of the copies stacked in neat little holders at the front of the booth. It showed the same girl wheeling her way through what looked like a haunted house with spooky eyes staring at her from the darkness. Trotting by her side was the same cat, its fur standing on end. "You do all of this?"

"Yep, pencils, inks, colors, and the writing. It keeps me hopping." Morris set down the pencil and shook out his hand, flexing his fingers.

"I can imagine." There were a number of comics in the holders as well as a small stack of books that looked like a compilation. "What's it about?"

"It's *Scooby-Doo!* meets *Dora the Explorer* with a dash of *E.S.P.*" Morris crossed his arms on the table as Theo picked up the compilation book and thumbed through it. "It's a kids' comic. The hero, Laila, is disabled from a car accident. She communicates with animals on a basic level, mostly her cat. And she goes around solving mysteries and generally taking life on at full throttle."

Car accident. Those two words struck an icy chord in Theo's heart and gut. He'd lost both parents, his dad to cancer and his mom from falling asleep at the wheel coming home late from the hospital. Too close together. Too fucking close. And the double punch still hurt.

Theo set the book down as he eyed the pencil drawing again. The way the girl reached as if she was on the verge of flying herself, the simple joy on her face called to him. He wanted the picture as a reminder that life went on, full of joy and pain in equal measure but still beautiful.

"Neat concept. I always wondered where artists and writers get their ideas and inspiration. Is it hard?"

"I have far more ideas than I have time to handle." Morris set the board down on the floor, propping it against the table, and folded his arms as he leaned closer. "The hard part is organizing the ideas into a usable form. It's like herding cats. You witnessed how well that goes."

"So if it's going to be a promotional banner, does that mean there will be lettering on it?" As much as Theo wanted the picture, he just wanted the image and not a lot of words all over.

"No. I used to do all my lettering by hand, but it's a lot easier to do it on the computer. You can even design your own fonts."

Theo's computer expertise ran to what he could do on his phone and even then not much. His sister Jill ran the books at the restaurant and had a sweet setup that intimidated him. She'd put in a new POS system that streamlined orders, but she'd had to talk him into it. At the time he was leery of the change, but now he was glad she had.

Theo looked around at the prints, impressed by the amount of work that went into a finished piece. Sure, he'd read plenty of comics growing up, though not nearly as many as Lincoln, but he'd never considered what went into making one. There was a little sign on the corner, like many of the other artists, advertising commissions.

"You get a lot of commissions?" Theo asked.

"Depends on the con. Brenden's shows are usually good for them and sales on the books. Other cons I'll get more interest off the prints or toys. Still others will be dead, but then I'll see increased traffic on my website and store. You never really know how it'll go until you're there."

Theo stepped back from the table as he looked over the show again. It was small, maybe fifty tables in all with a few vendors taking up more than one space. Though there had been a line when he'd arrived with his brother, there didn't seem to be a crowd thronging through looking to purchase. He couldn't imagine making a living doing this, though Morris didn't seem to be hurting.

It was a totally different world from the restaurant, but Theo could see how it all ran together, everybody knowing and doing their part to make the whole work. Theo wouldn't want to be in charge of running a show and getting everybody to function together. Bad enough dealing with his own staff. Thank the heavens for his sister, who was more than happy to deal with deliveries and vendors and everything to do with the front of the house. Theo just wanted to take care of his kitchen and cook.

"Brenden?"

"The promoter for the Chessie Cons." Morris pointed toward a tall, lean, bald man who examined a clipboard with an irritated expression as another man spoke with him, waving his arms in agitation. "He handles a few shows in Maryland and Virginia. The guy he's talking to is his foster brother, Dakota. He does a geek podcast, popular culture, game reviews, that sort of thing."

"Everything going okay?" Theo didn't see any obvious hiccups, but the two were definitely arguing, and the withering glance Brenden gave Dakota would stop anyone cold.

Morris craned his neck to look. "Yeah, they're often at each other's throats. Nothing to worry about. So this is my exciting life, art and cat chasing. How about you? What do you do?"

"I'm the head chef and co-owner of a restaurant." It was still strange to say, and as always, the words brought with them a mingled sense of pride, fear, and the dull ache of loss. "Chesapeake Bistro down in Solomon's Island."

"Hey, I know that place. Love the crab cakes. A group of us usually hit it up after this show." Morris looked at him again, his head slightly cocked. Theo had seen that expression before: curious to know how he'd gotten his own restaurant so young.

"Good to hear. We always like repeat customers." Theo gestured to the pad propped against the table and the half-finished drawing. "When you're done doing that for promo, how much for the original, fully colored?"

Morris sat back with a look of surprise. "You really want it? Not just pulling my chain?"

"Yeah, our living room is a little bare. I've been scouring everybody's portfolios here, looking for something that grabbed me that my brother would like too. I think this picture is it."

Morris looked down at the pad and then back up at Theo, speculation in his wide, dark eyes. "This isn't going to end up for sale online is it? 'Cause that would hurt, no lie."

"I swear." Theo could see Morris wavering, though hesitance lingered in the purse of his lips. Theo wasn't sure why Morris was so reluctant. Maybe knowing why Theo wanted it would sway his opinion. "I want it because it reminds me life goes on."

Theo felt silly for saying it. Out loud it sounded overly sentimental. But Morris's expression softened with understanding instead of laughter, and his gaze brightened. "Since that's some of what I was going for I can give it to you for eighty-five."

"That include a frame?" Theo asked as he dug into his pocket for his wallet.

"You're on your own there. I can give you the name of a place in Bowie that does good work. I've used them since high school. Gio who owns it is an old friend. If you drop my name he might give you a discount."

Matted and framed behind glass, the picture would make a nice centerpiece in their living room and maybe make it feel more like a home. Theo loved the house he'd grown up in, but without Mom and Dad, it felt empty. He had a dozen bills this money could go toward, but he didn't feel one speck of guilt over purchasing the picture. It wasn't like they were hard up.

"Do I pay you now or later?" Theo asked.

"Give me a couple weeks to finish it and get the promo together. Then I'll come up when you're home and show you the final piece. If you still want it, I'll take payment then."

"Fair enough. I want a couple prints today, though, and the first book." Theo looked them over and found a Spider-Man waving a rainbow flag over the Brooklyn Bridge. He plucked it from the rack and held it up for Morris to see with a questioning look, his interest renewed. Hot, great legs, and maybe swinging his way.... His new neighbor just got a lot more promising.

"Gotta represent," Morris said with a laconic shrug, though his gaze became wary.

"You're right. We do have to represent." Theo held up his fist for a bump. Morris tapped his knuckles with a slow smile. "I'll take this one and— Hold on. I need another one for my brother." He scanned through the offerings until he found one Lincoln might like. He wasn't sure who the ladies were, but Lincoln would know. Other guys Lincoln's age hung up hot pictures of women in their rooms. Lincoln hung up prints like these. When Theo had been fifteen, he'd been hiding Calvin Klein male underwear model photos under his mattress. Everybody had their thing.

Morris took out a Sharpie and signed his name with a flourish at the bottom of each print. "Is he a Scarlet Witch and Black Widow fan?"

The names sounded familiar, so Theo figured he must've picked the right print. "Not sure. To be honest, I didn't even know their names until you mentioned it. He's into all the geeky things."

"Does that mean you're not?" Morris asked, shaking his head with disappointment as he thumped his fist against his chest. "That hurts."

"Depends on the geek." Theo leaned closer, lowering his voice. "I'm an equal opportunity flirt."

"Good to know." Morris cast him a considering look, and Theo grinned back. Morris slid the signed prints into clear sleeves, then into a bag with the comic, and handed them back. "These are on me, as a welcome to the neighborhood gift."

"Thank you. I'll let you get back to work," Theo replied, conscious of the swirl of people around him pausing to look at Morris's wares. "If you do stop by the bistro tonight with your friends, be sure to ask for me and I'll return the favor."

"Will do." Morris picked up the pad and his lap table. "Enjoy the rest of the con."

Reluctantly, Theo turned away and checked his watch. He'd been at Morris's table longer than he expected, and Lincoln's panel should be over. He'd find his brother, talk him into getting something to eat, and then maybe he'd have another chance to flirt with Morris before they had to leave for the restaurant.

# Chapter Three

"YOU WANT the original Justice League as Minions?" Morris asked the woman standing before his table. He hadn't expected a last-minute commission. Most of the attendees had started draining out of the hall an hour ago, but he wasn't going to dismiss her either. It seemed like fewer people wanted original art these days.

"Yep, a two-page spread, full color." Sara dug into her backpack and pulled out a hardcover sketchbook. "I've been looking at your stuff for a few shows, but my book's been tied up with other artists."

She set the sketchbook on the table and opened it about halfway to where she'd marked the pages with a slip of paper. "Right here. I like to leave a blank page in between when I'm doing color so it doesn't bleed into someone else's picture."

"May I?" Morris asked, gesturing to the sketchbook.

"Sure." Sara handed over her treasure with a smile of pride.

Morris turned it to the beginning and flipped through the collection, his fingertips carefully grazing the edges of the paper as he turned. The sketchbook held all kinds of finished pieces in every style from the simple to the incredibly detailed. Some were ink only, others fully colored, most were single-page pictures, though a few were two-page spreads like the one she was commissioning. "You have a really sweet collection."

"Thanks. I got started last year. I saw some guy walking around Awesome Con with one of these. He said he'd been doing it for years. He even has a couple themed sketchbooks. It seemed like a really neat idea." She grimaced. "I love it, though it gets expensive."

"I think I know who you're talking about. I've done a few commissions for him. The guy with the service dog?" Morris tended to see familiar faces even though he attended cons from New York to Georgia. Whatever one he could get to within a decent drive that wouldn't lay him out.

"That's him." Sara closed her backpack and shrugged her arms through it. "Thanks for doing this."

"Thanks for thinking of me." Morris marked the page again with the slip of paper. "When do you want it by?"

Sara glanced around at the vendors, some of whom were already packing. "I was hoping for today, but the other guy took longer than I thought he would, and it is a two pager. I guess I could wait until the next Chessie Con if you're going."

The next one of Brenden's shows was two months away. Morris understood the hesitance in her expression. "You local?" Morris asked as he tucked the sketchbook into his bag.

"Sorta. College Park." She gave him a conspiratorial smile. "Don't let my parents know I'm spending my food budget on cons and art."

"That's part of college life." Morris had blown his semester budget more than once on feeding his own geek interests. His college experience contained as many art classes as he could get away with in between the courses for the education major his parents and advisers had talked him into. His mom appreciated that he was artistic like her, but as an art teacher herself she insisted on a major that would ensure a job after graduating. "I know College Park well, went to school there. I teach a class not too far away on Wednesdays. Give me a week or so. I'll email you, and we can arrange a meet up."

"That would be awesome." She grabbed one of his business cards and scrawled an email address on the back. "I can't wait to see it. Half now, half then?"

That was how Morris usually arranged it, but considering he had her sketchbook, he was sure she wouldn't renege on him. There was too much money already invested in it. He'd been burned in the past too many times not to have collateral. "If you want, or you can pay me when we meet. Up to you."

"Here." She dug into her back pocket and laid down some cash. "Not quite half, but splitting it will make it less of a bite later." She bounced off toward the exit with one last backward wave.

Morris scooped up the cash and put it with a note into the small moneybag. He pulled out his suitcases from under the table and began taking down the prints, humming to himself. All around him, other vendors and artists were doing the same with the exception of the few who'd ducked out early. He'd never understood that. Sure, there were cons where he did terrible, but he'd paid for the table and space, and he wasn't about to leave that commitment until he'd given it every chance.

There had been more than one occasion when he'd had a last-minute sale that made up for the day.

Today had been a good day. He had a few commissions lined up. He'd made enough in sales to pay back the cost of the table with a little extra. He'd been hit up with the possibility of a collaborative project. To make it even better, he'd had a chance to talk to Theo a couple of times and even meet his younger brother, Lincoln. That alone made his day. Morris didn't often get a chance to meet guys who flirted with him like Theo. His sister would say it was his fault for not getting out more, but Morris didn't enjoy meeting strangers unless he was sitting behind his table.

He had several gay friends among the convention circuit, but nothing had ever come out of those friendships. People outside of his circle often treated his interests and hectic schedule as if they were something he needed to be cured of, to the point where he almost swore off dating nongeeks. Most gay men he met assumed that because of his height he liked to top, when it was the exact opposite. He was a six-foot-three, black, geeky bottom. The struggle was real.

It wasn't like he never dated. He did, but it had been a while. Morris was the oddball among the men he met. The quiet artist who more often than not preferred the company of his cat and his pencils. He was usually content with his life. It was only periodic bouts of loneliness that made him question his choice to be a hermit. That and a gorgeous new neighbor who was easy to talk to and adorably sexy on the eyes. Who absolutely should be off-limits, considering the disaster the last time he tried dating someone who didn't share his interests.

"Hey, want to meet up for dinner in about an hour or so?"

Morris turned around at the sound of Felipe Suero's voice. The cosplayer was dressed as Link in a green tunic and tan breeches. He had an impressive array of accessories, from the ocarina dangling from his belt, to the shield strapped on his arm, to the green hat tilted at a rakish angle. But then, Felipe prided himself on the details, and he'd spend months handcrafting a costume and the weapons just for the joy of walking around a con and meeting people. Now here was one geek who was not shy at all.

Morris grinned as he straightened from his crouch. "Hey, Felipe, I'd love to. I didn't get a chance to catch up with you earlier. Who else is coming?"

"I'm sure Jackie is in." Felipe pointed toward Jackie's table, where the quiet redhead was busy rolling up her banner. "She mentioned wanting a few drinks tonight. Brett's family wants in as well."

"That works. I haven't seen Brett and Daphne in a while. I have to thank their son for saving me a couple times today. Jaydon covered my booth while I grabbed a drink and a bathroom break." Daphne crocheted geek-themed crafts, and Brett wrote sci-fi novels. They were often at the same cons as Morris, and they, along with Jackie and Felipe, formed part of their unofficial gaming group.

"That's what con rats are for, and Jaydon's been running around here since he was out of diapers. It's about time he helped out." Felipe patted down his pockets and the pouch at his waist before he found his keys. "I need to change first before we meet up. Once we decide where, I can figure out what to do. Might not make sense to head home."

"Cool costume," Morris said as he began to break down the wire frame into its individual squares. "Did you enter the contest?"

"Nah." Felipe grimaced. "Brenden said I take it too many times. He drafted me to be a judge instead. Which actually worked out because I was able to drum up some new business. There were some great entries. Some kid in a Kylo Ren costume won for the teens; an adorable little Hermione with afro puffs won the kids."

"What about the adult?" Morris had seen some amazing costumes today and some that were almost nonexistent, especially the older gentleman as Conan the Barbarian in nothing but a loincloth with a gigantic sword strapped to his back.

Felipe's grimace deepened. "Abby."

Felipe didn't need to say anything else. Abby Albion and Felipe had been in fierce competition since kindergarten, each of them striving to outdo the other. She would've gotten a kick out of him being banned from the competition as much as she would've sweated having him on the judges' panel. "Did you vote for her?"

"I had to, dammit. Her Alice in Wonderland meets Dorothy from Oz was fucking amazing. I hate her." He shook his head with a rueful smile. "I should've thought of it first. I look awesome in a dress."

Better to head off the rant before it got started. "Who else is coming? What about Dakota? You guys still a thing?" Morris asked as he stored the wire frames in their box before turning to organizing his supplies.

"Define a thing," Felipe said with a sigh. "We're still screwing if that's what you mean. He doesn't seem interested in anything more. Too busy kissing his brother's anal ass. It's a bomb ass, but I still wouldn't want to kiss it."

"Sorry, man." Morris threw a glance over his shoulder to make sure neither of them were nearby. Dakota and Brenden's feelings for each other were obvious to everyone who knew them. Well, obvious to everyone but them and their family and, bless him, Felipe. One day all that unexplored sexual tension was going to blow up in their faces. He'd had grave misgivings when Felipe set his sights on Dakota, but Felipe listened to no one when it came to following his own heart. Morris had tried until he'd caught the acid side of Felipe's tongue one too many times.

"Nothing to be sorry for," Felipe replied with a shrug. "I knew the deal when I hooked up with him, and it's still fun. We're friends with benefits until someone else comes along."

"Good luck with that." Morris hadn't been looking, but Theo made him give that a second thought. He'd solemnly sworn never to date a nongeek again, though Morris had to give Theo major points for attending a con with his brother instead of dropping him off at the door. He stifled a groan. He was reading too far into this already. One look at his neighbor, and he got all starry-eyed like an anime girl.

"That doesn't answer the question, though. Is he coming?" Morris wasn't sure if he wanted to sit in the middle of a Dakota-Felipe-Brenden triangle. It all depended on everyone's mood.

"Not sure. He's doing an interview tonight, so if he does meet up with us, it won't be until later."

"On a good note," Morris said as he closed the lid to his box of markers, "Brenden mustn't be taking exception to you seeing Dakota again or he would've found an excuse to boot you out with all the other attendees."

"Nah, he just hasn't seen me yet." Felipe looked over his shoulder as if searching for the bald promoter. "I still have to change anyway. What are you in the mood to eat? BBQ? Somewhere nearby, please. I don't want to head back to Chuck County yet."

Morris's stomach rumbled, reminding him all he'd had for sustenance over the day was a carafe of coffee and a mango juice. "How about the Chesapeake Bistro? We haven't been there in a while."

Felipe's eyes lit up. "Yeah, that will work. I've been itching for some crab cakes. I'll let Jackie and the Karlins know as I leave and have them send out the word to anyone else who might be interested. Hey, do you mind if I change at your place?"

"Nope." Morris dug out his keys and tossed them to Felipe. "Save me a seat."

Felipe snagged the keys with a grin. "Will do."

"Suero!"

Felipe adjusted his sword belt and winced as the deep, withering voice rolled through the hall. "There's my cue to leave. Brenden's got his boxers twisted up his ass again."

"Your tag doesn't say artist, vendor, or guest," Brenden continued as he walked up to them with his clipboard clamped under his arm. "You were supposed to exit twenty minutes ago."

"I'm going. I'm going." Felipe held up his hands as he backed away. "Chill out, man."

"It's my fault," Morris cut in. Brenden glanced at him, his mouth pinched with irritation. "I pulled him in for a conversation and didn't pay attention to what was going on around us."

"Suero's more than capable of defending himself," Brenden grumbled, but his expression lightened.

"I was trying to work on my pickup lines. I'm out of practice," Morris said as Felipe inched back and then headed for the exit as soon as he was out of Brenden's line of sight.

Brenden's brow arched in disbelief. "You and Felipe? For real? You and that trouble in tights and wigs? I thought he was banging the sense out of Dakota."

Morris would've paid good money to watch the fallout of that remark if Felipe had stuck around. Brenden glanced over when the comment failed to cause an eruption, and his scowl deepened. Felipe had made a clean getaway.

"Hell no," Morris replied. "I'd bore him to tears, and he'd drive me mental. I said practice, not for real."

"Ever the peacemaker." Brenden shook his head and eased his grip on his clipboard. "I repeat, Suero doesn't need you to run interference for him. I was itching for a good argument."

"Well, a bunch of us are headed to the Chesapeake Bistro for dinner, Felipe included. You're more than welcome to join us if you really want an evening filled with debate and needling." Morris lifted his suitcase onto the empty table beside him and began filling it up with the boxes that held his prints.

"Can't. I have a meeting with the other promoters. I'll text you if I decide to stop in later for a couple of drinks. Is Dakota going?" Brenden asked, his voice deceptively casual.

Morris sympathized with the triangle Felipe found himself in and he understood his friend was impatient with the situation, but he had to admit his sympathies were firmly with Brenden. He knew Felipe well enough to recognize his friend wasn't in love. As for Brenden, it was more complicated. If it was just lust between Brenden and Dakota, just scratching an itch, it would've blown over long ago, but there was more to their feelings. And anything more meant involving family. That was a can of trouble that didn't need to be opened by anyone.

"Not sure, to be honest. He's got a gig going right now. But he's more than welcome to join if you want to include him." Morris sent a silent apology to Felipe. They could sit on opposite ends on the table if they had to. Their local comic con world was small. They all had to work with one another.

"We'll see. I'll let you know." Brenden glanced down at his clipboard. "How was the show for you?"

"Good considering the location. I'll admit, I had my doubts when you first announced it. The crowd was steady, and there were new faces over the day, always a good sign. It gets a little old when you see the same people circling. The small stuff moved okay, and I landed a few commissions, which always makes me happy."

"Good to know." Brenden made a careful note and set his clipboard aside. "What would you think about doing a larger venue with me? Multiple days, bigger town?"

"More expensive table?" Morris added. He'd been scaling back on some of the bigger cons. After paying out for the table, hotel, and meals it didn't always pan out. There were a couple he always went to—Baltimore Comic Con, Awesome Con—because they were local and he could cut the costs. Besides, that was half work and half catching up with friends.

"That goes with the territory. Bigger venue, more days, more money. I've been considering the jump for a while." Brenden's eyes lit up. "I'd like to attract a few big names, get a real crowd going, but I wanted to feel you and some of the others out. The ones who've been with me from the beginning."

"Where would you have it?" Morris asked, intrigued by the possibility. He usually had luck with minimal hassle at the shows Brenden promoted. Brenden's ways might set some people on edge, but he got shit done smoothly. "DC and Baltimore already have big shows. I guess you could do Richmond, but that might step on the toes of the smaller cons. Unless you're thinking of venturing farther out."

"I'm looking at Annapolis. I'm hoping to keep some of the costs down since it's not a huge city." Brenden frowned in thought. "Though Richmond is still an option."

"That's a thought. Keep me updated." Morris zipped up his suitcase and glanced around to see what else he needed to do before he rolled out.

"What show do you plan on going to next?" Brenden asked.

Morris crouched and began stacking the rest of his gear onto the dolly, going over his mental calendar. "I'll be at Awesome Con, after that Allentown, then Hunt Valley. It's getting to be the busy season."

"Well, if I don't see you tonight, I'll see you at Awesome Con. I'll be there promoting our next event. You planning on going?"

"The one in Newport News?" Morris asked as he strapped everything down with bungee cords. "Yeah, I gave Dakota the cash earlier."

Brenden frowned as he flipped through the various papers on his clipboard, and then his expression cleared. "Yep, got you down. Thanks, man. You want a receipt?"

"You can email it, no rush." After his debacle with taxes last April, Morris was trying to keep everything organized electronically. He was not about to face his sister again with a bag full of receipts and a list of shows on his phone.

"Will do." Brenden held out his fist, and Morris tapped his knuckles against it. "See you around."

# Chapter Four

HEAT SHIMMERED in the kitchen as steaks sizzled on the grill, ovens poured forth aromas when they opened, and a battalion of pots and pans steamed and crackled. The vapor from the dishwasher in the back added to the humidity, as did the frenetic activity of the cooks. Theo loved it all, the glut of his senses from the clamor. It was like a dance, and he was the choreographer. Some viewed cooking as a science, and though that wasn't a bad way to look at it, Theo considered it art.

Jill walked to the line, where waiters deftly added plates to trays and whisked them away. His sister looked calm amidst the staff weaving and eddying around her. Her light brown hair was pulled back into a braid, wisps escaping around her face and frizzing slightly in the humidity. She stroked a hand over her belly, her summer dress starting to show off the little bump of her pregnancy. He'd expected hormones to turn her into a hot mess, but oddly enough, she seemed to be mellowing instead. She deserved a little mellowness after the last year.

"Theo, you have a tall, dark, and handsome throwing your name around in the dining room," Jill said, her expressive eyes lit up with curiosity. "Could it be you are finally taking an interest in the male species again?"

Morris showed up. A slow, quiet buzz of satisfaction went through Theo. "Wearing a kilt? Great legs?"

"I noticed the kilt, but I didn't pay any attention to his legs," Jill replied primly.

"Liar." Theo grinned and leaned his elbows on the countertop so he could get a better look into the dining room. But Morris wasn't visible from this angle. "I won't tell Craig you were eyeing."

Jill ignored his teasing with the air of a long sufferer. "He brought a bunch of people with him, so I put him in the back near the deck."

"Be a doll and offer a couple of appetizers to his table for free. I'll cover it," Theo added before she could object. It was a rule their parents had instilled when they were teenagers and started having friends hang out at the restaurant. One summer he and Jill had comped so much food their dad lost his temper. And that took quite a bit of doing. Now any offerings of freebies came directly out of their own pocket. The rule stuck when they assumed ownership of the bistro.

"He's caught your attention." Jill tucked a wisp of hair behind her ear and smiled. "Where'd you meet him?"

"Maybe I'm being neighborly." Theo gave his sister an innocent look. "He rents the apartment downstairs."

"Now who's the liar? If you were just being neighborly, you wouldn't have mentioned his legs first thing," Jill retorted as one of the waitresses called out an order and entered it into the system. Theo straightened and glanced toward the screen, where the order appeared in a neat line with the rest. Jill had been right to splurge. No more trying to decipher handwriting, no more lost slips or ones that got mixed up out of order. Theo wished their parents could see what a success it was for them.

"Scottie, need an order of hush puppies and corn balls, and an order of Old Bay wings."

"Order of pups, balls, and wings coming up," Scottie boomed back in his deep, bass voice.

Theo inspected a dish of fried oysters as they plated and nodded his approval. "Those look good, Letty," he said as she filled a small ramekin with their homemade remoulade and another with the cocktail sauce. Theo added a wedge of lemon and set the plate in the window with the rest of the order. "Order's up."

"Are you sure they're not underdone?" she fretted. It had taken weeks to get her to stop over-frying the food to unappetizing useless lumps, and he was not about to let her backslide now.

"They look perfect," Theo assured her. "Stop second-guessing the method so much."

He cast his sister an eloquent look, left Letty to handle the fish, and turned back to the grill. He enjoyed cooking at every station and made a point of switching around so his crew could have experience everywhere, but he had to admit, he had a special fondness for firing up a perfect steak. If the orders eased back, he might have a chance to slip out and say hello to Morris and his friends, but he wasn't holding his breath. It was a Saturday night.

It was after ten before the kitchen slowed down enough for Theo to take a break. He handed over control to Scottie, grabbed himself a plate of the special, and told himself not to feel guilty. He'd be closing the place down after Scottie left for the night. As he came into the dining room, he spied Jill and Lincoln sitting in a booth near the door rolling silverware. Theo recognized a couple locals at the bar, and the dining room was mostly empty except for a large party at the back nursing drinks and their dessert plates. Theo skimmed over the faces until his gaze landed on Morris. He was talking earnestly to the woman beside him, his expressive hands gesturing as he made his points.

He lingered over Morris's strong cheekbones and lush mouth and wondered if he could get away with stealing a kiss. It might make being his neighbor awkward, but then again, if Morris wasn't interested, they weren't likely to run into each other much. Not if it took them this long to meet. Morris glanced up, and their eyes caught and held. Morris grinned and waved Theo over. Theo held up his finger as he made his way over to his sister. Business first, then pleasure.

"Good night, we were crushed in the kitchen," Theo said, leaning his hip against the side of the booth.

Jill glanced up with a smile, though Theo could see the weariness in her eyes. "Yeah, the summer crowd is booming, and your new friends seem intent on racking up a nice tab. The group keeps diminishing, then expanding again."

"I think they're all con people." Theo winked at Lincoln, who was trying to twist his long body around to see the group. "Morris said a bunch of them like to hang out after a show."

"Morris? Is he the guy with the legs?" Jill asked with an amused smile.

Lincoln glanced at Theo with an expression of dawning horror. "You can't flirt with our new neighbor."

"Why the fuck not?" Theo retorted as a blush stained Lincoln's cheeks and Jill rolled her eyes.

"Because it would be weird," Lincoln muttered.

"Only for you, bro, so maybe you ought to stay out of it because it's really not your business." Theo sighed inwardly as Lincoln's expression darkened. He was so touchy. Theo remembered being moody as a teenager, but Lincoln took it to extremes. "But if it'll make you feel better, I won't flirt in front of you, unless he starts it. Then you gotta suck it up because I'm going to encourage him."

"Sounds fair to me," Jill said as she stacked the neatly rolled cutlery into the bin on the table.

"Yeah, I guess so," Lincoln replied, his long mouth sulky. "Is it okay if I spend the night at Jill's?"

"I don't see why not. Go home, both of you. I'll take care of closing," Theo said, eyeing the circles under Jill's eyes. She had brought up the idea of hiring someone new for the front of the house, leaving her to handle the books and everything else that went with management. Theo had been resisting. Partially because she also wanted him to hire on more help for himself, and Theo didn't want anyone else in charge of his kitchen. He also didn't want anyone other than family managing the front of the house. But they were both running themselves ragged, and Lincoln was getting lost somewhere in the middle.

Lincoln's eyes widened. "For real? But what about the last tables?"

"If you're all caught up in the kitchen, I'll take care of running the last of the dishes through." Theo tugged on the brim of Lincoln's cap. "Thanks for your help today."

Lincoln grinned at him, his sulks forgotten. "Thanks for bringing me to the show."

"I'm going to take you up on that," Jill said, struggling to wiggle her way out of the booth. He held out his hand to help her up, and she took it with a grimace. "It seems like my equilibrium is all off. At least I'm not as tired as I used to be."

"She'll be here by the time school starts," Theo assured her. "And the moment she can hold a spatula, I'm putting her to work."

"She has to be teething first, then I'll consider it." Jill rubbed the small of her back, gave Theo a tired smile, and waved Lincoln toward the door. "I'll bring him by for the lunch shift."

Theo glanced at the table and bit back a sigh. Lincoln's phone remained tucked beside the cutlery bin. He had the habit of taking it out of his pocket when he was sitting and then leaving it behind. Theo scooped it up. "Don't forget your phone, Linc."

"Don't worry. I've got it." Lincoln shot him a look of exasperation as he patted his pockets and his expression changed to one of comical confusion.

Theo held up the phone with a little wave and resisted the urge to toss Lincoln's words back at him. He handed over the phone without comment, shaking his head as Lincoln slipped it into his pocket without looking at him and made a dash for the door. Theo did not understand how someone could simultaneously live on something and forget it all the time.

As Theo made his way toward Morris's table, he made a quick note of who was still on duty. They were down to one bartender and two waitresses, all of them already starting the night cleanup. Once the doors shut all they'd have to do was grab some food for themselves and do the final scrub down and they could head home.

Morris grinned at him as Theo pulled out a chair, and some of his own tiredness disappeared under the warmth of that smile. "Hey, I was wondering if you'd get a chance to come out. It looked like it was busy. Then I saw you talking with your brother and that lady who hasn't stopped moving all night. Jill, I think her name was. She offered us an appetizer."

"We were hopping," Theo agreed, cutting into his fish. "That lady was my sister. She owns the bistro with me. Did you enjoy your crab cakes?"

"Best I've had in a while." Morris waved his hand at the group, who studied Theo with friendly curiosity. "Everyone, this is Theo. He owns this joint. Theo, this is Felipe, Jackie, Dakota—" Morris pointed around the table to each face, some of whom Theo recognized from the show. "You missed the Karlins. Their rug rat fell asleep almost as soon as he finished eating. Dakota, is your brother coming by?"

"Nah, he's still hanging with his gang, planning the takeover of the world," Dakota replied, giving Theo a once-over with a cool, assessing gaze. "Nice place you've got."

"Thanks." As Theo began to eat, the others continued with their conversation, which made little sense to him but seemed to involve tension between cosplayers and vendors. Theo figured they'd be as lost if he plunked them down in the midst of a group of restaurant people. "How'd the rest of the show go?" he asked Morris.

"Pretty good. I hope the summer season goes as well. You never really know how a show's going to go until you're in the middle of it." Morris looked around the restaurant at the pictures of the Chesapeake Bay and local life, the light wood bar top and well-scrubbed counters. "I can see why you're never at home."

"It's a busy time of year." At least with school ending soon, Lincoln could help more. Though Jill and he agreed they weren't going to pressure him to spend all of his time at the restaurant. Not all of their siblings had the same fire to keep the place going, and they didn't want Lincoln to come to resent it like the others had. "Though it helps to have family involved."

"Every quarter I have to talk my sister into doing my taxes for me. The amount of bribery she demands gets worse every time. This last April she made me do an entire spa day with her. It would've been cheaper to go to a local agent."

Theo grinned at the sorrowful shake of Morris's head. "She made you get a mani-pedi, didn't she?"

"The full works. She even let my niece pick out the color. Lime-green sparkles."

Felipe leaned over with a wicked snicker. "Maybe next time you won't wait until the day before the deadline."

"Shut up, you." Morris gave him a friendly shove before turning back to Theo. "Good luck with your siblings. Mine are the devil."

"Ah, the trials of being the youngest," Theo said, giving the bartender the nod to go ahead and start closing out.

Morris grimaced. "Man, they can mother hen a guy to death. They get on my dad too."

"Well, being the oldest has its own hang-ups, trust me. So what do you do after a show? Take a break?" Theo asked as he mentally ran over his schedule for the next day, wondering if he could sneak in some time for a quick date, even if it was just a cup of coffee down by the water.

"The problem with taking a break is that it's hard to get started again," Morris replied. "I'll be back at it tomorrow, working on a couple commissions and plotting out the next issue of the book. I want to make some real progress because I'm tied up the whole next weekend. I have a date with Laila that I wouldn't dream of backing out of. And she'll know if I'm distracted."

"Date?" Ah man, Morris was bisexual, and he had a girlfriend. Well, there went all thoughts of flirting with his hot new neighbor. Lincoln would be relieved, though Theo was keenly disappointed. Not that he really had time to date, but it had been a nice thought for the day. And Morris had been the first guy to pull his thoughts away from the constant cycle of family and the bistro.

"Yeah, my niece. I haven't been up to see her in a bit. That's what my sister was ragging on me about this morning. I'm taking her to the pool opening before we have a cookout at my parents'." A soft smile crossed Morris's face. "I've been a neglectful uncle."

"Not if you let her paint your toes sparkly green." That was sweet. Theo didn't know many men who'd take a day off to spend with their niece. He supposed he had that to look forward to with Jill's baby girl. "You'll have to give me some tips. My sister's having a girl this fall. A boy would've been no problem. I'm not quite sure what to do with a girl."

"Be prepared for her to have you in her tiny hands," Morris said with a knowing shrug. "They are masters of the adorable, and they know it."

"Thanks for the warning, though I doubt it'll do much good." Theo reluctantly pushed back his plate. He could give it another few minutes, but then he had to get back to the kitchen.

Felipe broke off from his banter with the others and turned toward Morris and Theo with an edge of irritation in his gaze. He scrutinized Theo. There was something about the slant of his mouth and the narrow spacing of his eyes that seemed familiar, but Theo couldn't place him. He must've seen him at the con earlier, but he would've remembered the thick raven-dark hair and smooth, warm complexion that made him almost pretty.

"You went to the show today, didn't you?" Felipe asked, cocking his head. "I'm sure I saw you wandering through the booths."

Now the sense of trying to place him really began to dig at Theo, but it continued to elude him. "Yeah, first time I've been to a show. It was actually better than I thought it would be." Theo shot Morris an apologetic look. "I've never been much of a geek."

"I guess, then, this neighbor thing isn't going to work out," Morris said with a pretend show of sorrow. "I couldn't possibly live in the same house with a man who openly disavows geek life."

"He can cook," Felipe pointed out as he glanced at the time on his phone. "And he's making no issue of us hanging out instead of shooing us out the door when they're about to close."

"Those are valid points, and your brother is one of us, so you have potential." A slight smile played on Morris's lips as he glanced at Theo through thick black lashes.

That was a definite sign of flirting if Theo ever saw one, enough that he was perfectly comfortable telling his brother Morris started it. "Sweetheart, I have loads of potential."

"I wouldn't kick him out of bed," Felipe murmured with a sideways glance at Dakota, who rolled his eyes.

"You kick me out of bed all the time," Dakota teased. Theo recognized him as the broad-shouldered, scowling man who'd been arguing with his foster brother at the show. He had a stubborn jaw and a hard slash of a nose that looked equally uncompromising.

"Enough, you two." Jackie leveled a glare at the couple. "Before I have to knock your heads together."

"It's okay." Felipe patted Jackie's hand. "Trust me, this is our version of foreplay."

One thick black eyebrow rose, and Morris's smile widened. "Potential, huh? Okay, quick test, then."

"Bring it," Theo challenged. "Only I get to test you in return."

"Sounds kinky." Dakota crossed his arms on the table. "But not appropriate for a family establishment."

"Seems fair enough to me." Morris ignored the byplay and leveled a finger at Theo. "Old-school or new-school *Doctor Who*?"

Theo's confidence took a hit. Morris wasn't playing softball, or Theo must've heard him wrong. *Doctor Who*? "What was his name again?" There was something vaguely familiar about it. Something Theo overheard at the show, maybe.

Morris shook his head sadly as his three friends exchanged amused glances. Theo should've brought Scottie along to back up his team. "Next question."

"Wait," Theo cut in. "It's my turn to even the playing field, to test these compatibility waters. How do you like your steak cooked?"

Morris grimaced and side-eyed him. "Well done."

"Ouch, wow." Theo bumped his fist against his chest. "I think that actually hurt."

"You two are hilarious," Felipe said with a laugh and elbowed Jackie. "Are you checking this out?"

Morris held up a second finger. "Marvel or DC?"

That one was easier. Theo had heard of both of them. Only problem was he wasn't sure which characters belonged to which company. "The one Spider-Man is from. He's cool. But I'm not sure why every time they make a new movie with a new actor they have to go through his origin story again. How many times do I have to watch Uncle Ben die?"

"That's not really answering the question," Dakota said, propping his chin on his fist. "I'm not sure if that qualifies for points or not."

"Hey, he offered a valid criticism," Jackie replied. "I think it counts."

"I have to agree. I don't want to see Uncle Ben die again either. If a nongeek knows it's time to move on to another story, it's definitely overplayed. It's not like Spidey doesn't have plenty of material to pull from." Morris turned back to Theo. "Your turn."

"What vegetables go into a mirepoix?" Theo asked, and Morris's eyes went blank. Since Morris had given him a question Theo had a chance of answering he figured he could give him a clue. "It's your aromatics, the start of many soups, stews."

"This is when we need Brenden. He'd know it," Dakota said with a you're-on-your-own smirk.

"You mean like a *ginisa?*" Felipe asked with a curious look. "Garlic, onions, tomatoes, sautéed in a bit of oil, a little meat for flavoring? My lola does that."

"I haven't heard the term before." Theo's interest was piqued. He was always looking for new recipes and techniques. "What kind of food does your lola cook?"

"All kinds, Filipino mostly, especially on big occasions or when she's feeling homesick." Felipe shrugged. "She likes to cook. She says it's relaxing."

"If she ever feels like sharing recipes, I'd be happy to take them." Theo didn't mind the input of others, especially since it seemed as if some of them were on his side.

"I'll let her know," Felipe promised.

"Sorry, man. My freezer is full of Hot Pockets, pizzas, and burritos, though I do cook a mean pot of ramen," Morris said. "Half of what you said is as meaningless to me as if I'd said Copic and Prismacolor to you."

"I will take a stab at it and guess it has something to do with coloring? Pencils?" Theo guessed, and Jackie caught his gaze with an encouraging nod. "Oh no, wait, I've got it. They are graphic art programs?"

"Yes and no," Morris replied. "Copic are markers, damned expensive ones when you're on a budget. I do have some Prismacolor pencils too. I'll count that as partial points again. So what's in a mirepoix?"

Two partial points in a row—that was grounds for taking a leap. "I'm off the Thursday after next. Come up to my place for dinner and I'll teach you." Theo met Morris's gaze and saw the temptation, but there was enough hesitance to make him wonder what held him back. Bad breakup?

"I'll consider it based on how you answer this," Morris hedged and held up a third finger. "Final question. *Star Trek* or *Star Wars*?"

Theo had seen movies from both franchises and enjoyed them even though they weren't his usual genre. But he was having too much fun with Morris's reactions to admit to it. "Hmmm." Theo drew his eyebrows together, pretending puzzlement, and stifled a chuckle as Dakota shook his head with an expression of disbelief. "I like the one with the little robot," he teased. "What's his name…? I took Lincoln to the movie."

"The little robot," Felipe said under his breath with a nudge to Dakota.

"*Star Wars*, aha, I got one!" Theo grinned. "Full points to me."

Jackie patted his hand in a pitying gesture. "That's debatable, but I'm on your side. Morris, you should take him up on his dinner offer."

"Well, you're not completely hopeless." Morris laughed with a shrug. Theo wondered if Morris actually had a preference with his questions or if he'd just been trying to gauge the depth of Theo's cluelessness.

"Yes he is," Dakota said. "Run screaming now."

"Please, we all have our issues," Theo cut in, focusing all his attention on Morris. "I for one am absolutely offended you could think to butcher a steak order the way you do, yet I'm still interested. Give a non-geek a chance."

A slow smile crossed Morris's lips. "I can't believe I'm doing this, but okay. Mirepoix at your place it is."

"You won't regret it." Theo grinned and stood up, casting a quick glance around at the rest of the group. "Last call for anything in the kitchen. I'm getting ready to shut it down."

Felipe eyeballed the smeared chocolate on his plate, all that remained of his dessert. "No." Dakota took his plate away and set it on the edge of the table. "No more for you."

Felipe shot him a fierce scowl. "You have no say. We're a casual thing, remember?"

"Bullshit. I have every say. Because I'm the one who has to listen to you bitch about the state of your thighs the next time you get into a costume." Dakota tapped his finger against Felipe's mouth as Felipe drew himself up, his eyes flashing dangerously. "For the record, I like your thighs any way I can get them. I don't like the rants."

Theo knew better than to get in the middle of that one. Felipe did not look mollified in the least. He beat a hasty retreat to the kitchen, taking the offending plate with him before Felipe launched it at Dakota's head.

# Chapter Five

LAILA PARKED her wheelchair under the shaded canopy of the pavilion as Morris set their cooler underneath the table. Before he had a chance to finish laying out their towels on nearby chairs and dig out the sunscreen, she'd already shucked her T-shirt and shorts. His niece might not be able to get around on land as fast as she wanted to, but in the water, she was an eel and always impatient to go swimming.

"Hurry up, Uncle Morris." Her voice was high with excitement as she eyed the cool water longingly. They were early enough that the pool hadn't yet filled up with the usual after-lunch crowd. With the exception of a few families getting a start on the holiday, they would have the lanes to themselves.

"Hold on. I need to get some of this on you." He held up the bottle of spray-on sunscreen.

"Forget that. I just need my swim cap and goggles." Laila wadded her T-shirt and shorts together and tossed them onto the chair with an overhand lob. Her arms and legs were rail thin from a recent growth spurt. Morris remembered those days when it seemed like he was a bundle of sticks shooting upward.

"Oh no, no way I'm going to explain that to your mom when you come back with a sunburn. Hold still, wiggle worm."

Laila gave him a long-suffering look but patiently subsided as he sprayed on the stuff. "How much longer do we have until adult swim time?" she asked as she stuffed her thick hair under the cap. His sister had a hell of a time keeping her still long enough to braid it back.

"Over half an hour," Morris replied with a quick glance at the clock near the lifeguard station. "Then we can bake in the sun for a bit and start all over again."

Laila's answering grin was pure sunshine. "And we can stay all day? Promise?"

"Right up until the time when we have to get ready to go to Grandma's house." Morris tapped her nose and handed Laila her goggles.

"Yay!" Laila lifted her strong arms and wrapped them around Morris's neck as he scooped her up. "I wish you lived closer, Uncle Morris. Then we could do this all the time."

"I promise, every weekend this summer I don't have a show, I'll come up at least one day," Morris said as he stepped into the pool. They must've just filled it that week because it was shockingly cold in the blazing heat of the day. He paused on the second step. "I'm not sure my body can take this."

"Uncle Morris! Don't be such a wimp."

"Ouch. I don't know what shocks me more, the water or your sass." Morris braced himself against the chill and carried himself the rest of the way in.

As soon as she was fully submerged, Laila let go of him with a squeal and eeled away, her slim body cutting through the water with astonishing quickness and agility. She pulled herself through with her upper body, her legs trailing behind her. If Laila could live in the pool, she would. Her head popped out of the water several yards away, and she twisted around to look back at him. "Race ya."

"Whatever, shrimp. You couldn't take me on your best day," Morris said, moving his arms in lazy circles. It wasn't so bad once his body adjusted, and the sun beating down on the top of his head added warmth.

"I betcha I can. I practiced at camp all last summer. Gonna do it again this year too."

Laila's summer camp had been the best thing to happen to her since the accident that left her paralyzed. They'd watched her confidence bloom as she was encouraged to dare and dream as much as she wanted without an overprotective family hovering over every move she made. Camp had also taught them they didn't have to treat Laila like a broken china doll, and once they stopped doing that, she stopped acting like she was one.

Morris came up alongside her and rolled onto his back. "What? Did they give you flippers and gills?"

Laila giggled and swam over to the wall. "I'll go easy on you."

"Hey, that's my line." Morris took a position beside her and eyed the length of the pool. "Okay, on my mark, one, two, three."

Laila couldn't push off, but that didn't stop her for one moment. She was gone, arms stroking smoothly as she swayed her body, coordinating her breathing with her strokes. Morris took off after her, moving at an easy pace until he realized he'd better push it. He was a little surprised that he had to work to catch up with her. She'd gotten to be fast, and he spent far too much time sitting on his ass at his art table. Then, as they neared the far wall, she put on a renewed burst of speed and slapped the wall a split second before him.

"Now I know they gave you gills. How the heck did you breathe the entire way?" Morris demanded.

Laila's eyes sparkled with delight. "You turn your face up as you lift your arm." She pantomimed it.

"What kind of Canadian voodoo is that?" Morris demanded suspiciously as she swam in circles around him.

"It's not voodoo, it's science." With that final say, Laila splashed off, leaving Morris in her wake.

By the time they left the pool and went to his mom's house for a wash-up and change of clothes, Morris was exhausted and ravenous. The lunch he'd packed didn't hold up to chasing Laila around for hours. And she acted like she had energy to spare.

This weekend off from work would leave him behind, but he had to admit he'd be better off for it. He'd be back at it Tuesday with a clearer head. From the top of the stairs, he could hear feminine chatter, the voices of his three sisters mixed with his mother's and the high piping of Laila. The scent of cooking food sent his stomach to growling. The chances of him being able to swipe a taste were nil. They'd either chase him off or interrogate him.

Quietly, Morris came down the stairs. Through the hallway, he could see the ladies moving between the kitchen and dining room. Morris slunk around the newel post and headed toward his dad's den. He always had some snacks hidden away. They could catch up until it was time to fire up the grill. Morris rapped on the door with the back of his knuckles.

"Come in."

The den smelled of leather, books, and his dad's cologne. Law reviews, binders of research, reference books, and all the other trappings of his dad's successful legal career lined the tall bookshelves. Morris remembered hanging out here as a kid, avoiding his sisters, and drawing in a corner as his dad worked.

In his dad's office, there was no talk about Morris's lack of a love life, his tendency to hole up at home and bury himself in his work. He knew it came from love and concern, but that didn't make it any less annoying. He was quite content where he was and saw no reason to change. Though his dad often did question him about the state of his finances, it was somehow different from the other questions. He wasn't trying to change him, Morris supposed, just his career. He was a quiet introvert. He could be outgoing when he was in his comfort zone or after he'd gotten to know someone, but he didn't seek it out. For all of their differences, his dad seemed to understand that about him and accept it as okay. Sometimes with his family, Morris had to pick his battles.

Augustus glanced up from his newspaper, grinned, and set it aside. "Hey there, stranger. How'd you get in here without being accosted?"

"They're occupied getting the rest of dinner together. I thought it would be safer in here until it was time to grill." Morris's stomach let out a loud protest as he sat in the chair on the other side of the desk. "I don't suppose you have anything to tide us over hidden away in here."

Without a word, his dad pulled open the bottom drawer and tossed Morris a protein bar. "What the heck is this?" Morris asked, shaking the bar. "What happened to the good snacks?"

"Your mother." His dad grimaced as he eyed the snack bar with disgust. "She's on a new health food fixation. She's been seeing this nutritionist once a week. She's tossed anything I can make out of a box and gone on a no processed food kick. Do not let her see your pantry."

"Oh man, that sucks." Morris's stomach didn't care if it would taste like cardboard or not, he wanted something now. The aromas wafting down the hall from the kitchen were pure torture. He tore open the wrapper, took a bite, and grimaced. It tasted like sawdust.

"Where do you find all of those skirts?" Augustus eyed Morris's black kilt. "I've never gone into a store and seen a man-skirt before. And since you've taken to wearing them, I've looked out of curiosity."

"It's not a skirt. It's a utility kilt." Morris wolfed down the rest of the bar and tossed the wrapper. "Mostly find them online. Occasionally there's a vendor with them at a show. Don't knock them, Dad. They're surprisingly comfortable, especially in the summer."

"If I showed up in court in one of those, I'd probably get slapped with contempt." Morris tried to picture Augustus Proctor arguing before the judge in a kilt and realized there were limits to his imagination.

"If I ever saw you in a kilt, I'd swear I was dead and gone," Morris said with a laugh. He got his height and breadth of shoulder from his dad. People said they were so much alike, but beyond those physical characteristics, Morris didn't see the similarities.

"I should do it just to see the look on everyone's face." Augustus sat back, folding his hands over his stomach. "Makayla said you did a show last weekend. How did that go?"

His dad didn't ask about his art much, though he did check to be sure Morris was okay, the bills were getting paid, and he had enough to eat. Morris didn't want to toss his job choice in Augustus's face either, that he, out of all his kids, his only son, went in the complete opposite direction of stable, steady income—or at least what his dad would term stable, steady income. Morris was sure his dad was proud of him, but he was a little afraid to ask. He definitely knew he baffled the man with his life.

"Good. Got some work out of it that kept me busy last week. It was nice to take a bit of a break from the book, but I have to start working on the next issue." Morris already had the outline of it in his head after his day at the pool with Laila.

"Laila does love being your main character. She talks about it all the time, to anyone who'll listen."

"She's my biggest cheerleader." It was one of the many things Morris adored about his niece.

"They're good stories. You always did have quite an imagination."

Morris's head jerked up as he stared at Augustus in surprise. "You've read them?"

"Of course I read them." Augustus sounded insulted. "My son wrote them. My grandbaby stars in them. Why wouldn't I read them?"

Morris glanced down at his hands, suddenly flustered. "I thought...." He shoved his hair back with a huff. He knew his mom read them and Laila, but he'd never pictured his dad getting into them. "I'm not sure what I thought. You never mentioned it before. I guess that maybe you wished I was doing anything for a career but this."

"Well, it is a worry, I won't lie. I wish you had a job that offered health insurance," Augustus said, tapping his fingers together.

"I have health insurance." It wasn't an expense Morris wanted. He was generally healthy, but after Laila's accident, he realized that something could happen to anyone at any time.

"What about a retirement plan?" Augustus asked with the air of a man getting ready to cross-examine, and Morris had to stifle the urge to squirm.

"I'm not sure if an artist ever really retires." The thought of putting the pencil down was too alien. Morris had been drawing as long as he could remember. He was sure that one day, many decades from now, someone would find him slumped over his art table with a pencil still grasped in his hand.

"What if an emergency pops up?" Augustus asked as he leaned forward. "Life does throw curve balls."

"I do have savings." It might not be robust, but Morris had managed to tuck away a little money here and there, enough that he wasn't having sleepless, anxious nights wondering if he'd make enough to cover the rent. He had steady work now that he supplemented by teaching. One thing he'd promised himself when he started this gig was he wouldn't go into debt to get his stuff out there. He had run successful crowdfunding campaigns to get himself started, and now he didn't need that. The sales from his last book paid for the printing of the next. He had an online store connected with his comic and deals with various local brick-and-mortar stores. While he wasn't going to be the next Jim Lee or Rob Liefeld, he felt he was succeeding in his chosen profession.

"I have to ask," Augustus said with a shrug of his broad shoulders. "And I know I ask often, but it doesn't mean I don't enjoy what you create. I just wish you had more of a backup, something steady you can build a budget around."

The door opened before Morris could reply that he did have a budget. He glanced over his shoulder to see who had rescued him as his twin, Makayla, slipped in. Augustus had passed his height down to all of his children, and Makayla carried it with a willowy grace. The corner of her mouth lifted. "There you are, Tree." She slid her arm around his shoulders for a quick hug and then caught him in a chokehold. "Next time I have to sic Laila on you to get you to come up for a visit, it's on."

"Jeez, I swear, violent much?" Morris replied when she eased up on him.

"I needed to make sure I made my point."

"The guilt trip made your point." Morris took a swipe at her, but Makayla danced out of the way.

"Too slow, bro." She stuck her tongue out at him. "And I emptied the house of all of your Nerf guns. So don't bother looking for them."

"Are you sure?" Morris leveled a look at her, and Makayla suddenly looked less smug.

"How many of those things can one man have?" Makayla demanded.

"As many as one needs when he's dealing with the likes of you, Tigger." Morris drilled his finger against Makayla's ticklish rib, and she swatted his hand away with a laugh.

"I thought all my children had become adults. What happened?" their dad said as he pushed back his chair. "Is it time to grill?"

"Yep. And we need mutant beanpole here to get down Mom's blue bowl from the top shelf." Makayla tweaked Morris's ear. "Why don't you whip us up some margaritas too?"

"Did someone bring limes and ice?" Morris asked.

"Strawberries too if you want to mix it up."

Augustus grinned as Morris rose to his feet. "We need to even the numbers around here. Where's your boyfriend? And Joe?"

"Yeah, where are the other guys?" Morris liked Sierra's husband, but his job kept him on the go and Morris rarely got to see him. And Makayla's Victor had become a close friend.

"Both will be here after dinner," Makayla said. "Joe's flying back into National in an hour. And Victor is volunteering at the shelter today."

Morris slung his arm around his twin as Augustus moved around them and disappeared into the hallway. He'd debated mentioning Theo to Makayla, but as much as her interest in his dating life annoyed him sometimes, she was still his best sounding board. "So I met this guy last weekend."

"Uh-huh. I take it that you don't just mean someone you ran into at a con, but someone who interests you." Makayla looked up at him, her gaze curious. "So what makes this guy different?"

Morris wasn't entirely sure. He'd managed to have a few quick conversations with Theo over the last week. Several text debates. It seemed like they didn't have a damned thing in common, but Theo drew him in. He was so easy to talk to. "Other than the fact that he's not a geek, he's also not my usual type. He's more laid-back."

"That's probably a good thing."

Morris eyed her suspiciously. "What's that supposed to mean?"

"Lately, your usual type doesn't tend to stick around too long," Makayla replied with a shrug.

Sadly, she had a point, another reason not to let his attraction to Theo get past a friendship level. Odd, he could picture a friendship with Theo quite easily, but the idea of anything more made him nervous. The last guy Morris had been with hadn't been bad. They'd liked each other. The chemistry had sizzled at first, but there hadn't been enough in common to keep the relationship going. Maybe that's what was holding him back. Or the guy before him who'd been awesome at first, until Morris realized he thought being a geek was something Morris needed to be rescued from or cured of. That hadn't ended well, and the memory still burned.

"Yeah, probably better not to scratch that itch," Morris said with regret. He wouldn't want their proximity to each other to be awkward later on. "He's my new neighbor."

"The one who's lived there for almost two months and you never saw?"

"Yep, he owns a restaurant. I get the feeling he's there a lot. He wants me to come over this week to cook some French-sounding thing." The idea still intimidated him. What was the point of learning to cook when he had a microwave?

Makayla laughed and pushed Morris after their dad. "Go, have fun, and relax. You worry too much about things like this. What-ifs get in the way of living."

"Don't you remember the guy who tried to completely make me over?" Morris stopped again, frowning at her.

"It wasn't his dislike of geek culture that was the problem. He was just an asshole," Makayla countered. "There was nothing about you that needed fixing other than your obsession with Nerf guns and self-inflicted exile at your art table."

"We're very different," Morris insisted. He heard the sounds of his family coming from the kitchen and his mom asking about his whereabouts. "He doesn't even know about *Doctor Who*."

"So? Neither do I, and you still talk to me. Seriously, relax dude." Makayla nudged him affectionately in the side. "Go, do something different. It's good for your neurons."

Morris halted and shot her a suspicious look. "What's wrong with my neurons?"

"You've gotten into a rut. You know it and I know it. A cute new neighbor will shake things up a bit, and the fact that you might not have the same interests isn't always a bad thing. Then you can really get to know him instead of getting comfortable. Relationships take work, dude, and commitment. The only thing you're committed to is your work."

Morris hated to admit she was right again. She could be insufferable about it. Unless there was a show, he rarely left his house now. He was going to become the crazy cat man. It wasn't out of introversion or fear of going outside. There was so much to do. Maybe it was time to cut back on a couple of deadlines before he burned himself out. "Fine, I'll go and check out my cooking lesson, but if I burn the house down, I'm moving in with you and Victor."

"Don't even joke like that."

# Chapter Six

THIS WASN'T a first date with Morris.

It helped Theo to tell himself that. Because having a boyfriend was not in the cards right now. Morris seemed leery of dating, too, and Theo didn't want to pressure him. This was a chance to feel each other out and to discover what they did have in common instead of everything they didn't. And maybe consider the idea of having a hot fling.

It was a damn good thing it wasn't a first date because Lincoln was home. Theo sighed as he took down the sea salt and black peppercorns. How could he seduce a guy with his kid brother around? He hadn't considered that. But he had to find a way because this was their new normal, and Theo didn't want Lincoln to think for one moment Theo considered him a burden.

The doorbell rang and Lincoln's bedroom door banged open before Theo could respond. "I'll get it!"

Theo tossed a hand towel over his shoulder and shook his head. Any other time and he'd have to drag Lincoln out of his room to interact with them. One hint Theo could be flirting with their new neighbor and Lincoln was determined to be underfoot to keep an eye on him.

"Hey, I wasn't sure what else I should bring," Morris said from behind him.

Theo looked over his shoulder with a grin. Morris juggled a bottle of wine, a six-pack of beer, and a two liter of soda. "Just yourself, but thanks anyway. Go ahead and stick the beer and soda in the fridge."

Morris surveyed the neat array of ingredients laid out on the counters and island. "That is a lot of food. I can eat, but I don't think I can eat that much."

"Theo likes to cook for the week on his days off," Lincoln said as he took a seat at the table. "There's something wrong with him."

"Hush, you." Theo snapped the towel at him, wishing his brother would shoo. "I don't always feel like leftovers from work, and I definitely don't want to make a full meal when I finally get home."

Lincoln gave him a cheeky grin. "So you reheat leftovers at home."

"How was your day with Laila?" Theo asked, ignoring Lincoln's teasing. Maybe it was a lot to cook, but once it was all started, he'd have a nice amount of time to spend with Morris before dinner was ready. He'd been looking forward to the break in his routine all week.

"Good. She swam circles around me and wore me out. Then my mom and sisters stuffed me silly with food, my dad and I plastered everyone with margaritas, and I ended up falling asleep on the couch like I was visiting from college again. It was like that through the whole holiday. By the time I made it back home on Tuesday, I felt like I needed a break from vacation."

Theo chuckled, though he didn't entirely feel it. The last time his entire family had been together like that was when Dustin and Robin had come home from school for an Easter holiday before their parents passed. Neither one of them had bothered to come home this year, and they all felt the additional missing spaces.

"I'm glad your sister harassed you into it, then." Theo exchanged a glance with Lincoln and saw the wistful look in his eyes. He wished he could ease the ache for him, but hell, he didn't even know how to do it for himself. "So, you ready to get your hands dirty?"

Morris tied his hair back and eyed all the ingredients on the counter. "I don't even know where to begin."

Theo shot him a grin and tossed him an apron as Lincoln began to inch his way toward the hallway. "Where do you think you're going, squirt? I thought you wanted to chaperone me. You can't duck out now and hide in your bedroom."

"How much trouble can you get into while sautéing?" Lincoln shook his head and backed up. "I get enough of kitchen chores at the restaurant."

"I forgot you said your brother lives with you," Morris said with a hint of curiosity in his voice, but to Theo's relief, he didn't ask. He wanted this to be fun and lighthearted. Morris tied on Lincoln's Think Geek apron. "What's this about a chaperone?"

"My brother thinks it would be wildly inappropriate for me to flirt with you." Theo scratched his stomach as he tried to remember why. "So, you are more than welcome to start things by flirting with me first."

Morris glanced away, his shoulders drawing together. He appeared disconcerted and a little shy. It intrigued Theo because he'd seemed completely confident at the show and at the restaurant with his friends. "Flirting's never been my strong skill, especially with a guy like you."

Theo tied on his own apron as he mulled that comment over. There was some history there. "Adorable non-geek?"

Morris laughed and his shoulders relaxed. "You say that without the slightest trace of embarrassment. I'm many things, but adorable is not one of them."

Morris clearly never looked at himself in the mirror while doing that little peeking through his lashes bit. "No... I'd classify you as damn sexy." Theo stole a glance at Morris's long legs and wondered if he wore anything underneath his kilt.

"It's the kilt. It brings all the boys to the yard," Morris said as he washed his hands. "So that's a mirepoix?" he asked, thrusting his chin out toward the ingredients on the counter.

"This is." Theo swept his hand toward the cutting board. "Two parts onion to one part celery and carrot. Only I changed the menu from what I originally intended. It's too hot for soup."

"What's on the menu?" Morris poked the meat that had been marinating all night and was now resting on the counter.

"Pork belly with gravy, roasted vegetables, and rolls."

"Mmm." Morris patted his stomach with a soft smile of appreciation. "Between you and my mama, I'm going to get fat and lazy this summer."

"I'm sure Laila will help you swim it off." Theo eyed Morris. For a man who sat at an art table most of the day and routinely ate frozen meals, he was remarkably lean. Swimming must pay off. Theo preferred a good game of basketball himself.

"True," Morris said with a laugh. "So what do we do first? It looks like you already started without me."

"I marinated the meat overnight to really get the flavors in there. First we want to get the pork belly going since that's going to roast on low heat for a while." Theo rubbed his hands together. It was a new recipe, and he was dying to try it. If it came out as good as he thought it would, they'd have a new special at the bistro. He flipped on the oven. "You start by rough chopping the celery and carrots while I get the garlic ready."

Morris located the knife block and drew out a blade. "What's a rough chop? I'm guessing it's not the pretty little strips or neat dicing."

"You've got it, big chunks. About the size of your thumb." Morris had really nice hands, too, large, capable hands with long fingers. Theo watched as Morris started on the carrots and celery, rocking the knife slowly to avoid cutting himself. "How's the comic going?"

Morris paused and stole a glance at him. "Good, spent most of this week laying out the pages for the next installment. My time with Laila always inspires me."

"You based your heroine off her?" Theo asked as he broke a garlic bulb into individual cloves. "I noticed they have the same name."

"Yeah. She was in an accident when she was four and it injured her spine. She still has some limited feeling, but she can't use her legs." Morris's expression grew thoughtful. "She's one tough girl. She's taught the whole family about living life and not letting circumstances limit you. Honestly, I think she's the most fearless person I've ever met."

"Some people deal with tragedy by avoiding it," Theo said, looking with new respect at Morris. "They can't handle it, so they distance themselves from their family at a time when they all need each other the most." He paused as he realized a bitter edge was creeping into his voice, and he lightened it as he continued. "I'm glad she's doing so well. Probably helped to have an uncle by her side rooting for her."

"I never thought of it that way." Morris smiled at him. "I don't often talk about her to guys I just met. Some have said the stupidest things. Like how I must be so uncomfortable around her. Or they assume she's incapable of anything or that it affected her brain. Bullshit like that."

Theo thought back to the strained smiles of friends and acquaintances, the awkward condolences, and how quickly the subject was changed anytime his parents were mentioned. He was sure their hearts were in the right place and they thought they were being kind, but in fact it was a little isolating when he had no one to vent his feelings to. They'd died, but people acted like they'd never existed at all. Remembering the good times, wanting to talk about it, didn't mean he wasn't moving on.

"It's terrifying when something like that happens and you don't want to show your fear 'cause you've got to be strong for them," Theo said thoughtfully as he pressed the flat of a blade against the garlic bulbs to pop the skins. It was crazy. He barely knew Morris, and yet he was finding it easier to talk to him than to people he'd known since he was a kid.

Morris began chopping again, his expression thoughtful. "You get it. You know, that's why I agreed to let you buy that picture. I could tell you got it."

"Yeah, I do. Maybe later I'll tell you why, but let's not bring the mood down." Struck by how intent Morris was at his task, Theo gave in to impulse and leaned over to brush his lips over Morris's cheek. His scent was earthy, of shea butter and sun-warmed skin. Theo liked the way he smelled, the way it mixed in with the scent of onion and garlic, scents that reminded him of home and work he loved.

Morris gave him a narrow-eyed, considering look, but before he could comment, Theo pulled back. "For now, toss those carrots and celery into the roasting pan, then start the onion."

"Do you want to see me cry? Is that it?" Morris demanded in a teasing voice as he popped a carrot into his mouth and then scraped the rest of the vegetables from the cutting board into the pan.

"I promise to kiss your tears away if you do," Theo replied with a perfectly straight face as Lincoln sauntered back into the kitchen to grab a soda.

"I heard that." Lincoln wrinkled his nose at his brother.

Theo exchanged an amused glance with Morris. "Morris started it."

"I did?" Morris raised one eloquent brow.

"You absolutely did. You, my friend, flirt with your eyes, not with your words." Theo dumped whole garlic cloves into the pan. He glanced at Lincoln, who popped the soda can top as he watched them. "Checking in on me?"

"Somebody has to." Lincoln took a sip of the soda.

"Just wait until you get a date, bro, just wait." Theo began tying small bundles of thyme together. "Everything you do to me, I'll do to you, then see how you like it."

Red colored Lincoln's cheeks. "I'd have to get a girl to look at me first," he muttered.

It had been an awkward year for Lincoln on top of the trauma at home. A sudden growth spurt left him with gawky, ungraceful limbs. He'd get used to it, but the in-between period sucked. "It'll happen, I promise you," Theo assured him.

"Seriously," Morris said, looking over his shoulder and blinking against the sting of the onion. "I was like you, a little shy and too tall, and braces on top of it. Be comfortable with yourself, that's all I can say. The rest will follow."

"Please tell me you have a picture of yourself with braces." Back in high school, Theo had shifted between a love for country rock and

Savage Garden and dressed accordingly. Then there had been his emo days. There was bound to be photographic evidence somewhere.

"Oh hell no. Look up insecure geek in the dictionary and you'll see a picture of me as a teenager." Morris stepped back from the chopping board. "How's that?"

Theo checked the vegetables while Lincoln shifted from foot to foot and glanced over his shoulder as if torn between staying or disappearing again. "Perfect. Add it to the pan, and I'll lay the meat on top."

"You know what this needs? Yeast rolls," Morris said after he tossed in the onions. "You should've said something. I would've grabbed some while I was at the store."

Theo shook his head as he drizzled olive oil over the vegetables and mixed it in before adding the thyme. "Don't you say you do everything for your comic? All the coloring and lettering? Same principal applies here."

"You're making them yourself?" Morris's chuckle carried a thread of disbelief.

"We're making them," Theo replied, sliding the roasting pan into the oven. "Then we know it's good."

"Wow, you haven't baked in a long time." Lincoln peeked into the oven before Theo shut it. "That looks good. What's for dessert?"

"There I will fully admit I got lazy." Theo ruffled Lincoln's hair. "There's ice cream in the freezer."

Lincoln grimaced and moved his head away. "What is it with you and desserts? You cook everything else. Is it so hard to whip up something sweet?"

"I've got to leave something for you to be a genius at."

Lincoln rolled his eyes. "I'm going to bike to the store and pick up something better than plain ice cream." He held out his hand and wiggled his fingers. "Since you muddled up this menu, you get to pay."

Theo dug into his pocket and pulled out his wallet. "It had better be good and not a bunch of processed shit either."

"I'm not going to dignify that with a response." Lincoln took the twenty Theo gave him with a lofty air and headed out.

"You're good with him," Morris said as the front door closed. "If you don't mind me asking, how do you have custody?"

"I split it with my sister. Our parents died last year." Theo rubbed his knuckles over his heart as if he could somehow massage away the ache.

"I'm so sorry. I can't even imagine what that must've been like," Morris said softly, his dark brown eyes warm with empathy, not pity.

There were no words, but Theo didn't feel like discussing it. He liked the mood they had going. Light and easy. "We all were living at our family's house, but I have to tell you, once my sister and her husband decided to have a kid, Lincoln and I realized we needed a place to ourselves before the 2:00 a.m. feedings started."

"Wise man," Morris said with a faint hint of a smile. He stared at Theo for a long moment, his expression unreadable, and Theo wondered what he was thinking. Probably that Theo had too much baggage on top of not being a geek. Then Morris leaned down and brushed his lips over Theo's.

Theo's negative thoughts scattered under the electric contact. Before he had a chance to react, Morris was already pulling back. No way. Theo wanted more than that quick taste.

"I have been thinking about kissing you ever since I first saw you standing in the driveway." Theo stepped closer to Morris.

"Is that right?" Morris leaned back against the counter, his posture an open invitation that Theo took. Morris's gaze heated as Theo pinned him there, his hands on the counter on either side of Morris's hips.

"That's right. I just wasn't sure if you were all that interested, not being as proudly geeky as yourself. You seemed to be resisting the idea."

"I was.... But I can't seem to remember why at the moment." Morris's voice was low and husky. The sound sent a tingle of anticipation through Theo.

"Good." Theo breathed in the scent of him, slid his hand around the nape of Morris's neck, and tugged him down. Morris settled his hands on Theo's shoulders as he met Theo halfway. Theo drank in the warmth of his mouth, the sweet pressure as they nibbled and tasted. Then Morris's lips parted and Theo swept his tongue in to tangle with Morris's. Morris's embrace tightened, and then it was all hot and heady sensation as their exploration deepened. Theo wanted more. He wanted to savor the touch and connection like a fine wine.

Morris drew in a shaky breath as they parted. "Damn."

Theo laughed softly. "Yeah, I think that about sums it up." His heart was still pounding as his gaze drifted from Morris's mouth to the bemusement in his eyes.

Morris traced his thumb along Theo's jaw. "You were teasing me about *Star Trek* and *Star Wars*, weren't you?"

"A bit. I couldn't help myself. Your reactions were priceless," Theo admitted. "I know the difference. After all, I live with Lincoln, and there are shrines to both in his bedroom. I even know some superheroes. I just never paid attention to who owned them."

"I think you're going to be trouble," Morris said with a shake of his head.

"You look like a man who can handle a little trouble." Theo kissed him again, long and lingering. Morris's kisses made him think of endless rainy afternoons, naked in bed, with nothing to do but each other. He wondered if a couple of heated kisses would be enough to convince Morris to give him the chance for a real date. If not, a home-cooked meal was always a path to seduction.

The buzzer on the oven rang, breaking into Theo's fantasy of dates and rainy afternoons in bed. He didn't know when he'd have an afternoon like that again. Reluctantly, Theo broke the embrace and flipped off the timer. His lips still tingled, and he could sense Morris's gaze on him like a slow caress.

"So what now?" Morris asked, hooking his thumbs into the wide belt.

Theo gestured to the rest of the ingredients. "Now we start the rolls and let the dough rise while I clean up. We should have time to see what movies might be playing on TV while we wait." Maybe neck a bit if Lincoln hadn't returned from the store by then.

"No, I meant you and me and the flirting and the kissing."

Theo cocked his head, studying Morris and the mix of bafflement and heat in his eyes. "I guess that depends on whether or not you've decided if I'm dateable."

Morris hesitated, and Theo felt a tinge of disappointment. Morris was going to be a tougher nut to crack than he thought. "It's not you. I'm haunted by the ghosts of jackasses past."

Theo held up one hand, palm out, and crossed his heart. "I swear not to be a jackass. Well, at least 95 percent of the time. Nobody's perfect."

That teased a smile from Morris. "I was thinking since you're so busy and I'm so busy and we're feeling this out and getting to know each other.... Would you be adverse to a sexy fling?"

The suggestion sent a hot punch of desire right to Theo's gut, but Morris's reluctance to commit to a date only challenged him. He kissed Morris, hot and claiming as the oven timer buzzed again, and Morris gave back as good as he got, leaving Theo breathless. "A fling is good. I've been so crazy busy, I haven't even had time for that this last year. And here I was worried you were going to shoot me down." Theo opened the oven to check on the meat. The aroma of melting fat and the aromatics from the vegetables and seasonings wafted out.

"You kiss me until I can't think and then you knock me around even more with a smell like that? There's no way I could resist." Morris gave him a shy smile that tickled Theo. He didn't know what it was about it that got to him, but it did.

Theo lowered the temperature on the oven, added a little white wine to the leftover marinade, and poured it into the roasting pan. "To kick off our sexy fling, do you feel like going out for dinner and a movie, or something a little different?"

"We're doing dinner and a movie tonight." Morris slid the dirty dishes into the sink and paused with a perplexed expression before shaking his head with a smile. "I see what you did there. Sneaky."

"We can incorporate the sexy fling by necking on the couch when my chaperone hides out in his room," Theo offered.

"Good luck with that." Morris pursed his lips. "I'll think of something for our next outing. When are you off?"

Theo frowned, mentally going through his calendar. "I'm not… not for a bit. Hell, I don't know when I'll have another weekend off until the end of summer."

"That's okay, because I've got a lot of shows coming up on weekends. Summer's a busy time, lots of cons all over the place. What about weeknights? I'm usually winding down by then unless I have a deadline."

Theo scratched his cheek. He was going to be closing until they could figure out how they wanted to handle getting extra help at the restaurant, and then they had to go through the training, which meant being on hand. Jill had been pressuring him to look into it. She kept reminding him babies had a mind of their own and came on their own timetable, not the parents'. If he ever wanted to have a life outside of the restaurant, he'd have to give up a little control.

"What's wrong?" Morris asked with a frown. "Already changing your mind?"

"Hell no." Theo caught Morris's hand and gave it a squeeze. "I'll finagle a night off."

Morris eyed him, his expression withdrawn, and Theo's heart sank. "Unless you wanted to sneak in time together during the day. It's easier right now for me to be off then. The restaurant isn't open for breakfast, and I can get someone to cover lunch."

Morris's eyes lit up. "Leave that to me," he said with a satisfied smile. "I have just the thing."

# Chapter Seven

MORRIS GLANCED at the thumbnails he'd sketched into the margins of his manuscript and pulled out a clean sheet of bristol board. He taped the corners down on his drawing table and began to measure out the panels for the next page. Once he got the pencils down, he'd call it a day. From his phone, Dakota's voice rang out in another podcast episode of *Geek Wars*. Morris tapped the volume up. He'd been waiting to hear Dakota's take on the *Shannara Chronicles* TV show versus the books, and the chances of it being picked up by a new network. People he found to argue both sides of a topic were always entertaining when Dakota egged them on.

He half listened as he transferred the thumbnails in the margins and the layout in his mind to actual images on paper. The page began to take shape under his constantly moving pencil. From time to time his gaze flicked up to catch sight of *The Mummy* running in the background on mute. "No harm ever came from reading a book," he quoted under his breath, and then chuckled at the thought of using that line on Felipe the next time they played *Call of Cthulhu*. Felipe would lose his shit. If they ever got a chance to get some role-playing in again.

Finally, he straightened, cracking his neck as he studied the penciled page with quiet satisfaction. Not bad. Not bad at all. One more page, and then he could do some inks. No… he was going to stick to his schedule. His back ached from hunching over the table, and his fingers were starting to cramp. He had the pencils done for the first seven pages. Morris set his pencil down and shook his wrist to ease the stiffness.

As if the motion summoned her, Cassie appeared and wound around his ankles with a plaintive mewl. "I just fed you," Morris said and scooped her up. She batted her cheek against him and mewled again as Morris's stomach started to rumble. "What time is it?"

Morris stood up with Cassie cradled against his chest and checked the clock. "Damn, boo, it's almost seven. I guess I didn't just feed you."

Cassie purred, her silky body rumbling as he headed toward the kitchen. The moment he reached for the kibble, her ears pricked up. "Yeah, you know what you want. Does this mean you're not going to plot my death tonight?"

He set her on the floor and scratched her head. She permitted the caress for a moment before she ducked away and sniffed at the remnants in her bowl with a tragic air. "Okay, okay, I hear you. You're eating better than me tonight."

He filled her bowl and topped off her water before eyeing his fridge. He was all out of the leftovers Theo pressed on him the other night. Not that there had been much left. The main dish had been meat nirvana, and the simple macerated strawberries and homemade whipped cream Lincoln put together had made a perfect topping as they ended their evening on the front lawn watching the stars and fireflies come out. They'd talked until they were both half asleep in their chairs, and Lincoln disappeared inside to play video games. Morris couldn't remember the last time he'd been so quickly comfortable with someone outside his circle.

Morris opened the fridge and stared glumly at the contents. He had half a leftover sub, but when he touched it, he discovered it had gone hard. How many days had it been there? Morris tossed it into the trash. There was a dish that looked more like an out-of-control science experiment than something edible. Shuddering, Morris tossed the dish. No sense in contaminating his sink drain. Besides, he was *not* putting his fingers in that to wash it.

Nope, nothing appetizing. Morris shut the fridge and looked morosely at the array of pizza coupons and delivery menus stuck on with cat magnets. Not one of them appealed to him. Not after having real meals again at his mom's and Theo's. And he was out of root beer. That had to be a capital crime.

"Sorry, Cassie, I'm going out."

Morris grabbed his keys as Cassie ignored him now that her immediate needs were met. He quickly cleaned up his workspace and tucked the newly penciled pages into a folder for safekeeping.

It was a beautiful evening. The day's heat hung in the air, and the cicadas roared in the trees, singing their mad song of mating before the summer ended. Morris always liked the sound. It was a comforting white noise that always brought him back to the endless summers when he was a boy and his biggest worry had been running out of books to read.

With the sun setting, the punishing heat had lessened, so Morris rolled down the windows of his car and headed toward town with the radio blaring. As he drove by the bridge and turned in the direction of the waterfront, he considered what he wanted to do for a date with Theo. Their evening together had convinced him they'd easily find things to talk about, so the idea of making conversation that didn't center around art or work wasn't so intimidating. Considering their schedules, maybe something that took them both as far away from work as possible.

The soaring bridge stretched out over the Patuxent River, a sparkling sheet of dark slate-blue glittering in the sun. Gulls dipped and swooped, hovering in the air before banking off again. Fishing boats bobbed in the water as pleasure boats skipped across the waves heading farther up the river or out toward the Chesapeake Bay. A boating trip might be an idea. Morris hadn't gone boating in forever. He'd met a group at a show that designed and built Viking ships, armor, and other accessories. They were based around here somewhere, and they did boat tours along the rivers.

Morris frowned and drummed his fingers on the windowsill. Nope, best not to scare off Theo with the extent of his geekiness yet. There would be time enough to do that when the Ren Faire hit in the fall. He still liked the idea of a boat outing. It had been far too long since he'd been on the water. If they left early, they'd have plenty of time to enjoy together before Theo had to return to the restaurant. And that would give Morris time in the afternoon and evening to work as well. Deadlines never ended; they only changed from one project to another.

Morris found a decent parking space along the waterfront sandwiched between the river and Back Creek. He checked his pocket for his wallet, worried for a second he'd left it at home until he found it in the glove compartment. He surveyed the waterfront, his stomach rumbling, and his eyes lit on the Chesapeake Bistro. The deck had been opened for the summer, the tables covered by cheerful white-and-blue umbrellas. There was a stiff breeze coming off the water, but it was warm and carried with it the scent of salt water and life. A chance to see Theo again coupled with a dinner outside on a night like tonight couldn't be passed up.

The restaurant had a steady crowd going for a weeknight. Morris spied Lincoln's lanky form bent over a booth as he cleaned up with quick, efficient movements. For all of his speed he didn't slack on cleanliness—the entire table was wiped down, condiments and napkin holder lifted. The booth itself was also wiped down before Lincoln grabbed a broom and carefully swept under as well. Then he hefted the bin full of heavy dishes and made his way toward the back.

Jill was at the bar, pen tucked behind her ear as she went over documents on her clipboard. The image amused Morris. Brenden would appreciate that approach. He wondered if Theo's sister had her carefully crafted check-off lists too. The hostess greeted him with a smile. "By yourself? Booth or table?"

"Would it be a problem if I sat outside?" Morris asked as he glanced toward the glass doors leading to the wraparound deck that had an amazing view of the water. It didn't look like it was filled up, but it had been his experience restaurants didn't always have small tables in prime locations.

"Not at all." She whipped out a menu and a roll of silverware and led him out on the deck. The breeze tugged at the umbrellas and whipped around Morris's legs, but it wasn't so obnoxious he wanted to go inside. He sat down and debated whether or not he should let Theo know he was here and decided against it. He didn't want to be a distraction when Theo was trying to work. It wasn't like he could pop out of the kitchen whenever Morris showed up.

He studied the menu, the scent of other diners' food making him even hungrier. He was sure he'd had breakfast, but lunch was another matter. He often forgot meals when he was on a roll.

When the waitress arrived, Morris ordered Old Bay wings and a root beer to start. Just to take the edge off before he decided he wanted every entrée listed, including the damn specials. He sat back, tossing his phone on the table as it buzzed with a message from Felipe.

*Don't forget. Yer turn to host game night.*

Morris tapped out a reply as the waitress returned with his drink and a basket of oven-fresh biscuits. He pounced on them as he considered his empty fridge. He'd have to make time to go grocery shopping before then or his gaming group would never let him live it down. As if Felipe heard his thoughts, his phone buzzed again.

*Real food motherfucker. Not beer and pretzels.*

*Whiner.*

He'd order one of those deli trays from the grocery store and grab some donuts from the bakery. That should be enough. Then he thought of the spreads the others usually laid out. Felipe and his lola always had several tasty options. Jackie went on a cooking binge. Even their old gamemaster, Glen, usually had a pot of chili or something else kept warm in the Crock-Pot.

*Beer we brought!*

Morris winced. Okay, he could do better. He thought of the little savories Theo had whipped up to hold them over as they waited for dinner to cook. Maybe Theo would give him a recipe or two. Something easy, and then Morris could have a nice offering to go with the deli platter and donuts. The savories had been little bite-sized things, and Theo had kept them in the fridge until they were needed. They couldn't be that hard to put together.

*I hear u. Trust me. There will b food.*

He was going to wow them all. Then all thoughts of what he was going to cook slid right out of his head as the waitress returned with his wings. "Theo says to tell me when you're ready for the entrée and he'll bring it out."

Morris blinked, a wing half-raised to his lips. How the hell had Theo heard he was here so fast? Morris hadn't even had a chance to say hi to Lincoln. "Sure, I can do that. Should I order now?" He still wasn't sure what he wanted because his stomach was demanding all the food.

She shook her head and gathered his menu. "I think you're getting chef's choice. Oh, I'm supposed to ask if you have any allergies." She gave him a questioning look, and Morris shook his head. "Good."

"But what if it's something I don't like?" Morris couldn't help but ask, not that there was much he wouldn't try at least once, but there were principles.

"Knowing the boss the way I do," the waitress said, patting his shoulder, "he'd look at you with that smile of his and ask you to trust him."

Yeah, Morris could easily picture that. Theo had enough charm for ten men. "Okay, I'll play his game. But fair warning, I can eat a lot."

"I'll give him a heads-up." She lifted her empty tray above her head and wended her way back inside, pausing to talk to another table. Lincoln waved to him from the long glass window, then went back to work. Morris broke open a steaming biscuit and slathered it with honey butter. This was so much better than whatever he would've discovered in his freezer. He looked out at the boats tied up to the docks on the creek, a blue heron wading through the tobacco-tinted water. It didn't get better than this.

He picked up his phone again and texted Felipe. *You off bridge duty yet?*

*Yeah, why?*

*Meet me at the bistro for some drinks.*

*Dude 4 real? Scratch that, on my way, but I'm crashing at your place.*

Morris frowned at his phone. Crashing at his place? Something was up between him and Dakota again. But he'd have to wait until much later if he wanted any hope of getting it out of his friend. As he ate and relaxed, his mind still buzzed from all the creative ideas racing through his brain. He pulled out one of his pencils and began sketching on the corner of the brown paper that covered the table, idly working out a new character concept.

"That's cool," a voice said by his side. "I wish I could draw like that."

Morris glanced up at Lincoln silhouetted against the lowering sky. "Do you draw at all?"

"A little, sometimes, not like that, though." Lincoln braced his tub on one skinny hip. "Mostly I do stuff on the computer. I like making new content for games. Stuff like that."

"That's art too, just a different kind." Morris pushed aside his empty plate and glanced at the sketch. It was okay, for a scrawl. "Practice at it. I've been practicing since I was a kid, and I'm still not happy with what I put out sometimes."

Lincoln shook his head. "You sound like Theo. He's always pushing to do things better." The slight grimace on Lincoln's lips spoke volumes.

"And always pushing you too?" Morris guessed.

The grimace deepened. "Yeah."

"Such is life. My parents were the same. Thanks for telling Theo I was here. I didn't want to bother him, but I would've felt like I was sneaking in and out if I hadn't said something."

"No problem." Lincoln grabbed Morris's empty plate and basket. "Better get back to work. I've been saving up for a new bike. Another few shifts and I should have enough. Do you want me to tell your waitress you're ready for another drink?"

"Yeah, and let Theo know I'm ready for whatever concoction he's come up with."

Lincoln grinned and took off as Morris mentally went through the menu, trying to decide what Theo was going to test out on him. Not long after, Theo appeared with a plate in his hand, and a flush of warmth went through Morris. He hadn't laid eyes on Theo since Thursday. He'd been chained to his desk trying to get content together for the next show. That hadn't kept him from listening for Theo's car in the hopes of a glimpse of him or the chance for a quick conversation.

"Hey." Morris rose to greet him, suddenly feeling awkward. Should he give him a quick kiss in greeting like he wanted to? But no, Theo was at work, and his job wasn't like Morris's. He had people looking up to him as the boss, so no kissing, but a hug was okay, right? Damn, Theo looked cute, even though his hair had wilted from the heat in the kitchen and his eyes were tired.

Theo slid the plate onto the table in the midst of Morris's internal monologue and then solved the issue by rising on his toes and hugging Morris first. "Glad you came. I've got to get back to the kitchen, it's busy, but I wanted you to try this first."

Morris glanced down at his plate at the seasoned bone-in steak, the little dish of what looked like creamed corn, and another small dish of greens. "I don't remember the corn as a side on the menu," he said as he sat back down again.

"It's something new I'm trying out. Tonight's the first night we're running it as part of the special."

Morris cut into his steak and juices poured out. "It's bleeding." He was hungry enough the temperature didn't matter, and he wasn't really that picky. He had to point it out on principal. He should've known his dinner would be a steak after the way Theo had reacted when he'd told him his preference. It was a silly thing to dig in his heels over, but the voice of his ex, the little slights and tricks he used to try to change Morris, still put his back up sometimes.

"No it's not." Theo grinned and leaned his hip against the table. "I promise you I didn't cook it rare, not even medium rare. I'll ease you into appreciating a good steak. It's warm all the way through," Theo assured him as Morris lifted a chunk of meat laced with pink on his fork. "If you don't like it, I'll make you another with zero judgment."

Theo seemed a little nervous, and Morris decided it was past time he got Theo back for his teasing over Morris's geek loves. He took a bite, frowning fiercely as he tasted. The well-seasoned meat and juice hit his tongue and Morris had a hard time keeping a straight face as Theo's expression fell. "You hate it." He reached for Morris's plate. "I'll get you a new one."

Morris caught his hand and gave it a squeeze. "I'm messing with you. It's wonderful." He dug his fork into the collard greens. The combined flavors were both sweet and smoky with a hint of heat. He couldn't resist sampling them again. They were tender and cooked perfectly without overdoing them. "Okay, whose idea was this?"

"Scottie, my sous chef," Theo said with a smile of relief. "He's a whiz at coming up with different sides. He wants to revamp that part of the menu seasonally."

"I think you should let him." Morris turned his attention to the creamed corn. He'd had it a few times, usually right out of a can, and it had never been a favorite of his. He suspected Theo was about to change his opinion on that as well. It had none of the mushy, sticky sweetness of canned cream corn. Instead it lived up to its name: creamy, heavenly goodness with subtle flavors Morris tried to nail down and failed. "Yes, you definitely need to let him."

"I'll let him know you think so. He'll be pleased." Theo straightened and clasped his shoulder. "I've got to get back to the kitchen. Enjoy."

Morris savored every bite of his meal and finished up as the shadows lengthened on the deck. Waitstaff came out to flip on the hanging lanterns, but the view wasn't the same. Morris paid for his dinner and headed inside, stopping at the bar. He spent so much time holed up in his apartment that sometimes he felt the need to be out. He took a seat at one of the stools and glanced at the Nats-Phillies game. Bottom of the seventh, he'd have a beer and stay to the end. If Felipe didn't arrive by then, he was either making up with Dakota or plotting some flashy and dire revenge.

He settled back, nursing his drink, half of his attention on the screen and the other half on the restaurant itself. It was neat to observe Theo's world. Jill stood at the long open staging area between the kitchen and dining room, checking food as it came up and directing the servers. There wasn't a dish that went by without her looking at it. Morris had no doubt she'd send something back that wasn't acceptable, but he couldn't imagine that happening often. Theo took pride in what he cooked, and the same pride in what they had built was in every gesture Jill made.

If there was a quiet moment, she was checking on the hostess stand or stopping by a table to chat up diners. She even stopped by the bar to see if the bartender needed anything and then directed Lincoln to get more ice, who did it without complaint. The Boarman family was a team in every way.

The restaurant's light wood floors gave it a bright ambiance. The walls were painted a pale blue and covered in pictures of the Chesapeake and surrounding rivers. There were several wide, long windows trimmed in blue that looked out onto the waters, and Morris could believe those vantage points were often packed.

Jill spied Morris and waved with a tired smile before heading right back to the window. No wonder Theo was trying to take so many shifts. Morris's twin and her boyfriend worked in the hospitality business. Maybe she knew a manager who was looking for some work, even if it might be part-time. He'd give Makayla a call tomorrow.

"So is this going to be your new permanent hangout spot?" Felipe asked as he slid onto a stool next to Morris. "If it gets us free food, I'm down for it. If it's about me watching you moon over a white boy, I'm out."

Morris leveled a look at Felipe as he gestured for the bartender. "I've been watching you moon over a white boy off and on for months now."

Felipe grimaced, and there was a deep-seated frustration in those eyes. "Yeah, well you don't have to worry about that anymore."

"I thought something might be up. This one's on me," Morris said as the bartender came over. He waited until Felipe asked for his Corona and an order of calamari. "So what happened?"

"We were supposed to hang tonight, but something with Brenden came up. That's the third frickin' time in as many weeks. Brenden, Brenden, Brenden. Damn, I'm tired of his fucking name."

Morris scratched his cheek as he debated whether he wanted to try to say something or not. "I always thought you guys were taking it casual. Maybe if you want it to be a little more, you should clue him in on that."

"Be real. If he can't take the casual seriously, then I don't even want to know how the hell he'd treat a commitment." Felipe took a long pull on his beer. "Think back, in all the years we've known Dakota, has he ever shown any inclination to sticking with one dude?"

Morris pondered that. Dakota's name had been noised around with this guy and that guy for ages, and he had to admit, Felipe was right— none of them ever lasted long. "True, but I thought he seemed to be coming back to you an awful lot lately."

"And then turning around and leaving every time Brenden gets a burr up his stick-in-the-mud ass that he needs Dakota to dislodge." Felipe shredded a paper straw wrapper to bits. "I'm done with taking second place to a man who treats Dakota like a lower-class citizen half the time."

Morris pursed his lips and decided not to touch that one. True, Brenden could be prickly, but Dakota gave as good as he got. Their bickering was the cornerstone of the brothers' relationship. "I'm sorry, man."

"It's okay." Felipe shrugged and dug into his calamari as it was set in front of him. "I need to blow off some steam before our game night. I don't want it to get weird. Dakota and I need to call it quits for good this time and give each other a little space."

That was definitely something Morris didn't want to see. He'd been in game groups before when a couple broke up. The tension got to be too much. It usually ended with one or both leaving if the group didn't splinter all together. Their group was already fractured now that their gamemaster was gone. Morris didn't want to see it go any further. He liked the bunch they had together.

"It'll be okay," Morris assured him. "Though maybe we shouldn't play Munchkin. That might get ugly."

A sudden grin flashed across Felipe's face. "There's a new version out. I bought it last weekend at that gaming table with the hot dude from the store in Richmond."

Morris tried to recall the guy Felipe was talking about, but he couldn't put a face to his description. "Wait a minute, you don't mean the hipster geezer from the Magick Den, do you?"

"Geezer?" Felipe rolled his eyes. "You need help. He's a silver fucking fox."

"Well, you've got the silver part right." Felipe's taste in men was seriously suspect. Trask was okay-looking if you were into tattoos, but he had to be decades older than Felipe. Maturity was nice and all, but Morris didn't see any reason to take it to extremes. "So you ready for Awesome Con next weekend?"

An avid gleam lit up Felipe's eyes. "Oh yeah. I've been working on my costume since January. I found out Abby is going as Ripley from *Alien*."

Morris rolled his eyes. "So what are you going to do? An alien?" Felipe had the skills to pull it off.

"Nah, I'll save that for when we do an *Alien vs. Predator* thing. I'm sure it'll happen. When we have the time to plan out every detail. I decided to go for something a little subtler. I'm doing the android complete with guts and white fluid spattered everywhere."

"Nice." Morris approved. "Ash or Bishop?"

Felipe shook his head. "We'll decide by my actions whether I'm the good one or the bad one. I even made a facehugger. I'm so fricken' excited. You ready for the con? You're staying in DC, right?"

"Yeah. It's too much to try to drive back and forth, especially if I go to any of the after-parties. I wind up exhausted. The hotel hooked me up with a double, so I have an extra bed if you want to crash." Morris didn't mind splitting his space with Felipe. His friend usually offered to pay for a couple meals in return.

"I might take you up on that." Felipe signaled the bartender and ordered a shot of tequila. Damn, he looked rough. It sucked to have a romance fall apart. "I'll let you know."

Morris leaned back on his stool and glanced toward the kitchen window at the sound of Theo's voice. Theo leaned one hand on the counter behind the staging area, talking with a large, heavyset brother with a squared-off jaw and a mouth that looked as if it smiled often. The man grinned and lightly punched Theo on the shoulder before disappearing deeper into the kitchen. Theo caught Morris's eye, winked, and blew a kiss.

"You really like that dude, don't you?" Felipe asked as Morris settled the stool back down on all legs.

"Yeah," Morris said after a moment's thought. "He's easy to talk to and there's not a lot of drama. Divas irk me."

"Yet you hang out with me." Felipe smirked.

"I'm not sleeping with you," Morris retorted. Not that he was sleeping with Theo either, but the thought of doing so sometime soon made the whole evening brighter. For the time being, Theo wasn't trying to change him—maybe change his taste buds, but not Morris. Just because he was a geek, it didn't mean he needed to be rescued or saved from himself. He certainly wasn't looking for this to last, but a nice, hot fling, one that would lure them away from work and stress a bit, would be good for the both of them.

# Chapter Eight

THEO LINED up the shot, jumped, and watched the basketball sail in a smooth arc to drop through the net. He darted forward, snagged the ball midbounce, and dribbled it back to the end of the driveway for another shot. Morning basketball beat the hell out of jogging or going to the gym, even if the air was already steaming with the promise of more heat and humidity to come. The trees arching over the driveway gave it a bit of shade but also kept the breeze from coming through. That didn't stop Theo from coming out on the mornings he didn't have to go to the market. This was his time—no contemplation, no stress, just him and the ball and the net.

He turned and caught sight of the strange car parked under the trees next to Morris's vehicle. He was not curious. He wasn't. After all, he and Morris hadn't even gone on a date yet. He had no claims to Morris's complete attention even if they were dating. Okay, so maybe he was a little curious, but not jealous. It did make him wonder if he had some competition, though. Could flings have competition? As silly as the emotion was, it was nice to mull over a concern like that rather than the constant worry about the restaurant and his family.

His concentration was off, and the ball banged off the rim and ricocheted toward the trees. Theo jogged toward it with a shake of his head. Sweat dampened his T-shirt, made it cling to his skin, so Theo stripped it off and tossed it to a corner of the driveway. He drilled the basketball off the backboard with a rattle and thud. He should've dragged Lincoln off his butt and made him go a couple rounds; it would be good for the twerp. Tomorrow morning he'd do that.

The back door banged open and Felipe came around the corner, his dark eyes hot with a vast irritation. He was disheveled as if he'd just roused from bed and dressed only in a tank and boxers. Well damn, maybe there was a little competition after all. And someone who shared Morris's interests as well. Unlike Theo. The reminder irked him.

"What the fuck is wrong with you, man?" Felipe asked with a snarl in his voice. "Do you know what time it is?"

Theo glanced at his watch. "Yeah, after ten. Rise and shine, sunshine."

"Nobody fucking rises and shines in the morning." Felipe stalked forward and attempted to swipe the ball out of Theo's hands. "It's amoral."

Okay, it was one thing to stalk out of Morris's apartment half naked. It was another thing to growl at him on a perfectly beautiful morning. But if Mr. Surly thought he could steal a ball from Theodore Boarman, he was having a wet dream.

Theo danced out of the way, dribbling the ball tauntingly within Felipe's reach. Felipe made another grab for it and Theo rolled around him, jumped lightly, and sank the shot.

"Look who thinks he's the king jock." Felipe glared, one hand on his hip.

Theo noted the dark circles under Felipe's eyes and the pallor beneath his golden brown complexion, and the irritation sloughed off. He took pity on Felipe and tucked the ball under his arm. "Hangover?"

"Like a bunch of damned djinn farting trumpets in my head." Felipe scraped a hand through his dark hair. "So if you don't mind not banging around out here, I'd really appreciate it."

That had to be the most colorful description of a hangover Theo ever heard in his life. Morris came around the corner, took one look at Theo shirtless and sweaty, then at Felipe half-naked and scowling, and stopped with a double take.

"Now I know I'm dreaming." Morris's gaze lingered on Theo's bare chest and Theo's cheer rebounded. Maybe they didn't have much in common on the surface, but Morris was interested. That had to count for something.

"Tell me about it," Theo said, giving him the once-over in return. Morris had foregone his usual kilt in favor of cargo shorts that draped him in ways the kilt never could, and a tight Batman T-shirt that showed off his broad shoulders. Theo liked that almost as much. Damn, Morris was easy to watch.

"Ugh, fine, you two flirt and make gaga eyes at each other." Felipe stalked back toward the apartment. "I'm grabbing my shit and heading home. I have a costume commission to finish up by tomorrow, and my whole family's getting together today for a celebration. Fuck me. Fuck!"

"Go, and take your attitude with you." Morris shook his head and gave Felipe a friendly push as he went by. Felipe shoved him back, but Theo noted the little smile on his lips and refrained from saying anything. Morris glanced at the backboard mounted over the garage. "You know, I noticed when it went up, but I wasn't actually expecting anyone to play."

"You mean you haven't heard me almost every morning?" Theo asked as he walked slowly toward Morris.

Morris looked a little embarrassed. "Sorry, once I'm in the zone, I tune out everything. And I'm usually hard at work by now."

"So the myth of the artist sleeping in until the afternoon and working into the wee hours of the morning is just that?" Theo stopped in front of him and tilted his head back to look at Morris.

"For this artist at least. Though I have pulled the occasional all-nighter and slept through lunch afterward." Morris glanced back toward the apartment. "Don't mind him. He's a little hurt and disappointed right now, and he tends to wear that out where everybody can see it until he gets over it."

"No worries," Theo said easily. "It didn't seem to be personally directed, so I didn't take it that way. Some men don't like mornings." His curiosity got the better of him. "I take it you had a bitchfest last night? Love problems?"

Morris blew out a breath. "I wouldn't go that far. I don't think Felipe loves Dakota, even if he's hurt and pissed. If he did, he'd be putting up more of a fight."

"Dakota…." Theo tried to remember him among the group of Morris's friends he'd met. "Stocky guy? A bit heavy on the country twang?"

"Yeah. That's him. Felipe and him have been hitting it casually for the last year or so. I think that's come to a screeching halt." Morris smiled as Theo touched his cheek. He leaned down and gave Theo a quick kiss with the air of a man greatly daring. Those little moments of shyness were a delight, and Theo suspected they'd disappear once Morris got more comfortable with him. He'd miss them when they were gone. "I was hoping to see you again last night."

"I'm sorry I didn't get a chance to come out. We were slammed." Theo hooked his arm around Morris's neck and kissed him in the dappled morning sun. Morris's lips were warm and inviting, and he deepened the kiss, pulling Morris a little closer.

"Get a room, you two." Felipe's tart voice whipped at them, but when Theo pulled back, a little breathless, he saw the hint of a smile on the man's face.

"Hush, you. It's my driveway. I'll kiss Morris if I want to."

Morris lifted his hand in a wave. "See you at Awesome Con, man."

"Yep, and then at your place in a couple weeks." Felipe pointed a finger at Morris, his eyes narrowing. "You'd better not let me down. I swear it, Proctor, there will be a riot."

"Trust me. Shut your trap and trust me. I've got this."

Theo watched Felipe drive away in his rattling old sedan and turned back to Morris. "What's going on in a couple weeks?"

"We have game night every third Saturday we don't have a con. And I'm hosting the next one." Morris popped the basketball out of Theo's arms, caught it, and juggled it from hand to hand. "I don't suppose you'd mind giving me the recipe for those deviled eggs? Maybe something else that would be easy and impressive? I really need to make up for the last time I hosted. You heard Felipe. If I don't deliver on my promise, I'm a dead man."

"How bad was it?" Theo asked, remembering Morris's description of the contents of his freezer.

"They haven't let me live it down and it's been six months." Morris swung the ball behind his back as Theo made a halfhearted swipe for it.

"Sure, come up with the menu you want, and I'll lay out instructions for you. Make sure you give yourself plenty of prep time. When you're doing several things for a party, it can get crazy." Theo wished he didn't have to work on Saturdays. He hadn't had a good game night in ages. "What kind of games? Poker? I play a mean hand."

Morris stared at him blankly for a moment and tucked the ball against his hip. "Poker? Hell naw. Tabletop games, or role-playing when we can, but we lost our GM so it makes it difficult."

Theo was almost afraid to ask because he had no idea what Morris was talking about. Role-playing sounded like a sex game to him, and he was sure it wasn't that. "So like Monopoly? Or is it dressing up in costumes?"

"Felipe is our costume guy. I only get dressed up for the Ren Faire, or maybe some conventions if we get a group going. Role-playing, like Dungeon & Dragons. That's the one most people have heard of, though we play all kinds. You make a character, sit around a table with other players and their characters, and the GM, gamemaster, comes up with the game scenarios." Morris tossed the ball in the air and cast a wary look at Theo. "Dressing up wouldn't be a deal breaker with our fling, would it?"

Dungeons & Dragons. Theo was sure there had been a club at his high school that played the game. It sounded like something Lincoln would love. "Nope, wear whatever you want. Just as long as you don't expect me to dress up. I don't think I can pull it off as well as you and Felipe."

"Don't be so sure. I think you could absolutely pull off a kilt during the Celtic Celebration weekend," Morris said as Theo reached for the ball. He held it up over his head with a teasing grin. "You've got to do better than that."

Theo had played this keep-away game many times before. His teammates in high school had been sure a short white guy couldn't hang with them. He jumped up and swatted the ball out of Morris's hand.

"Hey!" Morris leaped for it at the same time Theo did, and Theo shouldered him out of the way. Grabbing the ball, he swiveled, only to find Morris blocking him. Theo grinned, his heart pumping strongly both at the thought of a decent opponent and by Morris's nearness. Theo feinted and dashed around Morris as the taller man tried to steal the ball. Damn, those long arms had a killer reach. He went for the shot, and Morris blocked it again. Theo scrambled for the ball, caught it, and threw it from the far side of the driveway.

Morris put his hands on his hips and shook his head as the ball swished through the net. "You've got some sick moves. I can't believe it."

"Did you ever play?" Theo asked as he trotted forward to snag the ball before passing it to Morris.

"Not really," Morris said, dribbling as Theo faced off against him. "After my first major growth spurt, no one would shut up about me playing, so I did for a bit. Mostly with friends at the park. Never made the team at school, though. Coach was more likely to find a pencil and sketchbook in my hands instead of the ball. He told me to come back when I got my head out of the damn clouds."

"Coach told me I couldn't play, said I was too short. But I kept showing up for tryouts and practices anyway." Theo made a grab for the ball, and Morris bobbled it before recovering.

"Let me guess, you wore him down." Morris tried to go for the shot, and Theo jumped up to block him.

"Yeah. Played my junior and senior year, went to state," Theo said as Morris went for the shot again, bounced it off the headboard, caught the rebound, and sank it the second time. "Nice job."

Theo caught the ball and glanced at his watch. As much as he regretted it, it was time to go in and get washed up for work. "I've got to go. When you get that list together, drop it off upstairs. If Lincoln's off, he'll hold it for me."

"Before you go...." Morris stopped him with a hand on his arm. "You still interested in a day outing?"

Theo eyeballed Morris even as his heart thumped in anticipation. Morris had called this a fling several times, which Theo took to mean he wasn't looking for any kind of a commitment. And as much as he wanted the challenge of getting Morris to agree to more, it was probably for the best. Theo wasn't in a position right now to offer that to anyone. A fling—he liked the sound of that—a nice, hot, exciting fling.

"More than interested." Theo tucked the ball under his arm. "I have a late shift next Tuesday. I don't have to be in until four."

"Tuesday's good. That'll give me some time to set things up and I won't be worrying about this weekend's big con." Morris smiled slowly. "You're not the type to get seasick, are you? Have a deathly fear of water?"

Theo shook his head. "Water, not so much. Bridges tend to give me some trouble if they're sprung on me. Why?"

"It's a surprise. I'll text you the details if I can get them worked out." With that Morris turned and walked toward his apartment, leaving a mystified Theo to stare after him. For the life of him, he couldn't figure out what Morris had planned. His gaze dropped to the way those cargo shorts draped his fine ass as Morris glanced over his shoulder and caught him ogling.

Morris raised one eyebrow. "Enjoying the view?"

"What can I say?" Theo snagged his T-shirt and tossed it over his shoulder. "I'm only human. If you want to keep providing me eye candy with the kilts and the tight T-shirts and the cargo shorts, I sure as hell am not going to complain."

"Speaking of clothes, wear a bathing suit. You're liable to get wet."

That sounded even more promising. "Hey, Morris." Theo paused as Morris turned back to him again. "Any chance for privacy on this wet and watery outing so I can get my greedy hands on you?"

Morris's dark eyes lowered in that shy, seductive look he got. Theo wondered if he was even aware he did it. "I think I can guarantee that."

Whistling, Theo tossed the ball in the air as he headed around to his half of the house. Tuesday couldn't come fast enough.

# Chapter Nine

THE MAIN warehouse-sized room of the DC Convention Center was packed end to end with vendors and those hawking their personal creative endeavors, whether it was art, books, or crafts. Cosplayers and attendees crowded the walkways as staff in their Awesome Con T-shirts wielding walkie-talkies added to the cacophony. Brenden loved the whole mad spectacle as much as he loved the quieter shows only the die-hard attended.

He surveyed it all from behind his little table, where he was promoting the next Chessie Con. One day, Chessie Con would be this big. He'd made a name for himself in the Chesapeake Bay area, but after seeing Awesome Con explode, he realized the area was ripe for megacons. Why the hell not aim big? Brenden fully intended to leave his stamp on the local scene he loved.

He caught a glimpse of Dakota making his way toward the table, juggling a water bottle and some sodas. His chest tightened as he felt the unwelcome, oh-so-familiar tug of love and desire.

*He's your brother.*

The voice that nagged him had the tone of his foster mother, and Brenden looked away from the constant temptation. Problem was, ever since they'd met, Brenden never thought of Dakota as a brother. A continual burr under his skin, oh yeah. His oldest and most constant friend that he relied on, check. The man that haunted his dreams…. Brenden sighed. The universe hated him. It had taken the man who was perfect for him, who balanced him in every way, and made him his foster brother.

Didn't matter anyway. Dakota was taken, by that pain in the ass Felipe, whom Brenden desperately wanted to hate but couldn't quite bring himself to. He should thank Felipe for occupying so much of Dakota's attention and getting him out of Brenden's hair. Brenden couldn't find it in him to thank Felipe either.

He had to get used to the idea of them being a couple because Brenden hadn't known Dakota to stick with one guy until that kid came around. What was there not to like? Felipe was good-looking, insanely creative, and had enough attitude to keep Dakota engaged. He could be annoying, but he wasn't a bad guy. The truth was most of Brenden's annoyance came from the fact Dakota couldn't seem to quit him.

Dakota paused in front of the table, staring at the setup with a frown. Brenden's gaze slid over him, caressing the blocky shoulders and stocky frame, before lingering on his face. He'd never be pretty like Felipe or have the smooth good looks of Morris, but Brenden loved his face with its too square jaw, hard mouth, and equally uncompromising nose. Dakota's face revealed everything about the stubborn man… and dammit, Brenden was *not* going to stare at him.

"You need a new banner," Dakota said, handing Brenden the water he'd asked for. "No… not so much a banner, a new logo, something a little more eye-catching and creative. We've been using this one for years now."

Brenden twisted around to stare up at the banner. It was a little plain. A new logo might be a good idea. Then they could sell T-shirts at shows too. It would make their staff seem more like a cohesive unit. "I'll give it some thought." He scooted over as Dakota joined him, vitally aware of every move Dakota made. "Anything interesting going on?"

"Always. I ran into James Marsters. He lost his badge and the idjit at the gate didn't recognize him." Dakota rolled his eyes. "Which makes me think if we're going to do this con of yours, we're going to have to quadruple our staff and volunteers. Marsters was cool, though. We had a great conversation while we were waiting for his handler to show up to vouch for him."

Dakota bounced from one topic to another as thoughts came to him, and it always amazed Brenden he was able to stay on topic for a podcast. "You ask him to be on *Geek Wars*?" Brenden knew Dakota well. The man was always hustling a new angle.

"Yeah, but he's flying out midafternoon tomorrow. I won't have time to pull something together. Can you imagine if Boreanaz was here too? We could do a Spike versus Angel. Fuck, that would've been awesome." Dakota shook his head with a regretful sigh and rocked on the hind legs of his chair. "But he's letting me interview him in his room tonight."

Dakota had an innate knack for being in the right place at the right time. Two Awesome Con staff members went by, heading toward one of the curtained-off panel rooms. They looked harried. Dakota had a point; they would need more people. Brenden would start with his usual team and take recommendations from them for others. He was going to have to relinquish some authority and control if this was going to work. It would be utterly impossible for one man to handle all the details. The thought of relinquishing authority and control made Brenden twitch. The only one Brenden trusted with authority in his name was Dakota.

"I think you're right." Brenden narrowed his eyes as he caught sight of Felipe through the crowd. The young cosplayer had outdone himself again, dressed in a dark blue jumpsuit, splashed with white ichor. Brenden wanted a closer look at what Felipe had come up with for the rest, but he was a sad, terrible human being because he did not want to see Felipe and Dakota together. He should be happy for them, not covetous.

"Of course, I'm always right." Dakota smirked as Brenden raised a brow at him. "You know I am, so which part are you going to praise me about now?"

"Your ego needs no stroking," Brenden said dryly. "I was thinking about the staff and volunteers."

"And the banner," Dakota pressed. "You should have Jackie design it."

Brenden shook his head. "I know she's your buddy, and I'll admit she did a kickass job for you, but her style doesn't suit me."

"Are you for real?" Dakota scoffed. "What do you know about style? Her images pop. That's what you want, a pop."

"I'm not saying she's not talented, and she's got a uniqueness all her own, but her art lacks a little elegance, which—"

"Elegance?" Dakota snorted, and Brenden pressed his lips together, holding back the edge of his temper. Dakota knew which tone to use to get Brenden's blood simmering. "Your mascot is a damned mythical water monster. Are you fucking kidding me? Elegance he says, fuck me."

Brenden turned toward him, bristling. "Elegance can be eye-catching."

"Do you two morons ever give it a rest?" Felipe said in a tart, acidic voice. "How come you haven't killed each other in the last fifteen years?"

"Believe me, I've considered it." Brenden took in the rest of Felipe's costume. A rent in the side of his jumpsuit had ivory ropes of synthetic guts spilling out and a facehugger was wrapped around his arm. "Not a bad job, Suero. Where'd you buy all the props?"

Felipe drew himself up. "Buy? Bitch, I made this. Designed the molds and the jumpsuit." He held up the facehugger for closer inspection. "Did all the painting for this sucker."

The guy had talent, and he knew his craft. Brenden bet people would show up to his panels if he gave Felipe a slot, but his tendency to flout the rules made him hesitate. *Be honest with yourself, at least.* Brenden sighed inwardly. The only reason he shoved Suero away was because for the last year Dakota had been chasing him and letting himself be chased. Dakota never stuck with one guy that long. It was jealousy, pure and simple. And Brenden had to let it go before it ate him alive.

"What are you doing after the con tomorrow?" Dakota asked, giving Felipe a wicked smile that turned Brenden's insides to ice. It was time to walk away, let Dakota and Felipe talk all the sex they wanted while he checked out the show.

Felipe cut Dakota a cool glance. "Not you."

Brenden paused as he was about to get up. He'd never heard that tone of utter dismissal in Felipe's voice before. He took a cautious look at the two of them. Dakota had an engaging smile on his face, the expression he used when he was about to wield all of his charm to wheedle his target around to his way of thinking, but from Felipe's closed-off stance, he wasn't going to buy into it.

"Ouch." Dakota reached for Felipe's hand as Felipe drew back. "You're not still pissed about the other night, are you? I gave you time to calm down."

Brenden winced. Sometimes Dakota could be such a clueless ass. Okay, most of the time. Yet somehow, Brenden still loved the bastard.

"Time to calm down...," Felipe said in a dangerous voice. "Motherfucker, I am calm. I meant what I said. I'm done being the lower priority to him." Felipe jerked his chin toward Brenden as Brenden stared at him in astonishment. He recognized the glitter in Felipe's eyes. He'd seen it too often in his own.

"Wait a moment, you two. What the hell? Keep me out of your love spats." Brenden held up his hands. "I have nothing to do with this."

"Bullshit." The fury had drained out of Felipe's voice, and now he only sounded weary. "You have everything to do with this. Don't play innocent. How many times did you invent needing something when Dakota and I had plans? Don't even try to deny it."

Guilt silenced Brenden's tongue. He had done that a couple times. Maybe not as often as Felipe seemed to think, but it didn't mean his hands were clean. The thought he'd played a part in Felipe's genuine unhappiness pressed the thorns in deeper. He was a bastard all the way.

"Felipe, family comes first," Dakota said. "He's my brother."

Damn, Brenden hated that word. He'd never wanted a brother. He had been cool with being an only child. Then he'd wound up with Dakota's aunt and uncle as foster parents and he'd acquired three. Funny thing was, the two younger boys had become brothers to him. He loved them. It was just this one who stuck in his craw.

"You've made that clear. Now I'm making this clear, all this—" Felipe struck a pose, sweeping a hand over his lithe body as Dakota looked on appreciatively. "—is no longer your playground. Go find another sucker to sniff after."

"Any chance you'll think differently by the time game night comes around?"

"You don't ever give up, do you?" Felipe leaned over, his lips inches away from Dakota's. From his sudden grin, Dakota must've thought he was about to get kissed, but Brenden saw that hard edge in Felipe's eyes. He wasn't fucking around. "See these lips you like so much?"

"They are sexy lips," Dakota said in a lazy drawl, his gaze fixated on Felipe's mouth as he leaned in even closer. "Come on, let me buy you lunch. We can talk."

"Not. Going. To. Happen." Felipe straightened, spun on his heel, and flounced off.

Brenden shook his head. He had to give it to him—Suero knew how to make a scene. All eyes were on him, and he was eating up every bit of it. "Did you get dumped?" It was wrong of him to hope for a yes, and it didn't stop him one bit.

"I think we both did. He included you in on that little rant." Dakota followed Felipe with his gaze and then shrugged. "It's probably a good idea to back off anyway. Felipe was starting to think about commitments I'm not prepared to give anybody. I came into this world a bachelor, and I'm going to leave as one. Sticking to one person, marriage, is for romantic fools."

Brenden was a romantic fool, and Dakota was an idiot. They were a fucking pair. Brenden didn't feel like sitting around to hear Dakota's unique views on love. He didn't even seem upset over the dissolution of a relationship that had been a big part of his life for months now. Suero was better off without the aggravation.

"I'm going to go see if the Awesome Con promoters have a few spare minutes to talk. I want to pick their brains about going from a smaller con to bigger, maybe set up a few talks with their VIP guests if they'll let me."

"Don't forget to plug the podcast. And don't forget we have tickets to meet Matt Smith and get our pictures taken. Who's covering our table?" Dakota asked.

"Trask from the Magick Den is either going to come himself or send his guy. I'll swing by his table and double-check in case they're swamped." Brenden angled his way through the crowd, ignoring the temptations of the tables he passed. It was easy to drop money at shows like this between the cost of the tickets, the costs of the photo ops, the hotel, and food. It left attendees reluctant to spare money for original art or handmade crafts that were awesome, but not inexpensive considering the hours put into making them.

It was a conundrum he still hadn't solved in his plans for a bigger con. There was a balance that needed to be kept. The sale of vendor and artist tables helped to pay for the stars and convention rental, but every year he heard more complaints about how the vendors and artists weren't recouping what they spent. If they started to bail on purchasing tables, where would that leave the rest of the con?

Brenden worried over it as he passed by a section of tables that held his Chessie Con regulars. He paused at the sight of Morris with his eye-catching banner. Now he was someone to consider. Brenden liked his style. Morris waved him over, a serious look on his face that sparked his curiosity. The Karlins were set up by him, their son Jaydon asleep on the floor behind them, his head pillowed on his backpack, wrapped up in his mother's shawl. That kid had been coming to Brenden's shows since he was stuck in a sling on his mama's back. How he could sleep with all this going on, Brenden didn't know, but he supposed it was as familiar as a lullaby to Jaydon.

"How's it going, Morris?" Brenden asked as they shook hands.

"Okay, a little quiet right now." Morris looked down at a notepad by his elbow. "I'm running a poll with all my friends. I want your opinion."

Daphne leaned back in her chair and shook a crochet needle at him. "You're overthinking it. It's a date. A date you're looking forward to. Put a cork in it and go get laid."

Morris closed his eyes, and Brenden would've sworn he was blushing furiously. He made a mental note to never discuss his love life with either of the Karlins. What one knew, the other knew, and neither of them held back on an opinion. "Thank you for your input, Daph. Remind me you are not allowed to meet my sisters."

"Is this the guy Dakota told me about? The one with the restaurant?" Brenden asked as Morris set aside his notepad with a sigh and a nod. "He told me there were some serious sparks between you two."

"Yeah…." Morris smiled, his gaze going faraway. "Lots of sparks, but not lots in common, and I'm taking him out on a boat. What if we run out of things to say? I should've planned this better."

Judging from the look in Morris's eyes, Brenden didn't think talking was going to be much of a problem. He was sure Daphne had the right idea. "I think you'll be fine. You're a laid-back guy. Go with the flow and don't stress it too much."

"Yeah." Morris fisted his hand in his dreadlocks and shook his head. "Yeah, he's got me all tied up, which is a good thing, right? Otherwise, what would be the point?"

"Exactly," Daphne chimed in, going back to her project.

"I think my work here is done." Brenden grinned at Morris. At least one of his friends was dating. He wished him luck. Really, that's what he needed to do, go out on a few dates with somebody interesting. It had been a couple months. Other people's relationships would bug him less if he wasn't feeling so damned alone. "See you later. I hope all of Daphne's dreams for you come true."

"Thanks, man." A bemused smile tugged at Morris's lips.

A group of cosplayers trooped by dressed as characters from *Game of Thrones*. Brenden stepped out of their way as someone asked for their picture and they arranged themselves in a tableau. Daenerys Targaryen had a stuffed baby black dragon on her shoulder. Jon Snow looked grim in his dark armor with a White Walker hovering menacingly behind him. And Arya Stark held Needle to Cersei Lannister's throat. They'd practiced this setup. They probably couldn't get five feet without being mobbed for photos.

Brenden paused to get his bearings. At shows like this, he needed to walk through and make a mental map at the beginning to orient himself. Banners stretched out in a long line, creating ragged borders behind tables. Walls of T-shirts and prints soared toward the ceiling in splashy displays. The con buzzed with life, sung with the din of an indoor bazaar. Vendors hawking, writers spieling, artists haggling over commissions, and over all that, fans discussing their favorite geekery of choice. There was something for everyone at a con, and Brenden loved this life.

The Magick Den's booth took up a whole corner, and three people were manning the tables, doing a brisk business of dice sales, miniatures, and cards. Trask finished ringing up a sale and nodded to Brenden. "How's it going on your end?" The owner of the Richmond game store had been a fixture of local cons since Brenden moved into the area as a teenager. Back then, he had more black in his hair than silver and an edge to him that had mellowed, but he'd always been a cool dude.

"We're getting some interest for the next Chessie Con. A few new people signed up for tables." Brenden eyed the wall that had been set up displaying dice bags and game maps. A bookshelf on the end held games and manuals. "Looks like you're doing well." Trask had brought along a considerable amount of stock. But he had a system and years of practice getting set up and ready. He knew how to gauge a show.

"People can't seem to resist getting new dice." Trask looped his thumbs through his jeans pockets. "Including your brother. He stopped by for a set and to talk about the newest *Star Trek* game."

Dakota had always been a gamer, from board games to tabletop. He'd tried getting Brenden interested, but when he actually had some quiet time, he preferred reading instead of sitting around a table. "I'm not surprised. His group's still looking for a new gamemaster. I'm surprised he hasn't hit you up."

"He hasn't, but this cosplayer came by this morning and tried batting his lashes at me. I think he was angling for the same thing." Trask shook his head with one of his slow smiles. "I've been too busy for gaming with a regular group, which is a sad state for a man in my business." He rose on his toes as another customer waved at him. "Gotta go, but don't worry. I've still got you covered if you need me."

"Thanks man, I appreciate it." Brenden turned away, checking off another task on his mental to-do list. If only he could organize his own life as easily as he did a show. Dakota was single… and that didn't change a damn thing.

# Chapter Ten

MORRIS WASN'T sure how Theo would feel about being up this early when he usually worked so late, but he hadn't hedged when Morris suggested they meet at seven. Sure enough, when he got outside, Theo was waiting beside his car with a hamper and a thermos, not looking in the least bit sleepy. He had the inexhaustible energy of a mutant. That was the only explanation. Morris had nothing against mornings. He liked that quiet time to work, but he sure as hell didn't run around chasing basketballs when he first woke up or dive into making breakfast.

He took a moment to appreciate Theo's profile as his neighbor looked out toward the morning mist rising from the ground between the trees. His expression was relaxed without that little furrow between his brows that Morris realized was almost always present. He looked ready for the boat in sandals and dark blue swim trunks, with a pair of sunglasses perched on top of his tousled hair.

He turned toward Morris with a soft smile lighting up his face. "Mornin'."

Morris stared at the Georgetown Hoyas basketball shirt he wore and shook his head. This fling definitely wasn't meant to last. "Mornin'." He thrust his chin toward the hamper. "Please tell me you didn't get up extra early to cook for us."

"Nope, leftovers from last night." Theo's gaze slid over Morris in a way that reminded him how long it had been since he'd had any kind of action. As much as he was looking forward to more of Theo's stirring kisses, though, he was enjoying the thought of getting to know him better too. Perhaps the Hoya T-shirt could be forgiven, if Theo had a valid reason. Theo hefted the hamper into the trunk when Morris opened it. "You said there wouldn't be access to food, and I really like to eat. So I raided our kitchen as we were cleaning up."

"True, I was thinking of stopping by a donut place or something, but this works, thank you." Morris glanced down at Theo's upturned face, nerves suddenly jangling. Maybe this wasn't the best idea for a first date. What if they ran out of things to talk about or—

His worries were effectively gagged when Theo kissed him. It was a quick kiss, enough to leave him wanting more, and the way Theo touched the side of his face made him think of a long afternoon of lazing and cuddling. Anticipation made him a little breathless. Theo had all but promised to get his hands on Morris, and he knew the perfect place where they could go for a little private time with scant worry anyone would come across them.

"So, uh, why the Hoyas?" Morris asked as his thoughts cleared.

"Oh." Theo glanced down, that furrow appearing again between his brows. "My brother goes there. This fall is going to be his last year, I think."

Morris wished he could take back the question if it put the worried look in Theo's eyes. "Ah, family loyalty. I suppose I can forgive that," he said lightly, poking Theo in the shoulder to distract him from his long thoughts.

"I skipped the whole regular college thing, went straight to culinary school, and did some apprenticeships." Theo cocked his head. "Where'd you go to school?"

"University of Maryland, College Park." Morris thumped his chest with his fist. "Terp for life."

Theo winced and looked away. "I suppose now would really be a bad time to tell you I'm a Duke fan."

"Shut the fuck up." Morris stared at him in horror as Theo's lips twitched.

"I'm teasing, I'm teasing." Theo laughed and gave Morris a playful shove.

"That's not even funny," Morris replied, though he laughed too. He had to watch out for Theo. He had a way of teasing that made him seem so serious. It was easy to fall for. "I don't know, Boarman, teasing somebody when they've got a surprise lined up for you…. You *are* putting your life in my hands, after all."

Theo nodded solemnly. "I'll keep that in mind the next time I'm tempted."

Morris shoved the bottled waters into the trunk along with his bag, then clapped his hands together. This was going to be an awesome day. "Let's do this."

"I'm looking forward to your surprise. I've been racking my brain trying to think of what would involve most of the day, no access to food, and maybe a chance for a nap," Theo said with a wink that brought a welcome heat to Morris's thoughts.

"We're going boating out on the river, maybe the bay too, if the water's calm enough and we have the time," Morris said, fishing his keys out of his pocket. "So I hope you weren't joking when you said you don't have a problem with the water."

"You own a boat?" Theo asked, his eyes widening as he slid into the seat.

"Well actually, it's a friend's boat," Morris confessed, pulling the car out of the driveway and turning toward the marina. "I might make enough with my art to support myself, but I don't high roll like that."

"And he lets you borrow it whenever you want? I need a friend like that." There was a wistful note to Theo's voice.

"If he wants to date my twin, he does."

Theo shot a quick glance at him and then laughed. "Fair point."

"Just kidding, sorta. I had to get my boating license and log in many hours tooling around with him before he even considered it," Morris admitted. "There's also manual labor involved in the spring when we're getting it ready for the season and again in the fall to dock it for the winter. And it's my hide on the line if anything happens to it."

"Well, we can't have that. I'd be willing to put in whatever manual labor he wants if he lets us take it out once in a while. I love boating." Theo stared out the window for a long moment. "You'll probably think this is silly… and I'm not quite sure how to say it without sounding like an asshole."

Acting on instinct, Morris reached over and touched his hand. "Spit it out. It's okay."

"A part of me is thinking Lincoln would love to be with us and another part of me is happy it's just us. That feels wrong, but I…." Theo trailed off, his expression troubled.

"I get the feeling you haven't had time for yourself in a long while. After Laila's accident, my sister had a real hard time letting her out of her sight. We had to convince her sending Laila to the camp in the summers wasn't foisting her off on someone else. They both ended up being better for it. But I get it, it's hard. You feel responsible for him."

"Yeah," Theo said, his voice still a little uncertain.

"Besides, if he were here, we'd be scandalizing him with distressing regularity." Because Morris did not plan to keep his hands to himself, and he doubted Theo planned on it either.

Theo laughed, his expression brightening. "True that. And he's hanging out with friends. It's not like I've abandoned him at home alone for a week. I've got to stop hovering over him. Both Jill and I do."

"Sounds like today is a good day to start." Besides, Morris was also looking forward to it just being the two of them. He was sure he'd be able to convince Victor to let him borrow the boat again this summer if they wanted to go out. They could take Lincoln out another time.

"When did you get to be so wise?" Theo said with a teasing smile.

"Yeah, whatever, remind me of that the next time I'm a thoughtless jackass because it happens more than I'd like to admit," Morris said. In the distance, the wide river came into view, the far shore hazy in the early heat and fading mist.

"I have a hard time believing that. You seem to be so together and calm. You don't have any of that diva artistic temperament. At least not that I've seen."

Morris chuckled as he turned in to the marina. "Calm I may be, but I also get lost in my own head and forget important things, like dinner dates and engagement parties." That was another incident Morris would never live down.

Theo seemed calm and together too, which Morris considered amazing considering the stresses he was under. A morning off to relax seemed like a perfect first date. "You're laid-back yourself. Speaking of clichés, you don't fit the one of a bad-tempered cook or that guy who tries to overcompensate for his height by being a bulldog. We had a promoter like that once. He was a nightmare."

"I learned long ago getting pissed over short jokes only encouraged people more. Apparently, I'm known as a hardass at the restaurant. I prefer to think perfectionist, but as long as my people do what they're supposed to do, I don't give a damn what they call me." Theo rubbed his hand over Morris's bare knee. "So no kilt again today? I've been curious to see what you wear or don't wear underneath it."

"I am terribly sorry to burst your fantasy." Morris parked the car and turned to Theo. "But I do not go for being naked underneath. Too much could go wrong. A man shouldn't live in fear of escalators giving unintended peep shows or anxiety over wind gusts."

Theo gave him a grave look, though his mouth looked as if it wanted to smile. "Those are some heavy worries."

"Tell me about it."

Then Theo's gray eyes sparkled, and he touched his fingers to Morris's lips. "I can't wait to get you alone." Morris's whole body tingled at that, and then Theo was opening the door before he could respond.

Theo stretched and looked curiously around at the marina. Despite it being a weekday, there were many empty spots at the slips. It was too pretty to be inside working when the water beckoned like this. "Okay, which boat is ours?"

"It's the white skiff about halfway down on the left. The one with the small canopy. It's called *Into the Mystic*. Victor's a Van Morrison fan, and he's got me hooked." Morris threw open the trunk and hauled out the water. He'd learned his lesson last time. The bag he'd slung over his shoulder held other things he'd forgotten before and rued later: sunscreen, extra sunglasses, and something for the headaches that sometimes came when he stared at the sun sparkling off the water for too long.

Theo grabbed the hamper with a wide grin. "Man, I'm so jazzed. This is awesome."

"Yeah?" Morris paused with a quick look at Theo, and he smiled slowly at the pleasure on his face.

"Yeah." Theo hitched the hamper onto his shoulder. "You know, you're awfully damn cute when you give me that shy smile. It gets me going every time."

With that Theo strode off toward the boat, whistling softly and leaving Morris staring after him. He'd never met a man who tangled him up in so many knots and left him wanting to stay tangled. He wasn't sure what to make of Theo or of his own growing attraction to him. This was a fling, a dip outside of his comfort zone, and all he wanted out of it was good memories. Theo seemed perfectly content with the plan too.

Morris caught up with Theo as he reached the boat. It wasn't big and fancy like some others, but she handled well both on the river and the rougher waters of the bay. There was enough room for them to stretch out without feeling like they were crowded in. Morris loved Victor's boat. Every time he had the chance to take her out, he promised himself one day he'd have one just like her.

"There's a cooling box under the bench there in the aft. We can put the food and water there. There are life jackets in the bench beside

it. Victor keeps his fishing equipment in the storage on the port side."
Morris stored his carry-on bag by the center console and looked over the
controls.

"Do you ever take her out to go fishing?" Theo nudged open the
box and set the food and water inside. "I haven't been fishing… damn,
probably since middle school."

"Not really, no. Worms and hooks aren't my thing." Now that he
thought about it, he had zero interest in trying to get a fish off a hook
while it flopped and wiggled. Seemed cruel. "I like cruising around or
finding a good spot to lay out, relax, and enjoy the sun and scenery."

"I like the sound of that." Theo slid his arm around Morris's waist
and kissed his shoulder. "I have been looking forward to this date since
you asked me. Being out here makes it better."

"I can't believe I asked you." Morris looked down at him, struck
with embarrassment by how that sounded. "That came out wrong. I
meant, I'm not normally the one who does the asking." He paused and
huffed out a breath as he winced. That sounded even worse, like he was
full of himself.

Theo brushed his fingers along Morris's arm. "You can be a little
shy. I'm glad you did ask. I thought I was going to have to wear you
down with my persistence and charm. But if you took the chance, then
that must mean you are as interested in me as I am in you."

Morris turned to him, his whole body stirring at Theo's closeness.
"I'm glad I did too." He'd wanted the chance to sit back and be with Theo
again with no schedules hanging over their heads, just to talk and get to
know each other. He'd also wanted the chance to maybe do a little more than
kissing without worrying over being interrupted by overzealous brothers or
cranky friends. It had been crazy with Awesome Con looming and his trip
to Pennsylvania coming up. No, he wouldn't think about schedules today,
only Theo.

He brushed his lips over Theo's and then turned back to the boat.
With Theo's help they were soon moving slowly out of the marina and
heading onto the Patuxent River. "Which way do you want to go? River
or bay?" He glanced over his shoulder at Theo, who was resting his arms
on the side and leaning over to watch the water.

"How about by Calvert Cliffs? I haven't been by there in forever.
You ever go fossil hunting there?"

"Can't say that I have. I didn't grow up around here. My family's up near Bowie," Morris replied, turning the boat toward the Chesapeake Bay. "Do you ever find anything?"

"Oh yeah, mostly small stuff, but there's tons there. I don't know if you ever noticed the glass-enclosed picture at the restaurant with all the sharks' teeth." Theo gave him a curious look.

Morris thought back. The restaurant had a lot of art up, photos of the bay, drawings by local artists, and now he seemed to recall it. "The one behind the hostess station?"

"Yeah. That's all fossils we found as kids. Dad picked out the biggest ones and had them encased for us."

Morris had never been fossil hunting before, and the idea intrigued him. "Are there any boat slips nearby?"

"Not sure. I've never been by boat. But you have to hit it during low tide to get anything, otherwise it's all underwater." Theo came up to him as Morris opened up the throttle. He hadn't quibbled at all about wearing the life vest, for which Morris was grateful. He'd gotten to be a stickler for safety, and some found it to be a downer. "We can go another day. Just being out on the water with you is nice, and now that I think about it, Calvert Cliffs won't give us any privacy."

"Don't worry. I have just the place." The boat skipped along the river, the wind whipping at them. Morris lingered over the image of Theo standing in the bow, his hands on his hips as he looked out over the water. He slowed down as the river spilled out into the Chesapeake Bay and the tides and currents made the ride choppier.

The water was fairly calm today with no recent storms to stir it up. Morris drew in a deep breath of the salt-heavy air, his hands competent on the tiller as they were hit with a fine spray. While they headed north up through the bay, meandering and taking their time, Theo handed out water bottles and cold fish sandwiches slathered with the bistro's homemade sauce. Morris had forgotten how hungry he got when he was out on the water. Donuts from the bakery and the protein bars he'd shoved into his bag would not have cut it.

"Damn, these are good. Toss me another." Morris took a bite, trying to pin down the creamy, tangy sauce with a hint of heat.

"I don't understand how a man your size, who obviously loves food the way you do, can manage to forget about eating so much," Theo commented as Morris found a quiet spot in a cove, killed the engine, and dropped anchor.

"I wonder that myself sometimes. Especially when I finally look up from my drawing table and my stomach attacks with vicious intensity." Morris reached into the cooler for a brownie and then sat back on the bench with his eyes half-closed and his face lifted to the sun.

"You don't by any chance pack a lunch for yourself during a show?" Theo stretched out alongside him. "I noticed at the one I went to there were no food vendors."

"There is rarely any decent food at a convention unless you're one of the staff or a guest. It's mostly junk food and sweets." A little tingle of awareness went through him as Theo slid his arm around his shoulders. "Bringing snacks would be smart, and I've even done it once or twice, but I never get around to eating them, so it seems like a wasted effort."

"I'd pack you something if I thought you'd eat, but I'd be offended if you forgot."

Morris set his water bottle aside and looked at Theo. His cheeks were turning pink in the sun, and his clear gray eyes were more relaxed and calm than Morris had ever seen them. As laid-back as Theo seemed, Morris sensed an undercurrent of stress.

"Well, I wouldn't want to do that," Morris murmured as Theo slid his hand behind Morris's neck. Anticipation struck Morris with a breathless punch as Theo smiled at him and leaned up to kiss him.

Morris slid his arm around Theo's waist and kissed him back. This had been lingering in his mind all morning. Theo's kisses had a way of leaving Morris wanting more. He kissed as if all of his attention was on the moment, on Morris, and not on his worries. Morris speared his fingers in Theo's hair and tried to shift closer, but their life vests got in the way.

Theo skimmed his fingers over Morris's neck, making him shiver and making it hard for Morris to think of anything other than what he'd like Theo to do with his hands. He tried reaching under Theo's shirt and was blocked again.

"Okay, these things have got to go," Theo muttered as he undid the clasps on Morris's life vest before stripping off his own.

"Problem solved," Morris murmured, reaching for him again. Without those bulky obstacles in the way, Morris explored Theo with eager hands, touching him through the barrier of their clothes. He had an impression of a taut, lean body, but it wasn't enough. He wanted more. He turned his head, kissing Theo's throat, brushing his lips along the smooth skin of Theo's jaw as his heart beat faster.

Theo's hands skated under Morris's shirt, and he hummed in appreciation as fingers danced idly on his skin. He drew Theo as close as he could when the kiss broke, and Theo's lips began to wander. What could be better than the hot sun beating down on you, an ocean breeze cooling the sweat off your body, and a gorgeous man with his lips on your throat?

Morris shivered again, arching his neck a little more as Theo's mouth moved lower, his tongue tracing a hot path over Morris's skin. Damn, he wanted more. He wanted his fill. Then Theo pulled back to strip his shirt off him. Morris's breath quickened as he did the same for Theo. His chest was flushed pink from the heat and sun, a faint scattering of golden brown hair over his chest. He sat back to appreciate the view. Theo had given him a nice eyeful last week, but Morris didn't mind a repeat.

Theo slid his hand down Morris's side, his eyes warm with approval. "Nice," he murmured as he looked Morris over.

Morris grinned and caught Theo's hand, bringing it to his lips. "Same for you." He dug into the bag behind him until he found the sunscreen. It was a transparent excuse to touch, but he didn't care. He held it up with a little smile. "Shall I? You don't want to walk into a hot kitchen with a sunburn."

"That would be dire." Theo leaned back, his arms across the seat in an open invitation to explore. "Go right ahead, but I'll insist on returning the favor."

Morris poured some of the lotion into his hands and knelt in front of Theo. Theo watched him through half-lidded eyes glinting with banked heat as Morris rubbed sunblock over his chest and shoulders, then down to his flat stomach. "I like the feel of your hands," Theo murmured. "I've been thinking about those gorgeous hands of yours on me since I saw you drawing at your table."

"That's about as long as I've been thinking I wanted my hands on you." The reality was better than the anticipation. Theo was compact, lean without being skinny, not overly muscled, but his body carried a wiry strength Morris appreciated. He took his time, slicking sunscreen over every inch of him, even getting Theo to turn around so he could slide his hands down the back of Theo's shorts to massage his taut ass. The expression in Theo's eyes grew wicked and his cock pressed against his swim trunks when he stood up.

"My turn." Theo took the sunscreen from him and gestured for Morris to take his seat. He straddled Morris's thighs and poured some lotion into his palm. The way he looked at Morris made him feel sexy and not ungainly and too big. "I want my mouth on every sweet inch of you too," Theo said with a groan and laugh.

Morris leaned back on his elbows, his cock aching as Theo's hands slid over him in a slow massage. They lingered on his chest, and Theo lightly tweaked Morris's nipples until they stiffened. Morris moaned and caught his hand. "That is a highly sensitive area. I may not make it to nakedness if you keep doing that."

Theo shot him a serious look. "You wouldn't want them to get sunburned either."

"Tease," Morris said with a breathless laugh, his body still tingling.

Theo grinned in acknowledgment as he poured more lotion into his hands. He inched closer, until his cock pressed against Morris's stomach. Then he was kissing Morris again, slow and lazy as he massaged the lotion down Morris's back. Morris straightened and gripped Theo's ass. His entire body thrummed with the need to be naked beside him.

"Maybe it's time to move this off the bench," he whispered against Theo's mouth.

"Yeah." Theo nipped Morris's lip and slid off his lap. They grabbed a couple cushions off the benches, tossed them on the deck, and covered them with their towels. Morris's heart beat faster, and his hands shook slightly as they helped each other out of their swim trunks. The breeze was fitful down there and the sun beat down on them, but Morris didn't care. They could cool down in the water later. Right now, he wanted to get to know every inch of Theo's body.

They caressed more lotion over each other's legs, taking their time. More of those light golden brown curls gathered around Theo's erect cock and covered his legs. Morris stroked his hands over him, delighting in the feel of him. There weren't many lovers Morris encountered who didn't make him feel oversized or gangly, but somehow Theo managed to make him less self-conscious. Probably because of Theo's confidence in his own size.

Morris's breath caught as Theo gently pushed him back and hovered over him. "I have been thinking of this for weeks."

"You have?" Morris's thoughts scattered as Theo gently caught his earlobe between his teeth. "Which part exactly?"

"You under me with a needy look in your eyes and your hands on my body the way they are now."

"Wow." The heat setting him on fire with want had nothing to do with the summer sun and everything to do with the man leaning over him looking as if he was about to stake a claim on him. Morris had been waiting a long damn time for someone to look at him like that. He slid his arms around Theo, tugged him closer, and kissed him hungrily. "You make me needy," he whispered.

"Good." Theo nipped his lower lip and slid his hand up Morris's leg. "Next time we do this, you have to be wearing your kilt."

Morris chuckled. "You're obsessed with my clothing choices."

"I'm obsessed with getting my hands under them." Morris cupped Theo's cock, feeling the vital heat and energy as it throbbed against his palm. Theo touched him in return, stroking, teasing until Morris's hips moved into the touch, seeking more. "You are one sexy man," Theo breathed, his eyes alight with anticipation.

Morris never really thought of himself as especially sexy. He never really gave it much thought at all. And while Theo definitely got his juices going, he was more along the lines of adorable in that boy-next-door, heartwarming kind of way. He didn't want to tell him that, though, in case he'd be offended.

Theo teased Morris's mouth with his lips. "What are you thinking about so hard?"

Morris's cheeks heated as he lowered his gaze. "Too much." Like how he was going to tell Theo he was a bottom and the thought of topping anyone intimidated him. He should've brought it up before they were naked. Now they'd both be disappointed.

"I must be doing something wrong, then." Theo slid down Morris's body, and before he registered what Theo was doing, his lips were on Morris's cock and Morris lost all sense of coherency. His mouth was hot and demanding, and Morris's head fell back as he groaned.

"Oh fuck me."

Theo hummed around him as if he liked the thought of that. Morris slid his hand down, tangling his fingers with Theo's. Morris bit his lip, his breath coming faster, all his expectations and anticipation blown away. Theo made everything feel right, and the buildup had Morris making hot little desperate sounds that made Theo's gray eyes flash.

Theo tugged his hand free, and then he was touching Morris as well, gently cupping his balls, rolling and teasing. Morris felt a finger slide back to stroke over that hypersensitive area that always made him feel as if hot tingles of electricity were rolling over his skin.

"Wait… fuck…."

Theo hummed around him again, the suction increasing as Morris came with a shudder that left his heart hammering and his breath panting. Morris caught his arms, urging Theo up so he could kiss him. He tasted the musk on Theo's lips and groaned, eager to get his own mouth on Theo. He slid his hand between their bodies, gently tugging on Theo's cock until he moaned against his mouth.

Theo pulled back, his eyes hazy, his cheeks flushed. "Are you thinking now?"

Morris pushed him back on the cushions. "I'm thinking it's my turn. How the hell did you get to be so good at that?"

"I quit smoking. I have one serious oral fixation." Theo resisted Morris's gentle push long enough to lightly suck on his lower lip.

"Lucky me." Morris wasn't going to survive this fling. He was going to spontaneously combust before it was over.

Theo settled back, one arm tucked under his head as Morris kissed his throat, then his chest. He took his time, now that the sharp edge of his need to get off wasn't clawing at him anymore. He wanted to make Theo absolutely crazy.

He skated his hands down Theo's body, learning the feel of him, sighing softly as he did. Theo's scent hit him, musk and sweat and ocean air, and all thoughts of going slow left. Morris glanced up at Theo and their eyes met. Naked anticipation and need marked Theo's expression. Morris dragged his tongue across the head of Theo's cock, heard his barely there moan, before sinking his mouth over him.

Theo moaned again, louder this time as he brushed his fingers over Morris's shoulder. "You keep looking at me like that and this isn't going to last long."

The day was only half over. Morris figured they'd have time to get their hands on each other again. He'd make time. Theo's cock filled his mouth, filled his senses, stirring his excitement again. Morris concentrated on blowing Theo's mind until those strong fingers dug into his shoulders and Theo came with a strangled cry that was lost in the sound of the waves washing against the boat.

Morris lifted his head as Theo shuddered and tugged on his bicep. Morris eased over him, his gaze intent on the hazy pleasure on Theo's face. Theo fisted his hands in Morris's hair and kissed him long and deep. "Let's do this again," he breathed against Morris's lips.

"I think you're reading my mind."

# Chapter Eleven

THEO WOKE up as the breeze shifted direction and the label on the cushion he was resting against tickled his cheek. Lying sprawled out on the deck of a boat on top of the cushions and towels was a restful place to have a nap. Morris had extended the canopy over him so he was in the shade instead of the sun, and that consideration made him smile.

He stretched, conscious of the fact the cushions beside him were empty. He'd been hoping to wake up next to Morris. They'd curled up together, trading kisses and touches, until they'd both gotten off again. Then Theo had drifted off, completely at ease with Morris beside him. For once, he felt wonderfully rested and not as if he were racing to catch up.

He shifted his arm off his eyes and blinked, searching for Morris. He sat in the chair at the console on a towel, buck naked, with a sketchbook balanced on his lap as he scribbled away furiously. Theo grinned. And people thought he was a workaholic. He'd love to witness this sight again another afternoon. He nudged Morris with his toe and Morris glanced over, smiled, and nudged him back. "Hey there, sleeping beauty."

"Are you really drawing while wearing nothing but your skin?"

"I am. I wasn't wearing underwear with my swim trunks, or I'd be scribbling away in them. I often draw in nothing but my underwear," Morris confessed, tucking his pencil away. "It sometimes takes me a while to get around to being an adult after I start work."

Now, that was a lovely image to have in his mind. Morris's long body folded at his drawing table, all that beautiful exposed brown skin, and the sexy faraway look that he got on his face when he drew, like the look he'd just had.

"Good to know. I might have to stop by for coffee before I head to work." Theo rolled up onto his knees, unselfconscious in his own nakedness, and peered at Morris's sketchbook. "May I see?"

Morris drew the sketchbook a little closer to himself, a shy look entering his gaze. "It's silly. You're going to think I'm a creeper or something. I have a compulsion to sketch when my hands are idle."

Morris had been drawing him. Curiosity gnawed at Theo as he sat back on his heels. "I've never had anyone sketch me while I was naked," he said wistfully. "It was on my bucket list. If you show me, I can cross it off." Morris stared at him, his eyes widening, and Theo quirked a smile back at him. "Unless, of course, you drew me in a wild, physically impossible sexual position. Then I suppose you can keep your fantasy to yourself. We all should have some privacy when it comes to our kinks."

Morris cocked his head with a furrowed brow, realized Theo was teasing him, and burst out laughing. "I'll keep that in mind. Is that on your bucket list too? To be drawn in an impossible sexual position?"

Theo pursed his lips and nodded. "I think I'll have to add it now that you've mentioned it."

Morris shook his head and handed over the sketchbook. Theo tipped it up and smiled slowly. Morris managed to capture him in a few clean lines. He'd drawn Theo's torso and face. He was sprawled with one arm over his eyes and his hand resting lightly on his stomach. There was something sweet about the way he'd sketched him, so content and relaxed, and Theo realized Morris had a real gift for conveying emotion with lines on a page.

"Dude, you are really talented," Theo said, handing it back. "Don't let anyone tell you otherwise."

"Tell my dad that," Morris said, tucking the sketchbook away. "He thinks it's cool I make a living off my art. But he's an attorney. Deep down I know he'd be more comfortable seeing me in a job that had a stable paycheck, health insurance, and a retirement plan. He doesn't really say anything against it, but it's in the little comments and that hesitant smile he gets sometimes when I talk about a new commission or a book coming out that clue me in to his feelings."

"If you have a chance to do what you love, go for it." Theo shrugged. "We only live once. I suppose I could find something with better pay and less hours than running the restaurant, but I have zero interest in doing a different career. Honestly, if someone else wants to do the managing and leave me to do the cooking I'd be happier, but it's a trade-off. Besides, I wouldn't let anyone outside of family have control. I know myself too well."

"Yeah, that's what I keep telling myself, and I'm grateful for the support I get. Believe me. I've heard of some shit between artists and their families. It reminds me not to take my own for granted."

"How was the convention you went to last weekend?" Theo asked. It absolutely fascinated him there were people who did them on a consistent basis and worked their livelihoods around them.

"It lived up to its name, Awesome." Morris grinned. "It's always an exhausting madhouse. I usually have to hide away for a day or two afterward and enjoy the silence. I didn't make as much as I wanted to, but I got to network and see people who probably only pop up once or twice a year. And bonus, I didn't get the con crud going around."

"Con crud, it's a thing?" Theo shook his head. Morris and his friends even had their own language.

"Yeah, somebody shows up sick and passes their evil little cooties to everyone else. Add in the excitement and exhaustion, everyone returns home and starts bitching on social media about how they're dying." Morris cocked his head, his gaze sweeping over Theo in a way that made him remember how nice it had been to have their arms around each other. "You know, you're awfully adorkable when you sleep."

Morris closed his eyes, and Theo's brows rose. "Dammit, cute I meant." He opened one eye. "I told myself I wouldn't tell you you were adorkable. Not after all your comments about my sexiness. Now I feel bad."

One of these days Morris was going to tell him who made him so self-conscious of men outside of his group. Because Morris didn't seem to have any problems when he was in his element. "You shouldn't. Does adorkable push your buttons?"

"Every one of them," Morris replied without hesitation. "You're kind of like a short, less muscled-up Thor."

"Thor? The dude with the hammer? I'm not sure how Thor-like I am, but I'm absolutely fine with adorkable if it lets me get my hands on you again." Theo scraped his hands through his hair and leaned over to grab a bottle of water out of the cooler. "I didn't mean to drop off like that," he said ruefully.

"What time did you actually make it to bed last night?" Morris raised a brow. "It was definitely after midnight, because I heard your car pull up. Then you were up early this morning. No need to apologize."

"If you heard my car, you were up late too." Theo slid his arms around Morris's waist. "You could've napped with me. I liked having you near."

The corner of Morris's mouth lifted, and he nuzzled Theo's lips with soft kisses. "I dozed a bit, but then my fingers started itching for a pencil."

Theo chuckled. "I suppose I'll have to get used to that and seeing random doodles everywhere."

"It is a hazard. Besides, I wasn't thinking of only myself. Your best interest was on my mind as well." Morris rubbed his lips along Theo's jaw, and his body stirred.

"Do tell. Because if it's getting me all worked up again, you're definitely accomplishing your task." Theo wasn't alone. Morris's nakedness made his own renewed desire very apparent.

Morris smiled against Theo's skin. "I didn't want you to have to go to work tonight with a sunburn in uncomfortable places."

"That's very thoughtful of you. I should do something in return." Theo slid his hands along Morris's thighs.

"Maybe that something could include a bed where we could take our time all night," Morris murmured, rubbing slow circles on Theo's back.

"Mmm, I like the way you think, Proctor. Just you and me and nowhere we have to be and all the time we want to explore each other." Which sadly reminded Theo they did not have time today. He did not want to look at his watch. Reluctantly, he pulled back before they both got too worked up.

Morris hesitated, and Theo cocked his head when he seemed to decide not to speak. "What is it?" Theo could've sworn Morris blushed. He wasn't entirely sure, given Morris's complexion, but he'd seen the other signs before too. The look of embarrassment as Morris glanced away, the way he nervously rubbed his hand on the back of his neck. "Seriously, you can tell me."

Worry trickled down his spine. They hadn't discussed protection. In the past, Theo admitted he hadn't always been the most careful and he'd been lucky, but since he'd assumed custody of Lincoln and after everything that had happened with their parents, he'd vowed to be more cautious. He'd been tested and was clean and he planned on keeping it that way. Had he screwed that up?

"Well, I wanted to say something before we did anything, but I didn't know how to say it, and then one thing led to another. It's nothing bad. I swear," Morris hastened to assure him as Theo drew back even more with a stab of alarm. "I like to get assumptions out of the way."

Morris stopped with a groan. "I'm making it worse. Look, I prefer to bottom." Morris cast him that sexy, shy look through his lashes, the look that made Theo's blood heat. "Most guys look at me and assume top, but it's not really my thing."

Theo sat back on his heels with a wave of relief. Then what Morris said registered. Morris was a bottom. Theo had to admit he'd assumed the same thing and he figured they'd work around it some way. He'd dealt with the opposite assumptions often enough, so he should've known better.

"I think we're well matched, then." Theo dropped a kiss on his mouth. "Because bottoming isn't really my thing either. And if you keep looking at me through your lashes like that, I'm going to be very late for work, and I haven't done that in ages."

Morris's eyes warmed, and the shy look dropped away. "Maybe we're a little more compatible than I thought."

Theo laughed and pulled back before he gave in to temptation. A little regretfully, he began to put on his clothes. "Darling, we have loads of compatibility based on the way you blew my mind earlier."

"You do amazing things for my ego." Morris slipped into his own clothes and tossed Theo one of the life vests. "And for the record, since I saw that fear in your eyes, I am clean. I haven't had that many partners, but a friend of mine had a scare, so I went with him and got myself tested as a show of solidarity."

Theo smiled at him. "I'm clean too. I can't say I was all that celibate before Lincoln became my responsibility, but he caused me to change many bad habits."

Morris nodded his understanding and gestured to the dancing water. "Did you want to tool around a little longer?"

Theo shaded his eyes as he looked out on the expanse of glittering bay. Then he glanced at his watch and frowned. Time shot by too fast when he was relaxed. "We actually should start making our way back. Duty calls."

"Duty is a greedy bastard."

Buoyed by the look of disappointment on Morris's face, Theo realized he wanted more than a fling. Flings were okay for the short term, but he couldn't see himself walking away from Morris after a couple rounds with a vague promise to see each other again. Only problem, his life wasn't in relationship mode, and he didn't know when it would be again.

"What are you doing Saturday morning?" Theo had to open and close the restaurant, but maybe they could have breakfast before he headed out.

"I'll be in Allentown. Heading up to Pennsylvania Friday morning with Felipe in tow," Morris said as he pulled up the anchor. "I won't be back until late Sunday."

Well that sucked. "How about Monday morning, then? If you don't get in too late?"

"It all depends on traffic, but I think I should be back by midnight." Morris looked over the console and flicked a glance at Theo. "Why? Got something planned?"

"I was thinking I could make you breakfast. My days and nights are always hectic, but the mornings I don't go to the market are fairly quiet and relaxing."

Morris gave him a considering look. "It doesn't get old? All this cooking?"

Theo pointed at the sketchbook sticking out of Morris's bag. "Does that get old?"

"Fair point. Okay, I'll be there. Is there anything I can bring?"

"Just your appetite."

Morris frowned. "Are you sure? I can pick up juice or something."

"Juice is always nice, but you know what would be nicer?" Theo said, letting a wistful, forlorn note creep into his voice. "A couple kisses to see me through the day."

Morris shot him a startled glance and then chuckled. "I'll see what I can do about that."

Theo set about replacing the cushions and tying them down as the boat rumbled to life. As they took off, turning in a wide sweep into the bay, Theo straightened to stare at the water and watch Morris's profile from the corner of his eye. This had to have been one of the better days he'd had in a long time. Right on the tails of that thought came the guilt and heavy weight of his worries. Lincoln would've had a ball out here with them. Was it so selfish to want some time to himself?

"You're getting that look again," Morris called over the roar of the engine, the slap of the waves, and the tugging of the wind.

"Yeah? What look is that?" Theo asked as he made his way over to him.

"Weight of the world look." Morris flicked a glance at him. "Are you still thinking about hiring more help?"

Theo grimaced. "Jill keeps bringing it up. She's even gone so far as to start interviewing."

"And you're still resisting every step."

Damn, Morris read him rather well. "That nails it." Theo gave him a rueful smile. "I know it's a control issue, and I know I have to let go some. But knowing isn't the same as doing."

"Well, I guess recognizing it's the first step, and really, once you have some new hires in place, it'll be moot. If you want, my sister works in management at a hotel and she comes across many restaurant managers and kitchen staff in the properties she oversees. She might have a recommendation or two," Morris offered.

Theo hesitated and then sighed. "I suppose it wouldn't hurt to look into it." Maybe then Jill would get off his back.

"Treat it like a Band-Aid," Morris replied with a shrug.

"A Band-Aid?"

"Yeah, instead of fretting over it, rip it off and get it over with. Then the anticipation won't be hanging over you."

Theo leaned against the railing as he pondered that. Yeah… just hire someone and get it over. Then he could move on to adjusting. Sure… simple as that.

# Chapter Twelve

THE BREWERY hummed with the voices of attendees and vendors, and the scent of hops and yeasty beers underlined every transaction. Light filtered through the tall windows, burnishing the wood floors to a golden glow and caressing the leather-lined booths. Lamps hung from the ceiling in a row of colored glass that gave off more illumination. Morris had been to many a con in a strange location, but this one had to be the most inspired. He could get drunk off light like this even more than he could from breathing in the array of beers, lagers, and stouts. Tall metal vats lined up behind a glass viewing wall, each vat carrying a small chalked sign declaring its contents.

The signs tempted, and Morris had to remind himself he couldn't have a sampling fest at his own table, not if he wanted to recoup his money. He'd managed to avoid the partying last night, mostly because he and Felipe had gotten in so late, but he could tell from the bleary eyes of some of the artists across from him the drinking had been hard and heavy. Yep, inspired and very dangerous location. At least the attendees seemed mellow and inclined to spend as they lingered at tables with glasses in their hands. Now if he could keep them from setting those glasses down on top of his books and prints, it would be a near perfect day.

Morris was supposed to go out later with some of the guys from the 501st Legion, but he made a note to not get carried away. He did not want to run the table tomorrow with a hangover, and he definitely did not want a four-hour drive home after the con still suffering from aftereffects. He remembered a time when he'd ignored such considerations, and he hoped this wasn't a sign he was growing old.

He nodded to a passerby as they glanced in his direction, but they moved on without stopping. Morris's stomach rumbled. It was too late for lunch, breakfast had disappeared hours ago, and he couldn't see getting away to grab a bite until after they shut down for the night. One of these days, he'd remember to pack something.

Morris pulled out his phone and checked his empty text messages. Dammit, he had it bad. One afternoon of screwing around with Theo Boarman, and he couldn't stop thinking about when it would happen again. He was in serious trouble if he didn't get this under control. He knew himself. His heart got engaged too fast. Maybe it was time to pull back. The thought jolted him with a little surge of denial and rebellion. They'd really just started their fling. It was too early to pull back now. One more hot and heavy date. Then he'd let common sense return.

A shadow fell across his table, a welcome distraction from his thoughts that refused to obey. Morris glanced up at Brenden and grinned. "Hey there." He rose, clasping his hand, and noted Brenden's guest badge. "You doing a panel this weekend or scouting?"

"I'm moderating the wrestling panel." Brenden picked up Morris's latest book and flipped through it. "And promoting the next Chessie Con, which brings me to you."

"Oh? The next one is in Newport News, right?" Morris went through his mental calendar and tried to remember if he'd paid for that table yet or not. He really needed a better system than this half-assed one he had.

"That's the one. I wanted to do a role-playing panel. I know you and some others had that gaming group. I thought it might be interesting to get some players and gamemasters together for a discussion of favorite games." Brenden paused on a comic page and half smiled with a shake of his head.

"Dude, that would seriously be awesome. I'd love to." Maybe it would even help them find a new good gamemaster for their group. Morris really missed it. "Who else do you have in mind?"

"Well, Trask from the Magick Den already agreed to fill in one of the gamemaster spots. Dakota hasn't given me an answer yet about his schedule." Brenden tucked the book under his arm and pulled out his wallet. "That one chick who always does the kickass cosplay, Abby, I think, she agreed to take the other GM spot."

"You should include Felipe," Morris suggested, glancing around for his wayward friend. Felipe was going to kill him for this. Though once he got over his dramatic fit, he'd relish the idea. Abby made him twitch, and Dakota was his ex, but maybe ogling Trask would make up for those irritations.

Brenden grimaced. "I'd rather not."

Morris laid his elbows on the table, debating whether to address Brenden's ambivalence. Brenden wouldn't meet his eye as he carefully counted out his cash, and Morris decided against bringing it up. It really wouldn't serve any purpose, especially since Felipe was showing no interest in letting Dakota back into his bed.

"Felipe and Abby are dedicated rivals. They thrive on outdoing each other. They would make the panel lively."

"Yeah, and what's to keep them from going over-the-top?" Brenden asked with a cool glance in his direction.

Morris shrugged and took Brenden's money before scrounging around for a bag. "They don't usually get too out of hand, but if they do, I'm used to moderating squabbles." Not only Felipe and Abby. There were a few others Morris could name who needed someone to step in from time to time.

"Trask would shut it down quick too. He's not the kind of guy to put up with a lot of bullshit." Brenden handed Morris the book, and Morris signed it with a flourish. "I'll think about it. So are you on any panels at this con?"

Morris sighed as he slipped the book into the bag and handed it back. "They won't let me participate in the pop culture trivia panel."

"That's because you always win," Brenden said with a grin. "It's insane how much off-the-wall, obscure shit you have lodged in your brain."

"What can I say; I have hidden talents." It was a shame he couldn't enter because he coveted the prize, a sweet, pristine edition of Neal Adams's *Batman #232*. Morris loved Neal Adams's work, and the edition he'd had since he was a kid was banged up. "Daughter of the Demon" introduced his favorite villain. Okay, one of his top five. There were many kickass villains, which only reminded him he needed a new bad guy for a long arc he wanted to do for his own comic. "They're having me run it, though, and believe me, I'm going to make them work for a win."

Brenden laughed. "Okay, I'm going to have to sit in the back of the room for this. Who's watching your table? Your bosom buddy?"

"One of the volunteers. Felipe is working on a costume emergency for a friend of his. He's sewing his fingers off in the lounge they set up in the club." Morris glanced at his phone to gauge how much time he had before the panel started and couldn't stop himself from seeing no new messages had arrived. He really needed help, possibly therapy, all because of a gray-eyed cutie who had more charm than anyone possibly needed.

"How did the date go?" Brenden asked. "You didn't talk yourself out of it, did you?"

"It was amazing." Morris propped his chin on his hand, and Brenden laughed. "What?"

"You should've seen the look of dreamy adoration that came across your face." Brenden's smile widened, warming his usually stern expression. "You could be the poster child for a Hallmark card."

"It's not like that. It's just a fling." Morris glanced at his phone. Theo's quiet only proved that both of them wanted to keep it casual.

"I need a fling like that."

"So how goes the plans for your big con?"

Brenden's eyes lit up. "Good. We have the venue lined up in Annapolis and rooms blocked off. Struck a few agreements with some stars, and I have meetings lined up with others to try to lure them. I want to get a few more names in the pot."

Stars. They were cool and all—Morris met a number of really laid-back people who had made his day, others he would care to forget—but cons weren't any fun when all the focus was on the stars and cosplayers. "Are you inviting any guest artists and writers?"

"I have a few in mind. Tom King is local, and he agreed. There are others I'm reaching out to. Do you have any names you want to throw into the pot?"

Morris thought about the trivia prize with a rush of yearning. "Invite Neal Adams and I'll be your best friend."

"I thought I was your best friend," Felipe said as he sauntered up, stiletto heels clicking. How the hell anyone walked in stilts like that was a continual mystery to Morris. A long red wig fell to Felipe's waist, and the Dawn outfit he'd made was a fantastic rendering of skulls and roses, leather and lace. He cast Brenden a wintery look. "Wade."

"Suero."

Morris rolled his eyes. He did not want snark to break out at his table, and both of them were masters at delivering a cutting line. "Did you get the emergency fixed?"

"Yep." A satisfied grin crossed Felipe's scarlet-red lips. "And managed to make some sweet cash on the side. I'm getting blitzed tonight."

Morris was definitely getting older, because he did not want to contemplate driving back with a hungover Felipe any more than he wanted to deal with the symptoms himself. "Not too blitzed or I'm sticking you in the trunk for the ride back."

"Please, bitch, ain't no way I'm fitting in your trunk with everything you bring. It won't matter how fucked-up I get." Felipe's grin widened before he turned an insolent stare on Brenden. "You coming out for a drink with us tonight, or would that require an excavator team to get that stick out of your ass?"

Morris closed his eyes. They had actually managed to stand next to each other for fifteen seconds without incident. Which was probably a record and he should applaud them, but he did not want drama at his table, at least not this kind of drama. Maybe if they had capes and swords, that at least would be entertaining.

Brenden's eyes flashed, and when he spoke his voice was several degrees cooler. "I'll be there. The entertainment value of watching you make a fool of yourself as you attempt to replace Dakota in your bed will be more than enough compensation for having to put up with you."

Felipe's spine stiffened as his mouth fell open. "What the fuck is wrong with you? You sit there and judge me, imply I'm easy, when what really pisses you off is Dakota wants someone hot-blooded, not a dried-up block of ice like you."

Morris stood up to intervene before Brenden flayed Felipe open with his tongue or Felipe stabbed Brenden with a stiletto. "Hey, why don't we take a step back here and—"

"Don't bother to try to mediate," Brenden said to Morris in that same cool, dispassionate tone without taking his eyes off Felipe. "I don't give a damn who he fucks. And I never called you a whore. Desperate maybe, but not easy. Clearly, you're projecting as well as overcompensating considering you have your ass hanging out one end of your costume and your fake tits hanging out the other end. If you want to go ahead and keep trading shots with me, I'm game, but I'll eat you alive, Suero, so you might want to reconsider."

Felipe flushed an ugly red, his gaze glittering, but to Morris's surprise, he turned on his heel and stalked off instead of retaliating. Brenden watched him go, his face still set with scathing dislike, and then he sighed, an expression of shame crossing his face. "I'm an asshole."

"You both were assholes," Morris said with a shake of his head as he sat back down.

"I don't know what it is about him that gets under my skin so." Brenden rubbed a hand over his scalp.

"You're too different and too much alike at the same time." And they were fighting over a guy whether Brenden wanted to admit it or not, and that always got ugly.

Brenden shot him a baffled look. "What do you mean by that?"

"You're both fiercely protective, passionate, and have a tendency to say exactly what you think regardless of the impact. Neither of you back down from a challenge, and you're both masters of the cutting insult. You're as hot-blooded as he is, you just hide it better. He wears his emotions out there for everyone to see, while you only share it with a select few. Despite his age, Felipe knows exactly who he is, and what he wants out of life, and I think you're not entirely facing that. I think that's what irks you the most."

Brenden looked away, his jaw tightening. "Maybe you have a point," he said after a long moment. "So where do you think the little diva has gone? I need to apologize to him."

"I'd wait until tonight if I were you. Give him some time to cool down. He'll make you bleed if you try talking to him now."

"Yeah, you're probably right." Brenden sighed again as he studied where Felipe had disappeared. "Sorry for that bit of drama. I'll talk to you later."

Morris watched him walk away in the opposite direction, soon disappearing among the crowd moving through the narrow walkway lined with makeshift booths. There were a couple curious onlookers who quickly moved on when Morris caught their eye. Morris set up a sign announcing he'd be right back, grabbed his cashbox, and went looking for Felipe. Despite what he'd said to Brenden, it wasn't a good idea to let Felipe stew either. He was one who needed to bitch things out in order to move on.

Felipe couldn't go sulk in their hotel room since Morris had the car keys. Upset or not, he was not one to miss a costume contest or a chance to promote his work, so he had to be around somewhere.

The bar was darker than the restaurant, with smaller windows and cool tones in the marble-top bar and chrome-lined shelves behind it. The bartender was doing a brisk business, every round stool taken, and half the booths filled with attendees and vendors. Morris nodded to another vendor who had a sampler lined up in front of him, half the little glasses empty. The man wasn't going to be able to find his table again.

He found Felipe tucked back into a hidden corner booth, diving into a plate of nachos. He stopped by the bar, ordered a root beer, and joined his friend. Morris set Felipe's discarded wig aside, then slid into the booth across from him. Felipe glared at him as Morris selected a cheese-and-bean-filled chip and popped it into his mouth. Damn, he was hungry. He picked out another as he waited for Felipe to talk first.

"I'm the one who's emotionally eating," Felipe snapped, slapping Morris's hand away. "Go find your own booth and nachos."

"A true friend wouldn't let you emotionally eat all by your lonesome." Morris dipped a chip into some sour cream and studied Felipe's face. For all of his snaps and snarls, there was no anger in his eyes, just a vast frustration. "So what gives? You don't walk away from a fight you started."

Felipe flushed and glanced away. "Whatever. It was a stupid argument anyway."

"I'm glad you both recognize." Morris sat back, trying to figure out what made Felipe run. "Your costume is kickass. Don't mind what he said."

Felipe rolled his eyes and stabbed a nacho into the guacamole so hard the chip broke. "Fuck, for real? I'm not upset about the crack at my costume. It's amazing, and Brenden can suck my balls if he thinks otherwise."

Speculating would only irritate him more, so Morris decided to wait him out and hoped it wouldn't take too long. By the time they finished the plate, Felipe had slouched down in his seat, his expression changed from frustrated and angry to woebegone. If there was one thing that could punch Morris right in the heart and make him want to do anything to fix a problem, it was a pair of sad eyes.

"Come on, talk to me. What is it?" Morris finally asked in a low voice. "You're going to have me crying in my root beer in a moment."

That almost made Felipe smile. Morris saw the twitch, but then his friend bit his lip and glanced away. "Do I come off as desperate?" Felipe asked so softly Morris almost didn't hear him.

"As you would say, 'bitch please.' You're too confident in what you want to come across as desperate. If some guy doesn't want you, you don't give him another thought." Morris frowned. "Is that what's bothering you? Brenden's desperate comment? You're not still pining over Dakota, are you?"

"Fuck no," Felipe said, but it lacked his usual heat. "I'm not pining over him. I'm pining over what could've been if he hadn't been such a fucknut twit. I'm cool with Dakota."

Now Morris was really confused. He hated seeing Felipe like this. He could handle him hungover, pissed off, manic, and sulky. He could not handle him looking so damned sad. There was too much joy and passion in everything he did for him to be this upset. "So what gives?"

Felipe sighed and braced his cheek on his fist. "Don't you want happily ever after?"

Morris started to say no, it hadn't crossed his mind, but then he sighed as well and mimicked Felipe's pose. "If I admit to it, you're not going to rag on me, are you?"

A hint of Felipe's old mischief crossed his lips. "Afraid of ruining your rep?"

"Not really. I'm fine by myself. I've got things set up the way I want, and I don't have to compromise with anyone but my crazy cat." Morris met Felipe's gaze. "Sometimes, though, I think it would be nice. If I ever found someone who I can put up with and who can put up with me for an extended time. It's not something I put too much thought into, really."

Maybe those thoughts had been in his mind a little more lately, and Morris blamed it entirely on a gray-eyed white boy who was too damned adorable for Morris's peace of mind. It was irritating.

Morris glanced at Felipe and suddenly he understood. For all of Felipe's sass and living for the moment attitude, he was a romantic sap. He was a homebody. Morris could easily picture Felipe with a husband, fostering half a dozen dogs, and running a house. He'd be ecstatic dealing with all that domestic stuff that made Morris want to cringe.

"Don't rush it, man."

Felipe's eyes hardened. "If you remind me how young I am, I'm going to brain you."

"That's not what I meant." Morris leaned forward, catching his gaze. "What I'm saying is don't jump in and commit to the wrong guy because you're impatient for your happily ever after. You might miss the right guy. And that would suck worse than this limbo you're in now."

He saw it sink home, and then Felipe's eyes narrowed. "Okay, since we're here nursing our love lives and dispensing advice, let me give some of my own."

"I'm doing fine," Morris insisted, even as his gaze strayed toward his phone. Dammit! It was embarrassing to know he was being obvious. He was never obvious.

"Text the man before you bore a hole through your phone with your X-ray vision."

"It's a fling," Morris replied in a lofty voice. "I don't want to give him the wrong impression. That would be mean, and I don't do mean."

Felipe snorted and smirked as he grabbed his wig. "Yeah, well, we'll see about that. You'll be begging for my wisdom. Just you wait. Begging on your knees. Until then, text the motherfucker. You'll both be happier."

Theo was busy and Morris had told him he'd be out of town, so he probably assumed Morris was busy too and didn't want to bug him. What would it hurt to send one text? Morris picked up his phone before he could spin his thoughts into more circles.

*Thinking of you.*

The incoming text alert was almost immediate, and Morris's heart jumped. *Keep hoping to see you at the bar. Hurry home, breakfast is waiting.*

# Chapter Thirteen

*DUDE, GONNA be late. Sorry.*

Theo hit Send and set down his phone with a sigh of regret. He'd been looking forward to his semidate with Morris tonight. If hooking up after midnight and vegging on the couch with the hope of scoring if they caught a private moment was actually considered a date.

It seemed like Theo only ever got to see the man in quick snatches. It wasn't nearly enough to satisfy his desire for more, and Theo wasn't just thinking about sexy times either. He clicked with Morris in a way he hadn't clicked with anyone else before. The thought of this being only a fling was rapidly changing to a desire for something more—not that Morris seemed interested in a deeper relationship, and Theo couldn't blame him because he was never around.

Theo checked over the dining room to make sure all the chores had been finished even though the last bartender and waitresses had already left. He knew Jill would've gone over it, but he needed something to occupy his antsy thoughts. The dining room was as pristine as Theo's kitchen, living up to their exacting standards.

He didn't know what he was going to do without Jill to mind this half. It didn't matter his sister was only cutting back until the baby was toddling. It made the twin holes in his heart echo emptily. He kept looking up expecting to see his dad behind the bar, his mom tucked away at the back table she preferred as she went over receipts.

Theo craved a cigarette. It had been over a year since he'd quit, and sometimes he still wanted the taste and ritual. Not that Jill would let him have one in the restaurant anyway. His nerves jangled with the need, and he drummed his fingertips on the tabletop as he waited for Lincoln and Scottie to finish gathering their things in the kitchen and for Jill to come back with her husband. He'd go back to the kitchen to check on them, but Scottie would only chase him out if he saw Theo poke his nose back there again.

Theo's phone dinged, and he grabbed the welcome distraction. *No worries. I'm still up. Working on some concept sketches for a new idea.*

Theo smiled and scrubbed a hand through his hair. *Can't wait to see it. No drama at work today?* He glanced up as Scottie passed by, heading toward the front door. "Where the fuck do you think you're going?" Theo asked his sous chef.

"Skinny is done in the kitchen," Scottie replied with a perplexed frown. "I've got to prep in the morning. Where the fuck do you think I'm going?"

"We called a family meeting. You're family." Theo stabbed a finger toward him. "Sit your ass down."

"I don't want to weigh in on restaurant decisions. That should be up to you and your siblings." Scottie's frown deepened, but he slid into the booth next to Theo as Lincoln came out of the back. His brother looked tired from loading and unloading dishes, and damp from the dishwasher steam. Theo hated keeping him out so late, but he wanted Lincoln's input, and Lincoln wanted to use his own money for that new bike, so he wasn't quibbling about the extra hours.

"Half my siblings aren't here," Theo retorted. It stung. Dustin and Robin should be there. These were major changes they were implementing, and his wayward brother and sister still had a financial interest in the restaurant, but both of them said they couldn't make the drive and the decision was up to the rest. Theo refused to let it eat at him, but it was like acid in his throat. Every time he thought he'd beat that demon, it came back. "You are. Besides, we want your opinion. Isn't that right, Lincoln?"

Lincoln nodded and slumped into the booth across from them. "Better you than me, Scottie. You do the important stuff. I clean tables and wash dishes. I'd rather be playing a video game right now."

"I started out bussing tables too," Theo said. Their parents had been big believers in establishing a work ethic early on. And like Lincoln, Theo enjoyed saving up for things with his own money. In his case it had been a secondhand car. He'd loved that baby. It had been the perfect car to neck in down by the river.

"Yeah, but you like cooking and stuff. Freak. I don't." Lincoln gave him a moody smile before his gaze flicked to the front door as the bells chimed. Craig and Jill walked in, and Theo could tell from the expression on his brother-in-law's face he wouldn't accept any more hesitations from any of them. They were going to make these final decisions tonight. Theo's chest felt heavy. This sucked.

Craig hovered over Jill, his craggy face concerned. Theo supposed if he were a first-time father, he might be acting the same way. That at least was one worry he'd never have to face. Craig's gaze swept over the group at the booth, his eyes conveying his sympathy and the hard set of his mouth, his determination.

Jill waved off Craig's offer of support and lowered herself into the booth. "In another couple months, I'll need help getting up and down. Right now me and baby girl are fine." Her tone was as testy as her gaze, which meant she was in agreement with Theo on this total suckage. His phone dinged with a message back from Morris, and he pocketed it with a sigh. No more time to indulge.

Craig opted not to comment, grabbing a chair instead and straddling it backward. "Okay, I know you two don't want to make this decision, but it has to be made." He held up his hand, counting off his fingers as he went along. "First, Lincoln's going to be back to school by the time the baby gets here. High school is hard enough without putting in so many hours at the bistro. None of us want him to feel obligated to volunteer."

Jill and Theo's eyes met. "That's something we can agree on," Theo said. Lincoln's well-being came first. They couldn't count on him to take extra shifts all the time, keep up with his homework, and still have the normal teenage life he deserved.

"You won't hear me complain." Lincoln slouched back, tugging his cap low over his eyes.

"Second," Craig continued. "We had several really good candidates come through here for interviews. If we wait too long, they are going to be snatched up by other offers, and it's not fair to string them along. We should give them an answer, yes or no."

Theo had more of a quibble there. Didn't matter if they were qualified or not; they were outsiders. But he kept his mouth shut. If he got started, Jill would get started, and Craig might kill him. None of them were leaving until they made a decision, and Theo didn't feel like being here all night.

"Personally, I liked Rose Williams," Scottie cut in. Theo cast him a look of betrayal. "What? You wanted my opinion."

"You liked her because she was gorgeous and had that islands accent thing going for her," Theo accused.

"That didn't hurt," Scottie agreed with an easy shrug.

Craig frowned and went through the stack of applications in front of him. "She's the one your friend recommended, right?" he asked Theo.

Lincoln snorted. "Friend, right."

"Yeah, his sister works for a hotel in Annapolis. They worked together." Theo nudged Lincoln with his toe and Lincoln nudged him back, a smirk playing about his mouth. "She gave her a letter of recommendation. Look, I have to say this. I hate this. I hate giving up control to anyone who's not family, but I know we have to."

Theo looked around the table at each one of them. "And I know you all want me to either cut back on my hours some or consider closing the restaurant for one day a week. That has never happened, and I'm not willing for it to happen now. The weekends bring in our best revenue, and we make a killing at the lunch hour during the workweek."

Theo paused and felt his pulse jump. This part at least was something he could be joyful about. "So one of the changes I propose is for Scottie to split duties with me. We come up with a schedule, when I work dinner, he does lunch, with full authority over the kitchen staff. We already make the menus together. We split the time shopping at the markets. As much as I'll miss working beside him, there's no one I trust more to run my kitchen." Theo smiled at Scottie's stunned expression. "And I think he should get the pay to reflect it as well."

Jill beamed, the tension around her eyes easing. "That's an amazing idea. You two have both been doing double duty so long it's a miracle you're not ghosts of yourselves. What about days off, though? You two should still have at least one day off a week, preferably two."

Scottie was still staring at Theo with wide eyes, his sarcastic exterior stripped away for once. "You trust me with your kitchen?" he asked in a low voice.

"You're my brother from another mother," Theo replied. He tapped his knuckles to Scottie's. "I couldn't do this without you, man."

"Wow, okay." Scottie sat back with a shake of his head as Craig and Lincoln threw in their agreements. "Thanks, guys, seriously. I won't let you down. Theo and I can come up with a schedule tomorrow." He glanced at Theo for confirmation, and he nodded. "We'll each pick a day to do double duty so the other has a day off. I'm okay with starting out with one. It'll already be a big break after this last year."

"Yeah, I'm not comfortable with taking off two days yet. Once we get settled and school starts for Lincoln, then we can revisit it." The phone in Theo's pocket buzzed with another incoming message, and the temptation to take a peek was a siren's song.

Craig cleared his throat and tapped the stack of résumés meaningfully. "I'm glad to have a solution for the kitchen. Now we need to settle on a solution for the front." He held up his hand as Jill began to protest. "Honey, I know you want to keep working up until the baby is born. That's okay with me. That doesn't negate this decision. Let's face it, babies are unpredictable. They come when they want, so we need a plan in place. Hiring someone now gives you time to work with them. Then when you do take time off, you'll be at ease knowing there's someone you trust taking care of things instead of stressing about it. Not to mention you need a couple days off a week too."

Jill made a face. "I don't like you." She reached over and took his hand, giving it an affectionate squeeze.

"That's because you know I'm right and you can't come up with an argument against it." Craig patted her hand as she shrugged with a rueful smile of admittance.

Theo wanted to protest, too, but he didn't want to make Jill feel guilty about taking time off and easing back. It was hard. They'd never had anyone at the front of the house who wasn't family. It felt like he was letting his mom and dad down again. Bad enough he couldn't keep the family together after they'd buried their parents.

"As long as they aren't jerks, I don't care," Lincoln cut in. "That lady with the blonde hair and razor smile, Orit, I didn't like her."

Craig frowned as he pulled out her résumé. "She was the manager of that steakhouse for years. They have a good rep."

"That's a swanky, snobby place," Scottie said. "No lie, good food, but not the sort of atmosphere we have here. This is a family place, very homey. Even I could see her nose in the air as she looked around."

"She'd have us all in little uniforms," Lincoln said morosely. "Little soldiers jumping to her attention. I can imagine her expression if anyone steps out of line."

"Aren't you overdramatizing it?" Craig asked with a pointed look at Lincoln.

Theo remembered the flirt in her eyes when they'd talked. He didn't get the vibe the others did, but he trusted their opinion. He thought back over their encounter and recalled Orit being full of plans to "enhance" the bistro. He grimaced. No, he didn't care for that thought at all.

"Yeah, I didn't like her either," Jill added. "My impression was she'd rather change what we have instead of embracing it. I'm not willing to alter what works. We're successful because we're a place you can come to on a budget and bring your kids without worrying about feeling unwelcome."

"Okay." Craig sat her application to the side and pinned each one of them with a long look. "Before we discuss the next applicant, I want you to keep one thing in mind. Even your parents didn't do this alone. They had five kids to take care of. They split duties with others as well. It's not as important to keep it all in the family if you don't have enough family here to cover it, as much as it's important to have people you trust in these positions. So try to be open-minded."

Theo exchanged glances with his sister of mutual commiseration and then sighed inwardly. Time to do this. "We will, Craig. Who's the next one?"


THEO PULLED the car into their dark driveway and noted by some miracle there was still a light on downstairs at Morris's place even though it was so late. "I'm tired. You guys argue too much," Lincoln announced as Theo parked. "I'm going to bed."

"I'm going to go talk to Morris for a few minutes, if that's okay," Theo said, eyeballing the light as he held out the keys to Lincoln.

"Whatever." Lincoln snatched the keys out of his hand. "If you want to make a booty call on our neighbor, I'm not going to say anything."

Theo blinked. He didn't expect Lincoln to come out and say it like that. "Good to know."

"It's not like there could be a serial killer upstairs and I'm getting stalked while you're getting your freak on," Lincoln added in a huffy voice.

Theo wasn't sure if he was more unsettled by the fact he was that obvious or the thought he might be setting a bad example for his brother. Questions like that cropped up often now. He remembered when he didn't have a damn care in the world about whether his brother knew about his sex life. He and Morris were grown adults, responsible and all that. Neither of them was committed to someone else, and they were free to do whatever the hell they wanted. He needed to stop second-guessing himself so much.

"If we were going by horror movie rules, wouldn't I be the one getting killed? Not you." Theo threw an amused glanced at his brother, who rolled his eyes.

"Whatever," Lincoln muttered again. "That's fiction. This is real life. I don't want to move to a new apartment if this doesn't work out, that's all I'm saying."

Theo watched him climb up the hill to their place and disappear inside. He forgot how dramatic high school could be, when the thought of facing your ex every day was torture. He was lucky if he caught a glimpse of Morris over the week. He didn't think living upstairs was going to be a problem if it didn't work out.

Morris's door was unlocked, and he could hear the low murmur of the television. Theo stuck his head through the door. "Hey, Morris. You still awake, man?"

Silence greeted him, and Theo glanced at his phone to check the time of his last message. It wasn't more than thirty minutes ago. *Hangin' w/Sam and Dean. Come on in.*

Sam and Dean…. Theo tried to recall if they had been among Morris's friends he'd met after the con, but he couldn't put a face to the names.

He followed the sound of the TV and found Morris facedown on his couch with his cat curled up on the small of his back. Morris's long arm was draped over onto the floor resting on a discarded sketchbook with a pencil not far away. His dreads had half fallen across his face, and a faint snore came from behind them. Theo shook his head. "And they say I'm work driven."

He debated whether to slink back out and leave Morris a message but decided to wake him first. If Morris stayed like that the entire night, he was going to wake up with a painful crick in his neck.

On the TV two guys got into a black Impala before driving off down a creepy-looking street. It seemed like the kind of show that would give a man nightmares before bedtime. Theo shut it off and stepped over an empty box of tacos from the fast-food joint on the corner. Theo didn't know how Morris could stomach that shit; he really didn't. He must have a gut of steel.

Theo gently shook Morris's shoulder as the cat opened one eye with an evil glare. "Hey, man, wake up before your cat kills me or you knot your body into a pretzel."

Morris groaned and opened one eye in a scary impression of his cat. "You had really better be Theo and not some figment of my imagination, or I'm kicking your ass."

"It's really me." Theo crouched down next to him as the cat yawned, deliberately showing all of her teeth as if to warn Theo away. "Sorry to bother you, but you really didn't look comfortable."

"Comfortable is relative." Morris shifted and Cassie's tail thumped him as she let out an odd-sounding squawk of complaint. "I was having a really amazing dream where you and Idris Elba were arguing over who was giving me the best blow job and using my very willing body as a guinea pig."

Wow, Theo ranked with Idris Elba in a dream. That was kinda awesome. Theo grinned and brushed Morris's dreads back so he could get a better look at his face. "Don't keep me in suspense. Who was winning?"

"I was too deliriously turned on to judge." Morris shifted again, looking over his shoulder at his cat. "Don't you have your own bed?"

Cassie sat up, her baleful gaze on Theo. Deliberately she kneaded her claws into Morris for a few moments before stretching and jumping down. "I think your cat hates me."

"She hates everyone when she's woken up." Morris rolled onto his side and caught Theo's hand. "You look beat up."

Theo felt beat up. But the sight of Morris sprawled out on the couch erased the heartache of the night. He'd deal with that later. Right now, he'd rather get lost in the present. Morris tugged on his hand and Theo sat down next to him. "This makes me feel better."

"Glad to be of service." Morris brushed his fingers along Theo's jaw.

Theo skated his hand down Morris's side. He loved the long lankiness of his body and the breadth of his shoulders. He loved the weight of Morris's hair against his skin and the scent of him drowsy and warm. "I'd intended on waking you up so you could go to bed, but then you mentioned blow jobs." Theo shot him a hopeful look. "You wouldn't be teasing me, would you?"

Morris's brown eyes lit up with enthusiasm. He hooked his finger in the collar of Theo's T-shirt and tugged him closer. "You going to use me as your guinea pig?"

"Only if you say pretty, pretty please," Theo murmured before capturing Morris's lips in a heated kiss. Morris slid his arms around Theo, pulling him off-balance so he sprawled over him and their limbs tangled together. They shifted, laughing softly until they found as comfortable of a fit as they could get on the small couch.

"Pretty, pretty please," Morris said with a sigh as he slid his hands under Theo's shirt. He rubbed his hands over Theo like how he imagined a sculptor worked over an object of art he was making, patient and slow. Morris's lips teased his throat and Theo groaned, going dizzy as he felt the hard length of Morris's cock under him. Damn, the man could turn him on with a glance or a simple touch of his elegant hands.

Impatient, Theo tugged off their shirts and kissed Morris again with urgent lips. "I have been thinking of this all night. I'm sorry it took me so long to get here."

"The thought may have crossed my mind a moment or two," Morris said, eyeing Theo's body greedily as he continued to run his hands over him. "Hence the almost wet dream you interrupted." His gaze met Theo's, and the heat there made Theo's heart beat faster in anticipation. "Reality is far better."

Theo's gaze traveled over Morris's bare chest. "I have to agree with you."

Thudding footsteps shuddered over them as someone stomped around in the kitchen upstairs. Theo froze and glanced up as Morris's hands tightened on him. "What the fuck was that?" Morris asked.

Theo closed his eyes as the stomping died off down the hall. Man, he couldn't wait until Lincoln had his first date. He wasn't sure what he'd do yet to retaliate, but it was going to happen. "My brother. Rough night. We had to make some executive decisions about the restaurant, and I think he's missing his other siblings who elected not to come."

"Oh." Morris struggled to sit up. "No wonder you looked ragged."

Theo pushed him back down with a shake of his head. "Uh-uh, I've only managed to get half your clothes off. I have a dream reputation to live up to. Where were we?"

"Getting naked," Morris replied with a grin as he toyed with the button to Theo's pants. "We're still wearing too many clothes for the promised blow jobs."

"Yeah, that sounds about right." Theo leaned over him for a kiss as the stomping started again, this time accompanied by the discordant sound of an out-of-tune saxophone. Theo closed his eyes with a soft groan. He'd thought that sax was dead and buried at their parents' house.

Morris stifled a laugh against Theo's shoulder. "Well, that's attention grabbing."

"Were you this much of a little shit when you were fifteen?" Theo asked with a plaintive look toward Morris.

"I was an angel, but my sisters would argue otherwise." Morris looked up as the stomping and playing continued, marching up and down the hall. Cassie laid her ears back with a hiss of disapproval and streaked out of the room.

Theo touched his forehead to Morris's with a soft sigh of regret. "I've got to get back upstairs." Maybe between Morris's door and their own, he'd figure out a way to not strangle Lincoln.

A look of disappointment crossed Morris's face, but he nodded and brushed his lips over Theo's. "I understand. We have to plan to pick this up again very soon."

Theo rose and tugged his clothes back on. "If you have another dream of me, tell Idris Elba he doesn't stand a chance."

Morris chuckled, tucking his hand under his head. "I'll be sure to pass along the message."

# Chapter Fourteen

MORRIS SET the bags of groceries on the counter and eyed the clock. He had plenty of time to get everything ready before his friends showed up this afternoon for the games, and he was stoked. Wait until they got a load of this. They were going to die of surprise. Ha!

Humming to himself, he put the beer and cider in the fridge next to the mini-éclairs he'd picked up that morning from the bakery and then began unpacking and organizing. He checked Theo's list, amused by the emoticons he'd drawn on the margins. Okay, so not everything would be made from scratch, but it would sure beat his history. First, he needed to boil the eggs for the deviled eggs. He also needed to shred the rotisserie chicken he'd bought and prepare the ham-and-cheese rolls. Not a problem. Sexy-assed Marcus Samuelsson had nothing on him.

Morris pulled up his music on his phone and let Beyoncé blast as he began the prep work. He set the eggs in the water on the stove, turned up the heat, then moved to clean up. Laundry was strewn liberally throughout the living room. Towels were hung on his seldom-used workout bench. Morris sniffed them and tossed them over his arm to be added to the washer. Cassie followed him from room to room to see what all the fuss and activity was about, but when he didn't pull out the suitcases and boxes he used for a show, she sat herself down in the middle of a sunbeam and began cleaning her leg.

He dumped all the clothes in the washer, started the cycle, and returned to the living room to contemplate his art supplies stacked in untidy heaps around his drawing table and his favorite chair where he watched TV. Well, there was no sense in organizing that. It would get all disorganized again when he sat down to work. If he ran the vacuum cleaner around the piles, that would be good enough.

Bopping along to the music, he returned to the kitchen and looked at Theo's notes again. The water was definitely bubbling fast around the eggs, only he had no idea how long they'd been boiling. Pursing his lips, Morris shut the heat off and set the timer. Better overcooked than under, right?

He yanked out a baking sheet and referred to Theo's instructions again. Starting most of this early would save his sanity later on, but he wasn't certain he could actually do the prep now and then finish off cooking later for some of these.

*Are u sure i can make the ham thingies early?* Morris texted Theo. He set aside the crescent rolls he'd bought and contemplated the next item on the list, buffalo dip. The question was, did he have a baking dish? He knew he should've bought more tinfoil disposable cooking ware. Then he wouldn't have to wash dishes. They were going to make enough of a mess as it was tonight.

While he waited for an answer, he ran the vacuum through the living room and down the hall. He checked the bathroom and declared it good enough and then prudently closed the door to his bedroom, much to Cassie's indignation. She let out a meow of protest and batted at the door with her head. "Nobody wants to see that mess but you and me, baby girl. You can stalk that new cat tree I bought you instead of ignoring it."

She flicked her tail at him in response, giving him a good indication of how she felt about that, then turned her back on him. She lay down in front of the bedroom door and shoved her paw underneath. Morris shook his head at her antics and went back to work. There was no pleasing a cat.

He sprayed a good amount of air freshener around the whole apartment and opened a few windows to let in some fresh air. It wasn't that Morris considered himself a slob; he just stopped noticing his surroundings until something happened to make him look around. Once he got started, his cleaning binge would continue through the weekend until it was all nice and shiny from top to bottom and he'd made a dozen promises to himself not to let it happen again. A promise he'd forget within a week until the next time he needed to be sociable.

Morris returned to the kitchen to the sound of the timer going off, and still Theo hadn't responded to his text. Well, he was at work, probably slammed, so there would be no extra help from there. Besides, Theo had to know what he was doing and Morris clearly didn't, so he went ahead and started the ham-and-cheese crescent rolls.

He laid out the dough, slapped the ingredients down, and then rolled them into little bundles. They looked a little homely and awkward, and a couple of them kept threatening to unravel until Morris leaned them against another, but as long as they tasted okay, he didn't care how they looked. Most of his group wouldn't care about presentation anyway. They'd just be happy to have edible food.

Morris changed his song list to Prince and checked the time again. Yeah, he was on point. This was going to be the best game night ever. After scrounging around, he couldn't find a baking dish for the dip, so he set that aside and turned toward the eggs. First, he had to get the suckers out of their shell. Not a problem. He'd watched his mom do it a dozen times.

Fifteen frustrating minutes later, Morris had three mutilated eggs lined up on his counter. Instead of the freshly peeled clean look of his mom's eggs, he had forlorn lopsided blobs with bits of shell still sticking to them, chunks of egg white pulled off, and crumbling yolks.

Morris glared at the eggs and picked up Theo's instructions. There was nothing in there that mentioned egg peeling, and what the fuck was turmeric anyway? He'd forgotten that at the store, whatever it was. And what the hell did he mean by piping? What had seemed simple before had now gotten wildly out of hand.

Morris grabbed his phone and wallet. There had to be already peeled eggs at the store, and he could get the other things he'd forgotten and maybe he'd even run into somebody who could explain piping to him, because it sounded more like something Dakota would do with his marijuana instead of a cooking technique. He paused. He bet Felipe would know how to do this…. Morris shook his head and grabbed his keys. No, he was going to surprise them, and it was going to be awesome, dammit.

As he opened the front door, Cassie streaked outside from between his legs. "Fuck me!" He glared at his cat, who stopped a few feet away and turned to look back at him. "Why do you always pick the days when I don't have time for this shit?" Morris leveled a finger at her and then turned it back toward the apartment. "Do you want me to open the bedroom door for you? Fine, I'll open the damn door. Now get inside."

Cassie took one look at his pointing finger before turning and scampering underneath his car. Morris cursed under his breath and knelt down by the car. Cassie peered out from behind the tire, regarding him steadily with an unblinking gaze. "Please," Morris wheedled, slowly stretching his hand out on the ground. "I'll put some dice in a box for you. You know how much you love that."

Cassie yawned and glanced away.

"Something wrong?" Morris jumped at the sound of a voice behind him and narrowly missed hitting his head on the door mirror. He looked up at Lincoln, who watched him curiously from the edge of the driveway.

"Yeah, your brother and my cat are the devil." Morris pushed himself to his feet. "Keep an eye on her a moment."

"Who?" Lincoln asked as he crouched beside the car to peer underneath.

Morris brushed off his knees and stalked toward the house. "That evil imp that impersonates a cat," he called back over his shoulder.

He grabbed Cassie's favorite stuffed toy, a bear she carried around by his poor abused face, and the laser pointer. She only pulled shit like this because she knew how undignified he looked begging her to come back. He should've gotten a dog. You could train a dog. A cat did whatever she fucking pleased.

"So I get why she's the devil," Lincoln said when he returned. "But what did Theo do? Not that I think he's innocent. I know him. I'm curious so I can give him a hard time."

Morris eyeballed him, trying to decide if he'd freak out Lincoln with a bit of teasing. "You mean breaking out the saxophone to serenade us isn't enough of a hard time?"

Lincoln blushed, though he looked more abashed than mortified. He shrugged and shot Morris an apologetic look. "Sorry about that."

"It's okay." Morris gave him a reassuring smile. "I'm just going to start calling you Moodkiller Base One."

"That is awesome and awkward at the same time." Lincoln stood up and gestured toward the car. "So what's the plan to get her out?"

"Bait." Morris dropped the bear on the ground a few feet away from the car and stepped back, motioning for Lincoln to back away too. "As for your evil brother, he left instructions that made no sense and neglected to tell me how to peel an egg. Apparently it's not an instinctive skill."

Lincoln's expression became one of pity for a clueless caveman. "You crack it and peel it," he said in the condescending tone only a teenager could nail.

Cassie eyed the bear but still didn't move from her spot behind the tire. "I know that, but it won't peel cleanly. I made a mess of the first three, and I'm going to have to eat the evidence before my friends arrive for games." Morris directed the laser pointer beyond his cat's reach. Cassie's ears perked in immediate attention.

Lincoln shoved his hands in his pockets. "What kind of games?"

"All kinds. You're free to take a look. You off today?" Morris danced the light a little farther out as Cassie crept toward it on her belly, her gaze fixated on the dot.

"Yeah." Slowly Cassie moved out from under the car and then pounced on the light. Lincoln took another step back out of her way. "Wow, she is trying to slay that thing."

"She is the queen of laser dot hunting. I have claw marks on my wall from where she tried climbing it once to get at it." Morris flicked the light behind her, smiling at Cassie's acrobatics.

"Hey, maybe I can help you with the eggs and Theo's instructions," Lincoln offered. "Maybe I could borrow a game too? It's dead boring at home by myself."

"Sure." Morris led Cassie in a dizzying chase over the lawn. "I'll do one even better. If you want to hang with us tonight, you're more than welcome. It's nothing fancy, board games and food."

"What kind of board games? Boring stuff like Monopoly?" Lincoln asked, sounding like he wasn't sure if it wouldn't be more fun at home alone.

"Nah, man. There's so much more than that. I tend to like games where you have to work together like Pandemic, or if you want something a little creepy that doesn't take forever, Elder Sign is good too." Morris thought of Felipe and his mood lately. "Or we could get cutthroat and play Munchkin all night."

"Okay, Munchkin is fun. I have a couple different sets myself. I tried teaching it to Theo, but I think he was confused. It's not really a game you can play with two people anyway." Lincoln dodged out of the way as Cassie streaked by him.

"Bring them along," Morris said, luring Cassie closer. "Expansions are always fun."

"Really, you wouldn't mind having me along tonight?" Lincoln's eyes lit up. "I was supposed to go to a friend's house, but his parents are dragging him to a family dinner. They invited me, which was cool, but I wasn't really feeling it."

The note in Lincoln's voice said it all. The "I don't care" when deep down he did. Morris knew Theo worried about his brother, but Lincoln would open himself up to hanging with families again when he was ready. Right now, it was a still-healing wound.

"Not at all. We welcome geeks of all ages." Morris directed the light to Cassie's bear and she pounced on it so hard they both rolled over. He grinned as Lincoln laughed outright. She grappled with it, snuggling and purring loud enough for Morris to hear. "That's my little dot killer. You go, girl."

Morris glanced at Lincoln, and all of his earlier irritation vanished. "Say, you wouldn't by any chance have a small casserole dish for baking, would you? I seem to be short of kitchen supplies too."

Lincoln beamed. "Yep. I'll be right down. We'll eat the evidence and fix the rest of the eggs, and then maybe I could look at some of your games."

Morris gave him a thumbs-up, tucked the light in his pocket, and scooped Cassie up, bear and all. "You, my dear, are a troublemaker and a half, do you hear me? Troublemaker." He nuzzled her. "Do you know how I'd feel if you got lost out here? Huh?"

Cassie touched her cold nose to his cheek, still purring. "Was I ignoring you? Was that the problem? Bad Daddy, huh? Changing the house up with all the cleaning and not giving you attentions."

He carried her into the house, already feeling much better about the day ahead. Lincoln would help walk him through the mysteries of the kitchen, and in return, he'd keep the kid from dying of boredom. It was a win-win situation.

# Chapter Fifteen

THEO GLANCED up as an order popped onto the screen. It had to be frickin' kidding him, another six-top table. Who the hell declared tonight group date night? The kitchen scrambled as the front of the house overcrowded with a forty-minute wait for tables. No matter what they did, the flow was off, and Theo felt as if he was barely staying on top of things. At least they weren't behind. That was an extra layer of stress none of them needed.

"Scottie, can—" Theo cut off with a soft swear. Scottie wasn't here. Scottie had prepped that morning and then manned the lunch crowd. They'd had a chance for a quick chat as they passed by, and that was it. He'd not had a spare minute to think since then. Fuck. He had to start remembering he had a new sous chef now and try to not feel like his right arm had been cut off.

He rubbed his brow and focused again. "Jesse, sorry. Can you start on the salmon?"

"You can call me Not-Scottie, if it'll help." Jesse pulled out a tray and headed toward the walk-in refrigerator, patting Theo's back as she went by.

Bless her, she would accept it with her usual good humor and grace, and Theo was profoundly grateful for her stepping up the way she had. They'd find their rhythm again. This was their first weekend with the new system. The only thing making the change at all palatable was the extra few hours he had most days now. Hours to catch up on housework and errands.

He flashed her a distracted smile and shook his head as she passed by him again. "That's not right. I'll get it. It's just years of habit." And a friendship that stretched all the way to the start of high school.

He turned back to his station as he debated calling in Lincoln. The dish station was behind, with stacks of glasses and cutlery that needed to be run through before they ran out. No. He couldn't keep relying on him like that. He remembered his own teenage resentments. The other busboys would have to step up to Lincoln's level. Besides, if he got used to Lincoln's instant response, he'd regret it when school started. New habits, that's what he kept telling himself. Lincoln had a date with his video games, and he'd been looking forward to a rare Saturday off.

Theo checked the crab cakes, drizzled some of their remoulade, sprinkled some fresh chopped parsley on them, and slid the ramekins of sides onto the plate. The bacon-and-chive scalloped potatoes made his stomach rumble, and the zucchini medley looked perfect. He set the plate in the window with the others and looked up with a frown when they weren't immediately whisked away. The expedite station was empty of all servers, and Jill was nowhere in sight.

He reached for a knife as several plates of lamb chops slid in front of him. Where the hell was his sister? Someone needed to come grab this food before it started to go cold.

"Theo!"

The shout of his name didn't alarm him. The note of panic in the voice did. Theo jerked his head up and swore as he nicked himself. One of the servers, Erin, stood in the entrance to the kitchen, dangerously blocking the flow of empty dishes coming in. Only, Theo couldn't see any busboys either.

"What's wrong?" Theo asked sharply, wiping his hands on a towel. Her face was pale, and she was wringing her hands. Erin had a tendency to overdramatize things, but that didn't stop the tickle of unease. "Where's Jill? Dammit, get out of the way before someone slams into you."

"It's Jill…. She passed out and…."

Theo felt every drop of blood leave his face as his vision tunneled. Whatever else Erin said was lost in the roaring of his ears as he rushed to the dining room. A crowd of people gathered in a circle near the hostess stand, and as Theo approached, a small group of diners left the restaurant with irritated expressions on their faces.

"Where's my sister?" Theo demanded as he pushed his way through the curious onlookers.

"I'm okay, Theo." Despite her words, Theo heard the strain in Jill's voice. She gave him a wan smile from where she sat in one of the chairs meant for guests who were waiting for a seat, which drove home how serious this was. Jill would never take a seat and leave others standing. Then her face went tight with pain as she clutched her belly. "I think you need to call Craig."

Theo's thoughts stumbled over themselves as he searched for any sign of injury. Reaching for his phone with one hand, he held out his other to Jill. "What's wrong? Erin said you passed out."

"No, no. Just a little light-headed. I'm better now that I'm sitting down." She grabbed his hand, squeezing hard enough to make it hurt. "I'm having contractions."

Theo fumbled for his phone and almost dropped it as he stared at her with wide eyes. "You can't be. You have three more months."

Jill rolled her eyes, her mouth pinched with exasperation, and squeezed harder. "I'm pretty damn sure. They're kind of hard to miss."

"Okay, okay." Theo hit Craig's speed dial before she broke his fingers. "Are you sure they aren't the fake ones?" he ventured as the phone rang, steeling himself in case she started squeezing again.

An older woman with graying strands of blonde hair laid her hand on Jill's shoulder. "I'm a nurse. Let me help. You're going to be fine. I'm going to ask you a few questions, okay? When was the last time you had anything to eat or drink?"

Theo's throat squeezed even tighter, and he had to turn to block out the sight of the nurse before he stopped breathing. *It's a good thing. Nurses are good.* The sensation didn't go away. He kept thinking of his dad surrounded by hospital nurses. The hospital staff that came to talk to him about his mom.

Then his heart started beating again as Craig picked up. "Hey, it's me."

"Craig, you have to come get Jill. She says she's in labor." Theo tried to keep the panic out of his voice. If he panicked, she would panic. Then the panic would spread and there would be chaos. He shot her a reassuring smile as she continued to cling to his hand.

"I'm on my way," Craig replied, his voice cool and in control. Damn, Theo loved his brother-in-law. At least one of them had their shit together. He was two seconds away from sitting on the floor next to Jill to do breathing exercises with her. He'd be okay if she were a couple weeks early; it was the thought of another medical emergency in the family that kept threatening to make him fly apart.

"Craig is on the way, and he'll take you to see your doctor," Theo said as he pocketed his phone. He shot a look at the nurse, silently begging her not to say the word hospital. Theo could see the edge in Jill's eyes, and that might send her right over it. She'd calm down once she saw Craig. Their house was just down the road, so it wouldn't take him any time. He'd let Craig convince her the hospital was where she needed to be.

He waited until the nurse was done with her questions and reassurances and then crouched down next to Jill. "You do realize my niece is putting you on notice she plans on causing havoc right from the start?"

"Don't encourage her." Jill laughed shortly as Theo shot her an innocent expression.

"I'm sure there are any number of health code violations if you have her now. I'll make you fill out the paperwork, because I'm not dealing with it," Theo teased, reassured by the strength in her hands even if her grip hurt like hell.

"It'll add to the legend of the place." Jill clasped both of his hands now, her gaze locked on to him. "Tell me it's going to be okay. I'll believe you if you tell me."

Theo tried for light and flippant but failed. He squeezed Jill's hands back. "Hey, it's going to be okay. You're going to be fine, and Little Miss Impatient is going to be fine." He wished there was someone there to reassure him in return.

"You're going to be fine." The nurse chafed Jill's arm. "Your legs aren't swelling. The baby's kicking. Your pulse is strong. Just stop fretting."

"Okay." Jill drew in a deep breath that broke off with a groan. "Yeah, we've got this. Where's Craig?"

"I'm right here."

Theo's knees went weak as Craig eased through the crowd and slipped his arm around Jill's shoulders. "Can't keep you out of trouble for one moment, can I?" he said with a warm smile as he helped her to her feet. "I have the car waiting outside, ready to go."

The nurse stood up as well, talking to Craig in a low voice. Theo searched her expression but didn't see any sign of urgency or concern on her face. Craig nodded and turned Jill toward the entrance.

Jill shot Theo an anxious look as she grabbed his sleeve. "Keep everything running until I get back. Have Barb take over the front of the house."

Their head server shooed her with a wave of her hand. "Stop worrying. We've got this. See, Theo's even getting back to the kitchen."

She gave him a gentle push that had him moving a few steps before he looked over his shoulder again at Jill. It was crazy; she wasn't going to disappear on him, and if he trusted her in anyone's hands, it was Craig's. "Like Barb said, we've got this. Go wrangle my niece into line, okay? And don't worry."

"Call our siblings. Let them know I'm okay." Jill continued to shout instructions as Craig ushered her out the door. He glanced back at Theo and mimed a phone to his ear in a message that he'd call Theo later. At least that's what Theo hoped he meant. Then Craig and Jill were gone and Theo was surrounded by concerned employees and guests.

He let out an explosive breath. At least Jesse had kept everyone in the kitchen. He eased back as he let Barb take over. As much as he wanted to hover, making sure the food flowed was the best way to get the traffic jam unsnarled. Theo pulled out his phone and started making calls. None of his siblings answered. Lincoln was probably eyeball-deep in the middle of a game tournament. As for Robin and Dustin, hell, Theo hadn't heard either of their voices, except in a recording, since the funeral.

He leaned against an out-of-the-way corner in the kitchen. And that was precisely what he didn't want to think about right now. Theo composed his thoughts and sent a group text. *Jill's in early labor. Craig took her to the hospital. Right now everything looks good. As soon as I hear more, I'll let you know. Send her your love, but don't pester her with questions. Craig and I will keep you updated.*

Theo set his ringer on high and slipped his phone into his pocket, the need for a cigarette clawing at his nerves. He looked around at the kitchen and the frequent glances cast his way, but they kept on task. A lump of gratitude settled in his throat. He had the best crew.

"Just a heads-up, everyone. Our soon-to-be new line cook decided to tell Jill who's boss. Jill and Craig are on their way to the hospital to rein her in. She's doing good, though, and as soon as I know anything, I'll let you know. So let's make Jill proud. Jesse, where are we?"

Getting back into the rhythm of the kitchen gave him a much-needed focus. As soon as he got his stride back, his phone rang, and Theo's heart jumped back into his throat. It was too early for news. He murmured his apologies to Jesse and stepped away. He glanced at the screen and his heart panged again, this time with hope. Dustin was actually calling him.

"Hey, man, I'm glad you called."

"What the hell is going on?" Dustin's voice twisted with contained, sneering fury. "What happened to taking care of them?"

"Jill isn't hurt," Theo said in a tight voice as hope died. This was going to be as ugly as it was the last time. "She's having labor pains, but she's otherwise okay. Craig's going to call as soon as the docs tell him anything, and I'll pass it along."

"You always have to be in control, don't you?"

"What's that supposed to mean?" Theo demanded and then reminded himself to chill out. He did not want to get into another fight with his brother. "Look, if you want to contact them directly, go ahead. They might not answer right away, but I know Jill would love to know you're thinking of her," he said in a calmer voice.

"I bet you didn't shut down the bistro to go with her. This is Mom and Dad all over again." The level of hostility in Dustin's voice astounded Theo. It was like none of this had changed at all for him. "You have Lincoln chained to the dishwasher, or did you at least let him go with Jill?"

Theo closed his eyes as his blood pressure started to pound in his temples. "Actually, Lincoln is off tonight. No, I didn't close the bistro because if I did, Jill would murder me. Then it would scare her into thinking this might be deadly serious when she needs to be calm. If I scare her, Craig will murder me. I know as soon as Lincoln looks at his phone, he'll find a ride over. Then she'll have her husband and one of her brothers hovering." She didn't need more.

"Still a selfish—"

"Look, before you call me a bastard, think about what the hell you've been doing. You never visit, you never call unless you need something. You're only in DC and not taking any classes at the moment. If you're so damned concerned, why don't you put your ass in your car and drive down to check on her yourself?" Silence met Theo's angry, bitter words. "Yeah, that's what I thought."

Theo hung up the phone before more ugliness ensued. The urge to throw the phone and smash it into a million satisfying pieces grabbed a hold of him, and Theo slipped it into his pocket before he gave in to it. He'd already been enough of an idiot.

He could feel the cracks. A year's worth of worry and heartache making stress lines in his soul. Theo turned back to the line before the stinging in his eyes threatened to unleash the flood he'd been holding back. "All right. Sorry again. Where were we?"

# Chapter Sixteen

MORRIS OPENED the oven and smiled in satisfaction as heat and scent poured out. The buffalo chicken dip was bubbling, and the cheese on the ham roll-ups oozed from the sides of the flaky, golden croissants. Thanks to Lincoln and Theo, he'd nailed it. Dakota had fallen all over the deviled eggs, and Felipe kept wandering through the kitchen, checking the fridge with a bemused expression on his face. Morris had a slight burn on his finger, but it wasn't on his drawing hand, so he considered it a wound worth the effort.

"Smells good," Lincoln called from the living room, where they'd moved the table so they all would have elbow room.

"Thanks, man. I seriously owe you." Morris lifted the dishes onto the stovetop and flipped off the oven. Okay, this was perfect. He'd apologize to Theo for calling him the devil right after he kissed him senseless. Hell, he'd make sure Theo was floating on a cloud of gratification for a week.

He grabbed the tortilla chips out of the pantry and the stack of paper plates, and then stood back to survey the scene with satisfaction. The kitchen counters were covered. They wouldn't have to resort to his stack of fast food menus. The remainder of the deviled eggs was still in the fridge with the éclairs, sodas, and booze, but all the rest was laid out, waiting for them to dig in. This was awesome, just awesome.

Morris glanced into the living room where Lincoln sat at the table, deep in a conversation with Dakota, his face lit up with animation as they went through the stack of games together. It looked as if they were going for a horror theme tonight. Seeing the smile on Lincoln's face brought its own sense of pleasure. He'd stuck by Morris the whole day, not only helping him with the cooking and planning but some of the cleaning too.

He was glad he'd invited Lincoln to play with them, and the kid didn't seem at all disconcerted by being the youngest there. Though, really, there wasn't that much of an age difference between him and Felipe.

"Okay, who are you and where is the real Morris?" Felipe demanded as he came back into the kitchen and grabbed a mug of fresh-brewed coffee. "I've never seen your apartment this clean. And you cooked. You didn't order a bunch of stuff. You actually whipped up food I'm not afraid to try."

"I told you I'd bring it." Morris shook his finger at Felipe. "What's up with the coffee? I bought you some hard cider."

Felipe grimaced and shook his head. "I'm laying off that shit for now. I can't do another hangover like the last two."

Morris would never forget that drive home from Pennsylvania. They'd added at least another hour to the trip so he could let Felipe out for some stillness and fresh air. He'd been miserable after a night of drinking out his frustration and lingering anger. Morris was amused when he'd found Brenden and Felipe bitching about Dakota and toasting each other in drunken camaraderie. But then he got stuck with Felipe and wasn't amused any longer.

"For real, I can't handle that," Morris said as there was a knock on the kitchen door. "Now stop giving me a hard time about the food and get that. It should be Jackie. Hey, are Brett and Daphne coming?"

"Yeah. They found a sitter last minute," Felipe said as he leaned over and opened the door. "Get your ass in here, girl," he said, before glancing at Morris. "They should be here soon."

Jackie came through carrying a couple bags of chips and a two liter of soda under her arm. "Wow, what smells so good? Did we order from Ledo's? Did you pick up some toasted ravioli?"

Felipe snickered and hugged Jackie. "I love you."

Morris rolled his eyes and cleared off a space on the counter for her offerings before turning to hug her too. "No, I cooked."

Jackie's eyes widened, and she glanced at Felipe for confirmation. "Are you for real?"

"Personally, I think it's some kind of Canadian voodoo, as he would say." Felipe smirked. "But he insists it's not an illusion."

"If you keep teasing him," Lincoln called from the living room, "he might not do this again. Y'all got him worked up enough earlier."

"Yeah, but how does it taste?" Jackie dropped off the bags and soda, leaned over the dip, and sniffed it. "Sorry, I've never known you to cook in all the years we've been friends."

"Fucking awesome." Dakota came in and snagged another deviled egg. "Seriously, give it a try. Morris has been hiding some skills or banging the hell out of that chef and learning through osmosis."

"Shut your mouth," Morris hissed, smacking Dakota's arm with the oven mitts. "Don't embarrass his brother."

"Sorry," Dakota said over his shoulder to a red-faced Lincoln in a tone that indicated no apology at all.

"I had help." Morris gestured to Lincoln. "Jackie, Lincoln. He lives upstairs and kindly came to my rescue earlier."

Lincoln lifted his hand in a shy wave. "I didn't do anything other than keep you from panicking. You mostly had it."

"Bless you." Jackie grabbed a tortilla chip and sampled the dip. "Oh damn. I haven't eaten all day." She reached for a plate as she shot Morris an incredulous look. "This is really good."

"Don't look at me like that. I'm having a fling with a genuine chef. He's an insistent teacher." Morris glanced over at Lincoln, who pretended he wasn't listening, though the red tips of his ears gave him away. "Dating, I mean. Sorta, we've actually only had time for one date. But we're working on a second. When we both actually have time off at the same time."

Damn, this was a little awkward.

"The guy we met at the bistro?" Jackie asked, then grinned as Morris nodded. "Don't let him go."

Felipe patted him on his shoulder with an evil smirk. "Fling, right, he's already got you changing your ways. You're a goner."

Morris frowned at him, but Felipe's grin only widened. He wasn't changing his damn ways. He still had a pantry full of boxed meals and sugary cereals made of awesome. Just because he had a few more options now than he would've in the past didn't mean a damn thing.

Jackie reached over to snag one of the hot roll-ups. She juggled it between her hands and took a bite. "Mmm, these are good too. Do you have the recipes?"

Morris pointed at the much-abused scrap of paper covered in buffalo sauce fingerprints on the counter. "Feel free to copy it if you can read it."

Jackie picked it up and scanned it quickly as she absently reached for another roll-up. This was going even better than Morris had dreamed. Dakota could now be the problem child of the group.

Morris punched Felipe lightly on the arm. "All of this is not because of Theo other than I asked him for help. All of this is because you wouldn't stop ragging on me. I wanted to enjoy my games tonight instead of hiding in the corner in shame."

"Oh, ye of fragile egos," Felipe said with a shake of his head.

"Speaking of games...." Dakota cleared the stack from the table as Lincoln opened up the remaining box. "Who's in for a game of Munchkin before Brett and Daphne arrive? I want to check out Lincoln's Cthulhu expansion."

"I've never seen that one." Jackie grabbed a beer and carried her loaded plate to the table. "There aren't any cards that are going to make me sing, are there?"

"Only if the stars are aligned right... or wrong, depending on how you feel about it," Lincoln said as he laid out cards. "I don't think there are, but it's been a while since I played this edition."

"Hey, Felipe, grab my dice," Morris said as he searched for a serving spoon for the dip. "I have some new giant ten-siders we can use for level counters."

"And I thought Dakota had a dice problem." Felipe disappeared down the hallway to the game closet, but Morris could still hear his voice. "You have more dice than you can possibly ever use."

"It's really sad you can't understand. Aren't you supposed to be a gamer? Besides, it's not my fault." Morris filled a plate as his stomach started rumbling. All he'd had to eat were nibbles and bits he'd tasted as he cooked and a few maimed eggs. "Cassie keeps stealing them and chasing them under my washer and dryer."

"Blaming your cat," Felipe said, returning with Morris's empty cheese ball tub of dice. It was nearly two-thirds full and weighed as much as a small child. He really did need to find another home for his dice, maybe several. He could split them up into categories. "Now, that's really sad, man."

"Hey, some of those dice are classics. You'll never find them again," Dakota said as Felipe handed the tub to Morris. "I've started a new group, Polyhedron Anonymous. Morris and I are the founders."

"Respect." Morris bumped his fist against Dakota's, then pulled out the bag sitting in the top of his tub. "Check these out." He poured out half a dozen jewel-toned dice each about the size of an egg.

"Okay, that's cool," Lincoln said, picking up a royal-purple one. "Where did you get those?"

"Trask from the Magick Den was selling them at the last con." Morris selected the hunter-green one. "I've been waiting for a chance to use them ever since."

"Speaking of Trask…." Felipe turned a chair around and straddled it, taking the seat opposite from Dakota. "Did I mention if we play our cards right we might be able to talk him into being our new gamemaster? I've been dying to play again."

"Richmond's kinda far from here, don't you think?" Dakota asked as he dealt out the cards. "Our schedules are crazy enough as it is."

"Not really, when you consider how little we get together." Morris looked at his cards and shook his head. A cultist, figures, but at least he had some cards he could start with. "Going down to Richmond once every six weeks or so is manageable, especially if he's any good. Besides, we're already in Richmond for shows several times a year. Maybe we can schedule games around that?"

He agreed with Felipe. It had been way too long since they last played.

"What made you pick Trask?" Dakota asked. "He's not the most sociable guy."

"Felipe wants to—" Morris cut off what he was going to say after a quick glance at Lincoln. "Umm, ask him out on a date. He thinks he's hot."

Dakota cut Felipe a searching glance, but the other man ignored him. Felipe was the king of compartmentalizing. "He is hot, I'll agree. I've listened in on some of the games he's run at shows and his shop. I think we'd mesh with him."

"Is he even looking for a group?" Jackie asked. "If he runs a store, I'm sure he's not hurting for finding players. Hey, how are we deciding who goes first? I'm not playing rock paper scissors with you guys again. Bunch of cheaters."

"Rolling for it." Dakota grabbed his level counter die and let it bounce across the table. "Fuck, a two, lowest goes first?"

"No," Felipe scoffed as he rolled as well and smirked at Dakota as it landed on an eight. "You're going down, buddy."

"Oh it's on." Dakota smirked right back, then leaned over. "Forgiven?"

"Just as long as you keep your flirting ways to yourself." Felipe gave him an airy wave. "I think Trask would be open to the idea of having a group. Especially since we all know each other, sorta. I talked with him a bit at the last show. He's not really running with any other group right now, more overseeing the groups that come to his store. I'll hit him up again at the next con and see if I can get him to nibble on the idea."

"Ha. I've got a ten. Beat that," Lincoln crowed.

"Watch and learn youngling, watch and learn." Morris shook his head as he got a seven. "Never mind."

"Go ahead." Jackie waved to Lincoln. "You brought the cards and you're the newbie. What are you going to do first?"

"Kick in the door," Lincoln replied, reaching for the door deck with a happy smile. "Come on, give me something good."

# Chapter Seventeen

THEO TOOK one last check around the restaurant to be sure it was spotless and ready for the prep crew in the morning. His body ached, but that was secondary to the worries buzzing in his mind. Jill would be fine. She was having a baby. Women had babies all the time. She trusted her doctor, which was no small feat considering she didn't trust many.

He just wished she hadn't scared him so damn bad at the start of the dinner rush.

At least she was home resting, though Theo didn't envy Craig at all. Being confined to bed rest for the next couple of months was going to make her absolutely mental. Rest and de-stress, that was the key, though that was going to be difficult to manage. Theo would have to find some way to let her help, or she'd drive them all crazy. Maybe he could send her the books or have her coordinate food orders, tasks she could do sitting down because he knew she wouldn't stay in bed as ordered. Not after the initial scare passed.

He pulled out his phone, but there were no new texts from his brother-in-law. Unfortunately, there were none from Lincoln either. Theo had left several messages on his phone. He'd called the house, too, with no answer. Lincoln was probably holed up in his room, headphones on as he played his games, oblivious to the rest of the world on his night off.

Telling himself that did not help the anxiety clawing at him as he remembered another night when his mom didn't answer her phone and they'd all reassured themselves she was getting much-needed rest.

How wrong they'd been.

Why couldn't Lincoln have called back instead of Dustin? That conversation still made his blood pressure rise, only to be followed with more guilt. It was the first time he'd spoken to his brother in a year. Theo missed him. And the first thing they'd done was go for each other's throats. Theo pushed those thoughts aside before he worked himself up even more than he already had.

He tried Lincoln's cell and the house again, with no luck. He briefly considered calling Morris and then told himself to stop being ridiculous. Morris was entertaining friends. He didn't need Theo interrupting to check on Lincoln because he was being an overprotective, neurotic brother. Lincoln wouldn't appreciate it. Morris wouldn't appreciate it. Besides, it was a fifteen-minute drive home.

Theo locked up and made his way across the deserted parking lot to his car. He stretched, working out the kinks in his shoulders and back. Nothing seemed to relax the tension in them. He rolled down the window to let the summer air flow over him as he headed home. The radio was on, but he barely heard anything as he tapped his fingers on the steering wheel.

It would be okay. He'd get there, address the issue of Lincoln not checking his phone, and break the news about Jill gently after he'd assured him Jill was okay. Lincoln would fuss and worry, probably insist on calling her first thing in the morning, and then want to spend a couple days there. Which might not be a bad thing. Lincoln was more of a mother hen than any of them. He'd see for himself Jill was fine.

The trees parted, their house came into view, and Theo's heart jumped with a hard beat of panic. The upper part of the house was dark, not one light shining. Lincoln liked to leave at least the kitchen light on when he was home alone. More than one time, Theo had returned to find every light blazing.

Maybe he passed out early. He'd been working so hard. If he fell asleep before the sun set, he wouldn't have thought to turn on any lights. Theo pulled into their driveway and noted the other cars still there. Looked like Morris's game night was still happening. If he didn't have a little brother to chew out, Theo would check in and see how it was going, but there was a long talk coming between him and Lincoln. Dammit, he knew how Theo felt about having a phone on hand in case of emergencies.

Theo climbed up the walkway, his pulse thudding. The front door was unlocked, and his heart jumped again, harder this time, as his throat tightened. That wasn't like Lincoln. He was a freak about locking the doors after seeing one too many crime shows.

Theo opened the door and flipped on the living room lights. "Lincoln?"

The house was quiet, and the door to Lincoln's bedroom dark, and Theo's heart climbed into his throat. "Lincoln!" Theo called out a little more forcefully as he went down the hallway and opened the bedroom door. The room was empty, the computer off. Theo touched the back of his computer and game systems, but they were cold as if they hadn't been on for a while.

Sick to his stomach, Theo yanked out his phone as he searched the rest of his house. There was no note or any indication Lincoln had been there at all. He tried Lincoln's cell phone again and heard it ringing in the living room.

Theo pressed his lips together, his hands clenching and unclenching, as he tried to will himself to calm down. When he got his hands on Lincoln Michael Boarman, he was going to scare some sense into him.

Taking a deep breath, Theo debated calling his brother-in-law. He did not want to get Jill stirred up, but it was after midnight. If Lincoln had gone to a friend's house he would've called, even if he left his phone behind. But he might've forgotten if he had decided to bike over to Jill's. He wouldn't have thought twice about them not being at home and when they did arrive, straight from the hospital, Theo could see how checking in with him would've been the last thing on their minds.

As logical as it sounded in his head, the sick sensation gripping his insides wouldn't let go. He called Craig, pacing as he waited for an answer.

"Theo, what's wrong?" Craig's sleepy voice answered.

"Quiet, don't wake up Jill. I hate to disturb you, but you didn't by any chance pick up Lincoln after you got back from the hospital, did you? Or maybe he biked over?" Theo fisted his hand in his hair, a sense of acute failure hitting him. It was after midnight. He should know where his own brother was.

"No." Craig's voice sharpened, and the fear Theo had been holding back clawed its way up to his throat again. "When did you last hear from him?"

"When I went to work after lunch. I've been trying to get ahold of him ever since you and Jill left for the hospital." Theo drew in a steadying breath. This was not happening. "Let me call his friend's house, and I'll ask my neighbor if he's seen him. I'll get back to you in ten minutes."

"Okay, I'll check Jill's phone in case he texted her earlier."

His stomach churning, Theo called Lincoln's closest friends, trying not to feel like an abject failure. His brother was only fifteen. Theo should fucking know where he was. Finally, he hung up in defeat. None of them had heard from him either.

Anxiety ate at him as he headed back outside. The thought of calling the police and reporting him missing…. He couldn't go through this again. None of them could. It was too much. Lurking behind the terrible memories was the underlying worry the authorities might consider him unfit to care for Lincoln. That was a fight Theo never wanted on his hands. And Dustin would feed right into it if he heard. He'd been against Theo taking Lincoln from the start.

He heard voices and car doors opening as he went down the outside steps and walked around to the driveway. The party looked as if it was breaking up. There were a couple people Theo didn't recognize getting into their cars as Theo cut around to Morris's entrance. He didn't acknowledge them, too caught up in trying to figure out what to do if Morris hadn't seen his brother either. Morris stood in the doorway, and his smile widened when he saw Theo.

"Hey." The smile fell away, replaced by a look of concern. "What's wrong?"

The expression on his face, the obvious care in his voice almost did Theo in right there. His throat tightened and his eyes stung. "Have you—" Theo started to say and then Morris opened the door and turned his body to let Theo in. There was Lincoln, laughing at something as he carried a stack of games out of sight down the hall.

*Thank God. Oh sweet Jesus.*

Relief swept through Theo, making his knees wobbly. Lincoln was safe. He'd been here the entire time.

*That little fucker.*

Then a rush of fury steadied his legs again. Lincoln had been here the entire time, unaware that Theo had been frantically trying to get a hold of him. Oblivious to the fact that their brother-in-law had been dragged in when he didn't need the extra stress. He'd been here playing games while Theo had been making himself sick with fear. He hadn't thought once, *Hey where's my phone, maybe I should check in, maybe someone will worry.*

"You!" Theo pointed a shaking finger at Lincoln as he came back into view. "Get your scrawny ass upstairs."

Lincoln whirled around, his eyes widening as his cheeks reddened. His eyes darted around the room, and his cheeks darkened further when he saw Felipe watching. "Theo?"

Morris frowned and laid a placating hand on Theo's arm. "What's wrong? He wasn't intruding. I invited him."

"Don't," Theo cut in before Morris could offer more excuses and shrugged off his hand with a sharp glare. "I can't even right now… just don't." He tried to calm down, knowing he wasn't making sense, and he had to make sense to Lincoln. "I'm serious, Lincoln," he said in a calmer voice, though the hard edge remained. "Get upstairs now. We have a lot to discuss."

Lincoln's face set in stiff lines, and he grabbed a box with a jerky motion, hugging it to his chest. He opened his mouth as if he wanted to argue, but after a quick glance at a curious Felipe, a worried Morris, and a pissed Theo, he pressed his lips together and stalked past Theo out the door.

Theo shot Morris a fulminating look and the other man stared back, his brows drawn together, looking at him as if he didn't know who he was. Fuck this. Theo didn't need it. He turned his back without a word and followed Lincoln up to their place.

Lincoln jerked open the front door and turned on Theo. "You are an asshole!"

"I'm the asshole? After the stunt you pulled? I don't think so." Theo pushed past him and grabbed Lincoln's phone off the coffee table, where he'd left it under a comic. He didn't want to manipulate Lincoln and twist him up with guilt by mentioning Jill right away. He wanted to keep the focus on Lincoln's inaccessibility first. Jill was okay, but Lincoln would go to pieces when he heard, and Theo wouldn't get through to him at all until he calmed down.

"I've been trying to get a hold of you all fucking night. Craig has been trying to get a hold of you, but we couldn't because you didn't bother to have your phone on you. That's the first problem."

Lincoln flushed, reached for the phone, and winced as he saw the list of missed calls and messages. "I don't see what the big deal is," he muttered, shooting Theo an angry, sidelong glance. "I was right downstairs."

"The big deal is I didn't know where you were and it's after midnight, which is your damned curfew unless you clear it with Jill or me first. And as you can see from the number of messages, we needed to get a hold of you." Theo caught Lincoln's gaze and held it as Lincoln's flush deepened. "Second issue. I don't have a problem with you hanging out with Morris playing games, but you have to let me know first. A note, even a goddamned note left on the counter would've been nice. And since you didn't and you scared the fuck out of me and Craig, you're fucking grounded and by grounding I mean your games."

"You can't ground me!" Lincoln stared at Theo in utter shock, his eyes round and mouth gaping open like a landed fish.

"Like hell I can't," Theo retorted. He quickly texted Craig to let him know he'd found Lincoln before the argument went any further. "In case you've forgotten, I'm your guardian, which means you have to live by my rules. And you've broken two of them in one go. There are consequences."

"I'm going to Zack's house." Lincoln gave Theo a look that dared him to push it. "You can't stop me. You're not my dad." That last was said with a sneering stab.

"If you take one step outside that door, I'm locking up your game systems for the rest of the summer," Theo said in a cold, quiet voice as a fist squeezed around his heart. "And don't even think Jill won't back me on this."

Lincoln whirled around. "You can't do that!"

"Try me." This was a place he never wanted to be at with Lincoln, but he knew if he let Lincoln walk out so defiant, he didn't have a chance in hell of ever regaining a sense of discipline and boundaries with him again.

They stared at each other for a long moment as Lincoln tried to gauge how serious Theo was. He glanced at the door, then back at Theo. "You always say you love me and you'd do anything for me," Lincoln pushed, his lips twisting into a sneer. "What do you call this?"

"It's because I love you and because I'd do anything for you that I can't allow you to do this," Theo said in a gentler voice, trying to will Lincoln to see his side for a moment. "I needed to get a hold of you tonight. Ji—"

"I hate you," Lincoln stormed, outrage flooding his expression. The words hit Theo like a punch to the throat, robbing him of any chance to respond. "You take the fun out of everything. You don't care about anything but your stupid restaurant." He bolted into his room and slammed the door shut behind him hard enough to make the window rattle.

Theo sank down on the couch, his throat tight, his thoughts churning. How did this all get to be so damned complicated? The weight and strain of his relationship with Lincoln wore on him sometimes. He missed the easiness they'd once had with each other. Fuck, he missed his old family. Multiple holes had been carved out of him, and it seemed like every time he managed to get it triaged up, the healing wounds reopened.

His phone rang and Theo pulled it out. "Hey, Craig," he said quietly, eyeing Lincoln's closed door.

"What happened?" Craig asked in a soft voice.

"He went downstairs to hang with a neighbor. Left his phone behind in the living room. Didn't even remember to leave a note." Theo sank back into the couch.

"Oh." Craig sighed. "We were all dumbasses once."

"Yeah." Theo rubbed his chest, replaying it out in his head. "Now he's pissed because I grounded him and locked himself in his room." Theo let out his breath in a huff.

"Did you tell him about Jill?"

"Didn't get a chance. I was about to when he slammed the door in my face. I guess there's no point in scaring him or guilting him. She's going to be fine." Theo hoped he sounded more convincing than he felt. This was a routine thing. That was all. And she had been overdoing it. "She is going to be fine, right?"

"Yeah, she will, seriously, bro. I'll let you know if you need to worry." Craig sighed. "Hold up, Lincoln's texting Jill's phone. Maybe he checked his messages. I'll holler at you later."

Theo hung up the phone, tossed it on the coffee table, then scrubbed his face with his hand. Lincoln hadn't walked out of the house, so he supposed that was a win, but it didn't feel like a win. It felt like one fucking huge loss.

# Chapter Eighteen

MORRIS FINALLY managed to get Felipe out the door after the angry voices ceased upstairs. He desperately wanted to send Theo a text to check on him, but that look in his eyes earlier stopped him. Theo was so calm and easygoing, Morris never expected that fire. He suspected that anything he had to say would not be welcome until Theo calmed down.

And dammit, who the hell was Theo to make him feel like a bad guy anyway? He wasn't sure what had crawled up Theo's ass and died, but he'd killed the fine mood Morris had been in after the success of the get-together and a good night of hanging out and having fun.

Morris straightened up his apartment, tossing leftover bottles and paper plates, sticking glasses in the sink, and returning the table to the kitchen as he tried to figure out what had gone so wrong. They were having a great time. Once Lincoln had lost his shyness, he'd slipped right into being a part of the group. The food had turned out awesome. And then boom. A fired-up, pissed-off Theo came in like a bomb.

He hadn't given any of them a chance to explain or apologize. Though Morris still didn't know really what he had to apologize for.

Morris heard the sound of a car pulling into the driveway and went to the door. If that was Felipe again, he was going to lose his temper. Enough was enough, go home already, nosy bastard. He always had to be in the middle of things.

Morris stepped outside and saw an unfamiliar car as Lincoln hurried toward it with a bag thrown over his shoulder. He took another step closer, reaching for his cell phone with a sense of alarm. He hoped to hell Lincoln wasn't trying to sneak out. Unlike Felipe, Morris did not want to be in the middle of this, but he couldn't in good conscience look the other way either. "Everything okay, Linc?" he called softly.

Lincoln whirled around, clutching his bag to his chest. "Yeah, thanks. I'm going to my sister's." He hurried around to the other side of the car as the driver rolled his window down. A white man, about Theo's age, stuck his head out. He looked tired, and his mouth was set in an uncompromising line. Morris's heart sank. Wow, Theo and Lincoln had really gotten into it if Lincoln was skipping town in the middle of the night.

"Hey, you Morris?" the man asked.

"Yeah." A part of his brain said don't get involved, but dammit, he liked Lincoln, and he really liked Theo, as much as he did not want to admit that right now. There was something going on that went beyond a spat between brothers. He took a step closer to the car as the man smiled faintly.

"It's okay. Theo knows he's with me. I'll bring him back tomorrow." The man reached through the window, his hand outstretched for a handshake. "I'm Craig Zantzinger, Jill's husband."

"Morris Proctor." Morris clasped his hand. "Nice to meet you."

"I'm not going back," Lincoln's muffled, sullen voice came from the car. The man rolled his eyes, and his mouth settled in a hard line. Morris got the impression Lincoln's night was not going to go as planned by hiding at his sister's.

"I've got to get back home. See you around, Morris." Craig turned and began backing out of the driveway.

The sound of a door opening had Morris turning to see Theo standing on his front step, his hands shoved deep in his pockets. Morris took a step back from the retreating car and eyed him. He hated confrontations. They tied him up in absolute knots, and the memory of the way Theo had glared at him still stung. But the despondency in Theo's stance drew him. He wasn't sure of the reception he'd receive, but he couldn't leave Theo standing there like some forlorn puppy as Craig and Lincoln pulled out of the driveway and disappeared.

"I broke my jackass pledge already, didn't I?" Theo's voice was a rough rasp.

"I don't know. I suppose that depends on why," Morris said softly, searching Theo's face in the dim moonlight filtering through the trees. His eyes were dark and moody, his posture stiff, but the downward turn of his mouth was so sad Morris reached for him before he thought twice about it. Fuck it. He could be irritated with him later.

Theo didn't say anything, just leaned into him with a sigh. After a long moment, he eased back, his shoulders slumped, his head hanging. "I'm sorry I was a jerk," he said, not looking at Morris.

He sounded sincere, and that knocked another chunk off Morris's mad. "Want to talk about it?" Morris offered. "What set you off? He really wasn't causing any problems being there. He didn't invite himself if that's what you were worried about."

Theo sighed again and then sank down on one of the plastic chairs he had set out on the small landing. "Do you want the long version or the short version?"

Morris hesitated and then folded his body into a second chair. "Let's start with the short version." Now that Theo seemed willing to talk, Morris realized he was a little mad, a little hurt for being treated that way, and despite Theo's apology, he wanted some answers. A fling gave him the freedom to walk away anytime, but Morris would hear him out before he decided.

"Short version." Theo leaned back in his chair and rubbed his hands along his legs. "Jill went into early labor at work. Craig took her to the hospital and they were able to get it stopped, but now she's on bed rest until she hits thirty-eight weeks. I've been trying to get a hold of Lincoln since then as well as trying to act as both manager and chef in the middle of one of the busiest nights we've had in months. I didn't want him to come in, but I wanted him aware of what was going on."

"Wow, okay, that's a lot," Morris relented. And if there was a long version, that meant there was more to the story. Stressful, definitely, but there had been an edge to his voice that spoke of a much deeper pain. "Is she really going to be okay? Your sister?"

"Yeah. She's fine, actually, just doing too much and her body finally said enough." Despite his words, Theo still looked worried. "Otherwise, doc said her and the baby were both healthy."

"That's good. What else? Go ahead and lay it all out. I know there's more." Morris crossed his arms over his stomach. "So there was a personal and professional emergency and you couldn't get a hold of your brother."

Theo nodded. "I was already worried, okay, freaking out if I'm honest. So when he still didn't answer as I was locking up and I got home to find him not there, I panicked. There was no sign he'd been there all day, and he hadn't left a note. And goddammit, Morris, it was after midnight. Maybe I should've chilled out and checked downstairs with you, but when I saw he'd left his phone…." He broke off with a shake of his head.

"Understandable," Morris said before Theo could go on. "I've never had a younger brother, and I certainly have never been in charge of someone like you have responsibility for him. So I guess what to me wouldn't be a big deal is something else for you. I wish you'd've called. I wouldn't have been able to help at the restaurant, but I could've set your mind at ease about Lincoln. Even if he wasn't here, I would've been happy to step upstairs and check on him for you."

Morris did get it. After all, his own dad would've ripped into him too for pulling a stunt like that. But he sensed Theo was still holding back. He was sure there was more to the story, an underlying trauma Theo hadn't discussed before. He'd picked up hints of it, seen it in the shadows lingering in Theo's eyes when he looked at his brother. The only thing he could think of was it had to do with their parents' death.

"Doesn't excuse me for being a jerk to you. You didn't do anything wrong, and I'm glad he was here. It's a little easier to excuse going downstairs than if he'd popped off to a friend's house without a word. If he'd only had his phone on him…." Theo stared out at the driveway, his shoulders slumping again. "He said he hates me."

The lost tone in Theo's voice tugged at Morris's heart. This fight had really done a number on him. "Don't you remember being thoughtless at fifteen and a defensive little jerk when you were called out on being thoughtless?"

Morris wasn't sure in the dim moonlight, but he thought he saw Theo smile faintly. "God yeah. I remember one time we broke into the neighborhood association's pool for a little midnight skinny-dipping. My mom woke up, couldn't find me, and called the police. We might've gotten away with the breaking and entering, but they sent a patrol car around the neighborhood. We were caught and hauled in, and I blamed her for getting me into trouble. It was humiliating when she came to get me at the police station."

"Oh great, I'm dating a criminal," Morris said with a soft chuckle.

"Oh yeah, going off on her didn't help my cause. I ended up having to do community service on top of the epic grounding I received. That sucked." Some of the tension bled out of Theo's voice. "What about you?"

Morris thought about it, running through the many exploits of his teenage years. There had been no brushes with the law. If there had been, his mom and dad would've made sure he wouldn't have lived to regret it.

"My parents had this hard and fast rule about not having anyone over after school until they got home, and we couldn't go out either. We had to get our homework done, and then we could goof off until they came home. If everything was done, then we could go out or invite someone in."

"I take it you stomped all over that rule," Theo said with a faint smile.

Morris smiled too at the memory. He hadn't thought of this in a long time. "Well, I used to invite my friend over to play video games, but I wasn't the only one. My twin did it too. Whenever we'd hear our parents coming in, we'd throw our friends out the back door. Then they'd sneak around to the front door to ask if we could go out now."

"As a teenager I would've applauded that level of sneakiness," Theo said. "We usually had to go straight to the restaurant after school. I did my homework on a back table."

That was a life Morris couldn't imagine. His teenage years had been busy enough. "It backfired on me. One day, my sister's friend left her jacket over the chair and my mom saw it as soon as she walked in the kitchen. Makayla told my parents it belonged to my friend. Nobody can assume an innocent air like her. I couldn't even really say anything in my defense when I got grounded because I was as guilty as her, but damn, I was pissed at her for a week."

"I would've been too." Theo folded his hands on his stomach and leaned his head back to look at the sky. "But looking back at it from their perspective, they were in the right and we weren't. I wonder how long it's going to take Lincoln to see that."

"Well, you know how easily mortified teenagers are. Calling him out in front of everybody was sure to get his back up. Not that I blame you. I'm sure I would've done the same." Morris reached over and touched Theo's knee and caught his gaze. "I saw your face, Theo. You looked like you were about to fall apart."

"I overreacted. I shouldn't have done that to either one of you. And if he gives me a chance, I'll apologize to him for the scene at your place. But I'm not going back on the grounding." Theo buried his face in his hands. "I've got to find a way to reach him without backing down on the rules, you know?"

"I think every parent has a moment like this. I've seen my sister have a meltdown over a meltdown from Laila. Try not to beat yourself up over it. I mean, you didn't tell him you hated him back, right? Or that you wish he wasn't staying with you? Or anything else emotionally scarring?" Theo shook his head and remained silent. "Okay then, it'll work out. We've all been grounded at one time or another, and though it feels like forever at the time, we usually forget it pretty quick."

"I didn't realize it would be so hard," Theo said softly. "I don't regret becoming Lincoln's guardian for one minute, but damn, sometimes I really miss just being his big brother."

Morris couldn't even imagine a situation like that, losing both of his parents, having to be the head of their family. The thought was a nightmare. "What happened with your parents, if you don't mind me asking?"

Theo was silent a long moment, and then he shook his head as if struggling with himself. "My dad got sick. Stage-four colon cancer. He hadn't been feeling well but resisted going to the doctor's. Kept saying he was fine. Doctors did nothing but give you more and more medication. By the time my mom nagged him into it, it was too late to stop the progression, and they gave him a couple of months to live."

Theo stared down at his hands, rubbing them against his knees as if he couldn't keep still. "It was like the news sucked all the life out of him. He went downhill so fast after that. So fucking fast."

Morris inched his chair next to Theo's and slid his arm across his shoulders, bracing himself for more. "Mom spent so much time taking him back and forth from doctor's visits, stints in the hospital, looking for a hospice or a way he could come home for his final days, on top of trying to micromanage everything at the restaurant until we made her stop."

That sounded a lot like Theo himself, trying to do everything at once and not giving himself a little break. It sounded like Morris's oldest sister too. They depended on her to take care of things as they rode along in her wake.

"She was wearing herself so thin. Too thin. She lost weight, couldn't concentrate. My dad went back to the hospital for a bunch of tests, and whenever it seemed like they'd send him home, they'd change their mind and keep him for more poking and prodding." Theo went silent again as his voice hoarsened. Morris squeezed his shoulder.

"We were all so worried about her too. We managed to convince her to go home and sleep instead of spending another night tossing and turning in the chair by his bed. We should've picked her up. I don't know what the fuck we were thinking. We had someone to stay with Dad, but we didn't send anybody with her."

"What happened, Theo?" Morris asked before Theo could bog himself down in too much recrimination.

"She left late. I'm not sure how late. She was supposed to text us when she got home. When we didn't get a message, we all figured she'd gone immediately to bed. I mean, hell, who could blame her for forgetting?" Theo's body was tense, and his hands moved restlessly on his thighs, rubbing up and down in agitation until he stood up and began pacing. "I called I don't know how many times that morning. I texted. I checked the hospital, but she wasn't there. So I went by her house to make her and Lincoln breakfast. It was clear she never made it home."

Theo stopped moving, his hands falling to his sides. "She fell asleep at the wheel and ran off the road, head-on collision into a tree. They rushed her into surgery. I guess there was confusion about who to contact. They were looking for my dad at home when he was right there in another ward. By the time we heard about it, she was gone."

"I am so sorry, man," Morris said softly, his heart aching for the raw pain in Theo's voice, the lingering fear. No wonder he'd freaked out. He was surprised Theo had held it in as well as he had. Morris knew he would've had a hell of a time keeping his cool.

Theo sank back into the chair next to Morris. "Once my dad got the news, he didn't last long. He gave up." Theo dropped his head in his hands, his shoulders shaking. "Within a few days, I lost both my parents."

Morris rubbed his back, remembering when he'd heard the news of Laila's accident. The agony of waiting and not knowing the outcome. The uncertainty of trying to comfort his sister and brother-in-law and not knowing how he could. It had been a terrible time.

He waited in silence, wishing he could say something to help other than "I'm sorry." It seemed so inadequate at moments like this. Finally, Theo lifted his head and dashed the back of his hand across his eyes. "I'm sorry. I don't go all to pieces like this."

Morris squeezed his shoulder again. "You don't have a damn thing to be sorry for. Sometimes you've got to let it all out. I've done it. Hell, most guys have whether they'll admit it or not. How long have you been keeping that all in?"

"A long time." Theo heaved a sigh. "A very long time."

"Then maybe it was past time." Morris fiddled with the hem of his kilt. He wasn't sure he liked the thought of Theo being alone right now. But he also didn't want to take advantage of whatever emotional state Theo was in. He didn't want to send him the wrong message. Morris slid his arm around Theo's shoulders and tried to inch closer, but the plastic chairs were not meant for cuddling.

Theo looked up at him. "Invite me back to your place. Please."

Morris's heart began to pound. Slowly he stood up and held out his hand. "Do you want to come downstairs with me?"

"Yeah." Theo took his hand and rose, catching Morris in a rough embrace. He kissed Morris, his mouth hungry, leaving Morris no doubt as to his intentions. His pulse pounded, and his knees went weak.

"You sure about this?" Morris asked as he pulled back, breathing heavy. He hoped Theo was, because he was aching to feel Theo stretched out naked with him, to hold him. He tried telling himself it was hormones and his heart wasn't engaged, but he didn't quite believe that.

Theo caught his face between his hands and nipped his lower lip. "Yeah… I'm sure."

# Chapter Nineteen

THEO FELT wrung out like an overused dishrag, but the knots twisting and tightening inside of him had begun to unravel. And kissing Morris felt right. It felt so damn good. Theo was desperately greedy for more of something that felt right and good after today.

Still holding on to each other, Morris steered him in the general direction of his apartment. "I was really hoping you'd say that," Morris said in a breathless whisper.

They somehow managed to make their way down to Morris's place in between stealing more kisses and half stumbling over each other. Morris paused at the door, a pained expression crossing his face as he shot Theo a searching glance. Theo's stomach dropped. He'd changed his mind about taking this a step further. "What is it?"

"My bedroom's a mess," Morris said with an embarrassed grimace.

Theo nuzzled closer. He could handle a mess. Morris changing his mind about letting him in was another matter. "What level of a mess? Are we talking nuclear holocaust level or more like a natural disaster level?"

"I'm fairly certain it's safe to be naked if you haven't been inoculated," Morris replied with a slight smile. "But I'm not making any guarantees."

"Then I'm willing to risk it. Wait," Theo said as Morris started to open the door. Morris paused and looked back curiously. The outside light slanted across his high cheekbones and the elegant sweep of his brow. Theo really wanted to kiss him again. "Do you have any condoms?"

"Right next to the hazmat suits," Morris assured him, his eyes going hot as he tugged Theo into his apartment.

Personal responsibility, check. Before Theo could offer any pithy comeback, Morris was kissing him again. Oh God, good. Theo didn't have to think anymore; he could just feel.

He kicked the door shut behind them and tugged off Morris's shirt, throwing it somewhere in the vicinity of the counter. He touched him with greedy hands, skimming them over Morris's long torso and the broad expanse of his back. Those tight T-shirts he favored ought to be illegal. He smelled so damn good, and his skin was smooth and warm. Theo couldn't get enough of him.

Morris pinned him against the counter, gripping the hem of Theo's shirt. "We really have to make time for this more often," he said, easing his hands under Theo's shirt.

"Agreed." Theo nibbled on Morris's earlobe, smiling as he leaned into Theo with a soft moan. Then Morris exploited Theo's own weak spot, trailing his warm lips down Theo's throat. Theo groaned and maneuvered Morris toward the bedroom. He wasn't against kitchen sex, but he wanted something more comfortable than the deck of a boat, or the length of a small couch, or the hard edge of a kitchen counter.

They got as far as the hallway when Morris finally managed to untangle himself long enough to yank Theo's shirt off. He tossed it aside with a soft laugh. "I cleaned this place today, and now we're leaving a trail of clothes throughout the house."

"We'll pick up in the morning." Theo pushed Morris against the wall and pinned him there with another kiss. "Hold on. I have been dying to do this for a long time now." He slid his hands up the back of Morris's legs, under his kilt. "Very nice," Theo murmured as he gripped Morris's ass. He laid his head against Morris's chest, listening to his heartbeat, and slipped his hands down the back of Morris's underwear for another grip. "Oh yes, very nice."

Morris laughed and kissed the top of Theo's head. "Was it everything you wished for?"

Theo nodded against his chest. "Give me a moment. This is a dream realized." If Theo had the power, he'd make it so all men had to wear kilts. He never realized he had this fetish until he met Morris.

"I'm sure you'll have another chance. I promise." Morris unzipped Theo's pants and inched lower to take them off. "But you're hindering my efforts to get you naked, and I want to make sure my memory didn't lie to me about how sexy you are."

Reluctantly, Theo let go of him, stripping the underwear off him, and undid the wide belt around Morris's waist as he kicked out of his pants. Morris's eyes gleamed as he watched Theo undress. "That's what I'm talking about." They left the rest of Theo's clothes behind and finally made it to Morris's bedroom door. Morris paused, his hand on the knob. "How come you're buck-assed naked and I'm only missing my underwear and shirt?"

"Are you complaining?" Theo asked, sliding his hand along Morris's thigh and inching the kilt up.

Morris looked Theo over with a greedy gaze, and the corner of his mouth tugged up in an appreciative smile. "Hell naw."

Theo snorted, and Morris lifted his gaze again. "I'm wondering how far you are going to carry your fondness for my kilt. Are you planning to screw me while I'm still wearing it?"

Theo's cock throbbed at that thought, and he raked his gaze over Morris. "I hadn't considered it, but now that you mention it... I might." He fisted his hands in Morris's hair as he gently tugged his head down for a heated kiss. "I love the way your legs look in it. It really gets me going."

"You keep this up and I might insist you wear nothing but an apron," Morris said, fumbling the door open. "Or maybe assless chaps."

"For you, I would." Theo followed Morris inside and had the impression of belongings on the floor and an unmade bed, but those were forgotten as soon as they hit the mattress. "Fuck, I want you so damn bad, Morris."

He ached with it. Not just desire, but being with him. He had it bad.

Morris's artist hands slid over him, teasing, stoking the fire as Theo crouched over him. "Less talk, more doing it."

Good point. Theo would compliment him on his wisdom as soon as he was done kissing him. Morris's mouth was warm and inviting, his body hard and long and so fucking sexy. Theo loved the rough, scratchy feel of his thin dreds, the scent of shea butter and Old Spice, and the shape of his mouth.

He was falling for Morris, hard. When everything else in his life was so difficult... Morris was easy, natural, like a missing piece fitting right into place so smoothly.

Morris moaned as Theo pulled away. "Seriously, if I don't get naked soon, I might blow a blood vessel. I want skin to skin."

Theo laughed softly and knelt up. "Condoms, lube?" He glanced over at the nightstand covered in mugs and books, moonlight glinting over the hodgepodge and not a glimmer of what he wanted to see.

"Hold on." Morris twisted around, his kilt raking up one long thigh as he searched on the floor near his bed.

"Mmm." Theo inched the kilt up farther, exposing the bottom of Morris's ass, the plump cheeks and sexy-as-fuck cleft. Theo's cock jumped. That was the sexiest sight he'd ever had the pleasure to witness. He ran his palm over his cheek as Morris looked back at him, his lips curved in amusement. "Yes, naked is a good idea. I'm not sure I can handle the awesomeness of fucking you with your kilt on. We'll have to save some fantasies for later."

"You're such a dork." Morris tossed a shoebox on the bed, the lube and condoms spilling out onto the blankets. Theo picked up the box curiously, noting the variety of plugs, the dildo, and cleaning supplies. Morris really did seem to be into ass play. Theo could totally get into that.

He drew out one of the plugs and grabbed the lube as Morris rolled onto his back and lifted his hips to slide down the kilt. His hard, heavy cock lifted from his jutting hips and Theo groaned. He leaned over and kissed the shaft, inhaling his scent with a murmur of appreciation. He didn't think Morris really understood his appeal. Theo would have to make sure to tell him often.

"I'm okay with that, the dork and the geek, sounds like a good pairing." Theo hovered over Morris as he dropped his kilt over the side of the bed and kissed his chest. "Like a really good meal and a fine wine, the kind you want to savor. And I really want to linger over you."

"Trust you to bring food into this." Morris drew him closer and slid his foot down Theo's calf. "Now where were we?"

"Here," Theo whispered in a husky voice and kissed Morris, a quick taste that left him hungry for more.

"And here," he said again as he trailed his lips to Morris's neck.

"What about here?" Morris asked, reaching down to brush his fingers over Theo's cock. "Are we right here too?"

Theo moaned at the surge of heat that made it hard to think. "Oh yes." He kissed Morris more urgently, diving into the sense of him. Many nights when he went to bed, he thought about how awesome it would be to have Morris beside him. And not just because he'd get to indulge in this.

Morris kissed him back, wrapping his arms tight around Theo, and when they finally parted, they were both breathless. Morris touched him everywhere, exploring with that long reach of his, those gorgeous hands making Theo moan for more. "I love the way you touch me," he said against Morris's lips.

"I love touching you." Morris's hands skated down Theo's thighs. "I love feeling you on top of me."

"I think I had my hand on some toys a moment ago." Theo nuzzled Morris's jaw. "You game?"

"Nah." Morris wiggled out from underneath him and rolled onto his hands and knees. The sight drove away Theo's momentary pang of disappointment. "More foreplay later. I want you now. I haven't been able to get the idea of you screwing me out of my head since the boat."

Heat and naked need made Theo shaky. He hadn't wanted anybody as much as he wanted Morris. Theo kissed his side and reached for the lube and a condom. As he knelt behind him, he saw that Morris had reached back between his splayed thighs and was fingering himself.

Theo's mouth went dry and his cock ached. The moonlight coming in from the window was filtered by the trees, and the light from the kitchen was too far away to illuminate farther. He wanted to see more. The only thing that would've made it better would be if he could've watched the pleasure on Morris's expressive face as he touched himself.

"Okay, fuck, that's sexy." Theo rubbed a restless hand over Morris's flank. "I might have to watch you for a minute or two while I regain my composure."

"My fingers and toys aren't the same thing." Morris spread his knees a little wider, pushing that gorgeous ass back toward Theo. "You aren't going to leave me like this, are you?"

Theo was seriously trying to figure out how to think again. He'd discovered his sexuality through masturbation and pop culture magazines. He wondered how much of Morris's teenage years had been spent doing exactly this, becoming comfortable with his body.

"I think with either a yes or a no I win." Theo squirted some lube into his hand and warmed it up before stroking his fingers along Morris's cleft. "Let me help. Don't be greedy."

Morris slid his fingers free, and Theo rubbed his thumb over his entrance, circling and provocative as a small shudder went through Morris. "Tease," Morris panted. "Come on. Give it to me."

Theo grinned and slowly pushed his thumb inside of him, feeling the tightening of his muscles around it, the deliberate relaxation. "How often do you finger yourself? I need something to fuel my midnight fantasies when I get home from work."

"You can come down every night and watch." Morris pushed himself up to his hands and knees again. "More, come on, Theo."

Damn, Morris made it utterly impossible to think when he talked like that. A confident man was even more of a turn on than a sexy one, and fuck if Morris didn't tickle every one of Theo's happy places. He wasn't sure if Morris was joking or not, and he didn't care.

"How long has it been?" Theo asked, easing another finger into him, taking his time to make sure every moment was pleasurable. Like Morris said, it was one thing to play with yourself; it was another to be with someone who made you hot inside and out.

"Too long. Not many take you seriously as a bottom at six three." The frustration in Morris's voice was apparent, and it made Theo even more determined to make this good for him. He was out of practice himself. The last time he'd been on this end… it seemed like a lifetime ago.

As he fingered him, he searched for the spot that made Morris gasp and tremble. Theo ached to be inside him, but he continued until the resistance in Morris's body eased away and he was relaxed, making those low moaning sounds that had Theo's heart beating faster. "You ready?" he asked, hoping Morris said yes. As good as this felt, he knew it was going to feel so much better.

"Oh fuck yeah, been ready." Morris wiggled his ass at Theo and looked over his shoulder, watching as Theo slid a condom on. Theo slicked some more lube onto his cock, and his breath caught as Morris reached around him again to grip his shaft. "Let me."

Morris stroked him once, then gripped him lightly. Theo bit his lip and let Morris guide him, gripping his hips as he pushed in past the tight ring of muscle. Damn, that felt so good. Tight heat surrounded him, held him, as he slowly pushed deeper.

Morris groaned, settling his weight on his elbows as he rocked his hips back gently.

"You okay?" Theo paused, letting him adjust even as his body cried out for more.

"Yeah, fuck… it really has been awhile." Morris panted, clenching around Theo and then relaxing. "Give me a moment. Damn… feels good."

Theo rubbed his hands over Morris's back. The long shadow of his body in the dark, the warmth of him, fulfilled a long-denied need. The ache in his heart swelled even more. He had to convince Morris this was more than a fling. He wanted the promise of many more days and nights, whenever they could get time together.

"Okay," Morris said on a sigh as the tension eased. "I'm good."

Theo eased out of Morris's body, then thrust gently again, moving at the same slow pace until Morris was completely relaxed and rocked with him. Theo tightened his hands on Morris's hips, grinding against him as the heat rose higher. His body clamored for more, but his heart and mind wanted to draw out every moment.

"Fuck that feels good." The husky groan in Morris's voice made Theo long to hear more. As good as it felt to be inside him, it felt even better to hear Morris's pleasure. He thrust a little more surely now, the bed creaking and rocking with them as Morris's moans and groans spurred him on more than any dirty words could.

Morris lowered even more, crouching down, his ass in the air, and cried out softly, burying his face into a pillow as Theo snapped his hips. He tensed and trembled, then immediately pushed back again with another urgent cry. Theo held on to his hips, going for that same angle that made Morris tremble and clench so sweetly. Morris cried out again, a little higher, a little more urgent.

Fucking bingo. Theo found the spot.

Any sense of waiting and lingering vanished. Theo pounded into him as Morris writhed with wordless pleas and Theo's pulse raced. Fuck, fuck, fuck. He wanted to lean over and kiss his skin. He wanted to caress him. But he didn't want the sight and sound of Morris getting lost in his pleasure to falter.

Then Morris was stroking himself, and Theo felt the edge coming hard and fast. "No. Wait. More." Other unintelligible demands from Morris followed. They hit Theo on an instinctive level.

Theo clung to him, trying to hold on until Morris came. Just a little longer. "Oh fuck, Morris. Fuck, babe."

Morris wrapped his arms around the pillow, muffling the desperate sounds. Then Morris tightened around Theo almost painfully, and his rocking came to a stop as he twisted underneath Theo with a sharp cry.

Theo pulled free of him and yanked off the condom, jerking off as he came in a wild rush. He leaned against Morris for a moment, sweaty and breathless, and then Morris scooted to the side and they collapsed next to each other.

"Oh God," Morris groaned.

"Amen." Theo draped his arm over his forehead, his body still on a flushed high as he reached for Morris.

"I really have to change my sheets," Morris said, burying his face against Theo's shoulder.

For some reason, that side comment struck Theo as hilarious. He laughed, and a tension he'd carried all day broke. He laughed even harder as Morris joined him. He rolled over and kissed the top of Morris's head. "Come on. Let's clean up here and take a hot shower."

Morris caught his hand. "Tell me you'll stay. I don't want you being alone tonight."

Theo hesitated. What if Lincoln came home and couldn't find him? Then common sense returned. There was no way Craig would leave Jill again to ferry Lincoln home. Besides, his phone was right there on the nightstand. Anyone in his family would be able to get a hold of him. "Yeah, I'll stay." Theo squeezed Morris's hand. "Come on."

They lingered in the shower, washing each other tenderly. Stripping the bed didn't take long, and soon they were stretched out naked next to each other. Theo scooted closer to Morris, their skin still damp from the shower and Morris's lotion that they'd slathered over each other. Moments later Morris was snoring lightly.

Theo draped his arm over Morris's side. His body urged him to sink down and let exhaustion take over. His mind wouldn't stop circling around the same worries, touching on Jill and Lincoln before trying to figure out how things were going to go tomorrow. Then there was his argument with Dustin, and he was sure to drag Robin in on it like he had the last time. It made Theo sick to think he'd made things worse for everyone.

Maybe if he called and apologized tomorrow, maybe this time Dustin would hear him out.

# Chapter Twenty

MORRIS STIRRED, reaching for Theo across the messy sheets of the bed, but the other side was empty. It was still warm, as if Theo just left. Morris listened, stretching as he slowly woke up until he heard the sounds of activity in the kitchen. He frowned and half pushed himself up. Theo was trying to be quiet, but he was definitely moving about. Did the man ever sleep?

What the hell could he be up to first thing in the damn morning? Morris peered blearily at his alarm clock and then sat up with a groan. Half the morning was gone. He threw back the sheets and jerked on a pair of boxers and a Nightwing T-shirt. The scent of coffee hit his nose as he opened the door, and Cassie streaked inside to disappear under the bed. Poor girl had been locked out all night. Morris knew she was pissed about that and would spend half the day sulking in her favorite hidey-hole.

Morris scratched his stomach as he headed toward the kitchen, following the aroma of coffee. Theo was dressed only in his work pants and was busy stacking dishes into the dishwasher and wiping down the counter as he hummed to himself. He looked entirely too happy to be tidying up. It wasn't natural. The only thing that seemed right about the scene was Theo half-naked. He was supposed to be all the way naked and still in Morris's bed.

A pot of freshly brewed coffee waited on the burner, begging to be poured, and there was a clean skillet on the stove. "What do you think you're doing?" Morris demanded.

Theo looked over his shoulder with a crooked smile. "I literally cannot help myself. I see a kitchen in chaos and I start to twitch."

"I was going to do that," Morris said, not sure if he should feel miffed or not.

"I know. I saw evidence you'd started, and then I interrupted your efforts with my dramatic, angry fit last night. So this is an apology before

I have to run off to work." Theo folded the washcloth and draped it over the sink spout.

"You already apologized." Morris reached over him to snag a coffee cup from the cabinet. He was not awake enough to be mollified. He could clean after all, though he wasn't sure why he was so irked at the thought of Theo cleaning up after him. Then he saw the shadows under Theo's eyes and regretted his bad humor. "How's your sis? You hear from her or Lincoln?"

"Jill's fine and I'm not supposed to worry about her or check up on her every ten minutes. She's getting enough of that from Craig." Theo's mouth turned downward as his eyes went faraway.

Morris raised a brow as he filled his cup and went in search of milk and sugar. "Right. Good luck with that. You're going to worry and you're going to check up on her, just maybe not every ten minutes."

Theo nodded solemnly. "I think fifteen minutes is doable."

God help him, Theo was too adorably cute even when he was serious. Morris tried to figure out the appeal. He was good-looking, no lie—it was just the vibe he put out, the boy-next-door, the quiet friend who could be too easily overlooked for the flashier guy. Morris found that quiet steadiness greatly appealing. Even last night, he didn't go off the way others would have. They would've heard Felipe for miles if he'd been that upset. Still, that quiet, cold fury had revealed layers to Theo that Morris hadn't even started uncovering, and he really wanted to.

"Try out twenty, and then you can argue you doubled her allotment." Morris doctored up his coffee and took a sip, sighing in contentment. "What are you going to do at work?"

Theo shut the dishwasher door and leaned his arms on the clean counter. "I don't think I really got a chance to talk to you much since the last time we tried to get naked. We switched things around a bit. Scottie and I are switching off day and night shifts for five days and doubling up one day so we each can have a day off. I hate losing my right-hand man, but he's good. Hell, he deserves his own restaurant. At least then I have someone I trust in charge when Jill and I aren't there."

"Did you ever get around to hiring a new manager?" Now more than ever Theo needed to stop resisting the idea of someone new. Morris couldn't blame him, though. He'd thought a few times of bringing someone else on to help with his books since he had more ideas than time. But he couldn't see himself actually doing it.

"Yeah, thank God," Theo said with a tone of relief, though his brow remained furrowed. "She was supposed to start next week, but I called her this morning and begged her to start today."

"You ended up going with Rose?" Morris asked, taking another sip of his coffee as he looked around for his other shirt. He was sure Theo had removed it in the kitchen.

"Yeah, we met with her a couple times after going over her résumé. We wanted someone who'd embrace the locally sourced Chesapeake bistro idea." Theo topped his coffee off. "Plus we wanted someone who fit with the family. We all clicked with her the most. She even has ideas for expanding our hours while keeping with what makes us—us."

Personally, Morris thought Theo should shelve any ideas of expanding. He was overworked enough as it was, but who was Morris to judge? He'd come up with a whole new comic book idea that would double his workload unless he gave up taking more commissions or contracts for trading cards. "What kind of an expansion?"

"Adding breakfast hours and taking on the boaters, giving them an early breakfast or boxed lunches before they head out for a day of fishing and pleasure riding." Theo shook his head with a sigh. "It's a good idea, but not anything we're in a position to do right now. Maybe when Lincoln's in college."

"So, if the bistro isn't open until lunch, how come you're gone half the time in the mornings too?" Granted, Morris didn't wander outside much in the mornings, but he remembered being mystified by a neighbor who never seemed to be there.

"There's prep work every day. Scottie and I used to switch off on that. Then every third morning I hit up the farmer and fish markets. We took turns, Scottie, Jill and I." Theo scrubbed a hand over his face, his shoulders slumping. "Which I guess means every other day now."

Morris wished he could help, but he didn't know the first thing about running a restaurant. There had to be something else he could do to brighten Theo's day. Theo straightened and poured himself a second cup of coffee. "How did your party go yesterday? I forgot to ask."

"Great, but I had to get your brother's help. I had no damned idea what you meant by some of the instructions." Morris watched in disbelief as Theo got out some eggs and a bowl. "No. You sit."

"But…." Theo turned wide eyes on him as Morris gently pushed him away from the stove. "I don't get to make my boyfriend breakfast after a night of hot sex?"

Boyfriend. Oh God. No, Morris was not ready for boyfriend status, but he kept his lips shut. He was not going to pick at that issue with Theo after the night he had. He'd put them safely back into hot fling territory later on tonight.

"No, you don't." Morris deftly cracked some eggs into a bowl. "You already picked up the kitchen and made me coffee. And you're cooking the rest of the day. Let me do something." He did know how to make scrambled eggs and toast. It may not be gourmet, but it was good.

"You're awfully cute when you're irritated."

Morris glanced over his shoulder. Theo sat at the table, his head propped on his fist. He had that little smile on his face, the one he had to know was so appealing, all boy-next-door and innocently sexy. Morris was onto him.

"Bite me," he said, knowing it would make Theo grin, and it did, lighting up his face and erasing some of the exhaustion lining it.

The knock at the door startled them both, and Morris frowned. Anybody he knew would text before heading over. "Why don't you get that?" he suggested. "If I get it, I'll come back to find you overtaking my stove again."

"Fine, be that way," Theo said with a fake huff, "but if it's Felipe half-naked again, I'm dunking him headfirst through the basketball hoop."

Morris pulled out a fork and whipped up the eggs. He paused long enough to flip on the stove before turning toward the door, still mixing. Lincoln stood in the entryway, hands in his pockets in a gesture reminiscent of Theo, his shoulders hunched in misery. His gaze darted from Morris to Theo, and his cheeks turned red.

"I'm sorry," he said in a barely audible voice. "Am I allowed back home?"

Morris turned away to give them some privacy as Theo hugged Lincoln. He waited a moment and then looked back. "You hungry, Linc? I'm making breakfast if you want some."

"Actually, Morris, do you mind if we do this another morning?" Theo asked with an anxious glance his way. "I think Linc and I need a chance to talk before it's time to head to work."

"Yeah, sure, man, no problem." Morris lifted his hand in a wave as relief crossed Theo's face.

"Thanks." Theo disappeared down the hallway in search of his shirt. Morris couldn't remember where they'd tossed it. Lincoln shifted from foot to foot, his gaze darting around as if he didn't quite know where to look.

"Hey," Morris said, and Lincoln glanced at him. "If you ever want to, I don't know, talk. My door is open."

Lincoln flushed a darker red and nodded. Theo came back into the kitchen, shrugging on his shirt. He walked over and kissed Morris soundly on the lips. "Don't go to bed early tonight," he said under his breath and walked away, leaving Morris with a batch of eggs in his hands and one hell of a boner.

Bemused, Morris turned back to the stove. Somehow Theo managed to turn around all of Morris's preconceived notions and wiggled his way into his psyche. He poured the eggs into the pan, humming to himself, suddenly much happier with the day. He knew exactly what he was going to do.

After Theo's story last night, Morris understood why he liked that picture he commissioned from Morris so much. It was done. Morris had been procrastinating on scanning it and pulling his promo together. He'd finish that today, then go out and get the picture framed as a surprise.

Then he'd see if Lincoln was interested in a second job. He worked hard at the restaurant. Morris had seen that for himself. But it might be nice for him to do something that suited him and that would build his confidence. And Morris had just the thing in mind.

The tricky thing would be to find a way to make it work without taking away from Theo's help at the restaurant, because with the way things were going, only Theo and Lincoln were left out of the entire family at the place. And Morris knew how important that was to him. Maybe if Rose worked out, Theo and Jill would be convinced to hire a few more people before they both worked themselves to the bone.

# Chapter Twenty-One

THEO FOLLOWED a subdued Lincoln back up to their place, wondering what brought about this change. He'd been sure when his brother heard about Jill, he'd insist on staying to keep her company. "Your shirt's on backward," Lincoln muttered as he opened the door.

Theo glanced down at the tag sticking out. "It's inside out too."

Lincoln's face turned red. "Are you going to start spending the night there?" he blurted out.

"I wasn't planning on it." At least not on the nights when Lincoln was home, which made him wonder what he was going to do. He hadn't had a relationship since his parents died, and he'd never had to think about someone at home waiting for him if he did go out. It was something else to consider. Would it be too awkward for Lincoln at this stage if Morris stayed the night or would it blow over quickly? That would take some mulling too.

"Do you want to talk?" Theo asked, too tired to beat around the subject. Though he'd slept for a while next to Morris, his sleep had been troubled until he'd finally been driven out of bed to fix something.

"Not really." Lincoln shrugged. "Craig laid into me. I guess I should be grateful neither of you told Jill or she would've been on my case."

"She's got enough to think about right now, and we don't want her stressing more than she is already." They couldn't keep it from her indefinitely. She had a way of ferreting things out, and she'd be pissed. But they could wait long enough to take the bite out of it. "It might be best coming from you, though. Eventually, Craig will say something. Those two have no secrets."

Lincoln looked very uncomfortable at the thought and his mouth was downturned in unhappiness, but he nodded. "I'm still grounded, aren't I?"

Theo wanted to back off. Lincoln looked so miserable and the memory of the angry words between them still stung. But if he didn't show Lincoln he was serious about the rules, then there would be a lot more sleepless nights.

"Yeah, from video games." Theo clasped him on the shoulder. "But it's not the end of the world. Trust me, I've been grounded plenty, for pretty much the same thing."

"Then what's the point?" Lincoln asked in a sullen tone. "You know I didn't mean to make you worry."

Theo wondered if his parents ever felt this conflicted, because if they had, it never showed. "The point is the next time you go somewhere it may make you pause and remember to grab your phone, to send a text, something so we're not worried about whether or not you're safe. Sometimes it takes the thought of losing a privilege to remember the little details."

Lincoln nodded again, and though he didn't look happy about it, his stance lost that rebellious edge it had the night before. "How long until I can play my games again?"

Theo pondered that, weighing all the factors. "Until next weekend. Come Saturday, it's yours. Just please don't stay up till 5:00 a.m. on a binge, okay?"

"Okay." Lincoln's expression cleared. "That's not too bad, I guess."

"To be honest, I was so mad I was going to make it longer, but after looking back on it, you were only downstairs, and it started out with you helping a neighbor, and that was cool of you." Theo remembered some fragment of advice from some well-meaning friend of their parents about not setting punishments when you were pissed. He got that now.

"Just next time, please think ahead, Lincoln. Because I'm telling you now with complete honesty, I will freak the fuck out every single time I can't get a hold of you when I should be able to get a hold of you. Right or wrong, it's wired into me." If nothing else was drilled into Lincoln's head but that bit of knowledge, Theo would take it as a win.

"I'm sorry I said what I said." Lincoln scuffed his toe on the floor. "I didn't think you'd let me come back after that."

Theo squeezed his shoulder as an intolerable weight eased off him. "Lincoln, look at me." He waited until his brother's gaze lifted, his eyes stormy and troubled. "You will always have a home with me, got it?"

"Even if you hook up with Morris?" Lincoln fidgeted, shoving his hands in his pockets.

Now where had that bit of insecurity come from? Theo didn't know why Lincoln would think he wouldn't be welcome if Morris and he became more of a thing than they already were, but he hastened to reassure him anyway. "Morris and I aren't looking that far ahead. I like him. He likes me. But let's say we were to fall madly in love and want to shack up together, then yes, you would be more than welcome. Morris knows you and I are a package deal. He can't have one without the other."

Lincoln brightened a bit. "I like him too. He didn't have to invite me to stay with his friends but he did. It was fun."

"Was it all those geek games you try to get me to play with you?" Theo had tried, but some of them went way over his head. What was so wrong about a simple game of Monopoly or Life? Give him a deck of cards anytime.

"Yeah, some I never heard of before. Mostly creepy ones. That was cool."

As Lincoln started to relax, Theo realized he needed to apologize too. "I'm sorry I yelled at you in front of everyone. That was wrong of me," Theo said quietly. "I like to say I wouldn't do it again, but I can be a thoughtless jerk."

Lincoln nodded, looking down at the floor before meeting Theo's gaze. "I don't hate you."

A tightness Theo hadn't even known still lingered eased. "Thank you." It was bad enough he had the enmity of one brother. Theo couldn't bear the thought of another wanting nothing to do with him.

He glanced at his watch and winced at the time. The idea of having his mornings free worked better in theory than reality. "Our new manager is starting today, so I have to go in early and greet her and get things rolling on that end. Do you want to go in with me or catch a ride in later?"

"Might as well go in and pick up an extra shift. If I can't go anywhere, I could use the cash. Besides, it's my restaurant too, right?" Lincoln said with a smirk. "I need to keep an eye on my investment since you're running the show solo now."

"Yeah, you do that." Theo caught Lincoln in a rough hug, gave him a gentle noogie, and laughed as Lincoln shoved him away. He went off to make coffee, whistling softly, with a much lighter step.

By the time they walked into the restaurant, Lincoln was more like himself, as if the anger and argument from last night had never happened.

For all of his drama at times, Lincoln was not one to hold a grudge or sulk for long. In that way they were alike.

When Theo and Lincoln rolled in, munching on hastily thrown-together breakfast sandwiches, Scottie and his crew were hard at work prepping, and their new manager was early and talking with the waitstaff. The rush of gratitude Theo felt at the sight of her buried all the resentments he had about having to hire her in the first place. She was one of them now.

"Rose Williams," Theo greeted, coming forward to take her hands and kiss each one. "You do not know how welcome you are today. Thank you for agreeing to start early. I know we came at you from left field with this one."

"Theo Boarman." Rose smiled at him, and the expression lit up her lively eyes. "Do not try to charm me." Her shiny black hair was coiled into a neat braided knot at the nape of her neck and the musical, lilting accent of the Caribbean colored her voice.

"I can't help it. It's a part of me. Are you about done here?" Theo gestured to the waitstaff.

"Yes." Rose smiled at each one of them. Theo could see the uncertain and worried expressions many of them had. "I think we understand each other."

"I want to say a few words to you all," Theo started, still keeping a hold of Rose's hand. "First off, I know you've heard the news, and I want to reassure you Jill is fine. The baby is fine, and we appreciate all the texts and calls we've received. Second, I can see you've already met Rose Williams, our new manager, who has graciously agreed to come in today to woman the fort and keep me from crying into the appetizers. I want this to be a smooth transition. There will be other changes coming down the wire, but I want you to remember we're a family and we're going to take care of each other. Okay?"

He met each one of their gazes, trying to radiate all the confidence he could. The small group nodded and whispered among themselves, and Theo noted the few who were likely to try to test boundaries. He'd have to give Rose a heads-up. "Now, I'm going to be here until the dinner shift in Jill's office. If anybody needs a quick few minutes to discuss concerns, they are welcome to save me from paperwork, just please bear in mind, it's going to be an adjustment for us all, but I have every confidence in us."

"How's payroll going to be handled?" Erin asked, pushing to the front. "What about the days we already requested off?"

"Jill had already done the schedule for the front of the house for the month. So if you cleared it with her first, you're good to go. If you waited until the last minute, we'll have to see." Theo rubbed his temple as Erin's jaw tilted at a stubborn angle. "Jill's still going to do payroll from home. Her mind is completely sound, and if we don't give her something to do, she'll be on us like the Wicked Witch of the West."

He tucked Rose's arm through his before anybody else could pounce with questions. "Do you have a few minutes to sit and talk?"

"Absolutely." Rose flashed him a confident smile as the staff dispersed to finish getting ready.

Theo pulled a chair out for her. Thank God for small mercies. At least it wasn't Monday. They'd get the rush from after-church services, but not the crush they got during the week from all the businesses nearby. For two hours, it was nonstop with both those eating in and those carrying out, and then by midafternoon there was no one. "Lincoln, do you want to sit in on this?"

Lincoln shook his head emphatically. "I'll see if Scottie needs me." Theo watched him scurry back to get to work, and a rush of gratitude filled him. Lincoln really was the best brother ever. Even when Theo wanted to strangle him.

Theo massaged his temple again to ease the brewing headache. That's what he got for his lack of sleep. And it wasn't Rose's fault his stress level was climbing up the back of his throat and threatening to explode through his skull.

"I talked with Jill this morning," Rose said as she took the seat. "She gave me a very concise rundown of how things usually go on a Sunday. It sounds as if we'll have a busy day."

Theo nodded, mentally going through his list, reorganizing the next few days. Tomorrow would be early too if he wanted to hit the markets and create the menu in time to get everything to Scottie.

Rose patted his hand. "I've been doing this kind of work for a while now. You want to keep this a welcoming, local highlight for the area."

Theo smiled briefly. "You've got it. To be honest, I don't know as much as I should about this aspect of the operation or the business side either. I know cooking and menu planning and how to run a kitchen. I won't be as much help to you as I should."

"We'll muddle through. You've got a strong team. I can tell this place has been run well." Rose glanced over as someone tugged on the front door even though they weren't due to open for another fifteen minutes. "I'll come find you when we hit a lull in the afternoon, but right now, I think it's time to get started."

"Okay." Theo rose, his stomach jumping, and he regretted eating the sandwich. "I'll have all your paperwork ready by then. The taxes, etc." He'd have to figure that out, which meant he had an excuse to call his sister. And that wouldn't be violating her rule on checking in.

Scottie glanced up as Theo came into the kitchen. He came forward, enveloping Theo in a quick one-armed hug. "How's Jill? Why aren't you hovering over her?"

"Because I want to escape dismemberment. I'm letting Craig take that bullet for me."

A devilish smirk crossed Scottie's face. "She might let you keep your balls."

"Might is not a word I ever want connected to my balls." Theo leaned against the counter and crossed his arms. "I came in to greet Rose and to see if I could make any sense out of Jill's paperwork. Jill's doing good. I think the doctor who ordered her on bed rest is in more danger than she is."

"That's a safe bet." Scottie looked around the well-ordered kitchen with satisfaction. "We're all ready to go on this end."

"I love you, man. I really do." Theo scrubbed a tired hand over his face. It was time for some serious coffee. He couldn't go into a shift like this.

"Yeah, back at ya," Scottie said with a nudge that carried with it years of having each other's backs.

"What's the special?"

"Stuffed rockfish, fresh green beans with a bite of orange and almonds, cauliflower-couscous confetti for the first option. Chicken cordon bleu for the second." Scottie rubbed his hands together. "I'm trying out this new potatoes au gratin recipe to go with that and a tangy kale."

"Damn that sounds good." Theo loved the summertime: there were so many options. Going to the market was like Christmas morning. "What about dessert?"

"Strawberry-rhubarb pie." Scottie's dark eyes gleamed. "We haven't had that in ages."

"Theo?" At the sound of Rose's voice, he glanced up. "You have a call. It's Jill."

"Thanks, I'll take it in the office." Theo glanced at Scottie. "And she accuses me of hovering. The day hasn't even gotten started."

"Shoo." Scottie snapped a clean hand towel at him. "And if you step foot in here to work before it's your shift, I'm telling sis on you. I'll make sure Skinny takes a couple breaks."

"Thanks, man." Theo clasped his hand, and they exchanged another hug and parted. Jill's office was as neat as Theo's kitchen, nothing like how their mom had kept it. The file cabinet was meticulously organized, the desk cleared off, and the only clutter was the array of family photos scattered on every surface. Theo sprawled in her swivel chair and picked up the phone. "How you feeling?"

"How's my restaurant?" Jill asked at the same time.

"You first." Theo propped his feet up on the desk, leaned back, and closed his eyes. "You've vetted Rose, so there's not much suspense there."

"True, but I want to know what you think," Jill fretted. "I wasn't expecting her to have to start like this."

"She's a pro and it shows. She was holding a meeting as I walked in. And Scottie's running the kitchen like he's done it for years." Theo leaned back farther and crossed his feet on her desk since she wasn't around to yell at him.

"No surprise there."

"I might have to fight him for her undying affection. He's smitten." Theo had seen it in Scottie's eyes as he looked at Rose.

"How are things going with Morris?"

"Uh-uh, that's for later." Theo rolled his eyes. Trust her to hijack the conversation. "So tell me, how are you feeling?"

"Fine, other than the kicking and the gas and utter boredom already." Frustration was thick in Jill's voice. "You've got to give me something to do, Theo. I'm going nuts."

"Well for starters, email me what I'm supposed to do for new hires, 'cause I haven't a damn clue. And I'll send you the books so you can do that from your laptop."

"Bless you. My body may want rest, but my mind does not." She sighed. "I was surprised to see Lincoln this morning."

"Mmm-hmm," Theo said, at a loss for anything else to say to her probing tone. "It did him good to see you." Theo left it at that because he really wanted Lincoln to discuss last night's blowup with her first. "Speaking of Lincoln, other than a natural teenage aversion to thinking of family members hooking up, has he said anything to you about me and Morris? I can't tell if he's embarrassed or if it's something else."

"Hmmm." This time it was Jill's turn to equivocate. "I'd say a little of both. He gets weird around Craig and me too. Mostly I think it's insecurity. Too much has happened this last year. But we can't let it stop us living. At some point, I was going to have kids. At some point, you were going to get another boyfriend. If we'd halted our lives, it might've sent the message to him he had to halt his too."

"I guess you're right." Theo tried to see it that way, but he couldn't help but wonder if Lincoln felt shunted out and isolated.

"The other half is probably teenage squick. Anybody who's an adult cannot possibly have sex on the brain." Jill laughed. "Oh, the horror. Remember how I used to squeal when Dad would chase Mom around the kitchen?"

A smile tugged at Theo's lips. "I think he did it sometimes to hear us protest as much as to kiss her." He closed his eyes. Soon he'd have to tell her about his second blowup with Dustin, but not today. "Damn, I miss them, Jill."

The sigh from Jill was heartfelt. "Me too, but I'm glad we have each other."

# Chapter Twenty-Two

"WHAT DO you think?" Gio Viteri lifted the picture from beneath the counter and tilted it for Morris to see. Morris had cut the pale yellow matte himself and picked out the driftwood frame after spending a couple hours going through most of Gio's stock. Behind the glass the colors of the picture shone with stunning vibrancy. The frame was solid, and there was a sturdy hook for hanging that would last for a long time.

Morris studied the finished picture of Laila's character and her butterflies with a sense of quiet pride. He'd nailed it here. Normally he'd be reluctant to let go of a picture he'd poured so much of himself into, but it would be in good hands with Theo. He appreciated the sentiment Morris wanted to evoke.

"Beautiful work as always, Gio," Morris said with a pleased grin and dug out his wallet. "Do you have any of that plain brown paper and bubble wrap I can use? I want to give it tonight."

"I'll take care of it for you. Who's this for? Your lively niece? A client?" Gio set the frame down on the counter and measured out a sizable piece of protective wrap.

"A… friend," Morris said, feeling a little self-conscious over Theo's declaration about their status. "He saw me drawing it and wanted it for his new place."

"A new man?"

"He was supposed to be a fling, a wild affair for the summer." Not that they actually got to see each other enough for that to happen, and it made the time they did have together more precious.

Gio's thick silvering brows rose. "I've known you many years, Morris. There have been a few men who came in and out of your life. But this is the first one you've spent so much time over getting the look just right. Is it the picture that's special or him?"

Morris squirmed a bit under that steady gaze. Gio had been able to see through his bullshit since high school. He had become like an uncle to Morris and listened to his professions of love and heartbreak over the years. He'd known Morris was gay before his parents had. He couldn't evade this one. "Both, though I wouldn't read too much into it. He's had a rough time of it in the last year. If this eases that in any way, then it's well worth the effort involved."

Gio looked unconvinced but didn't comment any more as he finished wrapping up the frame in layers of bubble wrap and thick paper. "How is Ms. Laila?"

"Good. I took her out to lunch before I came here, and she's coming to stay with me next weekend. I can't believe it's almost August." Morris shook his head. The summer had flown by and was half gone. "I would've brought her with me because she asks about you often, but I knew she'd be bored with my lingering."

Gio's seamed face wrinkled even more with a wide grin. "I look forward to seeing her again." He handed over the heavy bundle. "It's always a pleasure seeing what you've brought me. Take care."

"You too." Going back to Gio's took so much time when Morris was already behind. He'd been dithering over finding a new frame shop nearer to home for years now. It was more than not wanting to take a risk on an establishment he didn't know. Despite the drive, Gio was like family, and Morris would've felt like he was betraying him if he went elsewhere for a picture this important.

Morris tucked the frame carefully under his arm and gave Gio a two-fingered salute as another customer walked through the door. He couldn't decide whether he wanted to give Theo the gift in person, leave it as a surprise, or, even better, he could swing by the restaurant, borrow the keys from Lincoln, and have it hung up when Theo came home. Morris grinned as he wrapped the frame in the blanket in the trunk. That's exactly what he would do if Lincoln okayed it.

Traffic was the usual Sunday heavy and it took Morris over an hour to reach Solomon's Island. As Morris turned along the waterfront, he looked out at the boats bobbing on the waves and realized they'd never gotten another chance to take out the boat. He wouldn't have a weekend free again until Labor Day, and then he'd be at his parents' cookout if he didn't want to get disowned. No chance there. And there was no telling when Theo would have most of a day to himself again either.

When Morris walked into the restaurant, it was starting to pick up with the dinner crowd. He noted Rose at the window, talking with Theo and his new sous chef. Theo lifted his hand in a wave, a tired smile lighting his face. Rose turned and noticed him with a shake of her head. His sister must've been telling tales of misdeeds again. He was going to find a way to get her back.

Theo turned to his sous chef and said something before making his way toward the kitchen door. Dammit. He should've planned this better. Now he'd have to have a quick bite in order to explain his presence or Theo would get suspicious. With that thought his stomach rumbled. Well, at least this would be better than the contents of his freezer. Morris had blown his budget on lunch with Laila and the frame, but he could get some soup at least. That would tide him over until he had time to defrost something.

"Hey." Theo came up with his easy smile and lifted his face for a quick kiss. "You hungry?"

Morris's stomach grumbled again, louder this time, and he gave Theo an embarrassed smile. "Actually, I just swung by to say hey. I was running errands most of the day, so I have to get back. Deadlines, man."

"Wait right here and I'll pack you something."

"Make it simple," Morris said to Theo's retreating back. "Laila cleared me out at lunch. For a skinny little girl, she can eat."

Theo shot him a reproving look over his shoulder. "I was denied the chance to make you breakfast, so allow me. Rose, if he pulls out his wallet, wallop him with a menu upside the head."

"I don't condone violence," Rose said with an easy smile as she walked up to Morris. "However, Makayla tells me you keep a secret stash of Nerf guns to terrorize her. Is that true?"

"Makayla exaggerates. Besides, how terrorizing is a Nerf gun really? It's foam darts," Morris scoffed. Unlike the picture she had of him when they were five and all the sisters had ganged up on him to put a dress and makeup on him. That was terrorizing.

"Hmm." Rose didn't look convinced. "How is Makayla?"

"Causing trouble as always." Morris caught Lincoln's attention with a little wave. "Excuse me, Rose. I need to talk to Lincoln real quick." Theo was distracted right now, and he wouldn't get a better moment than this.

"Hey." Lincoln propped his empty tub on one hip as Morris walked up, his expression both wary and pleased. "I'm not going to get another lecture, am I?"

"I think you've had enough, don't you?" Morris asked, and Lincoln nodded vigorously. "Actually, since it's quiet, I wanted to talk to you about two things. First, I have a picture out in my car Theo wanted to hang in the living room. Do you think he'd be excited or freaked if I hung it for him as a surprise?"

"That picture he saw at the con?" At Morris's nod Lincoln looked down at his feet for a moment and then shot Morris a measuring look. "I guess that would depend on what you mean by it. He's had a lot of people not stick around on him this last year. That seems like a sticking around kind of gesture. So if you mean it, he'd love it. If not, then maybe you shouldn't."

That was an insightful observation and deserved an honest answer in return. Morris searched for it, especially in light of Theo's declaration that morning. "Whether or not we keep seeing each other, we'll still be friends. I wouldn't walk away from a friendship, and really that's what this gesture is, one of friendship, not something more."

"Friends…." Lincoln considered that, his expression too serious for fifteen years. "I think it would be okay, then. He talked about having it over the couch. He said it would be the first thing we see when we walk in the house. That would really surprise him when he comes home tonight."

Morris glanced over his shoulder to be sure Theo was nowhere in sight. "Would it be a problem if I borrowed the house keys? I can be in and out in no time. I have all the tools I need at my place."

"Sure." Lincoln dug in his pocket, angling his body so the motion wouldn't be seen, and handed Morris the keys. "What was the second thing you wanted?"

"So in two weeks I'm doing a show in Newport News on Saturday. The promoter, Brenden Wade, is always looking for volunteers to help behind the scenes. If you can get off, would you be interested in something like that?"

Lincoln's eyes widened. "Are you for real?"

"Yes," Morris said with a laugh. "If you think Theo can spare you."

"I'd love to." Lincoln bounced on his toes. "I get every other weekend off. I'm supposed to be off today, but you know, I kinda felt bad, so I told Theo I would help." He was so excited the words were practically tumbling over themselves. "But I'm already off that weekend if you're serious. I wouldn't have to find anyone to cover for me."

"I'm serious." Morris was pleased he'd thought of it. "I'll check with Theo and make sure it's okay I keep you overnight. We'd probably head up Friday night. It'll depend on when Brenden wants to start setup. I'll talk to him today. Just a warning, there are boring parts to this gig. And times when you've got to deal with some real divas. On the upside, you'll get fed and you'll get to meet people. Brenden usually has a few pop stars at his shows."

"And I'll get to be at a con," Lincoln blurted, his eyes shining. "It can't be any more boring than bussing tables."

Probably not, but guarding a door for hours to keep people from sneaking in got old. However, Morris knew Brenden well enough to know he'd switch things up. "Good point." Morris glanced over to see Theo approaching with a decent-sized bag. He dropped the house keys in his pocket. "Okay, if Theo asks what we were discussing, this was it."

"Got it." Lincoln turned to one of the dirty tables and began bussing it with quick, efficient movements.

"You didn't have to do this," Morris said as he took the heavy bag. He peeked inside and sniffed speculatively. "What is it? Smells good."

"Spanakopita manicotti and roasted corn chowder. The market was good to Scottie today. There's an extra portion of both for you to freeze half."

Spanakopita, Morris had heard that before; it was some kind of spinach dish. Morris wasn't a big fan of anything green, at least not as a main dish, but Theo was offering and he was too hungry to argue. "Thank you. Sorry to grab and run."

"I get it, deadlines." Theo blew him a kiss. "Good luck, man."

"Will I see you after work? Movie at your place?"

Theo grimaced. "We'll see. I'm done in. I'm afraid I'd fall asleep in the first five minutes and you'd be offended."

That sounded like a sure bet—well, the falling asleep part. "I promise to not be offended." He just wanted to see Theo's face when he first glimpsed the picture hanging up. He caught Theo's hand and gave it a squeeze. "I'll see you tonight, even if it's only for five minutes."

Morris waved to Rose and Lincoln and then pulled out his phone as he headed toward the car. He put the phone on speaker and called Brenden before he headed down the road. "Hey, just the man I wanted to reach," Brenden said as a hello.

"What do you want?" Morris ran through his last few contacts with the promoter, wondering if he'd forgotten something he was supposed to do.

"Do I always want something?" Brenden asked with mock innocence.

"You're not one to call and chitchat," Morris pointed out. Brenden may be a friend, but he wasn't the kind of guy to hang around and shoot the shit. They hit each other up on social media, but that was the extent of it. "So if you wanted to reach me, you want something. Or I forgot to pay you."

"I am sadly misunderstood, but in this case you are right," Brenden said. "I do want something."

Morris headed out of town, stealing glances at the sun on the river as he drove. He loved living so near the water. He knew his family didn't get his love for the quieter pace, or his desire to live away from them, but it was the perfect work environment with no one able to drop in on him without warning, and the views were stunning. "Don't feel too bad. I called because I want something too," Morris confessed.

"What is it?" Brenden asked, his voice curious.

"I was wondering if Theo's brother could volunteer for you at the show in Newport News. He's almost sixteen."

"Theo? Your boyfriend?"

Morris sighed. It was easier to go along with it than to explain the complications. "Yeah. He's a good kid, loves the scene, works hard."

"Hey, if you vouch for him, that's cool. We can always use hands. Bring him to the loading dock and I'll put him to work. On time, Morris, we'll need hands from the start," Brenden said in a sterner voice. "We'll open the dock at eight."

Morris groaned inwardly. Eight, dammit, and Brenden would hold him to that. "We'll be there." At least he'd have plenty of time to get his table set up instead of scrambling at the last minute.

"Are you driving down the night before? We can catch dinner together, and you can introduce me to your young friend. Dakota will probably be there too."

"Yeah, probably, if I can get permission from his brother because, damn, I keep forgetting how long of a drive it is." It would be faster by boat than going all the way out to the highway to come all the way back in to the coast. "How come they haven't invented teleporters yet?"

"I'm not sure I'd entirely trust teleporters to humanity," Brenden said in a dry voice. "So, about the con in Annapolis, I want to revamp my

Chessie logo, and I was wondering if you could help me design it. I want to get a few of my closest friends in on the promo and program so I can showcase their work. Would you be interested?"

"Are you for real, man? That would be awesome." Especially if the con was going to be as big as Brenden wanted it to be. If it was done right, and they built a strong buzz, it could be a break for them all. Morris was leery of big cons. Independent artists had a hard time making back the money they put in, but he trusted Brenden's instincts.

"Yeah, for real. I don't screw around when it comes to business. You know me better than that."

Morris mentally went over his list of things he wanted to accomplish before the next show. He had the piece he had to finish for one of the prize giveaways. He really needed to think about new material for prints, but that would have to wait until he had his next books ready to go. He wasn't working on any commissions or card decks at the moment, so that gave him a little wiggle room.

"Okay, I'll have some concepts to show when we meet up in Newport News. Thanks, man."

"My pleasure, Morris."

# Chapter Twenty-Three

ONE OF these nights Theo wasn't going to trudge up to the door feeling like he'd been pummeled. He tucked the to-go containers under his arm as he searched for the right key one-handed. The lights in the living room were on, a welcome sight that told Theo his brother was right where he should be. Lincoln had caught a ride when his shift ended instead of hanging around in the dining room or waterfront like Theo had as a teenager. He didn't know what Lincoln planned to do without video games, probably hole up in his room with a slew of graphic novels.

Tomorrow was market day, which meant an early start. Theo's spirits dimmed at that. Sleeping in sounded like heaven right now. However, it also meant he could pick out all the specials, and that was awesome. It was a task Theo never tired of. Once he dragged himself out of bed and had some coffee, he'd enjoy the shopping trip.

As Theo pulled out his keys, he contemplated texting Morris and asking if they could hang tomorrow night instead. He wouldn't make it half an hour in front of the TV. In fact, face-planting on the couch seemed like a wonderful idea. But he really did want to see him, if only for a few minutes.

He opened the door and stopped in confusion. Morris sat on the couch, a drawing pad in his lap, a pencil in his hand. He lifted his head and smiled slowly at Theo. Lincoln sat next to him with a stack of comic books by his side. The sight hit Theo with a breathless punch of welcome home. He'd missed that sense so much.

"Hey, I—" Theo stopped, his eyes widening. Over the couch, perfectly lined up in a place of honor, was the picture Theo had coveted from the moment he saw it. The joy on the little girl's face as she reached toward the butterflies once again touched Theo's heart. "Oh my God, it's perfect."

Theo dropped the containers and keys on the small table by the door and bounded over, his exhaustion forgotten as he stepped on the couch between Morris and Lincoln to look at the picture more closely.

He ran gentle hands over the subtle browns and grays of the frame, the light pastel yellow of the matte that highlighted the bolder colors within the picture itself.

"You didn't have to frame it for me." Theo shot Morris a brilliant smile and crouched down to kiss him soundly on his upturned lips. "But thank you for doing it. I wouldn't have been able to make it so beautiful."

"Uh, no kissing when I'm right here." Lincoln got up, comic books tucked under his arm. "Gross. You're as bad as Jill and Craig."

Theo jumped down from the couch and caught Lincoln in a bear hug. "I know you were in on this." He pulled Lincoln's head down and gave him a gentle noogie. "You're the best."

Lincoln shoved him away, a pleased smile crossing his lips. "Maybe I abetted a bit." He nudged Theo's side. "It does look good, doesn't it?"

"Yeah, it does." Theo took another look at the picture, the sense of welcome and home stronger than before. He sat down next to Morris, his exhaustion momentarily gone under a warming glow. "So what else have you two hooligans been up to other than planning surprises?"

Morris shifted his sketchbook and slid his arm around Theo's shoulders. "I admit to nothing but work."

"I called Jill," Lincoln said, sitting down on the arm of the couch.

Theo snuggled into the comfort of Morris's half embrace. "Really? How'd that go?"

Lincoln shrugged. "We're cool. She's not mad, though I think you were right. If I hadn't told her and she found out, she'd be mad at us all."

"Yeah." Theo lightly punched his arm. "Thanks for your help at the restaurant today. I always know things will get straightened up when you're around without me having to oversee it. It was something I didn't need to worry about today. How was it working with Rose?"

"I like her," Lincoln said seriously. "Nothing fazes her, not even when Erin tried pulling her diva stunt and slacking off. You know how she tries to get away with everything."

"Yeah, Jill and I figured she'd try to take advantage and push back." She was good at her job when she wanted to do it; when she didn't, it was one complaint after another. "What did Rose do?"

"I'm not sure," Lincoln admitted. "I saw them talking a couple times, and she sent Erin in the back to cool down after she tried honing in on Kate's table, but Rose never lost her temper, and by the time I left, Erin wasn't complaining to her anymore."

"Fair enough." Privately, Theo thought they should've let Erin go a while back, but that was Jill's decision, not his. She understood the dynamics of the front better than he did. "Thanks again, Lincoln."

"No problem." Lincoln stood back up, comic books in hand. "Hey, Theo, would it be a problem if I went with Morris to a convention in Newport News the weekend after next?"

Theo frowned and glanced at Morris. "I guess I don't see why not if you won't be a bother. You're off that weekend. Is it both days?"

"Just Saturday, but we'd have to leave Friday if we didn't want to head out at 5:00 a.m." Morris shook his head. "Please tell me it's okay if we head out the night before. I'm getting too old for that crack of dawn shit."

Theo hesitated. He didn't want Morris to feel like he had to keep an eye on Lincoln. Before he could voice that concern, Lincoln spoke up again. "Morris said they always need volunteers to help out with all kinds of things. He said Brenden would be happy to have my help."

It was the undisguised eagerness in Lincoln's eyes that sold him. He couldn't ask his brother to give his life to the restaurant the way he and Jill had. The way their other brother and sister no doubt felt pressured to do. Maybe that's why they stayed away. They wanted their own lives away from Solomon's Island without having to fear being sucked into the family business. Theo and Jill probably would've done it too. They had been so frantic to keep things together, to keep strings on them all, they'd inadvertently cut them instead. It gave Theo something to think about and hope that maybe they could glue their family back together again. There had to be more to it than Dustin and Robin blaming him for Mom and Dad's death.

"I know you'll bust your ass, Linc. That's not a concern." Theo turned to Morris. "Are you sure you want to get saddled with Skinny? Sometimes when he starts talking, he never shuts up." Theo shot a teasing glance in Lincoln's direction.

"Try riding in a car with Felipe for a couple hours," Morris said dryly. "Seriously, it's okay. I'd like the company and somebody to boss around."

"I'm really good at being bossed around," Lincoln said with an earnest look in his eyes.

Theo stifled a laugh. "This is awesome of you, Morris."

Morris pointed at Lincoln. "You might decide this is not as cool as it seems."

"I'm sure I won't." Lincoln headed to his room with a wave. "Night, guys."

Theo waited until Lincoln's door was shut and turned to Morris. "Newport News, huh?"

"I hope I didn't step on any toes by asking him first."

Morris looked so solemn that Theo was struck with a moment of mischievousness. He frowned and looked down at his feet as he toed off his shoes and socks. "They feel trampled. I might need a splint or two."

"What—" Morris shot him a startled look.

"My pinkie toe is especially abused." Theo held up his foot so Morris could have a better view. "See?"

Morris shook his head and grabbed Theo's ankle. "You're terrible. I can't ever tell when you're teasing me or not. You look so damned innocent."

"That should be your first clue." Theo kissed his cheek. "Seriously, if you're good with it, it's okay. I don't want you to feel you have to entertain Lincoln when I'm not home."

"That's not it at all," Morris assured him. "He's a good kid, and he's one of us."

A geek. Something that, try as he might, Theo did not understand the devotion or hype. He enjoyed the movies and games Lincoln introduced to him, but he didn't seek them out. Then again, if he had his way, the only thing that would ever be on his TV would be cooking and home improvement shows. Not everyone's cup of tea.

"So what's with all the containers?" Morris asked, thrusting his chin toward the imbalanced stack on the table.

"Leftovers." Theo rose and sorted through them, leaving half more neatly arrayed on the table. "Let me go stick this in the freezer. The rest is yours."

"You don't have to keep feeding me," Morris called into the kitchen.

"We ran out of the stuffed rockfish, but there were a couple of the chicken cordon bleus left and the remains of the soup." Theo smiled and wondered if he'd catch Morris already peeking into the containers before he got back into the living room. "Better to share than to toss. I hate throwing away perfectly good food."

He glanced around the corner and sure enough, there was Morris. He didn't understand why he always put up a complaint. He liked the food. He smiled as Morris set them down and tossed him a guilty look. "It's not going to bite you from the freezer, I promise."

"The manicotti was good. I have to admit, I had my reservations about a meatless meal." Morris shook his finger at him. "You're always trying to change my mind about food."

"No, I'm trying to give you a better appreciation for food just as you're trying to give me a better appreciation for pop culture. Expanding our horizons is good for us, right? Because I don't know about you, but I can get stuck in my little rut of a world."

"Well, when you talk like that…." Morris came toward him and drew Theo closer. "You up to me introducing you to the Winchesters?"

"Winchesters? More friends of yours?" Theo fought a yawn. Damn he was tired, but he was also reluctant to say good night. "Not tonight, I think."

"No, it's a show." Morris chuckled and drew him toward the couch. "Since you were talking about expanding your pop culture knowledge. An episode is shorter than a movie."

"Good point." Theo stretched out on the couch and laid his head against Morris's shoulder. As tired as he was, he was tense all over. A show would help him unwind so he wouldn't be spending the night tossing and turning. He reached for the remote and handed it to Morris. "I have all the usual streaming services. If you can find your show, put it on."

Morris set the sketchbook down on the small coffee table, and Theo glanced curiously at the open pages. Half a dozen quick sketches of a swimming dinosaur covered the sheet. "Are your little sleuth and her cat chasing a brontosaurus now?"

Morris sighed and picked up the book, eyeing it with a critical look. "No, Brenden wants me to come up with a logo for his new con in Annapolis. I've been messing with this all evening and been unable to come up with anything that appeals to me."

"What does a dino have to do with comic books?" Theo looked over his shoulder. The sketches ranged from comic to sinister. There was one with the Bay Bridge behind it that caught his eye.

"It's not a dino, it's Chessie." Morris lifted a brow at Theo's blank look. "You've lived and worked near the Chesapeake Bay your entire life and you've never heard of Chessie?"

"Um…." Theo racked his brain, searching for anything that would make it seem more familiar, but it eluded him. "Is it a geek thing?"

Morris shook his head, his expression mournful. "No, a local legend, man. Our own version of the Loch Ness monster out in the bay. Her name is Chessie. Brenden named his con after her since most of his shows take place in the tidal bay area."

"That is a new one on me." A Loch Ness monster in the bay. He wondered if people chased after those rumors the way they did the Sasquatch or the goat man.

"You've really never heard of it?" Morris raised a brow, searching Theo's face to see if he was teasing.

"Is she edible?" Theo chuckled at Morris's incredulous expression. "If it doesn't fall into one of my loves, then it generally passes right over my radar. Besides, the whole idea is a little ridiculous, isn't it? I mean, the Loch Ness monster doesn't really exist."

"Sometimes ridiculous can be fun." Morris pointed the remote at the TV and flipped on the streaming service. "Let's see, your loves would be your restaurant and food in general."

"Good food," Theo corrected. "I have standards."

"Hmm, true. I can't deny that." Morris tapped the remote against his jaw. "What else, basketball?"

Theo nodded. "Especially college. See how well you know me?"

"Not as well as I'd like, I'm afraid." Morris ran his fingers through Theo's hair, and Theo dismissed the idea of watching anything. "You might have to tutor me. I'm drawing a blank on anything else. I promise, I make a very good student when the right teacher captures my attention."

Theo grinned and straddled Morris, the remote tumbling onto the floor. "You can't forget local artists and their work. I really love to get my hands on that."

"Oh yeah," Morris said, a little breathless as Theo nuzzled his lips with his own. "There is that. Silly me."

"Why don't you come on up Friday night and I'll give you a proper thank-you." Theo nibbled on Morris's lower lip, anticipation building at the thought of being alone with him all night long in his bed. "Lincoln is staying at a friend's. We'll have the whole place to ourselves after I get home."

Morris pulled back with a disappointed look. "I can't. My niece is spending the night. I usually get her at least once before the school year starts, and it has been so crazy between our schedules, I've been putting it off. All my other weekends are filled with shows up until the Labor Day party at my parents'. I usually stay the whole weekend."

Dammit. Theo frowned. He'd been looking forward to some alone time with Morris. Hell, just time with him period. "That's okay."

"I'll take her by the restaurant for dinner," Morris promised. "I'd love for you to meet her."

The pride in Morris's eyes softened Theo's irritation. He knew how much Morris loved his niece, and he didn't get to see her as often as he wanted. "I'd really like that, especially since she's going to be on my wall."

Morris slid his hands down Theo's spine. "Speaking of alone time, how about you and me the night after that?"

"Maybe." Theo was still trying to figure out how to balance his relationship with Morris and Lincoln's expectations of what to anticipate at home. Thinking of it was headache inducing, and Theo realized Lincoln might be embarrassed if he came out and saw them on the couch like this. Ugh, being an adult sucked.

He wanted something more concrete than a half-formed idea they'd get together. He'd find himself looking forward to it until something else came up that one of them had to take care of. Theo wasn't holding his breath. As much as he loved hanging out with Morris, trying to find time when they were both free was an exercise in frustration.

"Any chance you could get one of the days off over Labor Day?" Morris suggested. "You and Lincoln should come with me to my parents' house. You'd love one of my mom and dad's cookouts. There's food everywhere. My dad has a magic grill."

Theo's plummeting spirits lifted. "You want me to meet your parents?" That was a good sign.

An embarrassed look crossed Morris's face, and then he shrugged. "The whole family actually, my sisters will be there, and their families."

Theo was determined to go. He wasn't sure how he'd finagle it. He sat back, his thoughts racing. The bistro tended to be very quiet on Labor Day, and finding people willing to work was always a headache. Most of their Monday day sales came from the office workers who would be off for the holiday too. So many people took advantage of the last long weekend of the summer to bar-b-que and party that no one was looking for a sit-down meal in a restaurant. Not even one with a view of the water.

He should close the restaurant for a day and give everyone the time off. They could offer sides and desserts to sell to pick up the day before, the same way they did for Thanksgiving and Christmas. In fact, they could expand a bit, do it for Memorial Day and Fourth of July as well. They never did enough business to really justify staying open, and everyone was grumpy about it. It would give everyone a guaranteed day off without having to jockey for who would get it and who wouldn't. He was almost positive Jill would agree with him on every point.

"You're a genius," Theo said, giving Morris a sound kiss on the lips.

"I am?" The mystified expression on Morris's face was fucking cute. "What did I do?"

Theo had to steal another kiss. "You definitely are, and if this all works out, I'll tell you all about it."

# Chapter Twenty-Four

"SO WHERE are we going?" Laila asked, her nose practically pressed to the car window as they headed down the waterfront with the boardwalk on one side and a neat row of restaurants and businesses on the other.

"It's a surprise." Morris flipped the car around, searching for a parking spot. He didn't know why he should be nervous at the idea of Theo and Laila meeting. What if they didn't like each other? He couldn't think of one reason why they wouldn't, but there it was. He could handle it if his parents or sisters took a bit to warm up to him, though he didn't picture that happening, but not Laila. Maybe he should've told Theo how important this was. Yeah, like that wasn't pressure.

He'd been dodging this whole idea of a relationship, especially since Theo's offhand comment in his kitchen last weekend. But he had to be honest. This had gone far beyond a fling if he was running out to get portraits framed to put a smile on Theo's face. The fact he was this knotted up over Theo and Laila meeting was another clue to smack him upside the head. He really wanted this to work out, and it scared him.

"We always get pizza with extra pepperoni and sausage." Laila looked over her shoulder at Morris. "Do you have a new favorite place?"

"Yep, for a special lady." Aha, Morris turned on his blinker as a spot opened up.

"Is it your boyfriend's place?" Laila's voice was all sweet innocence as Morris braked in the middle of parking. He turned to look at her only to find her watching him with all too curious bright eyes.

"Who is talking to you about me and boyfriends?" Morris demanded.

"No one. I overheard Aunt Makayla and Mom talking." Laila shrugged as if it were no big deal. Behind them a car honked, and Morris muttered a few choice words under his breath as he turned his concentration back to maneuvering into the space. "They're trying to get Aunt Makayla's friend to give them some dirt, but she's not playing along."

God bless Rose. Morris made a mental note to thank her. He was having a hard enough time figuring out how he felt about Theo without his sisters complicating matters.

"Okay." Morris shut off the car and turned to Laila. "This is just between you and me. Solemnly swear?"

Laila grinned and held up her pinkie finger. "I swear I'm up to no good."

"That's my girl." Morris linked pinkies with her. "Yes, we're dating, but I have to have my best gal meet him before anyone else in the family. Who's my best gal?"

"Me!" Laila glowed, and then her brows came together in concern. "You know Mom's going to find out we came here. She's gonna ask me questions."

"True…." Morris considered the problem. "How do you feel about a little prank? A harmless one."

Laila nodded eagerly. "I love pranks."

Didn't Morris know it. She was a girl after his own heart. "Okay, here's what you do. When they start bugging you, you tell them I made you promise not to tell."

Laila's eyes widened. "But that will make them bug me more."

"I know." Morris smirked. "Hold out for a bit and then tell them he's turning me into a vegan."

Laila's eyes grew wide. "What's a vegan?" she whispered.

"Someone who only eats vegetables." Morris nodded at Laila's horrified expression. "Yeah, a nightmare, huh? Then tell them we're talking about forming a hippie commune in Montana where we'll raise alpacas and smoke w—" Morris cut himself off before finishing that one and hoped Laila didn't catch on.

"What's a hippie commune?" Laila asked. "And are alpacas the drama llamas?"

"Yes. The weird-looking animals with the long hair." Morris drummed his fingers on the steering wheel as he tried to figure out how to explain hippies to his niece. "You know the crazy white people who wear tie-dye shirts, have long hair, and believe in love, peace, and the power of a hug?"

Laila nodded solemnly. "That's a hippie? Then what's a commune?"

"Where they all live together and share everything. Now the key points are moving to Montana with alpacas. Got it? Oh and don't forget the vegan."

"They'll never believe me," Laila said, though her eyes danced with mischief.

"They will if you dole it out in little bits." Morris thought about it a minute. "Actually, your mom will probably get wise to it fast. But your Aunt Makayla will eat it all up." That was who he really wanted to get. He had to make sure he warned Theo to go along. There was no telling what Makayla would pass on to Rose.

"It might work better if you just eat veggies tonight," Laila suggested, all innocence. "Then if Aunt Makayla asks her friend, she'd be able to confirm you gave up meat."

Morris thought of the mouthwatering array of food Theo offered. That didn't even include the daily specials. There was bound to be red meat in there somewhere. "There's such a thing as taking a prank too far, Laila," Morris said loftily as he opened the door. "You have to learn the difference."

Laila's laughter followed him out as Morris popped open the trunk and unfolded her wheelchair. He made sure the wheels were locked and then let her be as Laila maneuvered herself into place. They'd all learned that though they wanted to hover, Laila was more than capable and much happier if they let her have her independence. He had no doubt one day she was going to be able to arm wrestle him into submission, because baby girl had gotten to be strong with all that swimming.

"Where are we going?" Laila asked, wheeling her chair around as she eyed the row of restaurants.

"See the one on the end with the blue-striped awning?" Morris pointed to the bistro alive with lights. "We have a table waiting for us on the deck. Theo promised to make it special."

As always on a Friday night, the bistro was hopping. Rose spied them as soon as they rolled through the door. "Morris and Miss Laila." She came forward, holding out her hands. "It's good to see you again."

Laila grinned, lifting her arms to hug as Rose stopped by her chair. Rose had been a frequent visitor to Makayla's house, so Laila knew her better than Morris did. "Uncle Morris said we could sit out on the deck."

"Your uncle is right. We have your table waiting for you." Rose tucked two menus under her arm. "Come right this way. It's a beautiful night to be outside. Theo is very excited to have you here tonight. He told me to make sure everything was perfect."

As they made their way through the restaurant, Morris noticed Theo's sister and her husband sitting in one of the booths near the front, talking with a steady stream of employees and guests as they ate. He lifted his hand in a wave as they went by. Jill looked good. The lines of exhaustion and worry had eased away, and she gave him a brilliant smile as she waved back.

The warm late-summer breeze and humidity flowed over them as they emerged on the deck. A table by the railing with a spectacular view of the creek was waiting for them with a bouquet of sunflowers in a pitcher adding a bright splash of sunshine. Morris plucked the card hidden among the blossoms.

*For Laila, because you make the sun shine for your uncle. Enjoy. Theo.*

Morris's heart pitter-pattered. It had never done that before. And with this one little gesture, Theo had him acting like a schoolgirl. "These are for you," he said to Laila, handing over the card. "May they be the only flowers you receive from a boy for the next decade."

Happiness shone in Laila's eyes, and a grin split her face as she read the card. Rose swatted him with the menus. "Ignore your uncle, Miss Laila. Receiving flowers from a boy, any boy, is one of life's simple pleasures."

Laila's grin widened. "Am I really your sunshine?"

"That you are," Morris said as Rose shifted one of the chairs aside so Laila had room to maneuver at her spot. "Thank you so much, Rose." Morris waited until Laila had settled herself before taking a seat.

"Our pleasure. I'll let Theo know you're here, and he'll be out when he gets a chance." Rose patted Morris's shoulder and handed Laila a little packet of crayons. "May I get you anything to drink while you wait for your server?"

"Can I have a soda, Uncle Morris?" Laila gave him a look of hopeful appeal.

"Totally. This is our night on the town. Let's go wild." Morris glanced up at Rose's laughing eyes. "Two root beers please, and if you see Lincoln, let him know we're here too."

"I think he's getting ready to clock out and sit with Jill until his friends get here." Rose glanced into the main dining room. "I'll let him know."

"Who's Lincoln?" Laila asked as Rose walked away.

"Theo's brother. He likes comic books too."

"Does he like my comic book?" Once Laila started in on her questions, they never stopped.

"I haven't asked." Morris knew Theo had bought a copy of the first book, but he didn't know what he thought of it, or even if he actually read it. That was depressing. Of course, Morris could've gotten some balls and asked him. And it went both ways. How often had Morris asked about Theo's job, unless there was an emergency? Or about the menu planning Theo got so excited about. The only time Morris asked about specials was when he was coming out to eat.

Morris frowned. That kind of a disconnect was okay for a fling, but they ought to do better if they were going to be dating. He'd warmed up to the idea of having a boyfriend.

"What are you going to draw?" Laila asked, handing him a crayon. "I'm going to draw Cassie."

"Of course you are. You two are like twins. I can't catch either one of you." Morris considered the blank brown paper in front of him and the green crayon in his hand. "How about the Green Lantern?"

"Nope, you always do him. Draw something funny, Uncle Morris." Laila bent over her paper and drew the blocky outline of a fat cat with spindly legs.

They were lingering over dessert by the time it calmed down long enough for Theo to emerge. Morris's heart gave a funny little leap when he saw him. God help him, Theo was turning him into a moody teenage girl who couldn't decide if she was ecstatic or depressed.

"Hey there." He rubbed his hand over Morris's shoulder in a warm welcome and grabbed a chair as he smiled engagingly at Laila. "You must be Miss Laila."

Laila beamed up at him as Theo sat down between them. "That's me. Thank you for the flowers."

"Pleased to meet you, and I'm glad you liked them." Theo took her hand and gallantly kissed her fingertips. "I'm Theo. Are you keeping your uncle on his toes?"

"He'd be too tall if I did that," Laila said with the pure candor of a child.

"Good point, I'd get a permanent crick in my neck then." Theo reached over and took Morris's hand, idly rubbing his thumb over the back of his knuckles. He leaned over, studying the artwork on the table half-buried under empty plates. "Okay, help me out there. Both are critters, I think." Theo tapped his finger against Laila's. "Cat?"

"Yep, it's Cassie. Do you like it?" Laila grabbed her crayon and added in a word balloon with "meow" in it.

"I do." Theo studied it some more. "But I think you forgot her horns."

"That's what Uncle Morris said." Laila cocked her head, then drew two spikes between her triangle ears.

Theo turned to Morris's and his brows arched. "Now, I'm at a loss for that green monster. Is it your new Chessie?"

Laila started giggling. "It's an alpaca with dreads."

"Really?" Theo looked at the picture again and shook his head with a smile. "Now I see it. So Morris tells me you like basketball."

Laila's eyes lit up. "I love it!"

Morris realized he shouldn't have worried one moment about the two of them meeting. Both Theo and Laila had the same teasing nature, and both dearly loved to be outside getting sweaty.

"Did you see the basketball hoop outside your uncle's house?" Theo asked, and Laila nodded eagerly. "What do you say tomorrow morning we have a scrimmage, me and you against my brother and your uncle?"

"Hey, wait a minute," Morris cut in with a laugh, "that's hardly fair unless Lincoln has some skills I don't know about."

"We can be the awesome shorties against the tall geeks." Theo smirked at Morris. "We will trounce you."

"Yes!" Laila pumped her fist.

"I have no doubt." Morris saw Lincoln and waved him over. "Please tell me you're a match for your brother in basketball."

Lincoln snorted. "Not likely. I mean, I can play, mostly because he makes me when he's bored, but I can't play like he can. Now our other brother, Dustin, plays for Georgetown. That's who you want."

Morris's heart gave a little twist in empathy. He wouldn't tease Theo about his Hoya T-shirts now. It was sad his brother was so close and yet still didn't come home. Maybe that's how his family felt about him sometimes. Like Morris was never there. He'd have to do better.

Theo had leaned over and was whispering something in Laila's ear, and she laughed as she shot Morris a wicked glance. "You realize they are conspiring to embarrass us," Morris said to Lincoln. It was really gratifying to see Theo and Laila hitting it off.

"Wear a kilt," Lincoln said with a shrug, "and go shirtless. He'll be too distracted to play at his best."

Theo turned toward him, his mouth dropping open. "I am shocked. Shocked, Lincoln, you would suggest such underhanded tactics."

Lincoln blushed but met Theo's gaze. "It would work."

"Laila, this is Lincoln, Theo's brother." Morris pointed toward the table inside, where Theo's sister was still entertaining. "See that lady with the brown wispy hair in a braid? That's his sister Jill. She owns the place too. How's she feeling? I thought she was stuck at home."

"She's allowed to move around, just not do any physical labor. She was driving Craig nuts, so he figured getting to hang out and see the place for a bit will relax her." Theo turned to Laila. "Some people always have to be moving about. I bet you're like that. Morris also tells me you beat him at swimming."

"I like swimming. But Uncle Morris swims good too." Laila pushed her empty dessert plate away. "Do you cook all the food by yourself? There's lots of people here."

"No, I have a team of awesome people to help me, but I did personally cook everything for this table." He squeezed Morris's hand in an affectionate gesture. "I have to make sure this guy stays fed. Did you like it?"

"I loved it." Then Laila shot him a guilty look. "Except for the vegetables."

"Did you try them?" Theo asked, and she nodded. "That's all I ask for. To be honest, and don't tell anyone, but I don't like carrots, not raw, not roasted, not any way."

"That might make it hard to live on your farm in Montana," Laila said with an impish smile at Morris.

"What's this?" Theo gave him a puzzled look.

"Never mind." Morris leaned forward and shook a quelling finger at Laila. "Troublemaker."

"I can definitely see how you based your character off of her," Theo said with a laugh. "You always have an answer, don't you, Laila?"

"You read the book?" Morris asked, immediately feeling bad for his thoughts earlier. Theo could've said something before now. "You never mentioned it before."

Theo looked down in embarrassment. "I'd forgotten I bought it, but after you hung the picture up for me, I remembered. I was curious, so I pulled it out. It's really good. I need the next compilation." He winked at Laila. "Then I'll know what you and his cat have been up to."

A warm glow filled Morris. He knew many of his colleagues whose significant others never read their work, and except for his mom, he was used to his family looking at it like it was more of a hobby than a job, so it meant something to him that Theo had taken the time to read it. "What do you think?" he couldn't stop himself from asking. "Other than liking it, I mean."

"I like the theme, the idea that obstacles can be overcome." He grinned at Laila. "I like someone's optimism. The mysteries are smart, not dumbed down, which to me gives credit to kids' intelligence. Lincoln was far smarter than me at a younger age. Still is."

"I knew you drew comics. I didn't know you write them too. That's cool," Lincoln cut in. "I like writing and drawing, but I'd really rather design video games."

"What do you want to do, Laila?" Theo asked. "You thinking of being a private detective?"

"Nope. That's boring. There's a lot of sitting around waiting and watching." Laila shook her head. "I wouldn't be good at that."

"Tell me about it." Morris tapped her nose and she giggled. "You can't keep a good woman down."

"For real," Theo said fervently. "God knows you can't get Jill to stop. So what do you want to do?"

"I'm not sure. I'm not grown up yet." Laila frowned thoughtfully. "I think I want to do sports. Maybe something with swimming. I really love swimming."

"Hey, Theo."

Morris glanced over at the waitress standing at the entrance to the deck. Theo shot her a warning frown. "Jesse needs you and Lincoln in the kitchen. It's an emergency."

"Thanks, Erin," Theo said, his frown deepening. He waved to Lincoln to sit back down. "You're off the clock now. It's probably just them getting busy again. We can handle it."

Morris caught his hand and kissed the back of it. "Don't work too hard."

Theo chuckled, a smile coming back to his face. "It was a pleasure meeting you, Laila. Tomorrow morning, you and me, okay?"

"Jill says you shouldn't be sitting down and hanging out with your boyfriend on a busy night," Erin announced from the doorway in a prim voice.

Theo's mouth hardened into a thin line, and his eyes flashed. Morris had only ever seen him angry once and quite frankly, he really didn't want to see it again. All traces of the affable, easygoing man he knew disappeared.

"Uh-oh," Lincoln said under his breath.

Theo stalked toward the door as Erin took one look at his face and wisely disappeared. Morris exchanged glances with Lincoln. "He's not going to make a scene, is he?" He remembered all too well how Theo called out Lincoln in front of all the party guests.

Lincoln shook his head. "She got out of his line of fire, and he'll want to check in on the kitchen. If she stays out of his way for the rest of the night, he'll probably leave it in Rose's hands."

"Is it because he's gay?" Southern Maryland was more open-minded than other rural parts of the state. But there was usually someone who couldn't help saying something because they disapproved.

Lincoln shook his head again. "No, she's upset by the new dynamic with Jill gone, and she blames Theo for it. Anytime something changes, she starts acting like a passive-aggressive twit. She thinks she should've been made manager with Jill out, and she sometimes forgets Theo is half-owner and tries to treat him like one of the staff."

"Is somebody in trouble?" Laila asked.

"Not you and not me," Morris assured her. "And that's all we need to worry about."

"And definitely not me this time." Lincoln got up and waved to Laila. "I'm going to go sit with Jill in case Erin tries to mitigate the damage by talking to her. Erin is not a fan of Rose." Lincoln rolled his eyes. "And Theo doesn't want Jill worrying about staff drama right now."

Morris hadn't had much of a chance to talk to Jill, but from everything he'd heard from Theo and Lincoln, he thought Theo might want to stop trying to shield Jill from work matters. She might make him eat his spleen.

Morris laid his elbow on the table and propped his chin on his fist as he eyed his niece. "So, what did you think about Theo and Lincoln?"

"They like you," Laila announced. "And I like anybody who likes you."

# Chapter Twenty-Five

THEO WOKE up suddenly out of a sound sleep and reached for the empty side of his bed. The image of Morris nuzzling at his ear and whispering erotic words lingered in his thoughts. He opened his eyes as his groping hand found only the pillow. His dream had been wrong. Morris wasn't beside him.

*Well fuck, that's disappointing.* Grumpily, he rolled over and eyed his clock. It was too fucking early to rise, and his brain was evil. He really wanted Morris in his bed and not downstairs in another apartment. Theo punched his pillow into more a more comfortable lump and started to close his eyes again.

There was a reason why he'd been thinking of Morris. Or maybe it was the bistro. Was it his day to go to the market?

Theo opened bleary eyes. He wouldn't get any more sleep until he figured it out. Then his gaze fell on the basketball and he woke up entirely. He had a game to play. With a grin Theo threw back the sheet and tugged on a pair of mostly clean shorts. He sniffed his underarm as he headed toward the bathroom. Okay, a quick cleanup was in order. No sense in knocking Laila out of her chair.

As he got out of the shower, he felt more awake. He paused in the hallway at the sound of someone in the kitchen and grabbed a tighter hold of his towel. "Lincoln, is that you?"

"Yeah," his brother called back.

"You're home early." Theo had expected him to show up at work and not before then. "Did you have fun?"

Lincoln poked his head into the hallway, half a croissant shoved in his mouth. He held up a thumb. Theo glanced at his watch. Okay, he definitely had not expected his brother to be up before 10:00 a.m. Much less home from his friend's house.

When he returned to the kitchen, dressed, with his basketball tucked under his arm, Lincoln already had coffee brewing and another croissant stuffed with ham and cheese waiting on a plate for Theo. Theo lifted a brow as he grabbed a mug. "What do you want?"

"Who says I want anything?"

Theo almost laughed at the insulted look on Lincoln's face, but he tossed Lincoln the basketball instead and poured himself a cup of coffee. "I was a teenager once too," he said, holding up the sandwich. "I recognize bribery when I see it. Does it have anything to do with why you're home early?"

"Maybe." Lincoln idly passed the ball from hand to hand as he eyed Theo. "I was wondering if I could get my video games back today." He tried to keep his voice level, as if it were no big deal, but Theo heard that hopeful note anyway.

Theo pulled out his phone and texted Morris as he considered it. *You ready for the can of whoop ass Laila and I are going to bring?*

"What's going on today?" he asked Lincoln, though he'd already made up his mind. Lincoln had been busting his ass at the bistro, and he hadn't complained or tried to wheedle his way out of his grounding once. He knew his brother well enough to recognize Lincoln wouldn't have snuck online anyway when Theo was at work. He couldn't say he would've shown the same restraint as a teenager. Besides, he had said a week.

"So a bunch of us talked last night about maybe hooking up online today and playing some *Star Trek*." Lincoln shot Theo a hopeful look. "They need an extra ship to take on the Borg Invasion."

"So you mean to tell me, you left hanging out with your friends in person so you can hang out with them online?" Theo asked and took a sip of his coffee. He was head over heels in love with a geek who was perfectly comfortable spending days on end alone. He had a brother who was a geek, but there were times when Theo didn't understand them.

He paused, pressing a fist to his heart as his thoughts registered with a skip in his pulse. Damn, he really was in love with Morris.

"What's wrong with that?" Lincoln bristled.

Everything, in Theo's mind, but to each his own. "How's this? You help Morris in his match against me and Laila, and I'll let you have your video games back again right after the game."

Lincoln's eyes widened. "For realsies?"

Theo laughed as his phone pinged. "For realsies. I actually have a few hours I can spend with you and Morris outside of work. You can spare some of that time out of a chair in front of a screen."

He glanced at his phone as it dinged. *I cry foul. You and Laila against me is not fair.*

"You don't really expect to play for hours, do you?" Lincoln asked with an alarmed look.

Theo laughed and finished his coffee. "No, best two out of three. You can't leave Morris hanging. He's already crying over it not being fair, and we haven't even started yet."

*Big baby*, Theo texted back.

"Okay, but I want to make one thing clear—I'm doing this for Morris, and video games, not out of any desire to make a dunk on you." Lincoln grabbed the ball and held it high out of Theo's reach.

"Big words, brother mine, big words." Theo checked his phone as it dinged again. *You realize Laila is already waiting outside?*

"Come on. Morris and Laila are waiting on us."

"Wait, before we go...." Lincoln paused, his expression worried. "Laila's in a wheelchair. What if I hurt her or trip over her or something? Won't it be hard to play against her?"

"I get the impression from Morris she's tougher than both of us. It's a friendly game of basketball. You block, pass, dribble, and shoot. You don't have to tackle her. Your and Morris's advantage is your size, and you're going to need that advantage. She's been playing on a team all summer."

"Well, if you're sure." Lincoln started to turn away, his arms lowering as he stopped paying attention. Then Theo rushed forward and snatched his basketball out of Lincoln's hands.

"Hey!" Lincoln raced after him out the door. "No stealing until the game starts."

Theo dribbled the ball down the long, sloping hill to the driveway, angling his body to keep Lincoln away from it. Laila was wheeling in circles on the blacktop with a happy grin on her face. "Hey, Theo," she called, waving her hand. "Hey, Lincoln."

"Hey there, sunshine. Catch." Theo lightly tossed her the ball. He paused beside her chair and glanced up at the portable hoop. "How high is the hoop you practice on at camp?"

"It's not as high as that one." Laila eyeballed the hoop and lined up a shot that fell short. "The older kids have one like that."

"Let's bring it down a bit, then." Theo reached for the handle to adjust the height and cranked it. "Morris and Lincoln could use the extra help. The only way Lincoln will land a shot is by dunking it."

"I heard that." Theo glanced over at Morris as he came around the corner, tying his hair back. Theo stifled a groan. Morris had followed Lincoln's suggestion, and Theo got a sweet eyeful of Morris's broad naked chest and sexy legs. "It's not our fault you two are shrimps," Morris said with a grin as he stretched.

Theo shook his head at the tactic. Morris was deliberately using his sexiness, and Theo couldn't even call him out on it in front of his niece.

"Yeah, you lost out on the tall gene." Lincoln reached up on his toes and touched the rim of the hoop.

"That's because you stop growing when you reach perfection. Obviously, it's taking you longer than it took me," Theo said with a superior sniff as he cranked the hoop down a few inches and eyeballed it.

"It took Uncle Morris forever," Laila said with an impish grin, and he shook a mock fist at her.

"You save that sass for your Aunt Makayla, girl."

Theo cranked the hoop down a bit more as Laila watched intently. "How's that?"

She rolled over and scooped up the ball. Theo watched how she maneuvered her chair and dribbled. The driveway had been repaved a couple years ago and there were no dips or cracks to throw her off, and she moved with the ease of long practice. She paused in front of the hoop and took aim. She made a face as it bounced off the rim. "I could've gotten that. Watch this."

Laila zipped after Lincoln as he went for the ball. He turned with it in his hands and let out a shout of surprise as she closed in on him. He stumbled back, launching the ball toward her, and she caught it neatly and spun her chair back around.

Morris shook his head at Lincoln as she headed back toward the basket. "She played you. She was trying to intimidate you and you fell for it."

"Believe me, I was intimidated," Lincoln said with a rueful expression. "She came after me like a rabid Jawa."

This time Laila sank the shot and lifted her arms in victory. "See, I said I could get it."

Theo high-fived her with a grin. "That was beautifully done."

"Thanks." Laila looked at Morris and Lincoln. "First to get to ten points wins? Best two games out of three?"

Morris shot Lincoln a questioning look and he nodded. "I think we can hang with that."

"Flip a coin to see who starts with the ball?" Lincoln suggested.

"We could do that. Anybody have a coin?" Morris asked. "I don't have any pockets."

"I didn't know skirts were standard basketball sportswear." Theo eyed Morris's knees again. He knew Morris wasn't showing any more leg in the kilt than he did in a pair of shorts, but damn, the sight always made him hot and bothered, and the man knew it. He flaunted those kilts.

"It gives me freedom of movement," Morris said loftily.

*Freedom of movement my ass.* However, Theo appreciated the strategy even if it was against him. And if Laila and Lincoln weren't around to witness it, Theo would make Morris understand the consequences of using sex as a distraction. Theo dug into his pocket and tossed a quarter to Lincoln. "Why don't you call it, Laila?"

"Tails!" Laila called as the quarter sailed up. Lincoln caught it deftly and slapped it down on the back of his hand to reveal heads.

"It's okay," Theo said as he passed the ball to Morris. "They need the head start anyway."

"You're going to eat those words, Boarman," Morris said, dribbling the ball. He feinted as Theo closed in on him to cover and then passed the ball to Lincoln. Lincoln tried to dodge around Laila, but every way he turned, she was on him. He passed it back to Morris. That was one thing Laila and Theo would have to strategize around. Their reach was incredible.

At first Lincoln was tentative around Laila, afraid to get too close, but when she kept outmaneuvering him and stealing the ball right out of his hands, he lost his uneasiness and got in the game. Morris had no qualms about being all over Theo. Every damned time he turned around, Theo was confronted by his very sexy naked chest.

The morning air turned steamy as the sun rose higher, bringing out the worst Southern Maryland had to offer. The air was liquid in their lungs, and Theo's shirt clung to his sweaty back until he stripped it off.

Morris was relentless in his attempts to block Theo's shots, and when he finally managed to dodge around him to sink a shot, it felt like the good old worry-free days when he used to go to the park to line up a game.

Laila seemed to be the only one completely unbothered by the heat, and she had to be working twice as hard. Theo was reminded how out of shape he was. Working in the kitchen kept him on his feet but did shit for cardio. Lincoln collapsed into a spindly heap as Morris scored the winning shot for their team, ten to their nine. "Can't we call it the best one out of one and y'all admit defeat?"

Theo exchanged a look with Laila, who shook her head. "We were going easy on you, lulling you into a false sense of security," he said, trying to catch his breath.

Morris snorted and retrieved his water bottle as a pained look crossed Lincoln's face. "How can you take it out here? It's worse than the dish station this morning, and I hate the dish station."

Theo wiped a hand across his brow and caught the fresh bottle Morris tossed him. "I'll admit, I'm a little out of shape for this heat. But it's fun."

"At camp we're outside half the day every day," Laila said with a shrug and sipped her own water. "I like it."

Theo finished his water, retrieved the ball, and tossed it to Laila. "Okay, let's do this." He helped Lincoln to his feet. "No more nice guys. Tear 'em up, Laila."

She grinned, her eyes lighting up with wicked delight, and Lincoln groaned. "I give. I'm a roasted tamale out here."

"Dude, you can't leave me hanging," Morris said as he nudged Lincoln's side. "Finish your water and let's nail them two times in a row. That'll shut them up."

Lincoln perked up. "Yeah, if we beat them, there won't be a third game and I can whoop some Borg butt online."

"What's a Borg butt?" Laila asked as she rolled and dribbled to the far end of the driveway.

"If you have a little time later, I'll show you," Lincoln said as he moved to intercept her.

Theo caught the pass, cursed under his breath at Morris's crazy long reach, and ducked under and around him to break away. This time he accommodated for the different height of the hoop and the ball sailed in on the first go. "One to nil." He pointed at Lincoln. "Better do more than that if you want to get online fast."

He tossed the ball to Morris, then went for a rush before he could pass it off to Lincoln. Laila nipped it out of the air with a war whoop and made for the basket with Lincoln hot after her. The ball dropped through with a heavy swish. "Booya, two to zip."

Morris glanced at Lincoln. "Did we get hustled last game?"

"Totally," Theo replied with a wink at Laila. He handed the ball off to his brother as his phone rang with Scottie's ringtone. He paused, glancing back at his phone. What if— Lincoln took advantage of his momentary distraction and passed the ball off to Morris, who rushed the hoop. "Hey!"

Even as Theo moved to block, Morris closed in and dunked the ball. He turned to Theo with a smirk. "Not nil any longer. Ever vigilant, my friend."

"Sorry about that," Theo said as he passed the ball to Laila. He should've shut his sound off. The phone dinged with a message notification and once again his eyes strayed toward it. No, if it was important, Scottie would call back. It made him twitchy to ignore a call from his go-to man, even if it was only for a short time. He tried telling himself Scottie was calling from his cell, not the bistro line, so maybe it was personal.

Laila passed the ball to him, and Theo rolled around Morris to pass it back. She zipped around Lincoln and they exchanged another couple of passes, keeping Lincoln and Morris spinning before she sank the shot.

"Those two move unnaturally fast," Morris muttered to Lincoln. "Is tripping illegal?"

"I think it's justified." Lincoln swiped the back of his arm over his sweaty face. "You distract Theo, and I'll tie his laces together."

Laila tossed the ball to Lincoln as Theo's phone rang again. He tensed at the sound of Scottie's tone. "Three to one, guys," Laila said. "We're going to beat you this time."

Theo jogged over and snatched up his phone, then frowned when he saw Scottie had texted too. He must not have heard that during the excitement of the game. "Hey." He lifted a finger to the others to let them know he'd be a moment. "What's going on?"

"I have Erin in your office," Scottie said in a flat voice Theo knew all too well. One that said Scottie was fed up. As if Erin's name wasn't a red flag already. Dammit, Theo should've talked to Jill about her last night. He was still irritated with the tone she'd used with him and the little games she'd played once Jill wasn't around to witness them. "She wants to talk to you now face-to-face."

"Now?" Theo asked with a longing look toward the trio watching him.

"Right now, for real, bro."

Theo bit back a swear and leaned over to scoop up the T-shirt he'd discarded earlier. "On a Scottie scale, how difficult is she being?"

"Not worth the trouble, boss man. She has a demand. It's basically her or Rose." Scottie sounded thoroughly disgusted. "Do you want me to take care of it?"

Tempting, it was so very tempting, but Theo knew Jill would want one of them to have the final word on an employee. Theo rubbed his temple at the headache brewing. He hated firing people, but he would if she pushed it. "Okay, on my way, but don't tell her that. Give her this option. Either she can get back to her shift and talk with me this afternoon or she can clock out and I'll meet with her earlier."

"You know which one she'll choose, but you've got it."

Yeah, Theo suspected she'd choose to try to force him to come in earlier. He'd hear her out, but if she didn't have a damn good reason for not wanting to work with the new manager, then she was out of there. He was done with the drama and games.

He turned and saw all three of them looking at him with disappointed expressions, even Lincoln. The disappointment twisted. He'd been having fun too. He really wanted to finish the game. It wouldn't hurt Erin to stew a bit. Then Theo sighed and shook his head. Responsibility was a motherfucker, and he still had to shower again and drive in.

"I'm sorry," Theo said, slinging his shirt over his shoulder.

"Yeah," Morris replied, his eyes unreadable, his tone impersonal. "See ya around."

# Chapter Twenty-Six

THE KNOCK on his door cut through Morris's concentration as he painstakingly inked his pencils, adding shade and dimension. The new brushes and inkwells were a pain to get the hang of, but once he had, he liked the end result. He sat back, studying the picture. Yes, this Wonder Woman was really going to be a hit for one of the prize giveaways. If he wasn't so pressed for time, he'd keep her for himself and start on a new project.

*Keep your damn eye on the job. You have enough of your artwork littering your apartment.*

The knock came again as Morris dipped his brush in the ink. *Go away. Please, go the fuck away.* With that thought in mind, he bent back over his table. Maybe whoever it was would get the hint. This was a do-or-die day, and he'd already shut off his phone to keep from being distracted.

"Hey, Morris, you home, man?" Theo's voice called from the kitchen.

Morris let out an explosive breath. "Morris is dead and stuffed in his closet. If you don't want the same dire end, back out now and lock the door behind you." Then reality filtered through the haze of his work. Morris glanced at his watch. "Wait a minute. What the hell are you doing home?"

He hadn't seen Theo since he bailed on them from the game last weekend. Which wasn't entirely fair. It wasn't like Theo had run off to hang out with someone else. But Morris didn't see how they were going to get beyond a fling if they didn't actually ever see each other. Talk about long-distance relationships. Theo might as well live several states away instead of just upstairs. And it sucked to get jilted when Theo had set up the game in the first place. Morris banked down his irritation over that before he worked himself up. He was already on edge with these multiple deadlines.

"I went in early and did the prep for Scottie so he could take care of some things. He's going to do the same for me this afternoon, so I have a few hours to myself." Theo came into the living room and paused by the art table. "Oh wow, that's sweet. She looks like she's about to kick some serious ass."

"It's what she does." Morris leaned closer, inking in the delicate lines of her lasso. He was still debating whether he wanted to leave it as a black-and-white picture or add color. He really needed to make a decision like yesterday. Normally he decided it before he started inking. He'd been thinking of adding color even if it was just a splash, but damn, he really liked the look of his inks. It was stark and edgy and added to the overall emotion of the piece.

"Huh, what? I'm sorry." Morris tore his gaze away from the page in front of him. Theo had been saying something.

A look of exasperation crossed Theo's face, and Morris stiffened. He was sick and tired of that look from his family, and he sure as hell got enough of it from the last dipshit he'd dated. He didn't need it from Bailing Theo Boarman too. What the hell kind of a reaction did they expect when he was in the middle of freaking working? It wasn't like he was tuning out people all the time.

"I was thinking since I had a couple hours off we could go catch a movie." A little hopeful smile crossed Theo's lips. It wasn't fair that one man could be so damned appealing and adorable. And right now, that was irritating too.

"Can't, gotta work." Morris bent back over his page, trying to figure out where he was going from here. He couldn't fuck this up now. It was going too well. "Deadlines."

"We could go see that new movie you insist you need to see because of work," Theo wheedled. "That new superheroes one."

Morris looked up with a frown, trying to analyze Theo's tone. "It is for work. Seriously, I've got a show coming up. Everybody's going to ask me if I've seen it and what my opinion is. I can't say it's been out for two weeks and I haven't gone." Though there was no way in hell he'd be able to get it in before he left for Newport News. Not unless a miracle happened.

"I understand, but I still call bullshit. You'd want to see it anyway even if you weren't doing comic books. Seriously, I don't have a problem with it. It's not the first time I've gone to the movies and saw something I normally wouldn't have."

If Theo said one more patronizing thing, Morris might lose his cool, and he didn't want to be like that. Damn, his ex said stupid shit like that and then made Morris feel guilty on top of it.

"Don't do me any favors." Morris's expression must've shown his frustration because Theo hastened to reassure him.

"Hey, relax." Theo rubbed his shoulder. "Just because I wouldn't have initially picked it doesn't mean I wouldn't enjoy it. Trust me. I'm laid-back when it comes to entertainment."

Morris hesitated. He really did need to see the movie and he really did want to be with Theo even if he was irritated with him. Dammit, the man was hooking him, and Morris still wasn't sure if he wanted to be hooked.

Theo sensed his weakening and pounced. "Come on, you're leaving for that out-of-town convention tomorrow night. You won't be back till late Saturday, and you're always exhausted after a show. This is a chance for us to be together."

*Until someone calls from the restaurant and Theo leaves again or Lincoln throws another foot-stomping scene or asks to tag along.*

At that unwelcome thought, Morris looked away to his drawing table again. The pressure of deadlines loomed over him and if he thought about it too much, it would scatter his concentration. He had to focus on one project at a time. First, he had to finish the Wonder Woman piece. Then he needed to finalize the conception work he was doing for Brenden. He still wasn't entirely satisfied with that. Then he still had to prepare himself for the show. That meant going through his inventory and preparing new pieces to sell, packing, and organizing.

"Sorry, man, maybe Sunday night if they have a late show." Morris picked up his brush again.

"You know they don't," Theo said, his voice tinged with the same frustration Morris felt. He rubbed both Morris's shoulders now, working out the tension and drawing his focus away from cleaning the brush. "You're going to permanently twist yourself into a knot bent over like that. Come on. Get away for a few hours."

Morris pressed his lips together. Theo owned his own business. He should understand being your own boss meant more work, not less. Morris could procrastinate with the best of them, but he also knew when it was time to buckle down.

Morris set his brush aside with a sigh and glanced up at Theo, who looked at him with an endearingly hopeful expression that both tempted and aggravated. He shouldn't feel guilty because he didn't have time right now to drop everything, yet guilty was how he felt. The same guilt he experienced every time his sisters called, making him feel bad for being busy. He hated it.

Setting his own hours didn't mean he could drop everything any time someone wanted something from him. Being a comic book artist didn't mean he sat on his ass all day long watching TV and being unproductive. "This isn't a hobby for me," Morris said, frowning at Theo as he gestured toward his table.

"I didn't say it was." Theo took a step back, his mouth thinning in an unpleasant line. "I just thought you might want to spend some time together. I haven't seen you in days."

That twisted too. Morris missed Theo. It seemed lately one or the other of them was always coming or going. It wasn't conducive to a relationship, which was probably one of the reasons why his relationships always bombed. He should cut his losses now if Theo couldn't understand. He was as bad about getting bent out of shape over Theo getting called away. This was doomed from the start.

"Can we talk about this later?" Morris asked, swiveling his chair back toward the table and picking up the brush again. "I can't right now. I have to focus." He dipped the brush in the ink and bent back over his work.

"You're going to shut me out?" The stunned incredulity in Theo's voice made Morris's stomach knot. He hated confrontations and arguments. It made him want to hide away. It was one thing to mediate between others, that he could handle; a situation like this twisted him up.

He paused, searching for a response as the brush hovered over the page. A small drop dripped down onto the paper. "Goddammit," he muttered, tossing the brush in his cup of water.

"You know what, never fucking mind."

"Theo." Morris pushed back from his table as Theo stalked out of the room, but he was at a loss for what to say. He couldn't skive off work because Theo was having a temper tantrum, and he didn't see how talking about it any more would change the situation. He told Theo he had deadlines. He'd mentioned before how it bothered him that his family saw his work as a hobby, conveniently pushed aside for their wants. Then the chance to say anything was gone as he heard the kitchen door shut.

Cassie lifted her head up from where she was napping in the sun and gave Morris a baleful stare. "What?" Morris lifted his hands as he glared at her too. "It's not my fault. Go back to sleep, you moocher."

She left her sunbeam, rubbed her face against his ankle, then leaped up onto her cat tree, where she curled up in a ball and went promptly back to sleep with her back to him. "Great, now my cat's pissed at me too," Morris muttered.

Morris rubbed a hand over his face with a sigh and turned back to fix his Wonder Woman. He'd deal with Theo later. Besides the deadline, he needed time to calm down and get his thoughts together or it would be another fight.

He stared down at the page without seeing it, the sound of Theo's voice replaying in his mind. He should go talk to him, or least send an apology text. But how could he word it so Theo wouldn't turn right back around to attempt to drag him away? Maybe if he waited until Theo was at work.

Morris rose and flipped on the TV, scrolling through his movie options. He put on *Big Trouble in Little China*. That was entertaining background noise and a movie he'd seen so often it wouldn't pull away his attention from his work, but it would keep him from feeling lonely. When it was over, he'd text Theo.

When Morris finally finished the last of what he wanted to get done, his hand trembled and throbbed, his eyes stung with strain, and his back ached with the knots Theo had promised would end up in his muscles, but all of his projects were done. He carefully tucked away the images of Chessie, then found sleeves for the dozen new trading cards he'd sketched, inked, and colored. It was always good to have new material on the table, the quick trading cards as well as the books.

He shook his hand as he rose and stretched up on his toes, and for a moment the room spun. Morris leaned against the wall as his stomach growled and he realized how thirsty he was too. How long had it been since he'd eaten or had anything to drink? In the background, the TV droned on with the next late-night movie option.

He made his way into the kitchen and grabbed a bottle of water, downing the entire thing in one go. Then he pulled out a box of crackers and a can of spray cheese and munched as he considered his mostly empty fridge. He really needed to hit the grocery store on Sunday. This was pathetic.

Morris opened his freezer, looking for something to pop in his microwave, and frowned. He hadn't realized how much food Theo had given him over the months. Instead of processed potpies, there were homemade empanadas. No more crappy but fast burritos, instead there were neatly labeled single-portion casseroles and soups. It was amoral.

Somehow, despite the plan that this was just a fling, they were beginning to blend their lives together. Morris even had his second-favorite sketch pad upstairs tucked against Theo's couch. Scowling, he dug through the freezer until he found a frozen pizza. Maybe it wouldn't taste as good as one of Theo's creations, but it was the principle of the matter.

Morris ate a few more crackers and cheese while the pizza baked, pondering the problem of Theo. Cassie came into the kitchen, pausing to stretch each hind leg before coming over to Morris. He scooped her up. "Why'd you let Daddy sit all day and not eat?"

She gave him her special patented look that said quite plainly he was an idiot. "Yeah, I know. I must've remembered to feed you, though, or you never would've let me alone." He glanced at her food and water dishes and noted they were half-full. As long as no part of the bottom of the bowl was visible beneath the kibble, Cassie was happy. But let one glint of silver show, and she was convinced Morris was starving her.

She accepted his nuzzling attention for a whole three minutes before wiggling to be let down. Morris crouched down with a sigh. "Fine, walk out on me. That's been happening a lot today."

He glanced at the ceiling. He couldn't remember hearing anyone move around up there, but then again, he'd been in the zone. Lincoln could've broken out his sax and Morris never would've known.

Restless, he looked in the freezer again. The cheese and crackers weren't cutting it. He could heat up some of Theo's tomato basil soup; that would be done before the pizza. He hesitated and then grabbed the carton. He was too hungry to be picky over principles. It was soup, not a life decision.

By the time he finished eating the soup, his stomach was happier and the pizza was steaming on the stovetop. Gooey cheese, pepperoni, sausage, and extra-thick crust. Maybe not as good as a fresh one from

Ledo's, but it would do. As Morris cut it, he couldn't help but wonder what kind of a homemade pizza Theo would make. He bet it would be awesome, whatever it was, probably have eggplant on it and it would still be good.

Morris leaned against the counter and bit into his first slice. The roof of his mouth was instantly scalded and Morris dropped the slice, swearing as he reached for a paper towel to spit into.

"Fuck, fuck, fuck." Somehow, the pizza on the floor seemed like a perfect metaphor for the day.

His hand ached, his brain was short-circuiting, and he was not in a good place. Grumbling, Morris picked up the slice and tossed it into the trash, then wiped up the mess he'd made. He glared at the rest of the pizza, his appetite for junk food gone. He wanted something home-cooked and comforting. Despite getting his work done, his day had sucked. He'd been stressed and upset, replaying his argument with Theo every time he paused to think.

He missed Theo. Maybe it wasn't too late to go upstairs and say hi. And maybe apologize. He wasn't entirely sure why he was apologizing, because there was no way he could've gone off with Theo for the afternoon, but maybe he could've handled it better.

Morris glanced at his watch. 4:00 a.m. Yeah, definitely too late. Fuck.

He eyeballed the rest of the pizza and sighed, going back into his freezer. He was being an idiot for no reason. His stomach knew what it really wanted. Not long after, he was sitting down to hot spanakopita manicotti, yeast rolls, and a tall glass of sweet tea.

He was willingly eating spinach in the wee hours of the morning. If that didn't say something for Theo's influence over him, Morris didn't know what did. But damn, it tasted good. Maybe a little change in his life wasn't such a bad thing.

As he ate he considered the problem of Theo. First off, he had to admit this had gone far beyond a fling. He had to stop mentally dodging that. Even if they didn't get to see each other as much as they wanted, feelings were invested, and that was part of the problem. His feelings had been hurt when Theo left the game. And instead of being an adult about it and talking to Theo, he'd sulked like a toddler.

Or maybe he'd sulked because he knew there really wasn't much Theo could do about it. It was his job, and being a baby about it would solve nothing. Morris also had to accept Theo and Lincoln were a package deal. This was totally new territory for him. Morris wasn't used to sharing his significant-other time with a dependent. Even if Lincoln was cool in his own right. He got it, but logic didn't mean a damn thing to emotions.

Theo accused Morris of tuning him out. He hadn't meant to, but Theo wasn't listening, and Morris hated an argument and getting upset. He just hated it. And he didn't have time for an argument then. Morris didn't go into Theo's restaurant and start shit about wanting time together while Theo was in the middle of dinner service. So why should he accept Theo coming to his work and doing it?

He dropped his head in his hands as he realized he was getting agitated again. He'd been playing it safe, keeping Theo at a distance, all because he was afraid of a repeat of his last relationship. And the entire time, Theo had been working his magic on him, getting Morris invested.

Morris closed his eyes against the ache in his heart. He'd fallen for the fool. Now he had to decide what the hell he wanted to do about that. He had to approach him in a way that wouldn't start another confrontation. He had to marshal all his arguments so his emotions wouldn't get in the way and stop his tongue. He had all the words running in his head, but he had to express them because Theo couldn't read his damn mind. Maybe then, together, they could figure this relationship out.

# Chapter Twenty-Seven

THEO TOSSED the ball toward the basket and cussed as it went wildly awry. He was totally off his game today. Basketball wasn't soothing him like it normally did. Theo trotted after the ball, scooped it, and threw it a little too hard. It careened off the rim and bounced off toward the trees. Theo glared after it, his hand on his hip. This day was already setting itself up for epic suckage. On top of a whole week of suckage, from having to tell Erin it was time to go, to his argument with Morris. All it would take now to make his week complete would be for Lincoln to have a teenage meltdown.

Theo stalked toward the ball. Fuck it. He was going inside. It was too hot, sticky, and lonely outside by himself. He was only frustrating himself, and the tiny hope Morris would hear him and choose to come out to be sociable died. He could annoy Lincoln while he packed instead.

"Your concentration is all off this morning."

Theo spun around at the sound of Morris's voice, bristling from the distant tone. "Yeah, what of it?"

Morris leaned against the side of the house, his dreads caught up in a messy topknot that was too appealing. He wore the same black cargo kilt Theo had first seen him in and a tight tee with a Captain America symbol on it. Theo had never realized how sexy geek could be until he met Morris. And the look of hurt that crossed Morris's face slapped Theo up short.

Theo pressed his lips together. Yep, he was an asshole. He'd been hoping Morris would come out, and the first thing he did was snap at him. Just fucking great. "Sorry." He scraped a hand through his hair and scooped up the ball. "I'm cranky."

Morris sighed, held out his hands for it, and Theo tossed it to him. This showed a willingness to stay and talk, the least he could do was hear him out.

Morris idly passed the ball back and forth in his hands, his brow lined. "I knew I should've come out to talk to you right away instead of holding off. But I did text you I was sorry."

Like hell he had. Theo had checked his phone several times throughout the day, and there hadn't been one peep from the overgrown jerk. "No you didn't," he said in a flat tone.

Morris frowned and tucked the ball under his arm. He pulled out his phone, and then his expression fell. "I meant to," he said in a plaintive voice. "It was on my to-do list."

"I am not a to-do list." Now he wasn't just irked, he was offended. If Morris really felt that a relationship was a damned checklist, then he had a lot to learn. Even as Theo's ego took the blow, he deflated. Morris had been saying from the start this was a fling. Theo should've listened.

"Of course you're not. That came out wrong." Morris dribbled the ball, his brows beetled together in a fierce frown. "Question for you. Say I came into your kitchen and told you to leave off the herbs you sprinkle over a plate or the goop you put on in a fancy pattern? What would you do?"

Goop? Theo glared at him. "That is not goop. It's all a part of the presentation, both for the eye and the palate."

"Exactly." Morris jabbed a finger in his direction. "Exactly. The finishing details are important, and running off with a job half-finished isn't what you do. I was in the zone, man, and up to my eyeballs in work that had to be done."

Morris sure as hell had a roundabout way of getting to his point. Theo knew what Morris was trying to say, his guilty conscience had bugged him enough, but he wasn't in the mood to have Morris rub his face in it. "I didn't say they weren't. I'm saying I swear Lincoln sees you more than I do."

"That goes both ways, Theo. The other day, with the game, it could've waited another half an hour while we finished, and I'm not just saying that because Laila was disappointed. You were too, and to be honest, so were Lincoln and I. Whether you fired the employee that morning or when you got in, it wouldn't have made much of a difference. Taking a short break for yourself isn't a bad thing. And I think that was part of my issue yesterday. I was still irritated over that when you came in, and I took it out on you instead of talking about it."

Theo wasn't sure if that was an apology or not. "It's not as easy as that. I can't ignore multiple calls from Scottie."

"I didn't say ignore the calls. And I don't think Scottie would've begrudged you half an hour."

It was clear Morris had given this a lot of thought, and his words made sense, but Theo wasn't sure he was entirely ready to let go of his mad. The problem was, any argument he played, Morris could turn right back around on him about yesterday. It was fucking aggravating. Theo pressed his lips together again, trying not to glare at Morris like a grumpy cat.

"I didn't come out here to argue about it again." Morris tossed the ball in the direction of the garage as he walked toward Theo. "I hate arguing. I came to apologize for my attitude yesterday. I overcommitted myself and I was frustrated and tense on top of my irritation. I should've stopped long enough to at least look at you when you took the time to see me."

Well, hell, how was he supposed to remain in a bad mood when Morris had such a sincere look in his eyes and looked sexily delectable to boot? And he'd apologized first, which he really didn't have to do.

Morris paused in front of him, searching Theo's face. "My defenses go into overload when I feel like someone's treating my job like it's a hobby. I should've given you the benefit of the doubt."

Theo had not been treating it like a hobby. But as soon as the protest leaped into his mind, he forced himself to reevaluate it. Sometimes it was easy to overlook Morris's job because he didn't have an office and because comic book artist seemed so cool. Theo tried to approach it from Morris's perspective. If Theo had been home, testing out a new recipe for a big dinner or for a new special at the bistro, and Morris came in midprep begging him to go out and not letting it go, he would've gotten pissed too.

If Morris could apologize, then Theo could too. It had been thoughtless, and he could see why Morris would think he didn't take Morris's job seriously.

"Yeah, well, I'm also sorry. If you'd come into my kitchen when I was slammed and tried to guilt trip me into taking off for a few hours, I would've gone off too." Theo reached up to cup Morris's face. "I guess you react to guilt trips about the same way I do. At least I'm not the only one who can be surly and snappy."

"I have my moments, not many, but I do have them." Morris turned his head and kissed Theo's palm. "Does this mean we're good now?"

Theo stroked his fingers along Morris's cheek and then let his hand fall. "Yeah. I guess it means we have some baggage to work through."

Especially if they went any further with this relationship, and Theo really wanted them to go further. He had fallen so hard for Morris there ought to be an imprint of his body in the ground. He could really see himself spending the rest of his life with him. It was a little scary how fast his feelings were moving.

"We have baggage? Both of us?" Morris's eyebrows came together. "What's my baggage?"

"I think someone did a number on you in the past. Whoever it was who made you feel like you have to apologize for who you are or suspect someone's always looking to change you." Theo didn't want to change Morris in the slightest. He wanted the chance to be with him, spend time with him.

Morris looked surprised. "I do that?"

"Sometimes. Most of the time you come off as crazy confident in what you're doing and content with who you are, but when you get defensive about it, you don't take any prisoners." A fact Theo would have to remember not to take personally, and maybe given time, Morris would relax the knee-jerk reaction.

"Yeah, there was somebody, and believe me, I dropped him fast once I figured out his angle. I think it's less him and more everyone else, my family especially," Morris said with a thoughtful look. "I guess I get really tired of having to convince people I'm happy with my life the way it is. I don't need an intervention or saving or whatever."

He was happy with the status quo, which meant Morris wasn't looking for any long-term engagements. Theo's heart sank. A point he had made more than once, and Theo hadn't wanted to listen. Theo shouldn't have allowed his heart to get this far into it. 'Cause the thought of Morris walking away now seriously hurt. "Yeah, I think I've gotten that picture," he said in a soft voice, his shoulders slumping.

"Except, I'm forced to admit recent changes to my freezer were very welcome in the wee hours of the morning last night," Morris said with a laugh. "So I guess not all change is bad."

"Yeah?" Theo straightened with a smile, damn his eternal hope. He had to get Morris to see they were perfect for each other.

"You had me eating spinach and soup instead of frozen pizza. I was a bit annoyed about it until I realized how ridiculous that was. It's actually nice that you think of me that much." Morris shook his head, and then his expression turned serious. "And speaking of baggage, I think yours is abandonment, being shut out and ignored."

It made him sound like a frightened kid, but there were times over the last year when he'd felt exactly like that. When Morris had turned away, completely tuning him out to concentrate on his work, it had slashed deeply in a way he couldn't control. He had to find a way to deal with his siblings' silence and shunning, for his own sake as well as Jill and Lincoln, but he didn't know where to start.

"Yeah, I guess so." Theo looked away, and Morris sighed, sliding his arms around him. Theo laid his head against Morris's chest. Couldn't the man see how they fit together, just clicked? Even when they were both being jerks Theo still wanted to be with him, and apparently Morris felt the same or he wouldn't be here.

"So we managed to hit every single one of each other's sore buttons yesterday, didn't we?" Morris said, setting his cheek on top of Theo's head.

"Seems like it." Theo tightened his arms around Morris. "So I say we've got our quota of arguing in for the year. Let's not do this again for a long time."

"Works for me." Morris held him a little longer until the sticky heat of the morning forced them to part. "Look, we have to decide if we're really going to make a go at this or not," Morris said, his gaze calm and steady.

"Of course we're making a go at this." The little spurt of anxiety Theo felt made his voice higher than he wanted. Great, now he sounded pathetically panic-stricken too. "I thought we already decided that."

"Maybe we did, but let's be honest, neither one of us really committed to it. We said we wanted more time together and went on our merry way doing what we do. We pass each other by every now and then, wham, bam, thank you, sir. We send texts, but not really much more than that. And we let everything and everyone interrupt us. I know some of it's inevitable, but—"

"What are you saying?" Theo interrupted, feeling miserable down to his toes as Morris kept rambling. He was going to get the friendship suggestion. He did not want to hear the fucking "let's be friends" spiel. "You want off this crazy train life of mine?"

"No!" Morris gave him an exasperated look. "Just because I like my life the way it is doesn't mean I'm not open to change. And last time I looked, you are a part of my life."

"Dammit, Morris, what are you saying?" But before he answered, Theo continued on in a rush. "I know you're worried I'm going to suddenly decide I don't want you for you, but the truth is I'm fucking crazy about you, Morris. All those things you think would turn me off are the things I…." Theo paused before the wrong L word could pop out. "That I really like about you. I like your geek/nerd love. I like the way you dress and look. The crazy number of hours you put into your work. Okay, that part may be frustrating, but I get it, because I love what I do too, and I have nothing but respect for someone else who's doing what they love."

Theo hesitated again. He hated being that pushy, insecure lover. It was a role he'd never played before, but he didn't know how to quiet the anxiety within him. "You keep saying this is a fling, and if that's all you want out of it, I'm not going to push you for more, but you need to know it's more than that for me."

Morris went still, and a cold knot formed in Theo's stomach. "Before we go any further… do I have a chance in hell with you? Like long-term, exclusive, me and you?" Because if he let himself fall in love any more, he didn't think he'd be able to handle having someone else disappear out of his life. Maybe it wasn't fair to lay that on him, but this was ground Theo had never crossed before.

"Can I talk now?" Morris demanded, his hands on his hips, and Theo nodded. He wanted to look away, but he couldn't. "I'm saying I love you, you clueless, adorable man, and maybe I might want to take this another step further if we can find the time together. I mean this—"

Morris loved him. The words hit Theo with stunning impact, and before Morris could get in another word, Theo latched on to him, lifted up on his toes, and kissed the breath right out of the both of them. When Theo finally released him, his knees were wobbly and Morris had a dazed look in his eyes. "I love you too."

"Yeah?" Morris asked in a breathless voice.

"Yeah." Theo kissed him again and then let Morris go with some reluctance. "I'm sorry I interrupted. You were about to say something else."

"I was?" Morris looked so sexily befuddled that Theo was tempted to kiss him again to keep that look on his face. Theo's heart was still beating a crazy rhythm from Morris's words, and he wanted to hear them again.

Theo nodded solemnly, though he doubted his serious expression was reflected in his eyes. "You were."

Morris held up his hands. "Fuck if I know. How's a brother supposed to concentrate when you come at me with octopus arms and anaconda lips?"

"How am I supposed to resist when you're standing there with your sexy knees exposed and you're all agitated as you tell me what I've been dying to hear from you for freaking forever?" Theo grinned and clasped his hands around the nape of Morris's neck to tug his head down. "Okay, time together. I can clear my schedule Sunday until it's time for my shift. And you'll be back from the show, right?"

"Late Saturday, I swear. I plan on a full day of relaxation on Sunday. My creative brain is short-circuiting, and I still have the show tomorrow." Morris wiggled his fingers. "So no pencil and table for me."

"Well then, I say we go crazy and spend the day…." Theo paused and thought for a few moments. He wanted to do something fun, but Morris's plan of relaxation sounded really awesome.

"This is going to be a really sad suggestion, but instead of running around, looking for a perfect date, why don't we just be us? We can fool around in bed. Maybe do something simple like going to the boardwalk and getting ice cream along the waterfront, nothing wild and over-the-top. No cooking for you and no drawing from me, and no answering work-related emails or calls." Morris pursed his lips, then continued, "But answering calls from family is okay, unless they're being annoying."

"Fair deal."

Morris glanced toward the house, then leaned forward. "Is Lincoln home?" he asked softly in Theo's ear.

Theo chuckled in return as heat slid through him that had nothing to do with the summer. "Yeah, but I don't see why that should stop us. We can be quiet, especially if we're at your place."

"Challenge accepted." Morris took Theo's hand and tugged him toward his kitchen door.

"You don't have to pack for your trip tonight?" That's what was keeping Lincoln thoroughly occupied. He wasn't sure what geek shirt he wanted to wear for the con. A momentous decision to be sure.

"Finished at dawn." A slow, wicked smile crossed Morris's lush mouth. "I thought you might be interested in me keeping the kilt on for this go-round, since you mentioned it a few times."

Morris did know how to tempt and tease a man. "There is that. I have had fantasies of you bent over your art table with your kilt rucked up."

"Absolutely not. I need to work there, and I won't be able to concentrate if I get horny every time I look at it." Morris wagged a finger at him. "You behave yourself."

Theo had zero intentions of behaving. He caught Morris's finger and nipped the end. Morris's eyes darkened. "You know, I've been craving a cigarette since our argument yesterday."

"Your oral fixation is going to be the death of me," Morris said as he fumbled for the door handle.

"Oh, but what a way to go."

# Chapter Twenty-Eight

FELIPE ADJUSTED his high-crowned fedora and made sure his bullwhip was firmly attached to his belt. It was too damn hot to do anything crazy. Like that lady dressed up as a Khajiit from *Elder Scrolls*. He didn't care if this con had good AC. Fuck that shit. Fur and clothes. If she made it through to the costume contest, Felipe would bow down to her perseverance. There were many things he'd do for a kickass costume, but roasting alive was not one of them.

He eyed her as she sauntered by. Damn, though, the matching tunic and boots were killer even if the prosthetics could've used a little more tweaking. She paused, then swiveled slowly to face Felipe. "Wrong costume there, Short Round."

Felipe's eyes narrowed. Abby Albion. He should've known. Bad enough she won at Brenden's last show. She'd definitely place this round too. And if anybody was stubborn enough to last out the heat, it was her. "I haven't done Short Round since elementary school, Duchess. I think I've earned the right to be Indy now. It's certainly a lot more sensible than running around in that getup."

"What you call sense, I call lack of creativity." She gestured a paw toward his costume with a dismissive flick.

Felipe had to give it to her; she had the arrogant bearing of a cat down pat. There was a reason why he'd given her his particular pet name. But he was in too good of a mood to be irritated by her words. And he wasn't the one who would be spending the entire day sweating. He'd been able to beg and swap his shift around so he could at least show his face at the con. Some might consider it crazy to drive all the way down to Newport News, only to turn back around and go home again, but he considered his Chessie Con crew family, and not getting to see them at all would've sucked royally. He would not let his childhood nemesis get under his skin. The Indiana Jones getup he'd put together was authentic from his battered hat to his scarred boots.

"Whatever, Duchess," Felipe said with an airy wave of his hand in return, refusing to rise to her bait. That alone would annoy her. "You might want to invest in keeping some cold packs in a cooler and slipping them underneath your fur from time to time. I'd hate for my best rival to get heatstroke."

"Wait, are you entering the contest?" Abby called after him as he turned away.

Felipe shrugged, then doffed his fedora with a little bow. "Maybe, maybe not. We'll see." He left her to puzzle out that exchange and headed toward Morris's table. She was probably taking a second hard look at his costume, wondering if her prosthetics would outclass his authenticity and recognizability. Not everybody played *Elder Scrolls*, but Indy was loved for life. Felipe smirked. Imagining her sweating it almost made up for the fact he'd miss the contest.

He spied Lincoln bringing drinks to the VIP tables and shook his head. Poor kid was still running the same shit he did at the restaurant, though Felipe supposed serving was better than picking up. Morris was a goner. Only a man seriously in love would drag around his boyfriend's brother to a show. Even if the brother was cool. Felipe would have to give Morris a hard time when his table wasn't so busy.

The con was hopping, the tables laid out in a meandering line, following the layout of the hotel, and the aisles were crowded with families. Felipe had already made his circuit three times, pausing to take pictures when people stopped him. He always tried to make it a point to do it so he wasn't blocking the vendors. Sometimes once he'd finish one shot, another person would ask, and the next thing he knew he'd been posing for a good twenty minutes. It was rude to do that in front of someone's table while they were trying to work too.

It was simple con courtesy. One of those unspoken rules that seemed to be dying out in the last few years. Like not crowding someone's table with your own stuff. Or freaking stealing someone else's artwork, making prints of your own, and then trying to hawk that shit. Jackie had caught someone doing that to her a few weeks ago, and the confrontation had been epic. Some promoters were more sympathetic to that than others. Felipe wished that had happened at one of Brenden's because he would've made the guy pack up and go. He might be a pain in the ass about rules, but Felipe couldn't deny his sense of ethics.

He passed by Morris's table once again, but Morris was deep in a conversation with Brenden, and Felipe didn't feel like dealing with the promoter at the moment. His anger toward Brenden and Dakota had cooled, and he realized he didn't miss Dakota all that much. The sex had been fun, but they never meshed that well outside of it. They made better friends than a couple. So maybe Brenden had been doing him a favor after all, but Felipe wasn't ready to thank him.

Felipe turned the corner and grinned as the table for Old Dominion Magick Den caught his gaze. They were usually crowded midday, but for the moment there was only one customer, which meant Felipe could shop and flirt a bit. Two of his favorite things. Trask Briscoe sat cross-legged on a chair, the container from a food truck balanced on his lap as the other dude from the Den, Ryan, talked with the customer.

Trask wore a faded Sex Pistols T-shirt and rugged jeans that had seen better days. His arms were covered in tattoos in splashes of color and whorls of black. Most striking, his hair had gone almost completely silver even though he didn't seem that old. Late thirties, early forties at the most. The man oozed sexiness, and he didn't even realize it. Felipe decided it was his job to let him know, a public service.

"Catching a breather?" Felipe asked, stationing himself near the corner where Trask sat. Ryan shot him a warning look that Felipe ignored. He wasn't in the way, and if the tables got swamped again, he'd duck out. This bullshit between cosplayers and vendors got out of hand sometimes.

Trask glanced up and wiped his mouth with a napkin. He had a silver beard too, just the right length, not overboard like some of the hipsters did. Trask's dark eyes warmed as he smiled at Felipe. "Trying to. Seems like everyone decided to hit the con today instead of the beach."

"The beaches get overcrowded this time of year. I'm not one to lay out and do nothing, and it's no fun bodysurfing when you're in danger of crashing into families playing in the waves." Felipe cocked his head, trying to imagine Trask laid out on the beach, working on a tan. It didn't quite fit. He could see him under an umbrella, with a book in one hand, a cold drink in the other, and a dog snoozing at his feet with a Frisbee between its paws.

"But you do go body surfing." Trask's gaze flicked over him, quick and appreciative, before meeting Felipe's eyes again. Felipe had wondered at first if Trask was gay or not. He'd never heard of him dating among the other convention folk. He definitely wasn't one to hang out and party, so it was difficult to get a read on him. But Felipe was slowly coming to recognize his signals. Trask never glanced at the female cosplayers other than with quick appreciation for a good costume, and if his gaze lingered on anyone, it was one of the guys. And Felipe had seen that admiring gaze in his direction a few times.

"Mostly in Ocean City at the start of the summer if I get the chance, or down in the Outer Banks for a long weekend after Labor Day. Sometimes I'll hit up Virginia Beach, but it's been crazy busy this summer. I haven't had much of a chance." Maybe his next day off, he'd drag Morris away from his art table long enough to go boating and hit the beach. The man needed to get out more and take his pasty boyfriend with him. Felipe wanted to get to know Theo a little better since he seemed as if he was going to be around for a while.

Felipe studied Trask, trying to nail down his attraction other than the fact the man was easy to look at. He was the exact opposite of Dakota, quiet instead of loud, confident, not brash. He definitely preferred the sidelines instead of being front and center. Everybody knew Dakota and Felipe had sometimes clashed over who would get the spotlight. Though, looking at him, Felipe didn't think Trask ever let himself be a pushover.

"Ever been parasailing?" Trask asked, gesturing with his fork. "It's a rush, and the views are amazing."

Felipe could picture Trask doing that. Something a little off the cuff and different, a little thrilling. "Not yet. I've thought about it a few times when I've seen others out, but never got around to doing it myself."

"You should." That was all Trask said as he began eating again. He wasn't much of a conversationalist, though he went along with one well enough. Felipe wasn't sure if it was shyness or a natural reticence in him. At first, he'd thought Trask was socially awkward. There were plenty of vendors with the same quirk. Morris could be shy sometimes, but the more Felipe talked with Trask, the more he thought the gamer was just a chill dude, content to observe everything around him from the sidelines.

It massaged Felipe's ego that he could get the guy to talk more. "So I was thinking, you GM, right? Run some of the role-playing games at your store?" Trask looked up with a nod. "I've caught your panels on gaming. I love it myself, been rolling the dice since fifth grade."

Trask's eyes gleamed with enthusiasm as he sat up straighter. "Do you run games too or stick to playing?"

"Stick to playing," Felipe said with fervor. "I do not have the mentality to run a game. The first time players ruined my carefully constructed plans I'd probably smite them. I, however, do love to screw up the carefully laid plans of others."

"So you're one of those." Trask shook his head, smiling slightly. "The players like you keep the game lively. You've got to plan for situations like that, because it always happens."

"How do you handle them?" Felipe asked. He really wanted to see if Trask would mesh with his group, and not just because he wanted the chance to ogle him during games. He'd had gamemasters try to force the group to behave with contrived scenarios that felt out of place. There was one who had a complete meltdown whenever the story didn't go the way he wanted it to. Felipe knew himself. That would be him all the way.

"You've got to be flexible and think fast. I like to go with the flow." Trask paused, and a glint appeared in his eyes. The evil glint only a gamemaster got. "And my villains have their own agenda, apart from what the players are doing. Their timeline for mischief and wickedness does not change just because the players go off on a tangent. So if a player character gets too wrapped up in side missions they invent for themselves, they're going to come face-to-face with reality real fast."

"That is devious." Felipe stared at Trask with grudging admiration. That was the type of shit that would land him into trouble. "I approve of your underhanded methods."

"You live nearby?" Trask asked. "You could always pop into the Den for a game. We have a schedule online. Not that I run a game all that often anymore."

That was the best opening Felipe was going to get. If Trask was like any other gamers, he knew he had to be missing rolling the dice. "You ever think of picking up a new permanent group? I have a group that's looking for a good GM."

"What happened to your last one?" Trask cocked his head. "You run him off with your shenanigans?"

"He was Army. Got sent overseas for a year. He thinks he'll be restationed when he's done." Felipe missed Glen. He'd been a good dude, a little squirrely sometimes but a friend nonetheless. "We play with him online sometimes, but it's not the same."

"And no one in your group is interested in stepping in? Usually there's one who wants to run their own game."

"Jackie does a quick campaign sometimes but isn't interested in doing anything with a long arc. So that's cool for a pick-me-up every now and then. Morris overthinks and overworries. He wouldn't have any fun doing it because he'd fret over every detail, and even though it's work, it ought to be fun for the GM too." Felipe mentally ran down the rest of their group as Trask nodded. "Let's see, Dakota and I would probably kill the entire party because we don't have the right mentality. And... Brett and Daphne have zero interest. I think they consider raising a kid gamemastering enough."

Trask closed up the rest of his food and tucked it out of the way as several people descended on the table. "Sounds to me like you know your group well. Good luck with finding someone, but I don't think I'm looking for a group at this moment."

At this moment. That left room for Felipe to discuss it again at the next con. And to get another eyeful, because damn, Trask and a pair of jeans and those rocker T-shirts made Felipe's hormones hum.

"I'll try to keep my disappointment to a minimum," Felipe said with an airy sigh and a deliberate ogle of Trask's ass. "And comfort myself by eyeing you with longing." He grinned at Trask's startled look and blew him a kiss. "See you around."

That didn't go too bad at all. Felipe glanced over his shoulder and sure enough, Trask was watching him saunter away, so Felipe added a touch more swagger. He'd planted the seed. Now it was time to sit back and let it take root. Trask didn't seem like the kind of guy to rush into anything, whether it was a date or picking up a group to play with.

Felipe turned toward Morris's table and saw his friend was free. Perfect. Now to gauge for himself how bad Morris had it for Theo. He should place a bet with their other friends. Felipe would lay down good money on the odds Morris would be shacking up with his chef by the time his lease ran out.

# Chapter Twenty-Nine

MORRIS CHECKED the speedometer as they started the steep roll down the Harry Nice Bridge. As impatient as he was to get home and maybe have a chance to swing by the bistro to see Theo, there was almost always a cop down at the end of the bridge, waiting to nab people as they entered Maryland. The last time Morris had been pulled over it was for a burned-out taillight and Felipe had ragged him for days. As they passed the tollbooths on the opposite side of the highway, Morris beeped the horn and waved out the open window.

"What was that for?" Lincoln asked curiously.

"Felipe has to work tonight. It's why he left the show early today." And bitter about it, no doubt. Felipe usually managed to finagle his way around a show, but it wasn't always easy to get the shifts he wanted. At this time of year, there was a show every weekend within driving distance. Felipe wanted to attend them all, but Morris was a little choosier when it came to the shows where he bought tables.

"He runs a tollbooth?"

"Yeah." Morris had to smile at the incredulity in Lincoln's voice. It was hard to imagine Felipe with his endless energy confined to an area that small for hours on end. "It's not an ideal situation. I'd hate to be his boss."

"For real," Lincoln said with true feeling.

It had been an excellent day. Morris had made more than he had at the same show last year, which was always a good feeling. His meeting with Brenden had gone well too. Brenden had been happy with the concept art, and they'd discussed tweaks to the Chessie design. Morris would make a nice chunk of change from that, and Brenden would have a whole new platform to run with for the launch of the bigger con. Morris was still a little hesitant on the idea of a bigger con, but Brenden's enthusiasm was catching. Lincoln had busted his ass, and Brenden was so pleased he'd urged Morris to bring him to other shows.

"Did you have fun today?" Morris picked up speed once they got past the danger zone. "I barely saw you."

"I did, but I think I ran around as much as I do at the restaurant. My legs actually ache." Lincoln slouched down in his seat and stretched out his legs as far as they could go in the cramped confines of the car. "I thought Brenden and his brother were going to start choking each other out during the setup, though."

"Oh?" Morris had missed that altercation, and he was usually attuned to their unique form of entertainment. "What about this time?"

"I guess Dakota didn't like where his table was located. He's scary, to be honest. He's an all-in-your-face kind of guy. I don't know how Brenden stands up to him. I was all ready to find a new place for him so he'd calm down."

Morris could see how Dakota could be intimidating if you didn't know him. He tended to gravitate to others with strong wills. He liked the challenge, but he was aware enough to tone it down when needed.

"Dakota will steamroll you if you let him. Brenden's more than a match for him, though. I don't think Brenden's ever let anyone steamroll him in his life. No need to worry about him. And Dakota's not the type to take his irritation out on you either." There were definitely jackasses at the shows who would, but Morris had warned Lincoln all about those.

"Brenden does need to get better food delivered, though," Lincoln said thoughtfully. "I heard complaints in the green room from some of his guests."

That was something Morris wouldn't know about. He rarely managed to scrounge food from the green room. He didn't have the clout at most shows, though he sometimes managed to get some by Brenden if he was feeling generous. "Did you tell him that?"

"Yeah, I passed it along because I had to agree with the complaints. He didn't look pleased."

Morris thought about that. It was the kind of conundrum that would bug Brenden. He wanted satisfied guests, but he wanted it at his budgeted price. "Maybe Theo can recommend some people in the areas where Brenden does shows. It's usually a set rotation in the Chesapeake area."

"Maybe." Lincoln fell silent, crossing and uncrossing his arms. He seemed relaxed around Morris most of the time. Which was cool because Morris planned on being around more often and he didn't want it to be awkward, but he was getting the increasing feeling there was something

Lincoln wanted to talk about. Morris wasn't sure how to address it or if he should ignore it until Lincoln broached the subject.

Maybe Theo had told him they were getting more serious. That could be worrying for a fifteen-year-old who'd lost his parents and whose sister was about to be distracted with a new little one in her life. He hoped Lincoln wouldn't cause a fuss over it, but he was prepared for Theo to pull back and slow things down if Lincoln did. Morris had zero doubts about Theo's commitment to his brother first.

"Can I tell you something without you telling Theo?" Lincoln asked in a low voice, as if he heard Morris's thoughts.

*Uh-oh.* Morris did not want to go down the road where he started keeping secrets from Theo, especially ones concerning his brother. That would only lead to bad things. "I'm not making any promises," he said, tugging on his earlobe. "I mean, if you tell me you're running a meth lab out of your bedroom, I'm sorry, I'll have to clue him in."

"I'll remember that in case it ever comes up." Morris heard the faint smile in Lincoln's previously solemn voice. "It's not illegal, but you'll probably end up thinking I'm an asshole."

"We're all assholes sometimes. Just strive not to be an asshole all the time." Morris cast a look at Lincoln as a smile of bemusement crossed the teen's face.

"I think that might be the adult advice of the year."

"I do try." Morris stole another quick glance at Lincoln, then looked back at the road. Once they left the interstate it was one country highway after another, monotonous, but with the constant threat of deer deciding to use the road for leaping practice. "Does it have to do with me and Theo?"

He really hoped not. This was not ground Morris had any experience crossing. If Lincoln had issues with how fast they were moving, or all the other changes hitting him over this year, Morris didn't know what he could say that would help.

"Oh no, you and Theo, that's cool," Lincoln said, though there was an odd note in his tone. "Is it serious?"

Serious enough to make Morris a little nervous. He'd never fallen for a guy this hard. "Yeah, we're pretty serious."

There was a long, thoughtful pause. "Theo's been happier since he met you. More like how I used to know him before Mom and Dad... you know, and before Dustin and Robin decided to be such jerks."

"He makes me happy too." Morris tapped his fingers on the steering wheel. "I know this last year's been rough for you all."

He caught a shrug out of the corner of his eye as Lincoln stared out the window. He was quiet after that until they turned down the long road toward Calvert County. Morris realized Lincoln had never got around to asking him the question that was bugging him. "So why do you think you're going to sound like an asshole? You can tell me."

There was a pause, and Morris sensed Lincoln's agonized tension. "Do you think it's Theo's fault Dustin and Robin don't ever come to visit or call anymore?" Lincoln finally asked.

Morris's hands tightened on the wheel. Theo didn't talk about his other siblings often, and when he did, he hadn't been able to hide the pain and anger in his eyes. He knew Theo felt guilty both for being angry with them and for their distance. He couldn't see why Theo should feel any guilt at all, but he didn't know the whole story either. He figured Theo would tell him when he was ready.

"Well no, but I'm guessing you think there must be something he's done to have caused it," Morris finally said in a careful tone. "Why do you think they're staying away?"

"He acts like he's head of the family now. Like he can take Mom and Dad's place." Lincoln's voice tightened as if it was going to break. "It's infuriating. He's not them, and he's never going to be them."

Oh boy, this got deep fast, and Morris couldn't help but wonder how long Lincoln had been holding on to it. He tapped his fingers again as he tried to gather his thoughts. "He's trying to feel his way through this new reality too. I don't think he's trying to replace them, Linc. Parents aren't something that can be replaced. But you can't hold yourself in a stasis either."

Lincoln's snort of scornful disbelief let Morris know what he thought of that, so he tried to go at it from another angle. "After your parents passed, who made the decisions, contacted the insurance company, made the arrangements for the funerals, all of that?"

"Theo," Lincoln muttered. "Which proves my point. He dove in and took control."

"Did he ask to do it all himself? Did anyone offer to help?" Morris paused and glanced at Lincoln. "Or were you all too shocked and stunned? Not that I'm laying blame, because I think I would've been in that state too." And pathetically grateful for whoever wanted to take charge.

"Nooooo…. I guess maybe Jill a little, but she was a mess too. Craig was occupied with her or I'm sure he would've helped." Lincoln was noticeably silent about his other siblings.

"Did something happen between Theo and Robin and Dustin?" Morris asked.

"There was some kind of an argument after the funeral." The note of accusation crept back into Lincoln's voice. "They tried to hide it from me, but I know it happened."

Laila had taught him how in tune kids were to the whispers and tensions of adults, especially if it concerned them. Morris wouldn't be surprised if there had been an argument. That might explain a lot.

Morris let out a breath he'd been holding on to. Why was Lincoln trusting him with these kinds of life issues? Probably because he was now at that unique point where he wasn't an outsider any longer, but he wasn't in the middle of the mess either. It also reassured him more than Lincoln's words that he accepted Theo and Morris as a couple.

"You've got to let up on him, Linc. He's doing his best, and you pushing at him the way you do is not helping either one of you. I know you're mad and scared and nothing feels stable anymore, and you have reason to feel that way, which is why you should be working together, not tearing each other down. You have to talk to him. If you talk to him, he might talk to you."

"I don't understand him," Lincoln exploded. "He's so calm and collected all the time. He never gets mad that Mom and Dad left us." His voice caught, and he angrily dashed a hand over his eyes. "You know he never cried once. Never. Jill cried all the time. He cares more about the restaurant than he does that they died."

"That you could see." Morris's cool voice cut through Lincoln's rage.

"What?"

Morris would never forget the sound of Theo's voice when he told him about his parents, or the raw pain on his face. It had broken his heart at the time, and hearing it in Lincoln's voice too broke it all over again. Theo had cried that night, and Morris had no doubt there were other times when he was alone that he'd allowed himself to break down.

"He doesn't let you see it," Morris said in a gentler tone. "He feels like he's got to be the strong face for the rest of you. He worries that if he lets you see it, it'll be harder for you than it is. But I've seen it. I've seen his anger, and I've seen his sorrow. He feels just as deeply as you. He cares about that restaurant in many ways because he feels as if he's honoring your mom and dad's legacy and trust by making sure it's successful and you are looked after."

"I never thought of it like that," Lincoln said in a near whisper.

"And if you feel like you have to see that side of him, his own sorrow, maybe try reaching out and sharing how you feel instead of the both of you assuming you know how the other feels."

Morris got the impression Theo didn't let many see that side of him. There was more to him than the easygoing face he showed the world, a solid core of steel and a shield for his deeper emotions. Those who were given the chance to see all his sides were few and privileged. Damn, Morris loved that man. He'd really snuck up on him, and Morris was still a little giddy over it.

He glanced at Lincoln to see if that was sinking in. Lincoln stared out the windshield with a thoughtful expression on his face. "You know, you two are a lot alike in some ways," Morris continued.

"Really?" Lincoln looked at him, and his voice was surprised. "How?"

"You're both loyal, you're both passionate. You go out of your way to make things easier for others even if it's at a cost to yourself. And you're both stronger than you think." Morris considered it a bit more as Lincoln mulled that over.

"If the situation had been reversed and you had been the oldest when your parents passed, I can easily picture you taking charge and taking care of your family."

"I'd do anything for them," Lincoln said, low and fierce.

"And Theo would do anything for you, don't ever doubt that, even play hardball, which I think we both discovered." Morris smiled ruefully. Theo did have a temper. Morris never would've guessed it to look at him, but having run up against it twice, he couldn't deny it.

Lincoln squirmed in his seat. "Don't remind me," he muttered.

"I can't speak for Dustin and Robin. I don't know them or their deal. Maybe they did have a fight with Theo and that's driving it. But people react in different ways to loss. Some cling harder to loved ones, and I think you, Jill, and Theo fall under that. Others try distancing themselves because they don't want to feel that kind of pain again. I don't know if that's the case with your brother and sister, but it's something to think about."

"Huh." Lincoln was quiet a little longer, but it seemed to be a thoughtful quiet, and the simmering restlessness had eased. Morris wished he could help more. He wasn't sure what else he could do.

"So do you think I'm an asshole?" Lincoln asked after a few minutes.

"Not in the least bit, buddy, not in the least." Morris smiled at him, then laughed as Lincoln's stomach growled. His own panged in response. "We're almost to the bridge. How do you feel about swinging by the bistro for a late dinner?"

"I thought you'd never ask." Lincoln patted his stomach. "You won't say anything to Theo, will you? About what we talked about?"

Morris sighed and shot another quick glance at Lincoln. "No, but promise me you'll talk to him, okay? That's the only way either of you will resolve this. And I hate feeling like I'm keeping things from him."

Lincoln bit his lip and nodded. "Okay, I promise."

Morris relaxed. He'd gotten to know Lincoln well enough to be confident he'd do as he promised. The rest of the trip was spent with them bopping to the radio and with Morris's thoughts centered on Theo.

When they walked into the bistro, the Sunday crowd was dwindling, Rose greeted them warmly, and the aromas from the kitchen just about knocked Morris off his feet. He glimpsed Theo in the kitchen, his expression intent as he made some final tweaks to the plates in front of him.

Morris chuckled as he headed toward one of the tables at the bar. The bistro was beginning to feel like a second home. Then Theo was there with a broad grin on his face, a rough hug for his brother, and a too quick kiss for Morris. "Hey, I missed you guys." Theo hooked another chair with his ankle and sat down for the brief time he'd allow himself to remain. "How'd it go?"

Lincoln immediately launched into a detailed description of the day, his arms waving as he gestured. Theo shook his head, a smile playing on his lips as he squeezed Morris's hand. Their gazes caught, and Theo's eyes were soft as he mouthed, "Thank you."

Morris's heart flipped as he squeezed Theo's hand back. "Anytime."

# Chapter Thirty

THEO POURED himself a second cup of coffee and leaned his hip against the counter as he considered the list of things he had to do today. He had to stop by the fish and farmer's markets to see what he could find for today's special. Then he could leave the prep to Scottie, come back here to catch up some on chores and laundry before he had to be back for dinner and closing.

No, fuck, he had the date with Morris. A mostly full day of relaxing. And Theo was not about to give that up. Morris was right; they had to start making each other a priority too, and he had been looking forward to this day.

Theo quickly recalculated as he glanced at his watch. If he left in the next five minutes and he talked Lincoln into helping him out, he could be back from the market by the time Morris would be caffeinated enough to want morning company. He could throw a load of laundry in after they returned, and the rest of the chores that didn't belong to Lincoln could wait until tomorrow. The world wouldn't end if the living room was left undusted for another day. Damn stuff just came right back.

"Hey, Linc, come on, man," Theo called. "I want to bribe you."

"What kind of a bribe?" Lincoln asked with heavy suspicion as he came into the kitchen, dressed for the day without Theo having to harass him. Theo lifted his mug to his lips and paused, blinking at his brother. He wore bright blue socks with a cartoon face on the front and white cloth spikes running up the backs of his calves. Theo lowered his cup, shaking his head in bemusement.

"What are those?" He pointed toward the insanity on Lincoln's legs.

Lincoln stiffened and thrust his chin out. "Sonic the Hedgehog socks. Morris got them for me at the show yesterday."

"He would. He probably bought a pair for himself too." Theo smiled and took a sip of his coffee as he tried to remember if Sonic the Badger was a comic book character or something to do with video games. "Cool, they'll make a statement when we're out and about today. People at the market are going to have a heyday."

"That's all you're going to say?" Lincoln asked, his brow beetling.

"Excuse me?" Theo studied his brother, not sure where he messed up this time. Nothing he said lately seemed to be the right thing. Maybe he shouldn't have implied he might get some looks at the market. Teenagers were so damn touchy. "Was there something else I should've said?"

"You're not going to suggest maybe I shouldn't wear them outside of the house?" Lincoln asked in disbelief.

"Nope." Theo eyeballed the ridiculous socks again. "Those things are awesome."

Lincoln's frown deepened, but he looked more confused than distressed. "But aren't they geeky?"

"Hell yeah they're geeky." Theo drained his cup and quickly washed it. "The real question is, do they make you happy?"

"Yeah." Lincoln glanced down at the socks again, admiring the cloth fins sticking out. "They are awesome."

"That they are. You have balls of steel, bro. I admire that." Theo could not imagine walking around in anything like that. He'd feel like an absolute idiot. The funny thing was, he didn't have one qualm at all about being seen with someone else wearing them. Each to their own. "You worry entirely too much about whether or not I'll find something to be too geeky."

Lincoln beamed at him, his shoulders straightening. "I guess I expected you to tell me to change before we went out. Like the suggestions you used to give me before school last year."

Theo went to stand before his brother. "Last year I didn't want anything else stressing you out. You have enough on your shoulders already, and high school can be rough. Being a teenager can be rough. I didn't want you to do anything that might make you be singled out even more. But in doing so, I probably stressed you out, so I was wrong."

"You were?" Lincoln stared at him, mystified.

Theo nodded. "You've got to be your own person. Not my version of you, or Jill's, or our mom and dad's ideal. You've got to be Lincoln, and Lincoln's a geek. So be a proud geek. That's something I learned from Morris. He is unapologetically himself, and he's not afraid to show off what he's into. I admire that about him, and I see the same quality in you when I'm not being an idiot about it."

Lincoln looked at him wordlessly a moment, then quickly hugged him and made a beeline for his room, moving at a gallop. Theo stared after him, analyzing the conversation. He wasn't sure he'd ever entirely understand Lincoln, but for the first time in a long time, Theo felt like he'd done right by him.

"I hope you're heading for the car," he called out after him. "Remember, I promised a bribe." He scooped the keys off the counter, and his phone dinged with Morris's message tone. Theo winced. He was a bad, bad boyfriend. He'd promised to clear his schedule today, and here he was already running out the door. He brought up the message and grinned. Somebody was definitely awake and grumpy about it.

*Your brother's a skinny twerp. How come he sounds like a herd of elephants in the morning?*

Theo began typing back as he heard Lincoln moving about his bedroom. *At least he doesn't have his saxophone.*

*No, he saves that for special occasions.* Lincoln bounded back into the living room, and a moment later, Theo's phone dinged again. *Like now. What's got him so excited?*

*Blame yourself, he's powered up by blue animal socks.*

*Ha!*

*Running to the market. I'll be back soon. Want to come along? Start the day off with a little shopping? I'll even offer you the same bribe I'm offering Lincoln.* He hit Send as Lincoln ran in circles around the living room. A day of working a comic book convention had seriously energized him.

"Can't find your sneakers, can you?" Theo called with a laugh. "Check under the couch. I think you kicked them there last night."

*Better be one hell of a bribe.*

*How about hot fresh donuts and the best coffee in So. MD?*

*You know a man's weakness. I'll be up.*

Theo didn't feel so guilty anymore. He shoved the phone into his pocket. He could throw a load of laundry in now while he was waiting for Morris, and then he'd be halfway done. As he came into the living room, he saw Lincoln staring at the family photos they'd set up on a little étagère. Theo's heart twisted at the wistful look on Lincoln's face. He often found himself doing the very same thing, standing right there, picking up each photo one by one.

Theo glanced at the picture Morris gave him, at the joy on the little girl's face. Sometimes looking at it really helped to remind him life went on. Sometimes when Lincoln had that look on his face, it was a little harder to believe.

"Theo, don't you miss Mom and Dad?" Lincoln asked in a soft voice, shoving his hands into the pockets of his shorts.

The ache that hit this time was swift and penetrating, knocking against the healing wound. Theo swallowed around the lump in his throat. "Every day... every damn day, Lincoln," he said roughly. "I miss Dustin and Robin too."

Lincoln looked over his shoulder at him, searching Theo's face. He seemed to be struggling with something, his eyes agonized, and it wrenched at Theo because he felt it too, and it wasn't something he wanted his baby brother to have to deal with. It made him feel so damned helpless, and Theo hated to feel helpless.

Then he replayed Lincoln's words and paired it with his tone. "You don't think I miss them?"

"You don't ever seem all that upset. Not like the rest of us were... are." Lincoln bit his lip. "I mean, I know you were upset, but you never showed it, and you don't talk about them a lot."

"Linc...." Theo dragged his hands through his hair. Did he really not talk about them? That's not what he wanted. He wanted to remember them. He wanted to talk about the good times, and he never wanted Lincoln to think he couldn't talk about them. "You ever been afraid that if you let yourself fall apart you might never be able to put yourself back together again?"

Lincoln's eyes widened, and he shook his head.

"That's how I felt. Like if I let go, I'd end up like Humpty Dumpty." He still sometimes felt that way, and it scared the hell out of him because if he fell apart, who would take care of Lincoln, the restaurant? He didn't want it all landing on Jill's shoulders even though she had Craig's full support.

"And as much as it hurts for me, I've always figured it had to be worse for you," Theo continued as Lincoln gave him his full attention. "I was an adult with my own life, my own place. You had every expectation of having your parents around until you became an adult too. I didn't want you to have to deal with a wreck of a brother on top of it."

Tears welled in Lincoln's eyes and he looked away, dashing his hand across his face. "It's just… I get mad sometimes. I get mad at them for dying, and I get mad at you for not being mad at them, and then I get mad at myself for being mad because it's stupid to get mad."

Theo gently squeezed Lincoln's shoulder. "Me too, Linc, me too. And I get mad at Dustin and Robin for deserting us, and I get mad at Jill for moving on with her life. You're not the only one who gets mad."

"Yeah," Lincoln said softly. "Sometimes it's like she's looking to replace our family. You too with Morris. That's stupid, huh?"

"No." Theo blinked back the stinging in his eyes. "But I'm not trying to replace them. Neither is Jill. If Mom and Dad were still here, I know they'd be ecstatic over a granddaughter and happy I've found someone like Morris." Someone he could lean on, who he could partner with, and who left him feeling less alone.

Lincoln looked at him again, his eyes worried. "Theo, can I ask you something?"

Theo steeled himself for some difficult questions he wasn't sure he had the answers to. He was still trying to figure out his future with Morris. All he knew for sure was he wanted a future. "Yeah."

Lincoln carefully set down the picture he was holding. "After the funeral, what did you and Robin and Dustin fight about?"

"What?" Theo stared at Lincoln in momentary incomprehension. That was not a question Theo had been prepared for. He sank down on the couch as Lincoln turned to face him.

Lincoln jutted his chin out at a stubborn angle. "I know you did. I saw you arguing."

Theo went back to that terrible day. It had already been hard enough, but when Robin and Dustin confronted him, it became so much worse. He often replayed it in his mind, wondering what he could've done that would've brought about a different outcome, and he came up with nothing every time. He looked up at Lincoln, who watched him in expectation.

"Yeah, we did." Theo leaned his elbows on his knees, his heart heavy. "They blame me, Linc, for Mom and Dad." And the truth was, deep down, Theo blamed himself too.

Lincoln stared at him, eyes round with disbelief. "Dad had cancer. How was that your fault?"

"They felt that if Mom hadn't died, Dad would've found the strength to pull through. They think I devoted too much time to the bistro and I should've taken off more to take over for her at the hospital. I should've driven Mom home that night." Theo also agreed with that. If he could go back, he would've insisted on leaving to go get her.

"But you and Jill took turns being at the hospital," Lincoln said in a bewildered voice. "And you took turns taking care of me. Most nights it was one of you two."

"They didn't see that. They were at school, and when they came home, both Jill and I worked to give them time with Mom and Dad, and to keep from wearing Dad out by all of us being there at once." Theo had hoped time would give them a clearer perspective, but so far, it hadn't happened.

Lincoln sat on the floor and folded his arms around his knobby knees. "Dad wasn't going to get better. That's what the doctors said. Mom explained it to me. I remember I kept thinking if I behaved and didn't make him mad, he'd get better. I think I scared her because I wasn't making a sound whenever I visited Dad. She said it was too late for him to get better, and we should be ourselves and enjoy our time together."

Theo nodded. "No, he wasn't getting better. The cancer was everywhere."

"I don't understand," Lincoln said with bewilderment. "How come they think it's your fault?"

"Jill and I knew how tired Mom was, which is why we urged her to go home and sleep." She never would've left if they hadn't made such a fuss. Theo chafed his hands together as he remembered how worn she'd looked. She'd been losing weight, and they were concerned she'd make herself sick too.

"We wanted to come get her. She was so damned independent. But she didn't want me to leave the restaurant or Jill to leave you." The medical bills had been piling up, and she'd been so worried about how they were going to cover it all. Still, it wouldn't have made much of a difference if they'd called someone in to cover for him while he got his mom. Hell, Scottie would've volunteered.

"So we let her come home alone and she had the accident."

Lincoln frowned fiercely and he wouldn't meet Theo's eyes. "Is there anything else?" Theo wished he knew what he was thinking. He wouldn't blame Lincoln if he agreed with Dustin and Robin, but he didn't want a wedge between him and another sibling.

Theo hesitated and then decided Lincoln deserved the whole truth since it concerned him. "They didn't want me to be your guardian. They figured if I was so careless about Mom and Dad, I'd be just as careless about you. I didn't fight them on the rest. I figured there was an element of truth to what they said. But I dug in my heels about you, Linc. I wasn't going to take the chance you'd wind up in Kentucky with Aunt Patti. You belong with me and Jill."

"Bullshit. Bullshit!" Lincoln's eyes flashed with outrage. "If they cared about me, they'd be here. They'd check in on me, but they don't, at least not very often. So don't you dare believe them. It was not your fault. And they never asked me what I wanted. You and Jill did. I didn't want to go to Kentucky. I wanted to stay here."

"I thought you talked to them online," Theo said with a frown. It was one thing to ignore him, but come on, Lincoln had done nothing to deserve their distance.

"Liking my posts doesn't count as communication," Lincoln said with a derisive snort. "Five-minute calls on holidays don't either. And neither do random texts. That's not enough."

Theo did not want friction between Lincoln and his aloof siblings. And he definitely did not want sides taken either. "I appreciate the support, and on one hand I agree with you. Despite how they felt about me, they should've checked in on you." The only time Theo heard from them was when they needed something, usually through Jill. "But I don't want this to be a new fight, okay?"

Lincoln's mouth settled in a pissy line. "Hard to fight with someone who's never here."

Theo felt the truth of that in every line of his aching soul. "True, but I'm still hoping they'll come around. Maybe when their niece shows up they'll rethink things." This had to come to an end. If he had to swallow his pride and go see them and beg them to let Lincoln and Jill back into their lives, he would.

The front door opened and Morris stuck his head in. "Hey, guys." He glanced at Theo, and Lincoln, then straightened. "Am I interrupting? I can come back."

"No," Lincoln said quickly before Theo could suggest Morris give them another twenty minutes. "We were just talking. We should hit the market before all the good stuff is gone."

Lincoln stood up and dusted his seat off. Morris stared after Lincoln as he brushed by him and then glanced at Theo. "Dude, I'm sorry. I thought we were heading out."

"Don't be." Theo scraped a hand through his hair. He couldn't decide if that conversation had been a good thing or not. "We were."

"Do you want to tell me about it?" Morris asked with a worried expression.

"I will later." Theo stood up and offered Morris a smile. "Lincoln's right. We'd better hit the market and the promised bribe."

The drive to the bistro to pick up the truck and then on to the market was quiet. Theo was still trying to digest his conversation with Lincoln, who sat in apparent unconcern as he played a game on his phone. Morris kept stealing little glances at him as Theo gradually relaxed. If Lincoln were upset with him, he'd know it by now.

"So how long have you been going to this market?" Morris asked as they pulled in. "Damn, it's huge."

"It's got everything," Theo said, maneuvering the truck around haphazardly parked cars and pedestrians who were paying no attention to moving vehicles. "Produce, Amish goods, that little building there has a first-rate butcher, and the fish market. I couldn't even tell you how long I've been going here."

"Mom and Dad used to take turns bringing us. Theo's probably been looking for ingredients here since he could walk," Lincoln said, shoving his phone in his pocket as Theo pulled up behind the market and parked by a back door. "I'll scout out the veggies. The fish market stinks."

"Where are the donuts and coffee?" Morris peered over at the long pavilions and the stands contained within them. "I can smell fried goodness."

Theo laughed and pointed toward the line. "There's also a stand that does a really kickass sausage and peppers. We can bring some back for our day of idleness and debauchery."

"If we're doing it right, we're not exactly being idle, now are we?" Morris said, the corner of his mouth lifting in a smile.

"Uh gross, sex talk." Lincoln made a face at Theo. "See you later." He headed off into the first pavilion, the socks covering his calves drawing more than one eye.

Theo gestured to them. "Lincoln told me you bought those for him."

"Oh yeah." Morris grinned as they turned toward the meat and fish market. "When I saw them, they screamed Lincoln."

"Good call. He was preening in them this morning." Theo opened the door and was hit with a wave of air-conditioning as he motioned for Morris to go ahead. "Look, I'm sorry about earlier. If I'd known Lincoln wanted a heart-to-heart, I would've given you a heads-up."

Understanding lit up Morris's eyes. He gave Theo a searching look as he entered. "How are you?"

"Okay, I think." Theo gave him a rueful smile. He headed for the fish counter first and stuck his thumbs through the loops of his jeans as he studied the offerings nestled on ice. "It started off because of the socks. I think I made Lincoln's day with my reaction. Would you look at those oysters?" He eyeballed the price and made swift calculations in his head. They'd do oyster stew for the soup special and speckled trout for the fish. They hadn't done trout in a long while. That would be a hit.

"Ever notice that oysters look like a pile of fleshy rocks?" Morris observed as Theo stepped forward to place his order.

"There's something wrong with you, man." Theo grinned at the woman behind the counter. "Hey, Terry, how's it going?"

A smile warmed the woman's eyes as she grabbed a notepad and calculator. "Theo, good to see you again. Who's that with you? New cook?"

Theo threw a mischievous smile at Morris. "That is the love of my life. I'm giving him a feel for my world before he comes to his senses and flees screaming. Morris, meet Terry. She runs this counter. I terrorize her world every other day."

"Truth. You and Scottie always run off with my freshest items first thing in the morning and then try to charm me into charging less." She shook a pen at Theo and smiled at Morris. "How's your sister?"

"Fat and impatient." Theo smiled at Morris's snicker. "I've got the truck parked out back, ready to be filled."

"I dare you to say that to her face," Terry said with a shake of her head. She pointed to a couple of young men in the back. "Okay, those two will help you load. They can get started while you're at the butcher. What's the damage going to be today?"

Theo gave her the order, argued good-naturedly about the price, and turned toward the butcher's counter, rubbing his hands together. "You are way too excited after the money you just dropped," Morris said. "Aren't you having heart palpitations?"

"Nope." Theo knew the specials would do well. "Though I'll admit when Jill first started handling the bills, she would have minor meltdowns."

"Steaks look good." Morris crouched down for a better look at the rib eye.

Theo had to agree with him, but he liked the price on the leg of lamb. He noted the farm it came from with a satisfied nod. He'd never been disappointed with their meat. "I was wondering if Lincoln would actually talk to you. I hoped so," Morris continued.

"You knew?" Theo turned to Morris in surprise. Lincoln didn't open up to many.

Guilt flashed across Morris's face. "Yes...." He drew out the word. "Sorta? We talked last night on the way home. He asked me not to say anything, but I urged him to talk to you." He paused, cocking his head. "Are you mad?"

"No... no." Theo studied the lamb again with a shake of his head. "Was it about Mom and Dad?"

"Yeah, your brother and sister too." Theo couldn't miss the curious look Morris was giving him. He supposed Morris deserved to hear that bit of ugliness too. He should know about what he was getting into.

"We talked about that. Dustin blames me for Mom and Dad. Robin less so I think, but she generally follows Dustin's lead. They're tight like that." He stepped forward on his turn and ordered the lamb, bantering with the man behind the counter, though his heart wasn't entirely in the moment.

Morris touched his hand. "Just as long as you don't blame yourself."

Theo gave him a rueful smile. "Wouldn't you?"

Morris considered that, his broad face solemn. "Yeah, I would."

"Sometimes I wonder if I'm doing right by him. Other times I think I'm nailing it. I'm just not sure which it is this morning."

Morris chuckled and nudged Theo with his elbow. "I think you're nailing it."

"I think you're biased," Theo replied. "Whenever I thought about possibly one day maybe being a parent or guardian, it was way off down the road, and I always thought I'd start from the ground up, you know? Then I'd have a learning curve as the little squirt grows."

"I think you're doing better than you think you are," Morris said more seriously. "You and Lincoln talk to each other, like really talk. How many teenagers have real conversations with their parents?"

"You've got a good point." Theo shook his head and decided to put that worry away for now. Lincoln was in a good mood and had opened up to him. Morris was with him. And they'd made a killing at the market. All in all, it was a good start to the day. "Thank you for being there for him."

"I like him. He's like the little brother I wish I'd had. It might've saved my sanity growing up."

Soon Theo would get to meet all those terrorizing sisters of Morris's. "Come on, let's get the truck loaded and check on Lincoln. Once we have the veggies, there are donuts with our names on them."

"Lead the way." Morris patted his stomach. "Standing here in the presence of all this bounty has made me hungry."

# Chapter Thirty-One

"Wow, swanky neighborhood." Theo leaned his elbow in the open car window to examine the houses as they went by. "I forgot your dad's a lawyer. This looks like a neighborhood where a high-profile attorney and his family would live."

The homes were tall and stately, the lawns and hedges neatly trimmed with plenty of space between neighbors. Close enough to be friendly but far enough away that each house was showcased. Morris loved his home growing up, but he wanted something a little less polished, a little more bohemian for himself.

"He isn't like one of those lawyers on TV, is he?" Lincoln asked in a worried voice. "All growl and intimidation?"

"Yes if you show up in court or come home with a bad report card, but I don't think you have anything to worry about." Morris remembered many times when he'd had to face his dad from the other side of the desk after a misdemeanor. It still made him cringe. "Or if you fuck up. I can't see you fucking up. It's only me and my sisters who get that side of him at home."

Morris tried to squelch the nerves that tingled his spine as he turned down the street toward his parents' house, but it didn't do a damn bit of good. He'd brought guys he dated to family gatherings before; this was nothing. He should be as calm and collected as Theo, who did not seem bothered in the least.

Who was he kidding? This was everything. He'd never been so serious about a guy, and including Lincoln made it seem like he was introducing his future family. His palms started sweating. Ugh. He was thinking about it too hard. If he kept this up, he'd have an ulcer before they parked.

"If you tug on your hair one more time, you're either going to pull it out or give yourself a headache," Theo said with an amused smile.

"You're abnormal. You do realize my sisters are going to tease and hound you and be incredibly nosy until they're satisfied," Morris said as he eased the car to a stop at the end of the spacious driveway, half-full of cars.

"That's what sisters do." Theo shrugged. "It would be worse if they didn't. That would mean they don't take me seriously as your boyfriend."

"If it makes you feel better, I'm nervous enough for all three of us." Lincoln leaned forward and poked his head between the seats. "I hate meeting new people. Why'd I have to come?"

"Jill is cranky and restless today. Craig warned you about coming over and you said you didn't want to deal with that," Theo reminded him.

"I could've stayed home and played my games," Lincoln muttered.

"I wanted you to come," Morris said. Again that little flutter of nerves brushed over him. "Because you and Theo are a package deal, and I want my family to know that." Morris twisted to look at him. "Besides, you know Laila, and you don't have anything to worry about. They'll mother hen you, but they won't give you a hard time."

"Just me," Theo said with a sunny smile. Morris suspected he was actually looking forward to the grilling to come. "I'm the one who has to pass the test, and when I ace it, we can go forward on the next part of my plan to get Morris to move in with us."

That was the logical next step. Morris had been spending most nights upstairs with Theo except when Lincoln was elsewhere and they slept at his place. But officially moving in was a big leap, and Morris was a little cautious about it. It wasn't just the two of them they had to worry about.

Lincoln pursed his lips, though he didn't look surprised. Either Lincoln had figured it out on his own or Theo discussed it with him first. Morris was thinking it was the latter since Lincoln's back wasn't up. "We'd need a new place. The apartment's not big enough for three of us."

"True," Theo said, his expression turning serious. "I'd hate to uproot you again so soon."

"Not like we're moving out of state." Lincoln rolled his eyes. "I'd rather have elbow room and Morris with us than not."

"Good to know," Theo said, his expression lightening. "Though it's all moot until our leases are up."

That gave them several months before they had to start making the decisions. Morris's wasn't up until January and Theo's until the spring. He pocketed his keys and got out of the car before his sisters could get curious and come looking for them. "Come on. Let's go meet the brood."

"It's probably a bit too late to ask you this, but did you tell your family I'm white?" Theo asked, resting his elbow on the top of the car.

Morris's mind went blank. He wasn't entirely sure he had. Probably, during one of the many conversations he'd had about the status of his life. "I'm sure Laila has already let them know, or Rose."

"Along with me being a vegan and a llama herder," Theo said with a perfectly straight face.

Morris grinned. "So you heard about that, huh? And it's alpacas, thank you very much. There's a difference."

"Oh yes, I heard," Theo said, his eyes lit up with suppressed laughter. "Rose was laughing so hard when she told me she could barely stand up. Your sis was bugging her for more details."

Morris was rather proud of himself for that little joke. Though maybe he should've remembered to clue his family in before he showed up with Theo. "Oh man, Makayla is going to kill me once you reassure them. I'm sorry, I probably should've cleared that up. Now that's all they're going to be thinking of when I introduce you."

Theo chuckled. "Who said I was going to reassure them? In fact, I think moving to Montana, raising alpacas, and learning to knit is a fine idea. We can mail them serapes for Christmas gifts." He opened Lincoln's door. "Hey, Linc, what do you think about opening up a new restaurant in Montana?"

"Don't even fuck around like that. My sisters would hound me all day long. Seriously, Boarman." Morris leveled a finger at him as Theo laughed. "You've got sisters. You should understand my pain."

Lincoln poked his head out of the car. "What's so funny? And what's this about Montana?"

"We're becoming vegan," Theo announced, his eyes still laughing, and Morris wondered how long he'd been waiting to pounce with this little joke.

Lincoln blinked and shot Theo a look of pure astonishment. "Like hell we are."

"Thank you!" Morris shook his finger at Lincoln. "At least one of you has some sense."

Lincoln smirked at Theo. "Hear that? I have sense."

"That's debatable. Seriously, though." Theo turned back to Morris. "Did you say anything?"

Maybe Theo was a little more nervous about meeting Morris's family than he let on, and that made Morris feel less nervous himself. His jitters about this meeting had nothing to do with race, though. He'd dated white guys before. It had everything to do with his wish for Theo and Lincoln to slip right on in like they belonged there.

"I didn't even think of it, to be honest. It's not going to be a problem, though. After I came out to them and Makayla moved in with Victor before marriage, nothing will faze them anymore. What you should worry about is showing up at this house wearing a Georgetown Hoyas T-shirt."

Theo grinned and held out his arms. "Maybe I'll find a few converts inside."

"Keep dreaming." Morris glanced toward the car, where Lincoln was digging out the side dishes Theo insisted on bringing and the bag of things he brought to entertain himself. Morris remembered those days, being the shy, quiet one at their family gatherings. It had never lasted long, and Morris was certain Lincoln would find himself involved with the fun before long. Laila would make sure of it. "What about your family? You think they might have an issue with it?"

Theo shook his head. "To be honest, I think Jill's happy I'm seeing someone period. She likes you. Lincoln adores you. And at this point, the others don't have a say."

"I can hear you talking about me," Lincoln said, kicking the car door closed. "I don't adore you. Adoring is for girls. We're cool."

Morris suppressed a grin at the prissy line of Lincoln's mouth. "Yeah, we're cool."

"And I don't get funny." Lincoln turned that look on Theo. "I know what you're worried about. I don't even get clingy. I'm okay with you two. I'm okay with the baby. I'm good, got it?"

"Got it." Theo gave him a little salute and then took one of the casserole dishes. "Sorry I offended your sensibilities."

Morris took the other one as he saw a curtain twitch. They probably had five more minutes before they sent Laila out to haul them inside while they pretended they hadn't been peeking out the window. He squelched the last silly flutter. Time to do this.

"How'd it go, when you came out to them, I mean?" Theo asked as they walked up the driveway. From the backyard, Morris could hear the music from his dad's new sound system. Vince and Joe were probably hanging out on the deck right now with Dad.

Morris grinned at the memory. He'd really gone about that the wrong way. "I may have announced my intention to major in art first. While they were still reeling from that and trying to argue me out of it, I let them know I was gay too. It didn't defuse the situation as much as I thought it would. They thought I was making it up to divert them from arguing about college. So then I got pissed and locked myself in my room to sulk over my misunderstood hurts." Morris shook his head as Theo laughed. His sense of timing needed work. "How'd you tell your family?"

"I was never really all that discreet about it. They figured it out long before I actually said anything. It was anticlimactic." Theo pursed his lips. "I think my dad said something like, okay son, pass me the paprika."

Morris started laughing. He had the feeling he would've gotten along fine with Theo's parents, just as he knew his family would like Theo. Especially his sisters, once they realized Theo was the only one alive who could tease him and get away with it. He was so damned sneaky about it. With that realization, his worries eased.

The front door opened and Laila wheeled herself out with a whoop of delight. "Uncle Morris!" She spun around in a circle around him and then turned to Theo and Lincoln. "Hey, guys. We don't have basketball here, but Grandpa has a cornhole game in the back. Want to play?"

"What's cornhole?" Lincoln asked. "Is it on Xbox?"

Laila shook her head with a laugh. "No. Come on. I'll show you. It's fun."

Lincoln looked back at them and Theo nodded. A relieved expression crossed Lincoln's face. Morris could read his mind—a chance to avoid the crush and not be accused of being unsociable and he was in. "Show me the way, Laila."

"It's probably better that he relaxes with someone he knows before meeting your parents and sisters," Theo said as Lincoln followed Laila around the side of the house.

"Yeah, we can be intimidating." Morris wouldn't want to be in those shoes. "You ready?" he asked as he reached the door. "It's going to be loud."

"Definitely." Theo held up his casserole dish. "This is my secret weapon, that and my charm."

Morris had to give him that. If he had Theo's charm, he'd be able to sell out his table at every convention. He heard activity from the kitchen, feminine chatter and the rattle of silverware. As he shut the front door, Makayla let out a whoop that matched the one Laila gave them. "They're here."

She came bounding out of the kitchen, a glint of mischief in her eyes. "Whoa, wait, holding goods." Morris managed to get his arms up and the dish out of harm's way before she pounced. She jumped up, wrapped herself around him, and bussed him on the cheek. "Hey, Tigger," Morris said with a smile.

"Hey, Tree." Makayla gave him another squeeze and let him go before turning appraising eyes on Theo.

"You must be the boyfriend." She held out a hand, all cool professional now with no trace of his playful sister. Oh boy, the grilling was going to start early. "I'm Makayla, this demon's twin."

"Theo." Theo took her hand and kissed it. "Thank you, thank you, thank you for sending me Rose."

Makayla's eyes suddenly sparkled. "Yeah, she's pleased with the job, and she's picky about those she works with. She told me to go easy on you."

"So did I," Morris said, hip checking her. "Everyone else in the kitchen?"

"Your dad's out back," his mom said as she came in, wiping her hands on a towel as Morris's other two sisters followed. Laverne Proctor had her graying hair cut close to her scalp, but with her round, smiling cheeks, she looked almost girlish. "So happy to meet you, Theo. I heard you were bringing your brother with you?"

"Laila took him out back. He's a little shy, so we'll ease him into it," Morris said.

His mom shot him a fond look. "Sounds familiar. Sierra, why don't you see if he and Laila want some lemonade outside. I think he'll be more comfortable with Laila's mama to start."

Theo greeted them all with an easy smile and a few words for each as Makayla called in their father and the rest of the guys. His family filled up the entryway, everyone talking at once in a mad cacophony of sound. Theo looked to be right in his element. Schmoozing. Him and Makayla ought to be best buddies by the end of the day.

"Come on," his dad said, lightly clapping Morris on the shoulder. "We have a fresh pitcher of margaritas outside. Let me pour you guys some."

"I'd love one." Theo lifted his dish. "Just let me stick these in the kitchen."

"You didn't have to do that," his mom said with a pleased smile as she took Theo's and gestured for Monica to take the other dish, "but I'll admit I'm glad you did. Morris raves about your cooking. What did you make?"

"Charred-corn salad and roasted-peanut slaw." Theo rubbed his hands together as a gleam came into his eyes and Morris knew he was about to volunteer to cook.

"Come on." Morris plucked his sleeve. "I'll pour you a drink and show you my dad's pride."

Augustus's eyes brightened in pleasure. "I have a setup that will make a grown man cry. Best grill there is and a small smoker on the side. Come on. You have to check it out and give me your opinion."

"I'd love to." Theo followed Augustus out through the bustling kitchen. He paused, his eyes widening at the long counters and stove with its six top burners. "You have a butcher's block counter and a farmhouse sink in an island? I have kitchen envy."

Morris gave him a light shove before he could get diverted. If not he'd lose Theo to the stove for the rest of the day. "It's your day off, remember? Drinks and a grill big enough to make even you happy."

Theo turned around and gave Morris an innocent look. "If I didn't know any better, I'd think you were afraid to leave me alone in the kitchen with your mom and sisters," he said in a low voice for Morris's ears only.

"A normal man would find that nerve-racking." Morris had to admit he didn't trust that gleam in Theo's eyes. "No, I want to introduce you to some serious pro-level relaxing. It'll be good for you. You make me eat green things and rare steaks, and I make you chill out for an afternoon." He gave Theo another push toward the deck door.

Theo gave in and let out a low whistle when he saw Augustus's setup. The long brick grill had been erected in its own space in the backyard on a bed of crushed stone. The pale yellow brick outlined in darker brick over the arched opening held firewood for the smoker built into the side. The grill itself was wide enough to hold a ridiculous amount of meat. And there was nothing more that Augustus liked to do on a hot summer day than grill. Even now the smell of smoking meat made Morris's stomach rumble.

"Come on, Theo. We can swap thoughts. Morris tells me you're a mean cook." Augustus poured them all margaritas and discussed the workings of his prize as Theo peppered him with excited questions. Morris sat down between Victor and Joe and stretched out his legs. He wouldn't get a word in edgewise for at least half an hour.

"So that's your new guy," Joe said, giving Theo a contemplative look. Morris's brother-in-law was a serious man whose work had him traveling often, so it was good to have a chance to sit back and relax with him. "He's not what I expected."

"Yeah, me neither," Morris said with a light laugh.

"Augustus is going to love him," Victor added in. "That grill of his is intimidating as hell."

Morris watched his dad and Theo, remembering how he'd been so sure a relationship with Theo would never work. On the surface, they were so different. But the same could be said for his parents. His dad was the no-nonsense litigator and his mom the art teacher who filled their home with the brightly painted abstract landscapes she was so fond of. He liked social gatherings; she preferred the quiet of her garden. He had his old cigars, rich food, and alcohol, and she was more into yoga and balanced diets. But if you looked deeper they just fit, like how he and Theo fit.

His gaze sought out Lincoln, who stood on the lawn next to Laila weighing a beanbag in his hand as he eyeballed the target. This sense of family was what he'd been missing in other relationships, the belonging and intimacy, and he wasn't giving it up for anything.

# Chapter Thirty-Two

THEO GLANCED at Morris, who was busy making more margaritas, and moved toward the deck door. He peeked into the kitchen at the four chattering women inside. The introductions earlier were a confused blur of faces and names, but Morris talked about them often, and there were pictures in his apartment. Theo used that to put faces to names. Morris's mama, Laverne, stood at the stove adding some seasoning to a pot. The three sisters were ranged around the room engaged in various tasks but chatting more than anything. Just the way the guys were poking at the grill and talking.

Theo couldn't forget Morris's twin. Makayla had Morris's broad cheeks and long legs. She was dancing in place, bopping along to the radio as she sliced pineapple for a fruit salad. She'd probably be the hardest to win over.

Laila's mama looked just like her daughter, and Theo had to rack his brains for her name. It was the only one that didn't begin with an M. Oh yeah, Sierra, which meant the pretty lady loading the dishwasher was Monica, the middle sister. He wanted a better look at that kitchen, and he'd only get a chance when Morris was preoccupied.

He slid the door open and slipped inside. "Hey, ladies."

As one they turned toward him with expressions ranging from confused to curious. "Do you need something?" Laverne asked as she glanced out toward the deck where the rest of the men were gathered.

Theo looked over his shoulder. Lincoln was occupied setting up what looked to be a croquet course with Laila, Augustus was adding a log to the smoker, and Morris was pouring another round of drinks. Theo wanted to get a chance to talk without him hovering and leaping to his defense every second. He would have to face the sister gauntlet sometime.

"I wanted to see if you needed any help in here." Theo had survived Morris's dad and brother-in-laws. Now it was time to face the real challenge.

"Well, we're wrapping up and about to join you on the deck, but I can always use another pair of hands," Laverne said with a welcoming smile.

"Yes." Theo rubbed his hands together in delight. He wanted to check out every nook and cranny of this kitchen. It was amazing. One day he would have the kitchen of his dreams at home, but until then he would tinker in kitchens like this.

Morris opened the sliding glass door and stuck his head through. "Do not let that man touch a cooking utensil."

"Hush, you," Theo said with a pointed look at Morris. "Cooking is a bonding ritual. I'm bonding."

Morris shook his head and came in, shutting the door behind him. "You have a problem. You see a kitchen you haven't touched and feel an insatiable need to lay your claim on it."

"You wound me." Theo laid a hand on his chest and assumed an innocent expression. "Similar to how you feel the need to check out every writing utensil you run across." He turned to Laverne. "Did you know he is compelled to test out every pencil and pen? One time when we were at the farmer's market, Morris left a doodle on the scratch pad the vendor had laid out for orders."

"Now that has a familiar ring to it," Makayla said with a hooting laugh. "Half my childhood books still have his sketches."

Morris shook his finger in Theo's direction as he came toward him. "You're changing the subject."

Theo caught his finger and kissed the tip. "Yep."

Laverne handed over a chopping knife. "Since you own a restaurant, I'm sure you're used to prep. I have a mound of peppers to cut up for the kabobs."

"I'd love to." Theo took it with a smile as Morris rolled his eyes.

"Does that mean you're helping too?" Laverne asked, raising a brow in her son's direction as she reached for another apron for Theo. "I'm sure I can find something for you to do."

"I'll help taste." Morris patted his stomach. "That's my official duty. And I'll keep this one out of trouble."

Theo gestured around the kitchen. "You grew up with all of this and you can't cook anything other than frozen pizzas?"

"Again, my job is taster," Morris replied in a lofty tone. "Someone needs to make that sacrifice."

"I've got to give it to you. You'll try anything once even if you side-eye it first." Theo leaned over a pot of gently bubbling greens and sniffed appreciatively. "Now, that smells good. Do you use ham hocks?"

"I like the ham, but I like smoked turkey even better." Laverne tapped her spoon on the rim. "Make the right kind of broth, add a little bit of fat and some heat—not really spice, just heat—and you have yourself a fine pot."

Smoked turkey, Theo might have to try that this fall when it got cooler and people started thinking of the holidays. He gathered the peppers and rinsed them off. "I can't wait to taste them."

"They're good," Morris assured him. "As good as your greens. You'll have to let him make them for you sometime, Ma."

"I guess this means that nonsense about you being a vegan wasn't true." Sierra glanced at Morris even as she continued to shape the rolls from the dough in front of her. Morris assumed an innocent expression as he swiped a fork and edged toward the fridge. She turned to Makayla. "Told you he wasn't a weed-smoking hippie. Morris got you again."

Theo laughed and shook his head. "I couldn't turn Morris into a vegan no matter how hard I tried, and I have zero interest in giving up meat." He stifled a grin as Morris shot him a grateful look—oh baby, you think you're safe. He began chopping the pile of tricolored peppers and onions with quick slices, tossing the cores and seeds into a waste bowl.

"I told you Morris was messing with you." Monica stamped her foot. "You always fall for it, 'Kayla. And this time you had me falling for it."

Makayla turned toward Morris, her eyes narrowing as he lifted the lid to one of the bowls in the refrigerator. "Mom, you'd better watch out, he's stealing bits."

Morris dodged out of the way as Laverne turned toward him. "God, 'Kayla, it was a joke. It's not my fault you're so gullible." He stuck his tongue out at her, and she returned the gesture. Theo watched the interchange with a little pang. Robin and Jill used to bicker like that, all in good fun.

Morris thought he was getting off easy, though. It was time to burst that bubble because Morris's reaction was going to be amazing.

"Now, I have this uncle with a farm in Montana. He raises all kinds of animals, some for eating, though mostly for other kinds of products." Theo hid another smile as Morris and Makayla's squabble stopped and all eyes turned toward him. Morris tried to catch his gaze and shook his head. Theo pretended not to notice as he continued to chop. This was going to be good. He'd been researching alpaca facts for days. "Goats for cheese and milk to make soaps and such. I've always loved visiting there."

"What about alpacas?" Makayla said with a quick glance at her brother, who stared at Theo in exasperation.

"Oh yes, a whole herd of them. Did you know alpacas sing to each other?" Theo turned and gave the room a wistful look. "I always thought about maybe moving there and setting up my own—"

"Theodore Boarman," Morris warned in an ominous voice.

Theo couldn't stop the smirk that crossed his lips. "Morris Proctor."

"You'd better cut it out right now," Morris continued. Damn he looked sexy with that stern expression. He resembled his father more than he realized.

Theo had zero intentions of cutting it out. He'd been waiting too long for this, and Morris's reactions were priceless. "You mean to tell me you don't want to run away to Montana to get married and raise cute baby alpacas?" A flustered look crossed Morris's face, and it caught Theo's heart with a sweet tug. He liked knowing he could get Morris all flustered. "Just think, you can draw alpaca portraits on the side. Imagine the little store we'd have with the artwork, homemade organic food, and wool crafts."

"He isn't serious," Morris announced to the quiet, watching kitchen. "You're not serious. Theo likes to tease, and he doesn't know when to stop."

"That also sounds familiar," Makayla said with a disgruntled look at her brother. "You don't know when to lay off either."

Theo leaned closer to Morris and lowered his voice. "I may have been teasing about the alpacas, but not the M word." Now that he said it, he knew he wanted it. Moving in might be the next step, but he didn't want it to be the last.

Morris's eyes went all hazy again. "If you ever tried talking me into eloping, I'd make you face my mom and sisters," he said with a tinge of desperation in his voice.

Theo gave the ladies in the room an assessing glance. "Fair enough. Don't forget, I'd have to face Jill too, so I suggest we plan it proper, when we get around to planning."

If Theo didn't know better, he'd swear Morris was blushing.

Makayla pointed a finger at Morris and snickered. "You should've seen your face when he started talking about Montana. Your dirty trick was worth it, just to see your face when Theo began messing with you."

"I wouldn't have had to resort to such tactics if you weren't trying to be nosy behind my back," Morris retorted. "I'm allowed a little privacy. If you wanted to know about Theo, you could've asked me."

"A sister's got to look out for her baby bro. And if you don't get out of that potato salad, Mama's gonna thwap you with her spoon."

Morris hid the fork behind his back as Laverne turned toward him. "You're a troublemaker, Makayla. Stop trying to get me into trouble because you fell for the whole thing."

"So who takes care of your books at the restaurant?" Sierra asked before Makayla could retort, and Theo remembered that she was a CPA.

"My sister, thank God. That is not a job I want." Theo swept the squares of pepper into a brightly colored pile and started in on the onions. He spied Morris getting his bite of potato salad and chuckled under his breath. "Though right now I'm taking on a little more of the management until my niece makes her appearance."

Sierra covered the rolls with a cloth before sticking them by the stove. "Laila came during tax season. My boss about had hysterics." She began cleaning the counter and shook her head at Morris as he investigated the next bowl. "You'd better be using the spreadsheet I gave you."

"I am." Morris crossed his heart and nudged the door closed with his hip. "And I'm keeping every receipt, filed away by month. I swear."

"You'd better or you'll have to find another sucker to do your taxes next quarter."

"You'll see. I'm the soul of organization." Morris palmed a brownie and turned to Theo. "And on that note, you are on your own. Don't say I didn't warn you when they go for your throat."

Theo watched in amusement as Morris retreated before any more comments could be made about how he lived his life. Sometimes a little mothering and sistering could get old, but damn he missed it. The sisters looked at each other, and Makayla smiled a feral little smile.

"Please don't go for my jugular. Morris thinks I'm adorable the way I am." Theo finished up the onions and looked around for something else to do. He really did love this kitchen. When he, Morris, and Lincoln looked at new places, they'd have to look for one with glassed-in cabinets like this. Theo eyed Laverne's well-stocked spice cabinet. "Would you mind terribly if I made a rub for the kabobs?"

"I don't see why not," Laverne said as she put a lid on the greens and wiped her hands. "Augustus usually takes care of that, but I don't think he'd mind picking up a new trick or two."

"What kind of meat are you using?" Theo asked, opening the cabinet and very aware of three sets of eyes on him. Maybe he shouldn't have teased Morris out the door.

"Half chicken, half shrimp."

"That'll be good." Theo began picking spices, envying Morris his stolen bites. He was getting rather hungry himself.

Makayla came to Theo's side and crossed her arms. "I don't know how many sisters you've got, but Morris has three. Hurt him and you're going to find all three of us on your doorstep."

"Makayla!" Laverne shot her a disapproving look. "What would you say if Morris threatened Victor?"

"Morris did threaten Victor, Mama. Don't you remember?"

Monica laughed. "Oh God, I'd forgotten about that. He tore Victor up in that silly wrestling video game and told him to remember that if he ever made you cry."

"That wasn't a threat. It was strategy," Theo said with a laugh. "I have siblings, so I can appreciate a good protective threat. The first time Jill brought Craig by when they were seriously dating and discussing moving in together, I may have done something similar. And Morris told me Lincoln already gave him a warning about me. It's okay."

Makayla leaned her elbows on the counter as she watched Theo concoct his rub. "His last boyfriend messed with his head."

Theo pondered the cumin as he considered her words. He knew part of the issue was Morris's family, though well-meaning, and Morris's own pride. And because of that pride, he didn't think Morris would appreciate him sticking his foot in. "We've talked about that, just as we talked about my own hang-ups."

Theo gave her a serious look in return. "Morris wants to be appreciated for himself, and I do."

"And what do you want, young man?" Laverne asked, pouring herself a glass of tea before putting the pitcher on a tray to take outside.

"I want someone who'll stick by me." Theo thought of Morris and smiled. "And I have no doubt Morris will."

# Chapter Thirty-Three

"I SEE you didn't manage to extricate him," Augustus observed as Morris emerged back onto the deck.

"No, he's in his element." Morris sat back in the deck chair and picked up his drink. "He's probably giving them alpaca facts while julienning something."

And thinking about marriage. Wow, that still made Morris's insides quake a little. That was the commitment to end all commitments, but Morris had to admit his thoughts had been dancing around that too. He wouldn't move in with a guy, give up his personal space and freedom, if he wasn't serious about their future. This was kind of making it official. He'd come here thinking he'd let his family get to know Theo and Lincoln, let them realize how important they both were to him. It looked like he was leaving with a set future, and despite the inner nerves, he was floating on a happy cloud.

"You mean the alpaca thing was real?" Victor asked, his eyes widening in disbelief. "Makayla's going to have kittens."

"Oh no, I was messing with her," Morris said with a light laugh. "I forgot to tell Theo about it and he found out. Now he's running with the joke for all he's worth, teasing me. I can't believe Makayla bought it."

"That's because she trusted that one." Joe pointed toward his daughter out on the lawn. Laila was laughing as Lincoln spoke earnestly to her, waving his hands to emphasize his point.

Augustus sat a platter of sliced grilled sausage and spicy mustard in front of them and took one of the empty chairs. "I didn't believe it for one minute. No son of mine was going to be a vegan."

Morris really wished he wouldn't use that particular phrase. It brought back too many uncomfortable memories of arguments over school, over his life choices. Arguments that had been settled but still lingered in his mind. Today was a good day, a new start, and he wasn't going to fall into the habit of getting pissy and defensive.

"I'm going to go harass Sierra and see if we can't get a little something extra to go with the sausages," Joe said as he stood up. "Anybody else want a beer?" He took orders, and Morris peered inside the kitchen as Joe opened the door. He caught a glimpse of Theo, still chatting away, looking completely at ease.

"Hey, Linc, there's some food here if you and Laila are hungry," Morris called to the pair on the lawn. Lincoln's hunger must've outweighed his shyness because after a hasty consultation with Laila, they both made their way to the deck, Lincoln lagging back. "Go easy on him, Dad. No interrogations. He's already nervous because I've told tales of your exploits in court."

"Theo survived," Augustus said with a good-natured grin. "I'm the easy one."

"Theo thrives off interacting with people," Morris said, giving Lincoln an encouraging smile as he started up the ramp.

"So he's shy like you," Victor said.

"I am not shy. People just annoy me, so I prefer my little cave more days than not." Morris high-fived Laila as she made a beeline for the food. "Work up an appetite?"

"I did, beating Linc in cornhole," Laila teased as she grabbed a plate. "He's making up for it in croquette, though. I think it's the angles. He's a math nerd."

Lincoln blushed and shoved his hands in his pockets. "Where's Theo?"

Morris pointed at the deck doors behind him. "In the kitchen, where else? But I wouldn't go looking for him," he added as Lincoln's body shifted toward the door. "I'm sure my sisters are digging out every secret he's ever had, or at least trying their hardest. If you go in, they'll focus on you next."

Lincoln's eyes widened. "I think I'll stay here instead." He straightened his shoulders and faced Augustus, Victor, and Joe. "Pleased to meet you. Thank you for having me. I'm Lincoln."

Morris knew how difficult that had been for Lincoln, and he was rather proud of him for not waiting to be introduced. Augustus gave him a measuring look, then smiled. "Good to have you. Pull up a chair. Do you help your brother out at the restaurant?"

Lincoln nodded as he filled a small plate and retreated to the other side of the deck, where there was an empty spot for Laila's chair. "Yes, sir. I bus tables and do all the odd jobs."

"You don't work during the school year, do you?" Augustus asked, his heavy brows drawing together in a frown.

"Oh no, not on school nights." Lincoln grimaced. "Theo and Jill won't let me. I usually work Friday and Saturday. Sometimes if I'm hanging out there after school and I'm done with my homework and it's busy I'll pitch in. I like the extra money for games, and I bought myself a new bike this summer."

"He started helping me out at cons too, Dad," Morris added. "Pretty much the same thing, though, glorified gofer."

"I love it." Lincoln flashed Morris a smile that animated his thin, narrow features.

"Really?" Augustus turned toward Lincoln. "You're not thinking of going into that life, are you?"

Morris bristled even as he tried telling himself to not take offense. It sounded worse than he was sure his dad meant, but still it rankled.

"Oh no." Lincoln shook his head. "I mean it was fun. I love comic books and cosplay, but I couldn't be a comic book artist. Morris is really good. You should see his table. There's always someone there looking."

Morris loved that kid. He really did. Augustus gave Morris a measuring look, and Morris refrained from comment. It didn't hurt for his dad to hear he was a success from an outside party. "I want to be a video game designer," Lincoln continued.

Augustus's heavy brows lifted. "What job prospects are there for that field?"

Okay, picking at him was one thing, but Morris was not going to let him start on Lincoln. "It's an ever-changing, robust field," Morris said in a level tone as he gave his dad a warning look.

"Is it stable?" Augustus asked skeptically. "You don't want to go through school, pay all kinds of money for a degree, and not have a job at the end of it."

"Bethesda Games isn't too far from our place, and they're huge," Lincoln jumped in. "I want to work there after college. I've made game mods for friends and designed some simple stuff. Game design is really neat because it lets you balance creative and tech. Like you have to know art and storytelling as much as coding."

"Think about it, Dad," Morris said before Augustus could add another argument. "Law school was expensive and there's no guarantee after you put in all that work and money a law firm will pick you up and pay you what you need to get out from debt. There are a lot of poor lawyers."

"You've got a point there," Augustus had to admit.

Joe returned, carrying a small cooler. "I've got lemonade, if you want some, Laila." He set the cooler off to the side and thrust his chin out toward Lincoln. "Who's your friend?"

Lincoln blushed to his ears, much to Laila's fascination. "That's Linc. He's Theo's brother. Theo's inside and Mama's making him squirm."

"Is that right?" Joe said with one of his slow smiles. "He didn't look like he was squirming that much to me."

"Probably not," Morris said with a shake of his head. "I've yet to see Theo squirm. Wait, I take that back. He definitely squirmed when he saw the state of my freezer and fridge. It was everything Mom won't let you have anymore, Dad."

Augustus sighed and gave the kitchen door a sour look. "A little preservative and processing keeps the body from decaying."

"I tried telling Theo the same thing." Morris thought of the new contents of his freezer with a rueful smile. "It didn't work either. And I get the feeling once we move in together, I'll never see a Hot Pocket again."

"Moving in, that's a big step," Victor said. "I remember you freaking out when I moved in with Makayla."

"I did not freak out." It wasn't freaking out; Morris was only expressing care and concern. He supposed that's just what his dad was doing too. Funny, when he thought about it that way, it made him look at all those irritating comments in a new light. "I wanted to make sure you were absolutely certain."

"On pain of death certain," Victor pointed out.

"I didn't outright say death." Morris might have meant it, but he knew there were limits to what Makayla would let him get away with, and threatening Victor on that level would've crossed a line.

"You didn't have to." Victor leaned toward Lincoln. "Did you give him a hard time about your brother? Please tell me you did."

Lincoln looked down at his plate and shrugged, but Morris saw the small smile. "I didn't threaten him."

"He expressed his concern." Morris gave him a wink. "He trapped me in a car, and I got the message."

"Well, don't jump down my throat, but I for one am glad you are going to be sharing your life with someone." Augustus made a point of fishing for a beer so he wouldn't have to meet Morris's gaze. "Does Theo have health insurance through the restaurant?"

"Dad," Morris said with more exasperation than irritation. "I can take care of myself."

"In a relationship you take care of each other." Augustus gave him a pointed look. "So sue me if I'm happy that you might have a backup plan."

"I can't sue you," Morris said with a grin. "You'd win."

"Your dad was like that with Sierra and Makayla," Joe observed. "Don't take it personal."

"Talk to Monica," Victor added. "I'm sure she can give you an earful about his hovering."

Morris had never thought about that before. Monica was the only other one of his siblings who also lived alone. She taught school in Baltimore. Though if there was anyone in this world who could take care of herself, it was Monica. He was sure she could take him out with three well-placed blows. It was a theory he never wanted to test.

"Don't get me started on your sister." Augustus pointed to the side of his head. "See all that gray? That's because of her, and I don't dare say a word because she's even more touchy than you."

"I am not touchy. I'm trying to point out I can take care of myself and I have been for a decade now. I'm doing what makes me happy, and I'm with someone who makes me happy." Morris met his dad's gaze and saw the bemusement there. "Got it?"

"I got it."

"So when are you giving up those skirts?" Joe asked, with a gesture to Morris's attire. "Don't you know black men don't wear kilts?"

"This black man does." Morris gave Joe an ominous stare, and Joe grinned back.

"See, touchy."

Morris opened his mouth to retort and then closed it thoughtfully. When one person said something he could ignore it. When several people commented on it, that was something else. He was living his own life and he was happy. He needed to learn to let other people's comments roll off his back.

Morris breathed a sigh of relief as Theo came back out bearing a vegetable tray as his mom followed with a pitcher of tea. Theo's eyes were sparkling, and he looked none the worse for having spent the last thirty minutes alone with his mom and sisters. Morris wished he could say he felt that unscathed. Theo set the tray down and sat next to Morris, accepting the margarita he held out. "Thank you for holding this for me."

"I see you survived." Morris leaned forward and grabbed a celery stick and some dip.

"I have war wounds and deep, lasting emotional scars." Theo took a sip of his drink. "I'm going to need some tender loving care when we get home."

Makayla perched on Victor's knee and poked Morris in the leg with her toe. "I took my vengeance out on him for the stunt you pulled."

"Oh, that's how we're going to play it?" Morris turned to Victor. "Sorry man, you're toast."

"Leave me out of your squabbles." Victor shook his head at Theo. "Word of advice, never try to get in between quarreling twins. It's dangerous."

"I'll keep that in mind." Theo took a sip of his drink. "This is really good. I—"

"Oh my God! Oh my God! Theo!" Lincoln jumped up, spilling the rest of his plate. He stared at his phone, his mouth agape, hand fisted in his hair.

"What?" Theo frowned, then pulled out his own phone. A stunned expression crossed his face, and he lifted his gaze to Morris's. "Oh my God, Jill's in labor. For real this time. They aren't going to try to stop it."

Morris stared at Theo. "Are you kidding me?" Then he looked at Lincoln, who was running his fingers through his hair until it stood on end. He took in a deep breath of wonderful food scents and resigned himself to hospital food. He stood up, checking to see if he had his car keys on him. "Are they at the hospital now?"

Theo nodded as Lincoln made a strangled sound. "Yeah, Craig says she's settled and it's going fast. Oh my God."

"Babies come at their own time," Laverne said with a laugh as she got up. "For Morris and Makayla, it was in the middle of an ice storm. I didn't want to leave my comfortable bed, and their daddy was in a panic we wouldn't make it on time."

"Don't remind me," Augustus said. "Delivering twins was never on my list of things I wanted to have to do."

Laverne lightly slapped him on the arm. "Do not talk to me about delivering twins, carrying twins, or anything else like that. You got off easy. Wait a few minutes, Theo, and I'll pack you up some plates. You helped cook it. You might as well help eat it."

"You've already heard my tale," Sierra said with a fond look at Laila. "You, young lady, almost got me fired."

"I'm so sorry," Theo said to Morris. "I know I promised you a whole day of me and you."

"It is going to be a whole day of me and you, just not in this spectacular backyard." Morris held up his keys. "I drove, remember?"

"How much have you had to drink?" Augustus asked, eyeballing Morris's glass.

"One margarita over the last couple hours, and I've been stuffing myself with whatever food I could glean. I never got into the second round," Morris reassured his dad. "I'm okay to drive."

"Linc, go grab your things. Morris, why don't you stay and I'll come pick you up before work tomorrow," Theo said with a dazed look in his eyes. "I don't want you to miss out on time with your family."

"It's okay, my alpaca man. I'm going with you." It was a good two hours to Southern Maryland and back. Theo would have enough on his mind today and tomorrow without having to worry about shuttling Morris.

"You are?" Theo continued to stare at him as if he couldn't seem to get his brain to work.

"Of course I am. One, you shouldn't be driving. You're going to want to spend every five minutes looking at your phone. My future brother-in-law is in the car with your adorable self, and I want you both to make it in one piece." Morris caught Theo's hand and gave his knuckles a kiss as Theo shot him a grateful look.

"I love you," Theo said under his breath.

"To quote the greatest smuggler ever... I know." Morris shook a finger at him. "And don't tell me you don't know who Han Solo is. That just may be a deal breaker."

Lincoln came up shouldering his bag, his eyes wild. "Is Jill okay?" he demanded as they made their way into the kitchen, where Laverne and Makayla were bustling around. Laila followed them, pestering Morris with questions he barely heard. He was glad this happened on a day off and not while Theo and Lincoln were at the restaurant.

"Yep. Craig is hovering over her." Theo pressed his lips together, his anxiety showing, before he offered him a tight smile. "You might be an uncle by the time we get down there."

"Ooohh." Laila wheeled into the kitchen and reached up to snag two rolls off the counter. She tossed one to Morris. "Be an uncle like Uncle Morris."

"No." Makayla shook her head. "Don't be an uncle like Morris."

"I am an awesome uncle." Morris took a bite of his roll and grinned at his mom. Then he nudged Theo in the side. "Ready?"

"Hold on," Laverne said. "Almost done." She closed up the to-go containers as Makayla came forward with a bag to put them in with some paper plates and everything else they could possibly need. "Hospital food is terrible. This should tide you over."

Morris took the bag with a rush of gratitude. He leaned over and kissed her cheek. "Thank you. I would've been miserable eating out of the cafeteria."

Laverne grinned in pleasure. "If you want to thank me, send on a picture. I love seeing new babies."

"Seriously, thank you," Theo said, catching her hands. "And thank you for having us. I promise to stick around later next time." He smiled at Makayla and gave Lincoln a light push toward the door. "If any of you are ever in Solomon's Island, come by the bistro. Dinner's on me."

Theo bolted out the door without waiting for a response with Lincoln right behind him. Morris shook his head and followed. The pair of them were one hot mess. He hoped they calmed down before they got to the hospital, or one look at them would probably send Jill into hysterics.

# Chapter Thirty-Four

"YOU DO know where the gas pedal is, don't you?" Theo asked tartly and returned to gnawing on his knuckle as he silently willed Morris to go faster. There was such a thing as being too cautious.

"We're almost there, in one piece. Let's not jinx it now," Morris replied in a patient voice. "I doubt Jill wants you in the delivery room, and I know you don't want to be there."

"Oh God no," Lincoln said as Theo shot Morris a panicked look at that thought.

No, he couldn't handle being in the delivery room. And he doubted Jill would even know if he was pacing the waiting room floor. It didn't matter. He wanted to be there. He wanted to be nearby.

"What is she doing in the hospital in Clinton? Why isn't she at the hospital closer to home?" Theo muttered for Morris's ears only. "I don't know where this hospital is."

"Don't worry," Morris said as he navigated through the bottlenecked traffic to get into the turn lane. "I know exactly where it is. It's literally right around the corner."

"Did Dustin and Robin answer?" Lincoln asked for the six hundredth time and Theo had to bite his lip to keep from snarling a reply that had far more to do with his resentment at his missing siblings than it did with Lincoln's pestering.

Theo checked his phone again and wished he could lie. "No. It's a holiday. They may be at a bar-b-que. Why don't you try to reach them?"

Morris reached over and took his hand, giving him a silent squeeze of support. "Were you teasing about getting married?" he asked in a low voice.

"Not that part." Theo turned to look at him, trying to gauge Morris's expression. He couldn't tell if Morris was trying to distract him or if it was a serious question. "I hope I'm not rushing you. I know what I want. I'm one of those people who just seems to know. I knew I wanted the bistro. I knew I wanted to be Lincoln's guardian. And I know I want you with me. That being said, I know this isn't entirely a normal boy meets boy situation, so I understand if you want more time."

Call him greedy or needy, but Theo didn't really want to wait for an answer. His heart pounded as a slow smile crossed Morris's lips.

"I should hedge to tease you for that bullshit you pulled earlier, but now's not the time for it. I don't need to think it over." Morris pulled into the crowded parking lot and found a space tucked into the back.

"Was that a proposal?" Lincoln asked, leaning forward. "Because if it was, that was the lamest proposal I've ever heard."

Morris chuckled softly. "Okay, let me do better." He turned to Theo and took his hands. His eyes were warm with a little amusement and a lot of love, and damn, Theo was lost. "Do you wanna?" The corner of Morris's mouth lifted in a shy smile.

"Oh hell yeah," Theo breathed and leaned forward to seal it with a kiss. Worry and resentment over his siblings faded away under the warm rush of happiness.

A yelp came from the back seat, and the sound of a door opening and closing followed. Morris laughed again and pulled away. "I think that was official enough for him."

Theo smiled and got out of the car, and his smile faded at the sight of the hospital. He saw Lincoln frozen in place a few steps away, his shoulders hunched, as he also stared up at the sprawling building. It looked different from the hospital where they'd visited their dad, a fact Theo was profoundly grateful for. Maybe Jill had made Craig drive here instead for that reason.

Theo couldn't blame her. They'd spent too many hours at the other hospital visiting, hoping, and praying. Theo walked up to Lincoln and touched his shoulder. "This is a good visit." This was welcoming new family, not saying goodbye.

Lincoln's shoulders hunched even more, and he seemed rooted to the spot. He turned anxious eyes on Theo. "But what if—"

"Don't say it, man," Morris said as he came to a halt on Lincoln's other side. "Women have been having babies for millennia. They are far tougher than we are. Come on." Morris nudged Lincoln's side. "We have to swing by the gift shop. You can't meet your new niece empty-handed."

That got Lincoln moving, and Theo shot Morris a grateful glance. He'd never gone by the gift shop before, so that was one place he wouldn't associate with his parents. He sent Craig a quick text message to let him know they'd arrived and to check on Jill.

In the gift shop Lincoln was going through each and every stuffed animal they had on display with the expression of a man on a mission. Morris touched Theo's hand and gave him a concerned look. "You holding up?"

"Yeah." Theo hugged his arms to himself for a second, squelching the jump of nervous energy. "I'm not that good at waiting. I like doing." It made his hands feel empty and useless. He stationed himself in front of the cards and began going through them without really seeing them. "Why hasn't Craig texted back?" he fretted in a low voice to Morris.

"He might have his hands full." Morris squeezed his shoulder. "You pick a card and I'll go ask. I know someone who works here. If Jill's pushing, then Craig is not going to have a chance to look at his phone. If he tries, she might make him eat it. Truth."

Theo was pathetically grateful Morris was there. He might've been coming out of this skin otherwise. He plucked a card out at random and joined Lincoln, who had a lamb and a lion in hand and was contemplating them as if the fate of the world depended on his choice. Theo turned the card over and over, his thoughts whirling.

"So you're getting married?" Lincoln asked. "That wasn't all for show?"

"No. I guess that's a jump from moving in together. Though I suspect it'll be down the road. At least a year away." Theo eyed his brother, trying to gauge his thoughts. "You okay with that?"

"Yeah." Lincoln flicked him a glance and then went right back to his decision. "But if you guys ever break up or this wedding thing doesn't go through, I'm moving in with Morris."

There was very little Theo was sure of, and he and Morris was at the top. "I'll keep that in mind," Theo replied with a perfectly straight face.

"Which one do you think?" Lincoln asked, holding up the stuffed animals. "These are the two softest in the bunch."

Theo eyed the offerings, then pointed to the lion. "That one."

Lincoln looked at it with a frown. "Are you sure? It seems fierce for a baby."

"Do you honestly believe Craig and Jill will produce anything lamblike?" Theo plucked the lamb out of Lincoln's hand. "The fiercer the better. Baby girl has already put her mom on notice, twice mind you, that she's doing things in her own time."

Lincoln's whole face brightened. "You've got a good point. This is Jill we're talking about. Everything's going to be okay, right?" For a moment, he looked at Theo for reassurance, and then he shook his head. "No, don't give me promises. It *will* be all right. You haven't heard from Dustin and Robin, have you?"

"Actually, I'm right here."

Theo whirled around at the sound of his sister's nervous voice. Robin stood a few feet away, rocking on her heels, a habit she always had when she thought she was in trouble.

"Hey," she said with a little half wave.

"Robin!" Lincoln gasped, dropping the lion. Theo bobbled and caught it, his heart suddenly pounding. Lincoln ran to her and engulfed her in an enthusiastic hug. "You're here. I can't believe you're here."

The joy in Lincoln's voice almost undid him. Theo watched them with a painful ache. God, it seemed like Lincoln had grown to be a yard bigger than her now. And she'd cut her hair. It hung in a sleek bob that framed her face. It made her look older and more unapproachable, but the way she clung to Lincoln told a different story.

They pulled apart, and Robin looked at him, the regret and pain so clear in her eyes that Theo was moving before he realized. She clung to him, shaking. "I'm sorry. I'm so sorry."

"I am too," Theo said and realized he was. He could've reached out more, done something else to heal the breach other than sit back and lick his wounds and sulk in his pride. He rubbed his hand over her back, his heart so full he thought it would break. "I've missed you so much."

"I thought I wouldn't be welcome after... after what we said." Robin clung harder and then pulled back with tears shining in her eyes.

"*You* are always welcome," Theo insisted, brushing a hand over her hair and pulling her close again for another hug. One more minute and he'd be crying too.

"Is Dustin coming?" Lincoln asked in a voice both hopeful and anxious.

Robin gave Theo an uncertain look. "He's planning on it. He wanted me to let him know if you were going to be here."

Theo sighed, his heart heavy once again at the implication. "I wasn't planning on going anywhere."

"Please, I don't want a fight between you two." Robin caught Theo's arm, her expression pleading. "Please don't."

"I don't either." Theo patted her arm. "I'm not ruining Jill's day. If after I see her, he wants to come in, I'll go."

"That's not fair," Lincoln objected, dark red spots flashing on his cheeks.

"It's okay." Theo looked up at him. "Seriously, it's a start, Linc, a good start. You can slay another dragon for me later. Jill should have the chance to see all of us today without drama or hurt."

It hung there, awkward and uncertain as Lincoln's shoulders stiffened more, and then he relaxed as he saw Robin's pleading expression. "Okay," he said softly and Robin smiled, hugging him again.

Lincoln met Theo's gaze, his eyes hesitant, and Theo smiled back. He'd never forget that Lincoln had his back, and that meant more to him than he could say. "It's okay," he mouthed again. "Thank you."

"It's go time!" Morris came back rubbing his hands together, breaking up the last of the awkwardness. He gestured to the forgotten lion in Theo's hands. "Go buy that and prepare to be a sucker when you first meet her. Nieces have their uncles wrapped around their tiny fingers." He shot Robin a curious look, then raised a questioning brow at Theo.

"You would know." Theo reached for Morris's hand, anxious on so many levels that he couldn't even express. He handed Lincoln his wallet and the gifts they'd picked out. "Would you get these rung up for us?"

"Sure." Lincoln cast a look between Theo and Robin, then made a beeline for the register.

Morris's long fingers closed around Theo's in silent support. Having Morris next to him bolstered Theo. If Dustin showed up, he wouldn't let it come down to a confrontation. "Morris, I want you to meet my sister Robin. Robin, this is my fiancé, Morris."

Robin's mouth opened in surprise. "When did you find time to date?" Then she blushed and held out a hand. "I'm sorry. It's nice to meet you."

Morris chuckled and shook her hand. "Trust me, finding time to date was an ongoing issue between us." He gave Theo a loving nudge. "But we worked out a system."

"So you're the one who texted me?" she asked, cocking her head. "You said you were a friend. I guess I should've realized."

Texted? Theo turned to Morris, narrowing his eyes, as Morris smiled cheerfully at Robin. "That would be me."

Before Theo could demand answers, Lincoln came bounding back, one long, lanky string of nervous energy. "Where do we go? Did your friend say if Jill's okay?"

"She's fine and I've got directions. Jill's in stage two of labor. I had to text Sierra and ask her what that meant, and she said it probably wouldn't be long now." Morris led them down one long corridor after another, and Theo walked beside him, his head down, trying not to look around as Robin and Lincoln chatted behind them in low voices.

"You okay?" Morris asked as they reached the waiting area.

"Yeah, yeah, I think so." Theo rubbed his hands on his thighs. There were a couple other families in the waiting room, and the air was filled with a mix of excitement and anxious patience. That was a step up from other hospital waiting rooms where a different kind of anxiety cast a pall over everything. "Robin said Dustin's thinking of coming if I'm not here. I told her to let him know I'd go if he did come, to give him some time with Jill. I don't want it to be an argument, but it pisses me off."

"Understandable." Morris steered him toward a couple empty seats.

"God, I want a cigarette." Theo shook his head, his jaw tightening. "I've got to let this mad at Dustin go because Lincoln's already about to get into it for me, and I refuse to be the cause of a fight between them."

Morris pondered that as he pulled out a sketchbook and pencil from his ever-present bag. "I wouldn't be so quick to leave if he does show up. It doesn't have to be an argument. Let him see you. Let him see you're still here, being beside your family, taking care of Lincoln like you promised. You are wearing that shirt for him, right? Because you're proud of him and what he's accomplished at school, show that. Let him see that generous heart of yours, and not the pain. There will be time later for the hard conversations. And maybe seeing you in that light will make him reconsider what he's missing."

Theo heaved out a sigh as Morris began to sketch, the pencil moving in long strokes over the page. "So don't get prickly with my family the way you get prickly with yours?"

"Exactly." Morris shot him an amused glance. "Though you have more cause, and I'm working on my knee-jerk defensiveness."

Robin and Lincoln were sitting in a corner, their heads together as they talked. He wanted to go to them, to join in, but he wasn't entirely sure of his welcome. He didn't want to ruin it for Lincoln. Let him catch up with her, and then maybe he would have a chance.

"So you texted her." Theo studied Morris, not sure if he should be irritated or not. He was sure that most of his irritation came only because he was on edge.

"Yep, Dustin too." Morris continued drawing in apparent unconcern. "I got their numbers from Lincoln. Did it right after we went to the farmer's market after you told me what happened. Never heard from him, but she responded a couple times."

Okay, dammit, Theo was annoyed. "How would you like it if I went behind your back and interfered with your family?"

Morris finally looked up, lifting one heavy brow. The man said so much with just a look. That was irritating too. "Last I checked we were working on being a family ourselves. And if things go the way we plan, they're going to be my family too. How would you react if someone in my family was causing me misery? Wouldn't you say something?"

Fuck, Morris had several points there. Theo crossed his arms with a scowl but couldn't think of a rebuttal. He could say it was crossing a boundary or they weren't engaged yet when Morris had sent the text. But Morris was right; Theo would've done the same damn thing. Yep, irritating, never mind that on a normal day he'd probably be overjoyed.

"You could've discussed it with me first," he grumbled.

"True, and I'm sorry I didn't, but I'm not sorry I sent the text because she's here. And you know what, she's probably not here because of my text either. I reminded them they were missed and welcome." Morris went back to his drawing. "So please don't be mad at me."

Theo huffed out his breath and then realized he didn't want to be mad at Morris, not when it was nerves fueling him. "What else did you say to them?" he asked curiously, watching Robin and Lincoln reconnect. He couldn't be mad seeing that.

"Oh, just that there was a new baby coming and what better time to come together with no worries about the past and that when you and Lincoln talked about them it was obvious how much you loved them."

Theo smiled despite himself and kissed Morris's shoulder. "You're too much, you know that?"

The corner of Morris's mouth lifted. "You too, Boarman."

Theo tried to sit still, but the inactivity soon had him on his feet looking for something to do. Morris shook his head and continued to draw, his lips pursed in thought. He could probably wait forever if he had enough paper and lead in his pencil. Robin broke away from her conversation with Lincoln and walked over to him as Theo paced restlessly about.

"How's school going?" Theo asked, searching for an opening. "You still studying business?"

"Yeah. I doubled down this last year. Buried myself in school. I think I'll end up graduating a semester early." Robin leaned against the wall next to him as Theo finally stood still.

"I guess that means you're not still dating that theater major?" Theo asked.

Robin shook her head. "He bolted not long after Mom and Dad's funeral. He said I had too much drama and he couldn't deal. Stupid bastard."

"I'm sorry," Theo said quietly. He didn't like the thought of Robin dealing with all of that alone. He really wished she'd let him be there for her.

"Artistic types." Robin shrugged. "They can be flaky as fuck."

"Not all of them." Theo glanced over to where Morris was still bent over his sketchbook as he talked to Lincoln.

Robin followed the direction of his gaze. "I have to be honest, that was a surprise. You haven't really dated since Dad got sick."

"It surprised both of us, too, but we fit each other. He's a good man. I'd like for you to get a chance to know him. Maybe you can come over for dinner after we leave?" Theo tried to keep his voice nonchalant but didn't succeed. "There's a pizza joint that Morris loves. I'm sure they have a branch nearby."

"Okay." Robin looked at him and offered him a tentative smile. "I'd really like that."

"Yeah, me too." Theo slid his arm around her shoulders and pulled her in for a hug.

"I hear there are some uncles waiting," a voice cut into the moment. Theo's head jerked up. A woman with a vaguely familiar face stood at the entrance to the maternity ward, clad in a nurse's purple scrubs covered with balloons.

"And an aunt," Morris said, stuffing his sketchbook away. "Hey, Mrs. Suero." He took Theo's hand as he approached as if he knew Theo needed that closeness. "Theo, this is Felipe's mom."

"I was trying to figure out why you looked familiar." Felipe had her eyes and the humor in them. "Nice to meet you. Is Jill okay, the baby?"

"Everyone's fine," Mrs. Suero said with a reassuring smile. "Mama's getting cleaned up, and Daddy's got the little one in the room if you want to meet her."

"You're not going to make me hold her, are you?" Lincoln shook his head adamantly at Theo. "I don't know anything about holding babies."

"You'll be fine," Morris said as the group followed Mrs. Suero down the hallway. "They're easy to hold at this stage. Wait until they get to the squirmy part and don't want to be held."

Craig sat in the rocking chair in the room, a blanket-wrapped bundle in his arms. He looked up with a huge grin. "Holy hell, Robin." He rose carefully and walked over to them. "Here, Theo, meet Olivia."

Theo took the baby with a combination of awe and a little fear. "Hey there." He looked down at the tiny wrinkled face. Olivia's eyes were closed, fair lashes fanning her cheeks, and her lips were pursed. Theo's heart squeezed. This is what they meant by love at first sight.

Lincoln crowded closer as Craig picked Robin up in a huge hug. "I'm so glad you came. Jill's going to be thrilled you're here."

"Oh my, isn't she a cutie," Morris said, stroking her cheek with his knuckle. He grinned at Theo. "I can see it already, a goner, the both of you."

Theo shot him a smile and looked at the trepidation and longing in Lincoln's eyes. "Want to hold her a minute before Robin steals her?" He laughed at the torn expression that crossed his brother's face. "That's about how I felt when I first held you, and I was almost your age. Sit down and crook your arm. I promise you won't hurt her."

"She doesn't weigh anything," Lincoln said after Theo nestled the baby in his arms. He cradled her as if she were made of delicate glass.

"Try carrying her on top of your bladder. Then you'll realize how much she weighs," Jill said tartly as her wheeled bed was pushed into the room. Theo straightened and examined his sister's face. She looked exhausted but radiant, and then her eyes lit up even more when she saw Robin. "Oh my God, come here, you."

Theo looked away, blinking back the stinging in his eyes, and Morris slid an arm around his shoulders. "Think we should tell them about us or wait?" he asked in a low voice by Theo's ear.

"Wait," Theo replied as he watched Robin and Jill's reunion. "There's so much emotion in this room, any more happiness and we'll all start weeping like we're in a bad soap opera."

When Jill finally released Robin, she looked in danger of a good cry. Theo had to do something about that because if she got started, they all would. He stepped up to the bed and squeezed her hand. "You weren't supposed to take Labor Day seriously," Theo said with a solemn expression.

Jill laughed and laid her hand over her stomach with a grimace. "Don't make me laugh, you big jerk."

"Good job, Mama." Theo leaned down and kissed her cheek. "She's perfect."

Jill's eyes welled, and she wrapped her arms around his neck. "Thank you."

Theo straightened as the room went quiet. He glanced at the doorway and saw Dustin hovering uncertainly just past the opening. Theo and him looked quite a bit alike, only Dustin was taller, his hair darker, and his eyes had a moody cast to them. So many emotions swarmed up that at first Theo couldn't identify them.

He looked at Morris, remembering what he'd said. Hard conversations could come later. Today was for welcoming. He smiled at Dustin and stepped back so he could approach. "Looks like someone is here to see you and Olivia."

Jill's eyes widened as Dustin stepped into the room and then she held out her arms, bursting into tears. Dustin stopped his advance with a panicked look, and Theo clapped him on the shoulder. "They're happy tears." For a moment their eyes met. Dustin glanced down at Theo's shirt and a bewildered expression crossed his face. Theo smiled again. "Good to see you, bro."

# Chapter Thirty-Five

LINCOLN BOLTED out of the car with the remainder of the pizza as soon as Morris killed the car engine. Morris watched him disappear around the corner of the house with a shake of his head. They wouldn't see him for the rest of the night.

"You think he's okay?" Theo asked.

"Yeah. It's been a busy, emotional day, and his introverted self was out dealing with all kinds of people, strangers and long-lost family. He's probably going to steal that pizza and hole up in his room playing games and decompressing."

"Do you need to do the same? Recharge, I mean?" Theo asked him. "I'll understand if you want some you time and space."

"When you find that right person, being with them is restful." Morris smiled at him. "All I need is you, that couch, and something on the TV, and I'll be good. On that note, I'm shutting off my phone. No more texts, emails, nothing. Just me and you."

"Don't forget your sketchbook." Theo tapped his bag. "That's part of the formula. And I'm stealing that sketch you did of Olivia and putting it on the fridge."

"You know me well," Morris said with a chuckle.

Theo's answering smile lit up his whole face. "Do you want to grab Cassie and bring her up?"

"Yeah, it's probably a good idea to keep getting her used to your space and you two. Then maybe there won't be drama later when we move in for real." Morris got out of the car, stretched, and patted his stomach. By the time they'd left the hospital, the leftovers his mom packed were a distant memory, and as a consequence, he'd probably eaten too much at dinner. "If Lincoln eats the rest of that pizza, I'm going to laugh."

"Don't even joke like that." Theo scrubbed a hand over his face. "If he manages that feat, it means he's going through another growth spurt, and I just bought him school clothes."

"My mom used to say the same thing all the time." Morris stretched, rising up on his toes to work out the kinks of the day.

"See you in a few minutes," Theo said with a tired wave, and Morris watched him head up to his place.

It awed Morris that Lincoln and Theo had made him a part of their circle. He'd gotten used to being alone, just him and Cassie, except for when Felipe crashed. He was looking forward to all the changes to come, and that was a major step for him. Change usually made him a cranky bastard.

Cassie sat in the window, giving him a measuring look as he unlocked the door. "You know you're not supposed to be on the kitchen counter." He leveled a finger at her, and she yawned, looking away as if what he said was beneath her consideration. Little brat.

Morris scooped her up and gently scratched under her chin as he retrieved her bag of treats. They'd already installed another cat tree, food dishes, and litter box upstairs in anticipation of the transition. Now it was time to test it out. "Neither one of us is sleeping alone tonight." Morris dug through her box of toys and pulled out her bear and a motorized mouse that never failed to elicit a reaction.

Cassie's purring ceased as Morris opened the door and her ears laid back. "Don't worry, you're not going to the vet. We're going to see your buddies."

Cassie remained vigilant until they'd passed his car and were walking up toward Theo's. Her ears pricked up when they walked through the door, and she twisted to be let down. Morris chuckled as she ran for the living room window and stationed herself on the ledge. She loved it there, a fluffy queen surveying her domain. Morris's apartment was downstairs in the back, and it didn't have the same panoramic view.

Morris looked around with a frown at the empty living room. A glance down the hallway showed Lincoln's door firmly closed. He peeked into the kitchen and sure enough, there was Theo, slicing strawberries into a bowl. He wanted to tell him to lay off, he couldn't eat one more thing, but he knew this was Theo's way of decompressing.

Morris walked up behind him and slid his arms around Theo. "How you doing?"

Theo added a little balsamic vinegar and lightly tossed the berries with some fresh basil he snipped off the plant in the window. "I'm…." He set the bowl down and leaned back against him. "I'm good. Today was a good day. I liked meeting your family. I wish we could've stayed longer."

Morris smiled as he rested his chin on top of Theo's head. "Yeah, that went rather well, didn't it? You survived my sisters' reign of terror."

"According to them, you are the terror." Theo stuck the bowl in the fridge and pulled out some heavy whipping cream.

"I was outnumbered and the baby. I did what I had to do." Vinegar and cream and strawberries? Morris eyed Theo's activity with skepticism. True, he had yet to taste anything bad that Theo concocted, but there was always that one time. "Okay, I've got to ask, what are you doing?"

Theo pulled down the mixer and smiled. "We missed out on dessert. Lincoln took the pizza. So I thought we'd have a little light sweet while we watched TV. Why don't you put on some coffee?"

Morris retrieved the coffee and some Irish cream to go with it. It was a spiked coffee kind of day. "I'm not quite sure if what you're making qualifies as dessert or anything edible."

Theo chuckled, whipping the cream into frothy lightness while Morris made their coffees. "You'll love it and beg me for more."

Morris dipped his pinkie into the bowl and sampled the whipped cream. "If you're right, I'll marry you."

"You're already marrying me," Theo said with a laugh in his voice, and Morris grinned.

"True." Morris poured two mugs of coffee and added the alcohol. "Come on. Let's stretch out in front of the TV. I need to digest before dessert."

Theo stuck the whipped cream in the fridge and took one of the mugs Morris handed him. "That works. I want to give the berries a chance to macerate. By the time they're done, you'll be hungry again."

They ventured out to the living room, and Cassie was nowhere in sight. Another peek down the hallway showed Lincoln's door cracked open. She did hate a closed door. She'd probably harassed Lincoln until he opened it. He settled on the couch as Theo clicked on the TV. "My family liked meeting you and Lincoln too," Morris said, picking up on the earlier thread of their conversation. "God knows my dad is happy I'm settled with someone. He truly thinks I need taking care of."

"Well, probably the easiest way to deal with that is keep on doing what you're doing and let him think it. You know the truth." Theo sat back with a sigh, propped his feet on the table, and took a sip of his coffee. "No sense arguing over something that's not going to change."

Morris stretched out his legs too and leaned his head back with a sigh of contentment as he realized with a smile how they'd mimicked each other. How the hell had a day off for both of them ended up so chaotic and busy? Babies, proposals, family. He didn't blame Lincoln for hiding in his cave, and it gave him a little alone time with Theo. It was nice to have some quiet time together.

"It was good to meet Robin and Dustin," Morris said as Theo flicked through the channels before settling on a cooking competition show. He glanced at Theo and saw his expression go thoughtful.

"I think that went rather well," Theo said after a long pause, his eyes hopeful. "How about you?"

"All things considered, yeah." Morris slid his arm around Theo's shoulders. "You know them better than me. But I think it was more regret and pride that kept them away, fear of being rejected like they tried to reject you. Now that the door has been opened again, I think it'll stay open."

The tension in Theo's body relaxed. "I really hope so. I wasn't sure, you know, but when Dustin also joined us for pizza, I really let myself start to think we could heal and be a family again."

"Hope is a good thing." Morris kissed Theo's temple, nuzzling as Theo cuddled in more. If someone had told him his summertime fling would've turned into an engagement, he probably would've run screaming. And he would've been an idiot.

"Yeah it is." Theo brushed his lips over Morris's and turned his attention to the mad chaos on the screen. Morris pulled out his sketchpad as Cassie wandered back in, dragging her stuffed bear by its face. Poor abused thing.

"Time for dessert," Theo announced as the first show ended and another queued up in its place. "Do you want some more coffee?"

"Nah, I'm good. Thanks, man." Morris watched Theo disappear into the kitchen with a shake of his head. He knew Theo had to be exhausted, but he wasn't going to stay still long enough to relax unless Morris made him stay still.

"Olivia is awfully cute, isn't she?" Theo said as he came back with two small plates. He handed one to Morris and sank back down again.

"That's how they get you. The cuteness. Then their personality sets in." Morris was going to enjoy watching Theo get totally entranced by a little being not much bigger than a french loaf. He warily eyeballed the slice of pound cake covered in strawberries and whipped cream. "That's when you're really in trouble."

Theo nudged him in the arm with a roll of his eyes. "Try it."

Morris broke off an edge of the berry-soaked cake and popped it in his mouth. It didn't taste like vinegar. It tasted amazing, light and summery. Like the kind of strawberry shortcake they'd serve at some fancy restaurant, not Theo's homey place. "I swear, Theo. Do you have an altar in your kitchen where you practice magic or something? This isn't normal."

Theo sat back with a satisfied smirk. "You love it."

"It's unnatural, but yep, I love it. Should we share some with Lincoln?" Morris took another bite, savoring the mix of flavors. Theo had added something citrusy as well, and he couldn't quite pin it down.

"I left some in the fridge for him." Theo looked over his shoulder down the hallway. "If he wants company, he knows where we are."

"You should have this at the bistro," Morris said as he set his plate down on the table. "You've made me a convert."

A slow smile crossed Theo's lips. "Oh the possibilities in that statement."

"For real. I'm sitting in another man's house, not my own quiet living room. I ate some crazy unnatural dessert, and there's a cooking show on TV." Morris tugged Theo over so he could give him a kiss. "What kind of Canadian voodoo have you worked on me?"

Theo shrugged. "Nothing more than what you've done to me. Thanks to you I've actually discovered a franchise pizza joint I like. I'm reading comic books, and you've got me hooked on reruns of *Supernatural*. I think you're the one with a hidden altar."

"Wait until Olivia's old enough to share in such geek fun. You have to buy your niece her first lightsaber. It's the number one rule of being a good uncle." Morris smiled up at him as Theo slid his arms around Morris's neck.

"If Laila agrees that a lightsaber is cool, I'll consider it, but I think I'll leave that honor to Lincoln." Theo trailed his fingertips along Morris's jaw, then tangled his fingers in the ends of Morris's hair.

Morris slipped his hands under Theo's shirt and rubbed circles on his lower back. "Speaking of Laila, I'm told she's already talking weddings and her plans to be a flower girl."

"I was thinking we could have alpacas with baskets." Theo gave him an earnest look as Morris straightened. "Did you know there are alpaca farmers in Virgin—"

Morris poked him in the side and Theo cut off with a snicker. "You are too much, Boarman."

"I'd like to think I'm just enough," Theo said with a smile as he leaned in closer so Morris could feel his breath on his lips.

Morris felt his whole being soften. "Yeah, you're just right." Theo's eyes lit up as Morris cupped his face. "You taught me there's more to life than the next deadline, the next show. I loved my life then. I love it even more now. Thanks to you."

Theo kissed the corners of Morris's mouth, teasing and sweet. "You helped me to realize life needed to be lived again, not just gotten through." He smiled softly. "Thanks to you."

Morris's heart began to beat faster as he felt Theo's body stir. "To quote another movie classic, 'Theo, you big stud, take me to bed or lose me forever.'"

Theo started chuckling as he touched his forehead to Morris's. "Is that right?"

"Damn right." Morris closed his eyes and pulled Theo closer before releasing him. "Please tell me you know what movie it's from."

"I have no clue," Theo said with another laugh. He clambered off Morris and held out his hand, tugging him up as their fingers joined. "But I approve of the message."

MARGUERITE LABBE has often been called both Trouble and Sunshine by those who know her. She's not sure how she manages to make both those nicknames work together, but apparently she does. She's a New Hampshire girl who married an Alabama boy, an Air Force brat who has somehow managed to settle herself firmly in Southern Maryland, with one overgrown son and two crazy cats.

Marguerite loves to spin tales that cross genre lines, where stubborn men build lifelong ties of loyalty, friendship, and family no matter the odds thrown against them, and where love is found in unexpected places. She has won the Rainbow Award for Historical Romance with Fae Sutherland, as well as the Rainbow Award for Paranormal and the Rainbow Romance Award for Excellence, also in Paranormal.

When she's not working hard on writing new stories, she spends her time reading novels of all genres, enjoying role-playing and tabletop games with her friends, and helping out her husband with Apocrypha Comics Studio.

Website: www.margueritelabbe.com
Twitter: @MargueriteLabbe
Facebook: www.facebook.com/marguerite.labbe.3
Email: margueritelabbe@gmail.com

# ALL
# BETS
# ARE
# OFF

## MARGUERITE LABBE

It only takes one night with Ash Gallagher to make Eli Hollister think he's finally met the right man at the right time. Good thing he doesn't bet on it, because Ash turns out to be a student in Eli's class at the local college. Eli can't deny he's attracted, but now it's complicated. He's already in enough trouble with the department head, a man who would like to see Eli denied his tenure and fired.

Ash is looking forward to taking his life in a new direction. After serving one active-duty stint in the Marine Corps and another in the Reserves, he's ready to put his military life behind him. The last new experience he'd planned for this semester was to fall in lust with his English professor, but the more Eli resists, the more Ash is determined to have him. Then he discovers Eli's playing for keeps, and Ash is only interested in a fling… or is he? Between these two, when it comes to life and love, all bets are off.

# www.dreamspinnerpress.com

Marguerite Labbe

# GHOSTS
## IN THE
# WIND

Andrei Cuza and Dean Marshall celebrated their tenth anniversary only to have their happiness shattered by a random, insane event: On his way home from closing a business deal, Dean stops on the parkway to help a young mother with her flat tire, and her ex arrives, murders them, and takes off with his two kids.

Ghosts have haunted Andrei all his life. He bears the guilt for his sister being stuck in limbo, because ghosts are frozen at the moment they died, unable to adapt to the changes in their living loved ones. When Dean returns to Andrei as a ghost, the double punch of losing him and having to watch him founder if he doesn't move on is almost more than Andrei can bear.

Despite dangers in limbo—Jackal Wraiths that devour souls are hunting him—Dean isn't going anywhere until he helps Andrei track down the missing children. Andrei is in danger as well when he pays dearly to feel Dean's touch one last time. Time is slowly running out as Dean and Andrei try to say good-bye while they track a killer who's more than happy to kill again.

# www.dreamspinnerpress.com

# OTHER SIDE
# OF THE LINE

## MARGUERITE LABBE

Caleb Hudson and Hal Zimmer became best friends the day they stood up against the schoolyard bully together. Life's complicated enough with their friendship crossing racial lines in 1960s Charleston, South Carolina, but as time passes, they realize it's more than their friendship that sets them apart from other kids. At first, Caleb denies his feelings for Hal could be more than companionship. He supports his friend when Hal admits he's gay, but Caleb isn't ready to face his own truth.

Hal becomes a staunch antiwar protester, and the divide between them widens after Caleb is drafted. But when Caleb returns from Vietnam, the time for denial is over. His homecoming sets off a series of events that force Caleb and Hal to confront their desires and what lines they're willing to cross to get what they truly want out of life.

# www.dreamspinnerpress.com